PRAISE FOR MELISSA FOSTER

"With her wonderful characters and resonating emotions, Melissa Foster is a must-read author!"

—*New York Times* bestseller Julie Kenner

"Melissa Foster is synonymous with sexy, swoony, heartfelt romance!"

—*New York Times* bestseller Lauren Blakely

"You can always rely on Melissa Foster to deliver a story that's fresh, emotional, and entertaining."

—*New York Times* bestseller Brenda Novak

"Melissa Foster writes worlds that draw you in, with strong heroes and brave heroines surrounded by a community that makes you want to crawl right on through the page and live there."

—*New York Times* bestseller Julia Kent

"When it comes to contemporary romances with realistic characters, an emotional love story, and smokin'-hot sex, author Melissa Foster always delivers!"

—The Romance Reviews

"Foster writes characters that are complex and loyal, and each new story brings further depth and development to a redefined concept of family."

—*RT Book Reviews*

"Melissa Foster definitely knows how to spin a tale and keep you flipping the pages."

—*Book Loving Fairy*

Maybe We Won't

MORE BOOKS BY MELISSA FOSTER

LOVE IN BLOOM ROMANCE SERIES

SNOW SISTERS

Sisters in Love
Sisters in Bloom
Sisters in White

THE BRADENS

Lovers at Heart, Reimagined
Destined for Love
Friendship on Fire
Sea of Love
Bursting with Love
Hearts at Play
Taken by Love
Fated for Love
Romancing My Love
Flirting with Love
Dreaming of Love
Crashing into Love
Healed by Love
Surrender My Love
River of Love
Crushing on Love
Whisper of Love
Thrill of Love

THE BRADENS & MONTGOMERYS

Embracing Her Heart
Anything for Love
Trails of Love
Wild, Crazy Hearts
Making You Mine

Searching for Love
Hot for Love
Sweet, Sexy Heart
Then Came Love

BRADEN NOVELLAS

Promise My Love
Our New Love
Daring Her Love
Story of Love
Love at Last
A Very Braden Christmas

THE REMINGTONS

Game of Love
Stroke of Love
Flames of Love
Slope of Love
Read, Write, Love
Touched by Love

SEASIDE SUMMERS

Seaside Dreams
Seaside Hearts
Seaside Sunsets
Seaside Secrets
Seaside Nights
Seaside Embrace
Seaside Lovers
Seaside Whispers
Seaside Serenade

BAYSIDE SUMMERS

Bayside Desires
Bayside Passions
Bayside Heat
Bayside Escape
Bayside Romance
Bayside Fantasies

THE STEELES AT SILVER ISLAND

Tempted by Love
My True Love
Caught by Love

THE RYDERS

Seized by Love
Claimed by Love
Chased by Love
Rescued by Love
Swept into Love

SUGAR LAKE

The Real Thing
Only for You
Love Like Ours
Finding My Girl

HARMONY POINTE

Call Her Mine
This Is Love
She Loves Me

THE WHISKEYS: DARK KNIGHTS AT PEACEFUL HARBOR

Tru Blue
Truly, Madly, Whiskey
Driving Whiskey Wild
Wicked Whiskey Love
Mad About Moon
Taming My Whiskey
The Gritty Truth
In for a Penny
Running on Diesel

THE WICKEDS: DARK KNIGHTS AT BAYSIDE

A Little Bit Wicked
The Wicked Aftermath

THE WISKEYS: DARK KNIGHTS AT REDEMPTION RANCH

Love, Lies, and Whiskey

BILLIONAIRES AFTER DARK SERIES

Wild Boys After Dark

Logan
Heath
Jackson
Cooper

Bad Boys After Dark

Mick
Dylan
Carson
Brett

HARBORSIDE NIGHTS SERIES

Catching Cassidy
Discovering Delilah
Tempting Tristan

STAND-ALONE NOVELS

Chasing Amanda (mystery/suspense)
Come Back to Me (mystery/suspense)
Have No Shame (historical fiction/romance)
Love, Lies & Mystery (three-book bundle)
Megan's Way (literary fiction)
Traces of Kara (psychological thriller)
Where Petals Fall (suspense)

Maybe We Won't

Silver Harbor, Book Three

MELISSA FOSTER

 Montlake

Published by Montlake, Seattle

www.apub.com

Amazon, the Amazon logo, and Montlake are trademarks of Amazon.com, Inc., or its affiliates.

ISBN-13: 9781542034920
ISBN-10: 1542034922

Cover design by Letitia Hasser

Cover photography by Regina Wamba of MaeIDesign.com

Printed in the United States of America

*Here's to leaving this world a little better
than we found it*

CHAPTER ONE

DEIRDRA DE MESSIÉRES lay in her childhood bedroom on Silver Island thinking about her upended life. She'd worked her ass off for the last several years as a corporate attorney for a tech firm in Boston, and after her promotion to assistant general counsel last year, she'd *thought* she was on the fast track to becoming general counsel when the slot opened up—until the GC had a heart attack and her slave-driver boss, Malcolm, had hired a referral from outside the company through his good-old-boy network.

The bastard.

He'd sprung that little nugget on her three days ago, after which Deirdra had announced her two-month hiatus, effective immediately. Everyone had been shocked, including Deirdra. She'd never taken time off and had made herself available in the evenings and on weekends since she'd first started with the company. She'd had to. It was a dog-eat-dog industry, and with six other attorneys on board—four of whom were men—she'd wanted to stand out. Yes, she was well aware that she was putting the company she'd given her all to in a pickle, especially since the new general counsel couldn't start for another two months. But *that* was the point. Let them suffer without her impeccable mind handling everything under the sun. She was confident in her game plan and certain Malcolm would quickly see the error of his ways.

Well, pretty confident, anyway. Ninety percent sure.

Okay, seventy-five percent.

The truth was, she'd thought he wouldn't let her walk out the door after her announcement. But her stern sixty-year-old boss had simply wished her a relaxing time and said she needed it. She'd already received dozens of calls and emails from colleagues who were shocked that she'd taken so much time off, but she struggled with disappointment over the ones that hadn't come from her boss.

She still couldn't believe Malcolm had said she freaking *needed* the break. As if she'd ever produced subpar work? That was a laugh. He'd had nothing but accolades for her jobs well done, and last year's promotion had been proof of that.

Her frustration simmered to the boiling point. *Ugh.* She needed to stop overthinking the situation. *Fat chance of that happening for a self-professed control freak.* Deirdra not overthinking would be as weird as her younger sister, Abby, *not* seeing the bright side of things or their older half sister, Cait, trusting everyone at face value. Deirdra had a better chance of trying to transform into a bird and fly away.

If only . . .

She and her sisters were quite the trio, and they'd had a whirlwind few months. She and Abby had only discovered Cait existed in the spring, when they'd come back to the island to go over their mother's will with one of their mother's best friends, Shelley Steele. While Abby had embraced and trusted Cait unconditionally from the moment she'd met her, Deirdra had been cautious, given that their family house, restaurant, and meager inheritances were on the line. It had taken Cait some time to open up and trust them as well. But they'd gotten through those trials and tribulations and had become close. Cait was a wonderful addition to their family, and like Abby, she'd found solace and love on Silver Island.

Deirdra would *not* be following suit.

Beyond seeing her sisters happy, Deirdra had no interest in their family restaurant, the Bistro, or in the island on which she'd spent too many years trying to hold together the pieces of her alcoholic mother's disheveled life, helping to run the Bistro and keep a roof over their heads. Deirdra had fled immediately after high school to attend Boyer University in Upstate New York with her bestie, Sutton Steele, and had *finally* started living her own life. But self-preservation had consequences, and Abby had been stuck caring for their mother in Deirdra's absence. That sucked, but what choice had Deirdra had at the time? Stay on the rinky-dink island running a restaurant she resented and putting her drunk mother to bed while her dreams went to pot? Besides, Abby had encouraged her to go, and Deirdra had clung to that support like a lifeboat in her sea of guilt as she'd set out to prove herself to Abby and maybe even to stick it to her mother and show that she couldn't hold her back.

Deirdra stared at the ceiling, discomfort simmering inside her. She'd thought her resentment toward the island and all that it represented might ease now that her mother was gone, but painful reminders lingered like ghosts in the wind, and the house and her bedroom were filled with them. Abby and Aiden had done a great job of sprucing it up. It was absolutely gorgeous. To anyone else it would seem warm and inviting, but there wasn't enough paint on the planet to obliterate Deirdra's painful memories. How many nights had she snuck out the window just to sit on the hill and look out at the water to keep from drowning in her mother's wake?

Maybe she shouldn't have come back, but she couldn't do that to Cait. The start of her impromptu hiatus had lined up with the day Cait and all their friends were fixing up her new tattoo shop. Deirdra wasn't big on manual labor, but she loved her sisters, and she'd needed to get out of Boston. She was glad she'd come, even if being on the island was uncomfortable. She'd gotten to witness Cait's boyfriend, Deirdra's childhood friend Brant Remington, get down on one knee in front of all their friends and propose. Deirdra couldn't be happier for them, but come hell or high water, she was getting off this island tomorrow and going on a well-deserved vacation, the destination of which was yet to be determined.

The sound of the front door jarred her from her thoughts, and Abby's giggles floated upstairs. She and her fiancé, Aiden Aldridge, couldn't keep their hands off each other. Deirdra glanced at her phone. It was almost one o'clock in the morning. In the spring, Abby had moved back home from New York, where she'd worked sixty-plus hours a week as a chef. She'd met and fallen head over heels for Aiden in a whirlwind love affair. Together they'd revived the Bistro, and they were getting married in November.

Deirdra tried to focus on the distant sounds of Silver Harbor sneaking in through the open window instead of the cacophony of laughter, low conversations, and prolonged silences, followed by loud lustful sounds coming from downstairs. If only she were back in Boston. She preferred her noisy neighbor's stereo blasting classic rock and oldies at all hours over *this*. At least *that* she could dance to.

Needless to say, she was a little jealous of her sisters' love lives. Not that she'd had time for a man, or anything else besides work, these last few years. More noises floated upstairs. She closed her eyes, willing them not to have sex in the living room or, worse, in the kitchen. She had to *eat* at that table. *Oh God, that's probably what Aiden is doing.* She squeezed her eyes shut. *Deletedeletedelete!*

What was she thinking, staying in her old bedroom? She should have stayed in the apartment over the garage. Why hadn't she thought of that from the get-go?

A loud *thud* rattled the walls, followed by more laughter.

Deirdra flew out of bed. She was *not* going to listen to a play-by-play of Abby and Aiden having sex. She put on her silk kimono and headed downstairs, praying she wouldn't catch them in a compromising position. She stopped on the bottom step, eyeing the trail of clothing that led past the steps and down the hall to their bedroom. *Thank God.* Hurrying into the kitchen, she snagged the key to the apartment off the hook by the side door and quietly slipped outside. She crossed her arms against the brisk September air as she climbed the steps to the apartment above the garage.

A streak of moonlight lit a path down the hallway to the bedroom. She took off her kimono and slipped under the warm covers, closing her eyes as she sank into the mattress. Something moved beside her, and her eyes flew open just as that *something* licked her face. She screamed and jumped out of the bed, flailing for the light switch. A bark rang out, and a cold nose hit her crotch. She swatted at it as she flicked on the lights, illuminating an amused Josiah "Jagger" Jones pushing languidly from the bed as his dalmatian, Dolly, nosed Deirdra's privates. The twentysomething hippie worked at the Bistro as a part-time musician and part-time chef.

"*What* are you doing here?" She twisted away from Dolly, her eyes catching on Jagger's *naked* body. Holy mother of hotness. Broad shoulders and a few wordy tattoos on his ribs vied for her attention, but her eyes locked on the dusting of dark chest hair trailing down lickable abs, and her thoughts skidded to a halt at the impressive cock dangling between his legs. She couldn't look away. Her loneliest parts clenched with desire, while her boggled mind tried to make sense of the perfect manscaping, which didn't fit the image she held of the hemp-clothing- and sandal-wearing, too-damn-laid-back guy for whom she had no patience. Not that she'd ever imagined him naked. *Well, not too often anyway.* He may not be her type—give her a man in a suit any day—but she couldn't deny that Jagger was hot, and he had a great voice, the kind that fantasies were made of. His hair wasn't bad, either: dark, thick, and wavy. The kind of hair she'd love to hold on to while his face was between her legs.

Dolly licked her, snapping her back to the moment.

Holy crap. She was losing it. She was thirty years old, and he couldn't be more than twenty-four or -five. She needed to get *off* the island and scratch that particular itch with a man who was more her speed . . . *age* . . . Holy cow, his body . . .

5

Dolly licked her again, jerking her mind back into submission.

"Dolly!" She turned away, glowering at Jagger, who was watching her with a big-ass grin.

"Like what you see?" he said far too casually. He lazily raked a hand through his hair, his leather and beaded bracelets slipping down his wrist.

"Why are you *naked*? Put some clothes on!" Dolly sniffed her butt, and Deirdra swatted at her.

"Chill, babe. Come here, Dolls." He reached for his glasses.

"Don't tell me to chill. Why didn't she bark and warn me you were here?"

"She's a lover, not a fighter." He put on his glasses, which made him look sharper than a man who said things like *chill*, *dude*, and *vibing* and couldn't commit to a permanent schedule because he liked to *keep things loose*.

Deirdra had no idea how Abby put up with any of that, but both her sisters loved the guy who had sauntered into town claiming to have been a good friend of their mother's and that he had worked at the Bistro from time to time. Deirdra had yet to make sense of his friendship with her mother. Nothing fit. Kind of like the hot body he kept hidden under loose clothing.

He took a long, lustful look at her, and her traitorous nipples rose to greet him. "Damn, Didi, you look good in silk."

"*Don't* call me that stripper name, and put clothes on!" She snagged her kimono and put it on over her camisole and matching sleep shorts.

"No one's forcing you to look." He reached for a pair of drawstring pants. "Why're you so uppity? It's just a naked body."

The hottest naked body she'd seen in a very long time. It was totally unfair that it was attached to *him*. He pulled on his pants, tying them low on his hips, which made him impossibly sexier, irritating her even more. "Don't call me *uppity*, either."

He chuckled. "Whatever. You're givin' off that vibe."

"Why are you here? I thought you lived in a van."

He sat on the bed, and Dolly jumped up beside him, resting her head in his lap. He petted her, but his eyes never left Deirdra. It must have been *way* too long since she'd been touched by a man, because she felt oddly jealous over the affection he lavished on his dog.

"It's a recreational vehicle," he corrected her. "And it's in the shop. Abby said I could crash here."

"Someone could have told me that this afternoon."

He shrugged. "You're the only one who's bothered by this. I'm enjoying the view."

"Don't look at me like that." She crossed her arms over her chest.

"You have a lot of pent-up anger." He patted the bed. "Lie down. I'll give you a massage, work it out of your system."

She scoffed. "Nice try."

"It must be hard, carrying all that distrust around."

He couldn't know how true his words were. He pushed to his feet, closing the gap between them. Her pulse quickened, his eyes holding her captive, all brown and gold and gorgeous, looking so deeply into hers, she had a feeling she was wrong, and he knew *exactly* how true they were.

"You've been living in a world of games for too long, Dee." He ran his fingers down her arm, sending heat slithering through her. "Trust is the foundation of everything good in this world. If I wanted to have sex with you, I wouldn't pretend that I didn't."

"I'm *not* having sex with you."

He arched a brow. "I'm not asking."

Great. Now she felt stupid and irritated.

"What's wrong with your bed, anyway? Abby and Aiden just redid your room."

"*Nothing.* They're just too loud."

He grinned. "Good for them. You can stay here. There's plenty of room for the three of us."

Deirdra rolled her eyes. "I'm not sleeping with you and your dog."

"Okay. You do your thing, but the offer stands if you change your mind."

"That's *not* going to happen." She stalked out the door, trying to push away the image of him naked. But just as no amount of paint could mask the ghosts of her past, nothing could take away the images that had seared themselves into her lust-addled brain.

She cursed at herself as she went back into the house. Murmurs came from Abby and Aiden's bedroom as she stepped over the trail of clothing by the stairs, and she was hit with the sense of longing for something more that had been poking its ugly head out recently.

Hammering that unfulfillable emotion down deep, she traipsed up to her room, determined to figure out where she should spend the next two months, because she sure as hell wasn't going to stay on this island.

CHAPTER TWO

JAGGER FINISHED HIS yoga stretches and gazed out at the morning sun glittering off the water. As he did every morning, he counted his blessings, starting with the big things: family, friends, and good health. Then he took stock of the little pleasures, like being granted another beautiful day on Silver Island, the grass tickling his feet, and the ocean breeze on his arms and cheeks. He looked up at the sun, tossing out another dose of gratitude for the run-in with Deirdra, with her long brownish-blond hair he wanted to feel brushing his body and sharp green eyes that he was sure never missed a thing. He had a feeling she was as sensual and passionate as she was quick witted and determined, but from what he knew of the uptight attorney, she probably never let herself be free enough to explore or enjoy it. He'd noticed she was never at a loss for words, no matter how cutting, as if her mind never turned off.

He probably shouldn't dig her sarcasm as much as he did, but he'd wondered about his longtime friend Ava de Messiéres's daughter *Didi* for a long time, and she was even fiercer and more magnetic than he'd imagined. As often happened when he thought of Ava, her voice whispered through his mind. *Didi seems like a storm bullying her way through life. But my darling daughter isn't the storm. She's everything beautiful in this world: the music in the air, the songs in the wind, the whispers from our hearts. I know she's going to do great things, but she's weathered my storms for too long and built an impenetrable fortress around herself. Because of that, I worry she'll miss out on the greatest beauty of all—love.*

Hit with a wave of missing his late friend, he let the emotions settle in, experiencing their weight and importance, allowing himself a moment to mourn her before moving on.

"Come on, Dolls." Dolly bounded across the yard. He loved her up, and she licked his face. "Want to go see Abby and Aiden?" Abby had invited him for breakfast when she'd offered the apartment to him last night. "With any luck, Didi will be there, too." *No doubt breathing fire.*

Dolly's tail wagged excitedly as they headed around to the side of the house. She also had a thing for the brown-haired beauty.

The scent of coffee wafted through the screen door. Aiden was reading the newspaper at the kitchen table, as distinguished as ever in dress pants and a polo shirt. He was an interesting dude, a billionaire who didn't flaunt his wealth. He looked like David Beckham without the tattoos, and though he'd loosened up in the few months Jagger had known him, Jagger had a feeling he'd always emit an air of dignity. Abby stood in front of the stove, swaying to a silent beat as she cooked breakfast. Her golden-brown hair always looked a little messy, as it did now, hanging loose over her shoulders, so different from her supremely well-put-together sister, who had looked like she'd walked off the pages of a Victoria's Secret catalog even as she'd bitten his head off last night.

"Knock-knock," Jagger said through the screen.

Aiden looked up from the newspaper. "Good morning, Jag. Come in. I just made a fresh pot of coffee." He was a serious coffee connoisseur. Importing coffee beans from northern Indonesia was his guilty pleasure, and his coffee maker probably cost more than Jagger's RV.

"Hey, Jagger," Abby said cheerily as he opened the door, and Dolly hurried to Aiden for some morning love, which he was happy to give.

"How's it going? Something smells delicious." Jagger made his way over to Abby. "Salsa verde eggs? *Mm.* One of my favorites. Has anyone ever told you that you should be a chef?"

"I keep telling her to quit stripping and become a chef," Aiden teased. "But she's got a mind of her own."

Abby pointed the spatula at Aiden. "You had no complaints last night."

Aiden got up to kiss her, and Dolly followed him over. Jagger loved their open affection. So many people plowed through life, missing out on all of the good stuff. *Just as Didi did.*

Speaking of the snarky vixen . . . "Have you seen Didi this morning?"

Abby handed him a plate of eggs. "Not yet, which is weird. She's usually up and working by now. I hope this hiatus does her some good."

He set the plate on the table, and as he poured himself a cup of coffee, a loud *thump, thump, thump* sounded from the stairs. Dolly scampered out of the kitchen to check it out just as Deirdra appeared in the doorway, wearing a dressy cream-colored tank top, expensive-looking brown slacks, and high heels. She was carrying a designer handbag and tugging a massive suitcase.

Dolly whined, her tail wagging as she pushed her nose into Deirdra's crotch. Deirdra set her handbag down and knelt, taking Dolly's face between her hands. "You cannot put your nose up in my business after hanging me out to dry the way you did last night. You and I are going to have a long talk about having each other's backs, girlfriend."

Dolly panted happily as Deirdra kissed her head, then pushed to her feet, scowling at Jagger. "At least you have pants on this time."

"Unfortunately, so do you." He handed her the cup of coffee he'd just poured, which she accepted with narrowing eyes, but there was no denying the electricity sparking between them. Or maybe that was just her fury.

"When did you see each other without pants on?" Abby's brows knitted, and then her eyes widened. "*Oh.* Did you two . . . ?"

Jagger grinned, and Aiden tried to hide a chuckle.

Deirdra's scowl deepened. "No. I did *not* sleep with the hippie." She slammed the coffee cup down, and it splashed all over the counter. She scrambled for paper towels, aggressively wiping up the spill. "Thanks for telling me he was staying in the apartment, by the way."

Abby looked confused. "It's only for a few nights, and I didn't think it mattered since you were staying in the house."

"Maybe you should have thought about that before you and Aiden decided to rock the house last night. I tried to escape your noisy sex-capade and ended up in bed next to *him*." Deirdra glowered at Jagger again. "Did you know he sleeps *naked*?" Her cheeks reddened.

Jagger had thought nothing could shake up Little Miss in Control, and hell if that blush didn't ramp up his desire to strip away that professional facade she wore like a shield and set free the sexy beast she fought so hard to chain down. What else was she hiding behind that armor?

"*Ohmygosh.*" Abby smiled awkwardly at Jagger as she set two more plates on the table. "Well, *no*, I didn't know that about him."

"Now you do, and *this one*"—Deirdra nudged Dolly's face away from her crotch—"didn't even bark when I came in. No doubt she's used to his revolving van door."

"Hey now, it's an *RV*," Jagger reminded her, amused by her anger and her assumption. "The door doesn't actually revolve."

"*Whatever*," Deirdra snapped. "I'm leaving after breakfast anyway, so enjoy the apartment."

"Wait," Abby said anxiously. "You *just* got here. I was hoping that since you have so much time off, and we're going to have an engagement party for Cait and Brant, you'd stay for a while. I thought we could finally spend time together when you don't have your nose in your computer and that we could go shopping with Cait for dresses for the wedding."

Tension riddled Deirdra's brow, her gaze shifting briefly to Aiden, who was looking at her hopefully. Deirdra's shoulders dropped a fraction of an inch. If Jagger hadn't been looking for any hint of softening, he might have missed it. "*Fine.* I'll stay for the week."

"The week?" Abby shook her head. "Didn't you get the group text from Jules last night? Gail is planning Cait and Brant's party, but Jules took the lead on coordinating everyone's schedules since she has all the phone numbers. She doesn't think we can have the party for two more weeks, and that's only a tentative date."

Gail was Brant's mother, and their bubbly friend Jules Steele had made quick work of getting Jagger's number when he'd first come back to the island. He'd learned she not only owned a gift shop in town, but she was also the unofficial Silver Island entertainment director, keeping everyone in the loop about gossip and events.

"I must have missed her text. I was a little busy traipsing between the house and the apartment." Deirdra glanced at Jagger. There was no missing the flash of heat between them, or the momentary slip of her gaze to his lap before she returned her attention to her sister. "Cait and Brant said they wanted a simple get-together. How hard can it be to make that happen? I'll go see Jules and speed things up after I get a room at the Silver House." The Silver House was a resort down the street from the Bistro.

"Why are you getting a room?" Abby asked.

Deirdra gave her a deadpan look, as if to say she'd already explained herself.

"You don't have to do that," Jagger said. "You can have the apartment."

Deirdra arched a brow. "And where will you sleep? Oh wait, let me guess, on the beach, warmed by the light of the stars?"

"*Dee*," Abby chided her.

Deirdra parked a hand on her hip. "I'm sorry, but is that so far out of the realm of possibilities for a guy who lives in a vehicle and goes wherever the wind takes him?"

Abby looked at her imploringly.

"I'm sorry. I'm just calling him as I see him."

"It's okay. I know my lifestyle isn't for everyone. It's hard for some people to understand how I can be happy with very few material things when everything around us sends the message that the more we have, the more important we are." He cocked a knowing grin. "And then there are those people who are jealous of the way I live."

Deirdra scoffed. "I'm *not* jealous."

"I didn't say you were." *It's just a gut feeling.* One he'd understand if true. Especially after trudging through a difficult childhood, when she'd had no choice but to work her ass off to make ends meet from the time she was a kid. It made sense that she'd carry a gigantic chip on her shoulder toward people she believed didn't work hard enough. "But you had a good idea. I haven't slept under the stars for a while. I might just break out the sleeping bag tonight."

"*Wait.* Dee, can't you stay here, in the house? We'll eat breakfasts together and do sister stuff," Abby pleaded. "We'll be quieter at night."

Deirdra sighed, as if just the idea of *sister stuff* made her weary, which piqued Jagger's curiosity even more. He knew she loved Abby. He'd heard Deirdra had given Abby her share of the inheritance their mother had left them, to help her renovate the restaurant.

"You and Aiden are just starting your lives together. You shouldn't have to worry about being quiet. Besides, you'll still see me while I'm staying at the Silver House."

"She won't see you enough." Aiden pushed to his feet and put an arm around Abby. "Abs misses you, and I haven't had a chance to really get to know you as well as I'd like. I apologize if we were a bit overzealous last night. We'd had a few drinks, and . . ." He looked at Abby in a way that said more than whatever he was about to. "What can I say? I adore your sister. But I promise we will be more respectful from now on. Please stay with us. Stay for Abby."

Aiden was so sincere, Jagger found himself hoping Deirdra would agree. "I'll even sleep in underwear if it'll help." He winked. "Just in case you get lost in the middle of the night."

Deirdra rolled her eyes, but a laugh bubbled out. "Fine. I'll stay here."

"Yay! I'll make a family dinner tonight!" Abby cheered and hugged her.

Dolly barked and went paws-up on the two of them. Jagger couldn't resist getting in on that action and put his arms around all of them.

"Do you *mind*?" Deirdra pushed out of his embrace, but at least she was smiling.

"Life's short, babe." Jagger petted Dolly. "Just soaking up the joy while I can."

"I'm not your *babe*." Deirdra reached for her coffee, and Dolly jumped on her again, knocking her cup, causing Deirdra and Abby to *yelp* as coffee spilled onto the counter again. After mopping up the mess, Deirdra pointed at Dolly. "*You*. It's time for that talk. Outside. *Now*." She marched outside with Jagger's pooch.

"Don't worry. She secretly likes dogs," Abby reassured him. "She always wanted one when we were growing up."

Jagger glanced out the screen door at Deirdra crouching in the grass, having a full-on, serious-looking conversation with Dolly, and wondered if she secretly liked hippies, too.

♥ ♥ ♥

Breakfast was delicious, and Deirdra enjoyed the banter with Abby, Aiden, and even the hippie, despite the fact that every time she looked at Jagger, she envisioned him *naked*. That was an image she wasn't likely to forget anytime soon. Especially after the dirty dreams she'd had about him when she'd gone back to bed last night. She'd had better sex in her sleep than she'd ever had in real life. Thoughts of those dreams had plagued her all morning as she'd unpacked and checked her email for the millionth time, hoping for something from Malcolm.

With all of that done, she visited with Abby for a little while, and now she was headed into town to see Jules. Everyone who came to the island fell in love with the colorful shops along Main Street, with OPEN flags at the entrances and window boxes bursting with blooms. Tourists could linger there for hours, window-shopping, meandering in and out of stores, eating at Trista's café, getting ice cream and eating it on the painted benches while people watching. If Deirdra had ever had those warm, fuzzy feelings about Silver Island, she'd buried them so deep, it was like they'd never existed.

She parked at the curb and walked down the sidewalk with blinders on, just as she had since she was eleven. She'd never had time to waste after her father had died and their mother had started drinking. There was always work to be done at the restaurant and homework to be finished. Not to mention making sure Abby was on task with her schoolwork and, of course, putting their drunk mother to bed at the end of the night. It was easier to focus on each chore, rather than to think about all the fun she was missing out on while she did all the things their mother should have been doing. Deirdra had carried that efficiency into adulthood. Nobody was better at time management than she was. It was the one good thing that had come out of her stressful childhood.

The bell above the door chimed as she walked into Happy End, Jules's eclectic gift shop. Cheerfulness overflowed not just from the joyful proprietor, who had beaten cancer as a little girl and believed in celebrating every little thing, but also from every table and shelf in the place, which boasted colorful displays of everything from clothing and signs touting the joys of beach life and the specialness of love, to toys, home decor, jewelry, and candles.

"Welcome to the—*Deirdra!*" Jules hurried across the store, her light brown hair bouncing over the shoulders of her red sweater. The top layer of her hair sprouted out from her signature water-fountain ponytail in the middle of the top of her head. She hugged Deirdra. "Wow.

You're all dolled up." She nudged her with her elbow, waggling her brows. "Got a hot hiatus date?"

"Here?" Deirdra scoffed. "Not a chance."

"Aw, come on. Don't say that. It might not be tourist season, but there are still single hotties around. You might get lucky and find a great guy like Grant. I saw the way Jagger looked at you yesterday afternoon at Cait's shop. He's so easygoing and super cute." She wrinkled her nose. "Although I'd bet my life savings there are no suits in his closet. Oh, I know! How about Fitz? He's single, and he wears a suit to work almost every day." Jules was engaged to Grant Silver, and Fitz was one of his younger brothers.

"No, thank you. Been there, done that."

"You *have*? With Fitz? How did I miss that juicy gossip?"

"It wasn't that juicy. We made out and felt each other up in the back room of the Bistro when we were teenagers." And now that she was thinking about it, Fitz had been packing heat back then, but he had nothing on Jagger. *God*, why couldn't she stop thinking about him?

"That's pretty juicy. But we'll find you someone else. Vacation flings are awesome."

"How would you know?" Jules had been a virgin before she and Grant had gotten together.

Jules lowered her voice, even though there were only a couple of customers on the other side of the store. "I read a lot of steamy romance novels, and the girls who have flings while they're on vacation have the greatest sex. Not as good as me and Grant, but not everyone can be *that* lucky."

"Well, I'm not sticking around long enough to have a fling. That's why I'm here. Abby said you were coordinating schedules for Cait and Brant's engagement party. I was thinking I could help Gail with the planning and speed things up a little." She'd never planned an engagement party before, but how hard could it be?

"I'm sure she'd love that. I have a ton of ideas, too." Jules went into a thirty-minute explanation about themes and games for the party, stopping briefly to help customers. Then she spent another half hour talking about menus and going into great detail on different types of food depending on the theme they chose and the time of day they had the party.

By the time she was done, Deirdra was thoroughly confused. "I thought Cait and Brant wanted something simple."

"They do, but this is Gail's first child to get engaged. I'm sure she'd like to make it special, and there's going to be a *big* crowd to please. Remember, Cait had a life with a whole group of other friends on Cape Cod before she and Brant got together and she moved here. I'm still trying to reach some of them. Didn't you see the group text I sent?"

"Sorry, I must have missed that one." The truth was, Deirdra didn't often read group texts. She loved Jules and their friends, but she wasn't that interested in what was going on around the island. And she was usually so busy with work, she barely had time to think, which was exactly how she liked it. "Thank you for trying to pull together everyone's schedules. Can you share their contact info with me? I'll track down the people you haven't reached, and then I'll get together with Gail and nail down the details."

"I have it all right here." Jules handed her a thick folder, as if she'd been planning for a month. "All of my ideas are in there, too. You might want to catch Gail at her house Tuesday evening. She's hosting bunco. Everyone will be there, and you know Brant's grandmother Millie, my mom and grandmother, and Mrs. Silver will also want to weigh in."

Jules's mother, Shelley, Gail Remington, and Margot Silver had been three of Ava's best friends, and they'd always been like surrogate mothers to nearly every kid on that side of the island, just as Jules's grandmother, Lenore, was like a grandmother to every kid who had grown up with Jules and her five siblings. Deirdra, however, had never relied on them to help after her mother had started drinking. She didn't want to be pitied and tried to show everyone that she and Abby could handle their family's issues. But no matter how she acted, they still had their children come to the Bistro to help when they could.

"Of course they will," Deirdra agreed. "*Silver Island, where everybody knows your name and your business.* That's what the welcome sign should say. I swear nothing ever changes around here."

"That's what I love about it," Jules said cheerily. "It's a really special place, isn't it?"

It was all Deirdra could do to keep from rolling her eyes. "Yeah. *Special.* Thanks again."

"I can't wait to see what you and Gail come up with. It's such a pretty day today. Where are you heading now?"

"I figured I'd go back to the house to look through your notes, then try to get in touch with the people who haven't responded yet. I'd like to firm up the guest list and ideas before meeting with Gail."

"Oh, *really?*" Jules wrinkled her nose. "You should take a walk in the park or go shopping. Spend time *hiatusing* before diving into all that."

"I'm trying to get off the island so I can go on hiatus someplace far away, like Europe or Hawaii or some other exotic place."

"Hawaii? I thought you didn't like beaches. You've always hated getting sandy and sweating."

"I know. But what if I only hate it *here?*"

"I don't know how anyone could hate it here, but if that's the case, I know *exactly* what you should do. You have to check out the virtual vacations the library offers. You can immerse yourself in all the places you're thinking about going and then make a decision." She plucked a flyer off the counter beside the register and handed it to her.

Deirdra scanned the flyer, which detailed one- to three-hour virtual tours.

"They offer private cubicles, and I've heard that sometimes they can give you one of their smaller conference rooms," Jules said excitedly.

"Last month Bellamy and I went on a tour of Greece." Grant's youngest sister, Bellamy, was Jules's best friend. "The tour was to die for, and Bellamy was in love with the host. He was really cute, and he had a sexy accent."

"A cute host with an accent? I'm sold. But first I've got a party to plan. Thanks, Jules."

"If there's anything else you need, I'm your girl." Jules hugged her.

Deirdra left the shop and took out her phone to google how to plan an engagement party, but first she scanned her email notifications, opening one of several from her assistant. Deirdra had left so abruptly, she knew there would be ongoing questions about projects she was handling. As she typed a response, her phone rang, and Sutton's name appeared on the screen. Sutton was one of Jules's older sisters. Deirdra answered as she walked to her car. "You're just the person I need to talk to."

If anyone knew how to figure out how to do something for which they had no experience, it was Sutton. She was a former fashion editor, and she was basically faking her way through her job as a reporter for the World Exploration Network's *Discovery Hour* show. When Sutton had taken the job, she'd had no reporting experience, and she rarely knew much about the projects on which they asked her to report, but she was great at research—and she'd mastered the skill of faking it until she made it.

"That greeting is so much warmer than the *you again* look Flynn Braden gives me every time I walk into his office. If he wasn't so good-looking, I might have already quit."

"No, you wouldn't have. You've wanted to be a reporter since you were six years old, interviewing anyone who would let you. Is Flynn still trying to get you fired?"

"Yup. I'm pretty sure it's his life mission. But more importantly, how are you? Has your boss come crawling back yet?"

"No. Do you think he's waiting for *me* to go crawling back to him?"

"Who knows. He has a big ego, and we both know men are bizarre creatures."

"Too true." She climbed into her car. "Speaking of bizarre creatures. I accidentally ended up in bed with Jagger last night, and he was *naked*." A shiver of heat skittered through her with the memory.

"You did *not*. You got naked with the hippie? I mean, *I'd* do him, but you?" Sutton laughed. "Take it from a girl who has had quite a few of those *accidents*—he's supposed to be naked."

"Ohmygod. *I* wasn't naked, and we didn't have sex."

"Well, that's disappointing. Why not? He's hot."

"Because it's *him*, and it wasn't like that. Abby and Aiden had a ridiculously loud sexcapade, and I went to the apartment to get some sleep. I didn't know Mr. Kielbasa was waiting between the sheets."

"Really? He's *that* big? I might need to take a trip home."

Deirdra laughed, but she felt a pang of something akin to jealousy, which annoyed her. She kicked that awful feeling to the curb. "Go for it. I can't even look at him anymore without seeing *that*."

"The man cooks, plays guitar, travels, *and* he's well hung? Sounds like the perfect hiatus partner to me."

"Not me. We have absolutely nothing in common, and I have to get off this island, which is why I need your advice. What do I need to know about planning an engagement party for Cait?"

"I'm better at attending than planning. You might want to ask Jules instead."

"I just left Jules. She gave me a folder an inch thick with ideas. But she was talking about party games and themes. Is that really necessary?"

"Oh, my sweet business-minded friend, a girl is only supposed to get married once. It should be special, right?"

"Yes, of course, and I want to make it a big deal for Cait. She's been ripped off her whole life." Cait had lost her adoptive mother when she was just a little girl, and her adoptive father was an asshole who'd hurt her instead of loving her and showing her how amazing she was. "But party games? I think Cait would hate that."

"Then there's your answer. Ask Cait what she wants. But first, just to make sure you don't miss anything, contact my other bestie. Her name is Google, and she's awesome."

"I know that chick. I'll see what she's got for me, and I'll ask Cait for ideas tonight. Abby's making a family dinner."

"They must be so happy you're there. How long are you staying on the island? Until your boss breaks down and begs you to come back?"

"I don't know, but I told Abby I'd stay a week, which means I have to get this party together by next weekend."

"Did Jules tell you that Leni and I can't be there next weekend? You can still have the party, but a few of us will miss it. I think Jamison couldn't make it, either. Check the group text." Leni was Jules and Sutton's sister and Abby's best friend, and Jamison was one of Brant's younger brothers.

"Shoot. Okay. I'll check the text. How are you? Are you good, other than the whole hot-boss-hating-you thing?"

"Yeah. I just wanted to check on you. I have to run, but do you want my advice on how to survive being back on the island?"

"Please."

"I hear snacking on kielbasa does wonders for bad attitudes."

"I hate you."

Sutton cracked up. "You know you love me. *Bye.*"

The line went dead. Deirdra pulled up the group text from last night to check everyone's availability. There were dozens of messages. Had everyone responded except her? She opened the folder to grab a piece of paper and found a neatly printed guest list on top with hand-written notes about each person's availability. Jules had even written down how each of Cait's friends from the Cape knew her, and she'd added what Deirdra assumed were comments that had come from those people about things they'd done with Cait or knew about her.

She felt bad for not paying attention to the group texts. Apparently orchestrating a guest list took a lot more time and attention to detail than just checking off a list. She paged through the other papers in the file. There were printouts from engagement-planning sites with dozens of ideas circled and highlighted and notes about why Jules liked each of them for Cait and Brant. How the heck had Jules gotten all of that done since Brant proposed yesterday afternoon? She had a business to run and a new fiancé, and she'd gone full hilt for *Deirdra's* sister.

If that wasn't a reality slap, she didn't know what was.

She should have offered to coordinate the schedules of their friends, not Jules. She thought about Abby and Aiden's engagement party, which had taken place shortly after the grand opening of the Bistro. Deirdra hadn't been involved in the planning of that party, either. Aiden's sister, Remi, had planned it with Cait and Leni. All Deirdra had to do was show up, but she'd gotten stuck at work and had arrived late to the party. Abby had understood, but still . . .

She sat back, thinking about her motives. She hadn't come to see Jules out of the goodness of her heart or wanting to help plan her sister's party because she wanted it to be special. She'd just wanted to get off the island as quickly as she could.

I really do suck as a sister.

That harsh reality stung.

That was not the sister she wanted to be. She was going to fix this. She'd plan the best damn party Cait and Brant had ever seen—right after she bought Abby's favorite chocolate-cherry lattice slab pie to bring home for dessert.

CHAPTER THREE

DEIRDRA'S MIND WAS all over the place as she and Aiden set the table for dinner on the back patio. She still hadn't heard from Malcolm, and she had no idea what she was going to do for two months without work to focus on. She'd made good headway on the party planning, and with all the information Jules had compiled, she couldn't imagine it taking more than a few hours to pull together the rest. She'd also stopped by the library and signed up for virtual tours of Italy, France, and Spain over the next three days, but then what? She hoped if she traveled far enough, she'd think less about work and more about vacationing, but she wasn't even sure she knew how to do that. She hadn't taken a vacation since before her father died. She was pretty sure she'd lose her mind if her boss didn't ask her to come back soon.

She set down the plates, trying to push away her worries, but when she wasn't thinking about work, her mind zipped right back to Jagger's lustful gaze strolling down her body as he stood beside the bed, far too comfortable in his nakedness. The only time Deirdra was that comfortable in her own skin was when she was fully dressed, sitting behind a desk conquering a pile of work.

She needed a distraction and admired the twinkling lights Aiden had strewn overhead and the patio furniture he'd surprised Abby with a few months ago. When that didn't get her mind off Jagger, she gazed out at the gardens Abby had resurrected. Abby and Aiden had made the place that held so many bad memories into a home as warm and inviting as if it had been rebuilt from the ground up. Deirdra looked beyond the hill to the ocean below, wondering if she'd ever be able to move past the ugliness she'd experienced in there. It was like her mother's failings had become a part of her, digging their nails in deeper every time she came back to the island.

Anxiety prickled her limbs. Sometimes she hated her own shortcomings more than her mother's. What if Malcolm decided he could do without her while she was gone? What if she didn't plan a special enough party for Cait and Brant? And why had Jagger seeded himself in her mind? Her perfectly orchestrated life suddenly felt like it was spinning out of control. She pulled out her phone to check her work email, hoping for the usual sense of calm it brought, but with her job up in the air, all she felt was a rush of anxiety.

Aiden sidled up to her. "It's not easy, is it? Figuring out what to fill your time with when you're not working."

If only it were just work that was bothering her. She was determined not to let her bad mood ruin their family dinner, and Aiden didn't need to be burdened with her issues, so she played along. "Is it that obvious?"

He slid a hand into the pocket of his dress pants. "As a former fellow workaholic, it's easy to spot the signs." Before meeting Abby, Aiden had raised his much-younger sister after losing their parents in a tragic accident, while also building an empire out of his father's financial business, and after a few years, he'd added managing his sister's acting career to his already overburdened schedule.

"Do you have any tips? Twelve steps maybe?"

He laughed. "Unfortunately, no. According to Abby, it all starts with the shoes. Apparently loafers are not conducive to relaxing." He lifted a leather-sandal-clad foot. "I don't know if she's right or not, but my love for Abs is the only thing other than Remi that has ever spoken louder than my need to work."

"Well, love is not on my agenda, so I guess I'm screwed."

"It wasn't on mine, either. Come on, let's see how dinner's coming along and get your mind off work."

They followed the heavenly scent of her sister's cooking inside and found Abby pulling a rack of lamb, potatoes, and a plethora of vegetables from the oven. Cait and Brant hadn't yet arrived.

Deirdra peered around Abby. "You made my favorite dinner? Thank you. It looks like it should be in a magazine. Too bad it's going to end up on my hips."

"That's okay, that pie you bought is going to end up on mine." Abby drizzled something over the lamb. "You've spent too many nights eating takeout at your desk. It's about time you had a home-cooked meal."

"You're the best." Deirdra plucked a cherry tomato from the colander in the sink and popped it into her mouth, watching Aiden put his arms around Abby from behind and kiss her cheek. They made love look appealing. She couldn't imagine ever feeling that way about anyone. "How can I help?"

"Why don't you pour us some wine while I get the salad together." Abby added broccoli to the mix of vegetables and poured something over them. Deirdra grabbed wineglasses from the cupboard as Abby put the food back in the oven. "This needs to cook for a little longer, and Cait and Brant should be here any min—"

"*Hello*," Cait called out as she and Brant came through the front door. Their Yorkie, Scrappy, barked. He made a beeline for the kitchen and tried to climb Deirdra.

"What is it with me and dogs?" Deirdra scooped him up, holding his tiny wiggling body away from her face as he tried to lick her. "Stop with the tongue."

"My girl never says that," Brant said as he and Cait strolled into the kitchen hand in hand. He flashed a charming smile, bringing out the dimples that had always made girls go wild, and leaned in to kiss Cait's reddening cheek. "That's just one of the many reasons I love her."

Deirdra smirked. "It's more likely one of the many reasons *she* loves *you.*"

"Dee." Cait looked imploringly at her, her straight black hair framing her pretty face. She looked the most like their mother, tall and thin, with high cheekbones, and she had a sweet demeanor.

They all laughed.

Deirdra kissed Scrappy and set him down. He scampered over to Abby, who knelt to love him up.

"Who's ready for wine?" Aiden filled glasses and handed them out.

"Wow, Cait, that sweater really brings out your eyes." Deirdra and her sisters shared their mother's green eyes.

Cait looked down at her forest-green sweater, which she'd paired with dark jeans and white Converse. She pushed up her sleeves, revealing her colorful tattoos. "Thanks. I got it when Abby and I went shopping a couple of weeks ago. Remember? I texted you pictures when we were at that shop with the fancy earrings."

"I remember." Deirdra had been working when she'd texted. She vaguely remembered the text, but she would never forget the FaceTime call with them later that night, when Abby had asked her to walk her down the aisle at her wedding. Maybe she should have expected that, but she hadn't even thought about it and had been so touched, she'd relived the moment for days. Abby had also asked Cait and Leni to be co–maids of honor.

"We had so much fun shopping," Abby said. "I was just telling Dee this morning that I wanted to find time to go shopping for your dresses for the wedding. I talked to Faye and Jagger this afternoon, and since Dee's not staying long, they're willing to fill in for me whenever I need it. Cait, do you have any free time coming up?" Faye Steele was another cook at the Bistro. She was as maternal as her ex-sister-in-law and best friend, Shelley Steele.

"You don't have to take time off for me." Deirdra sipped her wine. "I have two months to find a dress. I can always pick something up while I'm away, or find a dress online."

"Where's the fun in that?" Abby asked.

"I agree. I have some time Thursday or Friday afternoon," Cait said. "But what about Leni?"

"She's swamped at work, so we're going to look for a dress when she comes home for your engagement party," Abby explained. "I can do Thursday. Dee?"

If Abby's wedding-dress excursion was any indication of how many dresses she'd want Deirdra and Cait to try on, they were in for a long day. But the hope in her sister's voice was a great reminder that she needed to put her sisters first, and this would make Abby *so* happy. "Sure. That sounds fun."

"Great!" As Abby and Cait began making plans for their girls' day, Aiden and Brant joked about having a guys' day while the *girls did their thing*, and Deirdra finished her wine.

There was an easiness between the four of them that made Deirdra feel a little like an outsider. When had that happened? Was it just that they were coupled off now? She texted often with her sisters, but as the four of them shared inside jokes she wasn't privy to, she felt a widening divide. Had it been there all along, and she'd just been too wrapped up in work even when she was there to notice it? Or was this new?

She didn't know the answers, but it suddenly became even more important to bridge that gap.

"How does that sound, Dee?" Abby asked. "We'll go to Chaffee after lunch Thursday."

"Perfect. I'm looking forward to it. Cait, I wanted to talk with you and Brant about your engagement party. I'm going to try to help Gail plan it, and I wanted to get some input from you guys." Her phone rang, and she pulled it out of her pocket as Malcolm's name flashed on the screen. *Finally!* "I'm sorry, but this is my boss. Can you excuse me for just a second?"

"Of course. Go," Cait said.

Deirdra answered the call as she headed through the living room and out the front door. "Hi, Malcolm." *Ready to grovel?*

"Hello, Deirdra. I'm sorry to bother you, but we've hit a snag with the Dipco merger, and with Madeline King's bloodhounds on the trail, I wanted to pick your brain to make sure we don't miss anything." Madeline King was the vice president of one of their strongest competitors.

"Absolutely. What's going on?" Fueled by adrenaline, she paced the lawn as he filled her in and they discussed strategies. When Abby peeked out the front door to let her know dinner was ready, Deirdra waved her off, too entrenched with the conversation to break away.

She didn't know how much longer they talked, but by the time the call wound down, Malcolm sounded relieved. "I'm glad I called. I had a feeling I was on the right track, and you've just solidified it. Thank you."

Her pulse was soaring. "No problem." *I knew you'd need me.* "That's what I'm here for."

"Yes, well, enjoy the rest of your time off, and thanks again for taking the time to discuss it with me. Have a nice night."

Deirdra ended the call and grinned up at the sky. *Yes! My plan is working!* As she headed around the house with a bounce in her step, the sounds of silverware clinking and upbeat conversation brought a spear of guilt for missing some of the family dinner Abby had been so excited about. But she would understand, wouldn't she? She knew the importance of Deirdra's work.

"I'm sorry that took so long." Deirdra sat at the table. She must have taken much longer than she'd thought, because they were halfway through dinner.

"It's okay. Is everything all right?" Abby asked.

"Yes. He wanted to talk about a merger I was working on." She hadn't shared her plan to make her boss grovel with anyone other than Sutton, and she wasn't about to now. The last thing she wanted was for Abby, who had always looked up to her, or the others to see her as a failure for not having been chosen for the job in the first place.

"I'm sure they're lost without you." Abby passed Deirdra the platter of lamb.

"Thanks." Deirdra loaded up her plate. "What did I miss?"

"Abby was just telling us that Cait's old apartment above the garage saw some interesting action last night." Brant arched a brow. "So, you and Jag, huh?"

Jagger's face *whooshed* through her mind like the wind, and her thoughts stumbled. But it wasn't his naked body taunting her this time. It was his piercing and somehow also *soft* gaze fracturing her ability to think straight. She tried to push his image away, but those enticing eyes beckoned her, and she finally snapped. "*No*, not me and Jag. What kind of name is that, anyway?" She looked at Abby. "I can't believe you told them."

"Sorry. It was too good not to share."

"For what it's worth, we think Jagger's awesome." Brant put his arm around Cait. "Right, babe?"

Cait nodded. "Yeah. I like him."

"He's a good guy," Aiden said. "I had my reservations at first, like you did, Dee, but he's solid."

"Solid as a leaf blowing in the wind." Deirdra stabbed a potato with her fork. "Can we talk about something important, like planning Cait and Brant's party? I want to make sure the party is everything you guys want."

"We don't need a big party," Cait said.

Brant's brows knitted. "Baby, you're marrying a Remington. My family alone makes it a big party. And you know Joni will make up a theme for the party if there isn't one, so we might as well have some input." His young niece, Joni, had a big personality and an even bigger imagination. She loved to dress up and had been making up stories about people and events practically since she'd learned to talk, and Brant's family was known for playing along with her antics, including dressing to match her themes.

"He's right about Joni," Deirdra said. "Remember the under-the-sea dinner you told us about when Brant's family wore scuba masks and bathing suits?"

"How could I forget? When I first saw them all dressed up, I wasn't sure what I was walking into. But by the end of the night, I was a goner for all of them." Cait leaned closer to Brant. "I'm not very good at party ideas. Do you have any themes in mind?"

He nuzzled against her neck. "Several, but none are acceptable for public consumption."

Cait blushed again. "I'm serious."

"So am I." Brant kissed her.

"I see this is going to be fun." Deirdra sipped her wine. "Can you give me a hint? I know Scrappy sort of brought you guys together, but a dog-themed engagement party doesn't sound romantic. We could do something with boats or artistry. What else are you guys into?"

Brant smirked, and they all chuckled. They tossed around ideas as they finished eating. It was nice being part of their group. Deirdra had been working so hard, she hadn't enjoyed dinner with friends since the last time she'd visited the island, months ago.

After dinner, everyone helped clean up, and Deirdra carried the pie out to the table. "Who's ready for dessert?"

Brant drew Cait into his arms and kissed her. "I'm always ready."

"Lucky Cait." Deirdra's phone rang, and Malcolm's name appeared on the screen. Adrenaline rushed through her. "I'm sorry, you guys. This is Malcolm again. Go ahead and start without me. This shouldn't take long." She hurried around the side of the house and answered the call. "Hello."

"Hi, Deirdra. I wanted to thank you again for your insight earlier. I value your opinion and appreciate how you've always gone above and beyond for the company."

Damn right I have. "Thank you. I enjoy my job."

"It shows, and your efforts are admirable."

Here it comes. She couldn't suppress her smile, even though way down deep she was bothered about having not been his first choice.

"Would you mind if I give Ted Garber your number in case he has questions?" Ted Garber was the new general counsel. "In light of your hiatus, he's agreed to start part time next week and full time in three weeks, after he completes his contract with his current company."

Are you freaking kidding me? Deirdra was speechless.

"Deirdra?"

"Yes. That's fine," she said tightly.

"Wonderful. He's going to be a great addition to our team. Thanks again, and have a good night."

She ended the call and stared at the phone, unable to believe that was *it.* She felt gutted, torn between disappointment at not being good enough and pissed off because she knew she was far above *good enough.* Tears of anger and frustration burned, but she gritted her teeth, staving them off. She was not a crier, and that bastard was not going to make her into one.

The sounds of laughter broke through her frustrations, driving her anger deeper. Only this time that anger was directed at herself, for slighting her family and friends once again. She took a few deep breaths, pushing all those uncomfortable feelings down deep, and lifted her chin, forcing the mask she'd perfected over the years—the one that said *I'm Deirdra de Messiéres, and nothing can sink my ship.*

She walked around the house, and when she realized they'd already finished dessert, her stomach knotted up.

"Did you save the day?" Brant asked.

"Of course she did," Abby added, but there was no mistaking the disappointment in her eyes or the pitying *been there, done that* look Aiden was giving her.

"I'm *so* sorry. You know how crazy work is."

"It's okay. We're used to it." Cait patted the seat beside her. "Sit down and have some pie. It's really good."

Good Lord. Even Cait, who had known Deirdra only since the spring, was *used* to it? Her sisters asked for nothing other than a little of her time, and she'd screwed them over for a boss who had already made his choice clear.

Aiden passed her the pie as she sat down. "Pie makes everything better."

Not everything. She took the pie she'd been so happy to bring for Abby, but she'd lost her appetite. When had she turned into someone who disregarded the feelings of the people who mattered most?

Holy shit.

When had she become her mother?

CHAPTER FOUR

JAGGER SAT ON the deck of the Bistro Sunday night well after the restaurant had closed, playing a new song on his guitar that he'd written for his younger brother, Gabriel, over video chat. Gabriel was a year and a half younger than Jagger and lived with their parents in Boston. His curly brown hair had a mind of its own, his smile could steal anyone's heart but was rarely seen, and he absolutely loved music. His left thumb rubbed the side of his index finger as he listened to Jagger play, eyes trained downward. Their mother sat beside him, swaying to the music, her loving gaze moving between her two sons. She tucked her light brown hair behind her ear, and when Gabriel made an indiscernible noise, she asked him what he wanted. Jagger continued playing, having learned long ago not to stop midway through a song unless Gabriel wanted him to. Gabriel had autism and was nonverbal, and over the years Jagger had learned to avoid many of the things that triggered discomfort for him. Although, as with everyone, Gabriel would learn and grow as years passed, and those triggers might change. Jagger would be right there, learning and growing with him.

Jagger finished the song and set the guitar beside Dolly, who was sleeping by his feet. "What do you think, Gabe?"

Gabriel rocked forward and back in his chair, his head bobbing. Their mother moved the iPad on its stand into position in front of him so he could use a special software program to communicate with Jagger.

Gabe knew some sign language, and he could say a word or two here or there, but the iPad was his main device for communicating. As he typed, an automated voice spoke for him. "Good. I like it."

Jagger lit up inside. "Awesome, man. I wrote that just for you."

"It was lovely, honey," his mother said. "It's too bad your father is at a meeting tonight. You'll have to play it for him sometime."

"I will, the next time we practice for the holiday concert." His parents were musicians, and he joined them in holding concerts a few times each year to raise money for various autism charities.

"Perfect. How are things going? Are you eating enough? You look a little thin."

Jagger laughed. "Mom, I've always been thin. I'm eating plenty. Faye pushes food on me all the time. You'd like her."

"I'll have to thank her if we ever meet. What else is happening? How's work?"

"Work is good. Cait and Brant got engaged yesterday." His mother had always been interested in his travels and the friends he made. When he'd told her about Ava's passing, which he'd only learned about when he'd returned to the island to see her in late spring, his mother had called often for the next few weeks, making sure he was okay.

"That's wonderful. You said they were really good together."

"They are, and Ava's daughter Didi showed up yesterday. The lawyer. Should make for an interesting few days." *And if he had it his way, a few fun nights, too.*

"The mouthy but cute one?" she asked.

"*Feisty*, Mom. There's a difference."

His mother smiled. "*Ah*, I hear that now. You like her, don't you?"

"You know me. I like everyone—right, Gabe?" Gabriel was staring off to the side, and he didn't acknowledge Jagger's question, but hopefully he'd sidetracked his mother.

"You know what I mean, honey," his mother said.

Dolly's head popped up, and she looked down the beach. Jagger petted her.

"Hi, Dolls," his mother said, and Dolly stood up, pushing her nose into the screen, making his mother giggle. "We love you, too, sweetheart."

Gabriel poked at the iPad again, the robotic voice saying, "Hi." Dolly pushed her nose toward the screen as the robotic voice said, "Eat dessert. Bye."

"A'right, buddy. I love you guys."

"We'll talk soon, honey." His mother blew him a kiss. "Love you."

As Jagger ended the call and pocketed his phone, Dolly went to the edge of the deck, tail wagging. Jagger followed her gaze to Deirdra stomping toward them in the sand, her arms crossed over a thick sweater. *Always so mad.* She stopped to take off one of her shoes and dumped sand from a high heel, which made Jagger chuckle. Only Deirdra would wear heels on the beach. "Go get her, Dolls."

Dolly bolted toward her, and Jagger slung his guitar strap over his shoulder, watching with amusement as Deirdra tried to dodge Dolly's excitement while simultaneously trying to take off her other high heel.

"*No*, Dolly. Stop, sweetie." She turned away, but Dolly moved with her, pushing her nose into Deirdra's face every time she bent to pick up her high heel. "*Jagger*, do something."

He sauntered down the steps to the beach. "She just wants some love."

"I'm not in a very loving mood." She looked down at Dolly. "*Sit.*"

Dolly sat on Deirdra's high heel, tail wagging wildly, tongue hanging out of her mouth with great anticipation of the love Jagger usually lavished on her when she obeyed his requests.

"Good girl, but you could have chosen a better spot." Deirdra petted her as she yanked her high heel free, and Dolly tried to lick her hand.

"A little love goes a long way." Even in the moonlight he could tell Deirdra's nose was a little pink and her eyes damp, like she'd been crying. He wondered who or what could make a woman as strong as her cry. "You look like you could use some, too. Want to talk about it?"

"I don't know what you're talking about. I'm *fine*. I'm just taking a walk."

"You mean a *stomp*."

She rolled her eyes and continued stalking toward the Bistro. "What are you doing down here, anyway?"

"I like it here. It's relaxing."

"So . . . *what*? You just hang out on the deck of the restaurant until a woman walks by, then send your wingdog in? I bet most women fawn all over her."

He laughed. "I've never needed a wingdog, but now that you mention it, what's *not* to fawn over?" When Deirdra didn't respond, he shifted his guitar around his body, whistling as he played "Don't Worry Be Happy."

She looked at him out of the corner of her eyes. "Can you *not* do that, please?"

"Not a Bobby McFerrin fan? What else would you like to hear?"

"The sounds of silence."

"Cool. I can chill." He moved his guitar behind him again.

When they reached the Bistro, Deirdra headed up the steps. "You've got a key, right?"

"Yeah. Why?"

"Because there's alcohol in there, and I need it."

"That bad of a night, huh?" He opened the door, and she strode past him with Dolly on her heels. Dolly went to explore with her nose to the floor.

Deirdra dropped her heels by the door and went to the bar. Like everyone else, Jagger knew she didn't like being on the island and wondered if that was all this was, or if there was more to it.

He set his guitar on a table and went to join her at the bar. "What's going on with you, Dee? Did your family dinner go awry?"

She opened a bottle of tequila, giving him a serious stare. "Are you staying or going? Because if you're staying, you're doing shots." She poured a shot, holding the bottle over the second glass. "What's it going to be?"

"I'm not letting you drink alone. I'm in. But give me a second." He went around the bar and set the salt beside the glasses. Then he grabbed a few limes from the fridge, quickly cutting them into wedges, and placed them in a bowl, eyeing her playfully. "And don't think just because you get me tipsy, you can have your way with me."

She laughed, and *man*, that made her sexier than ever, but she quickly schooled her expression. "Dream on, hippie boy." She poured his shot and handed him the glass. "Here's to shitty bosses."

As she lifted the glass to her lips, he grabbed her wrist, earning a scowl. "First of all, I have a great boss, who I happen to really like working for."

She rolled her eyes, trying to pull her arm free.

"But more importantly, have you ever done tequila shots?"

"Once," she said, chin held high. Then softer, "Well, I *almost* did them once."

"Almost?" He set her glass on the bar. "You can't just down the tequila. This is a *lick*, *sip*, *suck* situation."

Her jaw dropped. "I am *not* licking or sucking anything."

"Cool, then *sip* remains in play. Body shots it is."

She glowered.

He smirked. "Chill out, babe. I already told you I'm not going to let you take advantage of me, so there will be no body shots tonight."

"Oh *darn*." Her words dripped with sarcasm. "Let's get to it."

He gave her a slow, suggestive grin, and she laughed. "That's a good look on you, Dee."

"*Shots*, Jagger."

He chuckled. "Lick the skin between your index finger and thumb, like this." He licked that part of his hand.

"You just want to see me lick something."

"Now that you mention it . . ." He took her half scowl, half smile as a win.

With another eye roll, she licked her hand.

"Now put salt on the wet spot."

"*Ouch.* I bet you don't get many second dates with that line." She tried to stop a grin from taking over.

He took her hand. "A gentleman always takes care of his lady, but I wasn't sure you'd let me." He sprinkled salt on the area she'd licked.

She tried to scowl, but laughter bubbled out, making him laugh, too.

"Jesus, Jones. You are *bad.*"

Their eyes collided, turning the tease in hers into something dark and hungry. *Oh yeah. There's no mistaking this sizzling heat for fury.* "I guess you bring that out in me."

She swallowed hard, and as if she'd caught her guard slipping, she lifted her chin and drew back her shoulders. "Yeah? Well, this island brings out something bad in me, too."

"*Bad* as in wicked and naughty? Or *bad* as in you might need bail money?"

Her expression turned serious. "*Bad* as in, I'm realizing things about myself that might lead to me needing bail money, which is why I need *this.*" She lifted her glass. "Lick, sip, suck, right?"

"Absolutely." He winked to make her smile, but it didn't ease the heaviness her confession had caused or the desire to figure out why she felt that way. "Lick the salt, drink the tequila, and then bite into a lime." They did the shots, and she scrunched up her face. "You okay?"

"*Whew!*" She shook her head, sending her silky hair whipping from side to side. "Yup. I'm good, and that's nasty."

"You don't have to drink it."

"Oh yes, I do." She poured two more shots. "Lick up, Mister."

He leaned closer, wagging his tongue, and she pushed him away, laughing.

"Hey, you sent out the invitation."

"I didn't *send* anything. Less talking, more drinking." She held up her glass.

He gave her a coy smile. "It's my turn to toast." He lifted his glass. "Here's to shitty nights that lead to you laughing."

They did the shots, and she scrunched her face again. "God, that's so gross."

He was about to make a comment when she said, "Don't even think about lecturing me about drinking. I never drink unless I'm on this freaking island." She refilled their glasses and slid his across the bar. "Here's to trying not to be a crappy sister anymore."

Aw hell. Shitty bosses? Being a crappy sister? She had some pretty heavy stuff going on. "I take back the toast about shitty nights. Sorry, Didi. You really must have had an awful night, and that's nothing to joke about."

She blinked several times, a little glassy eyed from the tequila. "What'd I tell you about calling me by that stripper name? Hush up and drink."

"How about I lend you an ear instead?"

"You wouldn't understand."

"Try me."

She eyed him doubtfully and lifted her glass toward her mouth.

He touched her arm, stopping her. "You might want to slow down. That tequila's going to kick in and knock you off your feet."

She narrowed her eyes. "No lectures, remember? It's okay if you can't keep up."

"Oh, I can keep up. But you've made no secret of hating your mother's drinking."

"You're right. I definitely don't make a secret of that. And *yes*, I realize I'm a freaking hypocrite for turning to tequila tonight, but like I said, I *never* drink unless I'm here."

"I'm not judging you. I'm a firm believer that people know what they can handle."

"I think my mother disproved that theory." She picked up the tequila bottle and waved it at him. "Grab the stuff. Let's take this party outside." She headed for the door with a little extra sway in her step, leaving the full shot glass behind. "Come on, Dolls."

Oh yeah, that tequila was taking her down a notch. Jagger dumped out the shots, gathered their drinking supplies and his guitar, and headed into the breezy night. Deirdra was sitting in the sand in front of the deck with one arm around Dolly. The tequila bottle lay between her bare feet. As Jagger lowered himself to the sand beside Deirdra, Dolly stretched out, resting her jaw on her paws. He swore his pooch was smiling. Deirdra, on the other hand, was gazing absently out at the water.

"Want to talk about your shitty boss?"

She shook her head. "I need another drink." She snagged one of the shot glasses and fumbled with the bottle, pouring herself a drink. "I admit that I suck at some things, like cooking, and apparently being a sister, but I'm damn good at my job." She shoved the bottle into the sand and licked her hand.

"I've never heard about you being a sucky sister, but I have heard that you're an incredible attorney." He put salt on her hand and gave her a lime wedge.

"Thank you." She did the shot and dropped her glass in the sand and the lime into the bowl. "Do you know why I didn't get hired for the general counsel position?"

"I didn't know you were up for a promotion."

"I wasn't, but I *should* have been. I'm the best attorney in that place. I moved right up the corporate ladder." She moved her fingers as if walking up steps. "But I don't have the right plumbing to be part of top management's freaking boys' club. So what does my misogynistic boss do? He hires a *dude* from outside the company."

Jagger knew she was pissed, because she never used that word.

"I mean, what the hell was he thinking? He had *me*." She smacked both hands on her chest. "I work harder and smarter than anyone else. I put everyone else to shame."

"I'm sorry to hear they passed you up. That had to sting. I'm sure they'll regret it."

"That's just it." She leaned closer, like she was sharing a secret. "They're too stupid to see what's right in front of them. Why are men so stupid? Why am *I* so stupid? I missed most of dinner with my sisters and Aiden and Brant because I was dead set on hearing my boss say he was wrong, which makes me an ass for giving *him* the time I should have spent with *them*." She started pouring another drink but missed the glass.

"I think you've had enough." He reached for the bottle, but she pulled it away, shaking her head. "Didi, you're going to regret drinking too much."

"Don't pretend you know me. I never do things I regret."

He had a feeling even she knew that wasn't true, but he wasn't about to call her out on it when what she really needed was a friend and an escape from her own head.

She started to bring the bottle to her lips, but he grabbed her wrist. "*Jagger.* It's only one night."

"Listen, if you want to drink yourself numb, that's cool. I get it. Your boss is a jackass, you slighted your sisters, and you need to disappear for a while. But what did I tell you? A gentleman always takes care of his lady." He took her hand.

"I'm not your—"

He licked between her finger and thumb, turning the scorn in her beautiful eyes to liquid heat. Her cheeks flushed, and that enticing look climbed right up to the top of the *Great Looks on Deirdra* chart, next to blushing. "I can't let you drink that swill without at least trying to make it better." He sprinkled salt onto her hand and offered her a lime. "Now you may carry on."

She didn't go for the salt or the tequila. She just sat there staring at him, brows knitted. "Who *are* you?"

"Just a guy with a guitar and a dog."

"No. You're more than that. You're a pretty nice hippie."

She drank the shot, and when she put down the bottle and looked up at the sky, he discreetly moved the bottle to his other side, hoping the old adage "out of sight, out of mind" would hold true.

"Where was I?" She looked at him.

"You said you never do anything you regret."

"Obviously that isn't true. I screwed over Abby and Cait. They're two of the sweetest women on the planet, and I didn't just do it tonight. I *always* screw them over."

"I think you're being a little hard on yourself, don't you? You came back to the island to help Cait with her shop, and Abby talks about how much fun she had wedding dress shopping with you guys."

Deirdra shook her head and whispered, "Can you keep a secret?"

He'd been keeping her mother's secrets for years. "Sure."

"I didn't come back only to help Cait. I came back because I was screwing over my boss. When he told me he'd hired someone else for the position, I wanted him to see how much he needed me. So I took off." She pushed her hand out and up, like a plane taking flight.

"But you could have gone anywhere, or stayed in Boston, and you came back here and helped your sister. That has to count for something."

"I'm not sure it does. Because where would you go if you realized you weren't as great as you thought you were? To be with the people who believe in you and would tell you you're *all that*, even if you weren't, right?"

He noticed she didn't ask if he'd go *home*, which spoke volumes about her feelings on that topic. "Yeah, I would. It's called seeking solace, and it still counts, Dee. That's what family is for, being there when you need them."

"That's just it. It shouldn't count for me because I'm never here when they need me or when they just want me. I always put work ahead of them, and they *still* love me." She stared out at the water, her voice softening. "I don't get it. How can they? Even when I'm here, I'm not really *here*. I can't wait to leave. And you know what else?" Sadness washed over her face. "Tonight, when they were talking about color schemes and menus for Abby and Aiden's wedding, I realized I don't even know the details of the biggest event in my sister's life. Abby has probably told me a million times, but always when I was working and only half listening. I *suck* as a sister, Jagger. I've made myself an outsider in my own family."

The pain in her voice brought his arm around her, his heart breaking for the woman who resented her mother so deeply, she couldn't forgive her, and in turn, he was fairly certain she didn't trust her own sisters' unconditional love. It was no wonder she pushed away anyone who tried to get too close. "You don't suck, and you're still here. The fate of your relationship with your sisters is in your hands, Dee. You have the power to make it anything you want."

"I don't know if I have what it takes to fix it," she said softly. "I'm not selfless like Abby or insightful like Cait. Look how selfish I've been, even tonight, unloading on you like this." Her eyes dampened. "I think I've become my mother, and I hate myself for it."

A tear slipped down her cheek, and he braced himself, fearing she'd cast thunder and lightning at him to hide her vulnerabilities. But she didn't make a snarky comment or stalk off to escape the sadness emanating from her, and when he pulled her into his arms, she rested her head on his shoulder. When she sniffled, he held her a little tighter.

"I'm *not* crying," she snapped.

He smiled at her vehemence. "I didn't think you were."

She drew back, just a few inches, their faces so close he wanted to lean in and kiss that tear away. But she was tipsy and studying him as if she was either waiting for him to judge her or debating walking away.

"I don't blame you for your feelings toward Ava," he said carefully, assuming that was on her mind.

She sat up taller and looked out at the water. "Why? Did she tell you everything? How we lost our childhood? That I sent her money every week like clockwork, even when I was in college?"

"No." Ava had told him a lot, but not about the money. He wasn't surprised to hear it, because, despite her fierce resentment for her mother, he still saw love for her in Deirdra's eyes. "She didn't tell me everything, but she knew she wasn't the best mother after your father died."

Deirdra looked down at the sand. "That's putting it mildly."

"She never tried to hide her failings. She was up-front with me about her drinking. I know she was a functioning alcoholic by day and nearly drowned in her sorrows at night."

"I really don't want to talk about her."

"Okay, but you should know she loved you and your sisters very much."

She met his gaze. "She said that?"

He nodded. "We talked a lot. I know she had issues, and I don't like how her drinking affected your family, but she was a good friend to me, and I liked her."

"Yeah? Well, she wasn't a good friend to us. What was your relationship with her, anyway? Were you really only friends? *Wait.* I don't want to know if you slept with her."

"Do you seriously think I'd sleep with a woman old enough to be my mother?"

She shrugged one shoulder. "I don't know what you two could've had in common, but I don't want to talk about my mother, and you're two shots behind me." She reached around him for the bottle, their chests brushing. Her eyes flicked up to his, and just like that, flames ignited between them. She tore her gaze away and poured him a shot, sitting up a little taller as she handed him the glass. "Are you even old enough to drink?"

So sassy. "That's a sneaky way to find out my age. I'm twenty-five."

"You're so young. You'd better drink that before I do." She watched him drink and licked her lips as if she could taste it, too. "You probably go after twenty-two-year-olds, don't you?"

"There's only one woman floating my boat lately, and she's definitely not twenty-two."

"That was about as smooth as gravel."

"Really? I thought it was pretty cool." They both laughed. "I've lived a lot in my twenty-five years."

She gave him a disbelieving look. "Banging coeds doesn't count as living."

"Why are you so uptight?"

"I'm *not.*"

He arched a brow. "Prove it. Tell me something you've done that'll surprise me."

"No."

"Come *on.* I'll go first. I once modeled in the nude for an art class."

"Lucky students," she said under her breath, her cheeks reddening. "If we're going to play true confessions, I need another drink."

"How about no more shots, and we just live in the moment, right now, as tipsy as you are?" He was enjoying this side of her and didn't want her getting too far gone.

"Fine." She leaned against his shoulder. "I made out with a girl once."

"That's funny. So did I." They shared a smile. "Did you like it?"

"All we did was kiss and feel each other up. What's not to like? But I couldn't do more." Her voice softened. "I'm not into *V.* I'm into *D.*"

He chuckled. "Good to know."

"Your turn."

"Okay, let's see. Well, I haven't made out with a guy, so I can't meet you one-for-one. But I had a mad crush on a girl in middle school and dyed my hair bright pink because it was her favorite color."

"No way."

"Yup, and I wore all black for two weeks because she thought it was cool."

"Wow, you really took dating seriously. Did she go out with you?"

"No. She went out with my best friend."

"Aw, that's sad."

"Not really. Her older sister felt bad for me, and I got to third base for the first time in her basement." He did a fist pump, and she laughed. "Who was your first crush? The guy who you could barely breathe around, who you dreamed about and lusted after?" He picked up his guitar and started playing "Jessie's Girl."

She gasped in surprise. "I *love* that song."

"Sing with me."

"I suck at singing."

"That'll make it even better. Come on. Don't be chicken."

"Chicken, my ass. I sing *and* dance all the time to my neighbors' music when they blast their stereo." She began singing, swaying closer, and a minute later she was leaning against his side, belting out the words horribly off-key.

She bobbed her head to the beat and stood up, nearly falling over before finding her footing and breaking into a dance. She whipped her head around, singing as if she'd just been freed from prison. Dolly barked and howled as they sang. Deirdra laughed so hard she fell to her knees, holding her stomach, her smile a mile wide. "If I laugh any more, I'm gonna puke."

He cracked up, and she swatted at him. He caught her hand and pulled her into his arms. They fell to the sand, bodies tangled, her carefree laughter the *best* music to his ears. Dolly ran back and forth beside them, barking, but when Deirdra looked up at Jagger, the air pulsed with heat and happiness, turning those barks to white noise, their laughter silenced by the pull of desire.

"Didi—"

"*Don't*," she pleaded.

"Ah, you want to remember our first kiss."

She giggled and pushed at his chest. "*Off*, hippie boy."

He rolled onto his back, and Dolly dove for Deirdra, covering her face with sloppy dog kisses. Deirdra shrieked, laughing and covering her face as she rolled in the sand beside him. "Dolly! *Jagger!* Help!"

He nudged his pooch away from her. "Come on, Dolls. Save some kisses for me." He pushed to his feet and helped Deirdra to hers. She was always beautiful, but sandy, smiling, and clinging to him with her guard down? She was utterly and completely captivating. If she weren't borderline drunk, he'd lean in and take that first kiss, knowing it'd be so damn good, neither of them would *ever* forget it.

"You can have *all* the doggy kisses." She stumbled back.

He caught her, pulling her into his arms. "I wasn't talking about Dolly's kisses. Who knows, maybe one day we will . . ." He grinned.

"Or . . ." She pressed her luscious curves against him, whispering, "Maybe we won't."

"Always so sassy . . . I like it."

She leaned back, swaying a little, her gaze as soft and curious as it was hot and wanting. "Why are you so good to me, much less want to kiss me, when I'm such a pain?"

"Because I have a feeling that beneath that prickly exterior is the woman Ava raved about every time I was with her. Come on, tipsy girl, let's get you home."

"I'm *not* going home with you. I wanna dance, and sing, and drink." She plunked herself down in the sand, and Dolly went in for kisses again. Deirdra giggled and petted her. "Save those for your hippie daddy."

"How about you save some for me, too?" He winked at Deirdra.

She rolled her eyes and began singing "*Dah, dah, dah, dah, dah*" to the tune of "Sweet Child O' Mine" as he gathered their things, and she burst into song as he went to lock up the Bistro. He stopped on the deck to watch her sitting in the sand playing the air guitar and whipping her hair around. She was so cute and unguarded he could barely stand it, but he knew that song came from a place of sadness she'd probably never admit to. It was Ava's favorite, and Ava had told him all about Deirdra's father, a Frenchman named Olivier, who had come to the island and opened the Bistro with nothing more than a backpack full of money and a dream. Olivier had loved classic rock, and Abby had been his daddy's girl. But what few people knew, or seemed to remember, was that before Olivier died and Ava started drinking, Deirdra had been a mama's girl.

Jagger looked up at the sky, sending a silent message to his lost-but-never-forgotten friend. *Hear that? There's a crack in your girl's fortress, and that beauty you raved about is spilling out.* He gazed at Deirdra, singing softer now and petting Dolly. *If I'm lucky, she might even let me help her take down those walls.*

CHAPTER FIVE

AS WAKEFULNESS TRICKLED in, Deirdra's throbbing head paved the way for images from last night in her periphery. Did she really spill her guts to Jagger and almost *kiss* him? Her body heated with desire. *Oh yeah, I did.* She'd wanted to do a heck of a lot more than kiss. She shifted on the mattress, but she was squished between two heavy bodies. Her eyes flew open, and she found Jagger's sleepy eyes and scruffy cheeks smiling down at her.

"Morning, crooner." He was leaning on his elbow, and Dolly was lying on her other side.

"Ohmygod. I'm in *your* bed? I *sang*? Did we . . . ?" She covered her face with her hands, and Dolly licked her cheek, her tail thumping happily.

"You sang, you danced, and you tried to have your way with me." He pulled her hands away from her face, and she groaned. "Remember that? You were singing when we got home, and you didn't want to wake Abby, so you asked if you could stay with me."

Her cheeks burned as those memories pushed their way to the forefront.

"You were pretty convincing once we got in bed." He lowered his voice to a whisper. *"Come on, Jaggy, we won't tell anyone."*

She cringed. *Jaggy?* Lord have mercy, she'd lost her mind. "I'm *never* drinking tequila again." Dolly jumped off the bed, and Deirdra suddenly realized Jagger was shirtless. She held her breath as she peeked under the sheet, relieved that she was still clothed, and he had sweatpants on.

"Don't worry, I kept you an honest woman."

"How chivalrous of you," she said sarcastically, and climbed out of bed, looking around for her heels.

"We had fun last night."

She remembered that, too, having more fun than she'd had in years and feeling a connection with the least likely guy on the island. Even three sheets to the wind, that oddly matched connection had felt solid and real, which rattled her. "Where are my heels?"

"With your phone."

"My *phone*." She'd thought about her heels before her phone? That tequila really had messed with her head.

"Yeah, you asked for my number, and then you took the phone into the bathroom and sent me some *very* enticing pictures."

"Oh no. *No, no, no.* Where is it?" she snapped.

He laughed. "I put it by the front door, with your heels and your sweater."

"Delete whatever I sent you."

"Your dirty voicemails, too?"

She winced. "Please tell me you're lying."

He stepped from the bed, looking like sex on legs, and stretched, the bulge in his sweatpants becoming more pronounced as he arched his back. "Nope. Want to hear them?"

"Good God, *no*." She stalked out of the bedroom in search of her phone, and he followed her down the hall.

"Hang out with me this afternoon."

She pocketed her phone, afraid to look at the pictures, and grabbed her sweater as she pushed her feet into her heels. "I can't." She opened the door, taking one last look at his deliciousness and hating herself a little for doing it. "Thanks for not letting me make a bigger fool of myself."

"You didn't make a fool of yourself. You set yourself free for a few hours, and we had a great time. Let's have some more fun. Stick around and do some yoga with me, or meet me after work. I get off at three. We can explore the island, and I promise not to let you anywhere near alcohol."

A voice she barely recognized as her own whispered through her mind. *Okay! That sounds fun.* As she'd done a million times after her father had first died, she kicked that frivolous girl to the curb, forcing her responsible self to take charge. She met Jagger's gaze, but those playful, alluringly sexy eyes weakened her resolve. The urge to throw caution to the wind and drag him back to bed to while away the morning together was so strong, she had to force herself to look away and break whatever spell he'd cast on her.

"I can't. I'm going to Italy." She hurried down the steps, feeling him watching her, and willing herself not to look back as she headed in the side door. She hurried past Abby, nearly knocking into Aiden, and sprinted up the stairs.

"Are you *just* getting home?" Abby called after her. "Where were you all night?"

Apparently trying to molest Jagger.

Deirdra closed her bedroom door and leaned against it, breathing like she'd been chased by the devil. *Devilish charmer, maybe.* It had taken her thirty years to do the walk of shame, and she hadn't even gotten sex out of it.

She *really* needed to get off that island, but how could she fix things with Abby and Cait if she left? And then there was Jagger, the only man who had ever been able to make her forget work. She was so screwed. She *always* had a clear direction, but she was too confused to think straight right now, so she focused on the things that mattered—taking care of a few plans for Cait's party. Then . . . *Italy.*

♥ ♥ ♥

Classic rock played on Olivier's old boom box in the kitchen of the Bistro, a tradition Jagger was glad Abby had continued when she'd taken over the restaurant. Ava would sometimes leave it playing long after the restaurant had closed, while she drank to remember—and to forget—the love of her life and the pain she'd caused.

Pushing those harsh memories away, Jagger put garnishes on two entrées and rang the bell, alerting the waitstaff that they were ready. He was thankful the Bistro had been busy all day, giving him less time to think about Deirdra leaving. He was bummed she'd decided to take off to Italy rather than trying to fix her relationship with her sisters. He'd thought she was sincere in wanting to make things better, and he'd hoped she'd felt the same growing connection with him as he had with her. But maybe it had been the alcohol after all.

He heard Abby and Faye chatting and looked in the direction of the open back door, where they'd stopped to pet Dolly on their way in. He didn't like to tie up Dolly, but he had no choice. At least if she was leashed outside the kitchen she'd get attention from the Bistro staff and customers, and he could see her from where he worked.

"I told Lenore I will *not* use one of those dating apps," Faye said as she and Abby washed their hands. "Can you imagine? At my age?" She grabbed an apron and handed it to Abby, then slipped one over her head, past her layered blond hair, her apple cheeks growing rounder with her smile as she tied the apron around her thick waist.

"You're only in your fifties. I think you should go for it. You never know who you'll meet." Abby looked at Jagger. "Dating apps aren't all bad, are they, Jag?"

"I don't use them." He began fixing a sandwich for an order. "But, Faye, you might want to stay away from Tinder unless you're just looking for a good time, if you know what I mean."

"Oh, honey. I might be old, but my libido is still intact." Faye walked over and bumped him with her hip. "Now, get outta here. It's five after three, and I'm sure the hot young ladies on this island would much rather you were hanging out wherever they are than slaving away in here."

"Speaking of hot ladies," Abby said conspiratorially. "Dee didn't get home until early this morning. Jagger, did you happen to see her when you were out last night?"

"Maybe she's using Tinder." Faye giggled. "Can you imagine Dee's profile? *Beautiful attorney seeks smart man who will keep his thoughts to himself so as not to piss her off.*"

Abby laughed. "She's a tough cookie, but one day I hope she finds a man who loves her as much as Aiden loves me. I don't know who she spent the night with, but she was pretty wigged out when she got home. When Aiden and I left for our walk this morning, she said she was catching an early ferry to the Cape to talk to some of Cait's friends about the engagement party, but I'm worried she's heading to Boston and going back to work instead of taking time off. She got two calls from her boss last night. I know they need her, but I was looking forward to spending time together."

"Maybe we should have made her a dating profile," Faye suggested. "We could have kept her busy so she wouldn't want to leave. We'll have to remember to do that next time she visits."

Jagger felt a pang of jealousy he had no business feeling. He wanted to own up to being with her last night, but if Deirdra hadn't told Abby, he had a feeling he shouldn't, either. "I highly doubt she'd give up Italy for Boston or work."

"Italy? What do you mean?" Abby asked.

"I saw her this morning, and she said she was leaving for Italy today."

Abby's eyes widened. "*What?* She doesn't even like to fly. That's why she always takes the ferry. I'm calling her." She pulled out her phone and made the call, holding up her index finger as she waited for Deirdra to answer. "Dee? Hi. Where are you?" She paused. "Oh, good. Okay." She was quiet again, listening. "That's great news. Okay, see you later. Love you." She ended the call. "Looks like I misjudged her. She's back on the island."

Jagger took off his apron and tossed it in the hamper.

I guess I misjudged her, too. I never thought she'd lie to avoid me.

Forget waiting for Lady Luck to step in. Come hell or high water, he was going to help Deirdra tear down her walls, because while she might be afraid, or untrusting, of their connection, or scared of who she might be when she came out on the other side, Jagger had gotten a peek behind her curtain. Ava was right. She had music in her heart, love in her soul, and far too much goodness to be left drowning in a swamp of resentment.

After leaving the Bistro, Jagger headed over to the library with Dolly. Like most places on the quaint island, the library was dog friendly.

Shondra Mellinger, a sweet, fortysomething brunette who had once tried to set him up with one of her nieces, greeted him from behind the desk. "Hi, Jagger. It's nice to see you and Dolly." She got up to pet Dolly. "Hello, sweet girl. What are you two up to today?"

"I need to do some research on old Silver Island newspapers. Is there a computer and printer I can use for a little while?"

"Let me check." She went to her computer, and a minute later she said, "All the computers on the floor are in use, but you're in luck. The history room is free, and that's where you need to be to check the archives. I'll walk you back."

He followed her through the library. Sunlight poured in through the glass walls of offices around the perimeter. People sat in cubicles poking at computers and at tables, reading. Rows of bookshelves lined the middle of the floor like a path to the aisles of books in the back. They walked past an office, and Jagger spotted Deirdra sitting at the computer. Her long legs were crossed, and she was sitting at an angle, one elbow leaning on the arm of the chair, her chin perched on her fist, eyes glued to the computer. *Italy, huh?* He wondered if she was job searching, although she could do that on her laptop at the house.

"Any idea what Deirdra de Messiéres is doing here?"

"Yes. She's taking a virtual tour of Italy. It's part of a new program we started this summer."

His clever girl hadn't lied after all. "Did Deirdra sign up for other tours?"

"Oh yes. She's trying to decide where to spend her hiatus." She lowered her voice. "She's taking a three-hour tour of France tomorrow at two, and I believe she signed up for a three-hour tour of Spain at five on Wednesday."

"Interesting."

"She seemed excited. I still can't believe she's taking time off, but good for her. She deserves a break. I've never met anyone who works as hard as her." Shondra unlocked the door to the history room. "Here we are."

There was a computer desk and a printer on the left side of the room, flanked by floor-to-ceiling bookshelves, a set of cabinets and drawers to their right, and two tables by the interior glass wall.

"You can sign on using your library card identification number. If you search *Silver Island Gazette* you should come up with all the historical data, but if you have trouble finding what you're looking for, just let me know."

"Perfect, thank you. I'd love to hear more about those virtual tours."

"I thought that might pique your interest. I've already taken *five* tours to places I'll surely never have a chance to see in person . . ."

CHAPTER SIX

TUESDAY AFTERNOON, DEIRDRA shoved the folder from Jules, and all of her own notes for Cait and Brant's party, into her tote bag, while talking on Bluetooth with Sutton. "I'm still trying to decide on a theme for Cait's party. This is harder than handling a five-million-dollar acquisition."

"You can always hand it over to Jules and be done with it."

"No way. I want to do it. I just never expected it to be so complicated. I spent yesterday morning on the Cape tracking down Cait's friends who hadn't responded to Jules's texts. I don't know if you've met Cait's biker friends Zander and Baz Wicked, or their brothers and cousins, but they are wild. They *both* hit on me, and Gia, who Cait worked with at Tank Wicked's tattoo shop, tried to talk me into getting a tattoo. It was funny, and those guys are *hot*."

"So I've heard. Maybe we need to spend more time on the Cape."

"They're totally not my type." For some reason Deirdra kept comparing them to Jagger, who also wasn't her type. But she couldn't help noticing that the badass bikers' brash flirtations didn't hold a candle to Jagger's easygoing charm. "At least now I've reached everyone on the list, and I've confirmed the party for a week from Saturday."

"Have you talked to Gail?"

She headed through the living room to the front door. "Not yet, but tonight I'm going to crash their bunco game and get all the moms' and grandmothers' opinions at once. Hold on." She peeked outside. "Okay, the coast is clear. Where were we?" She hurried out to her car.

"What *coast* is clear?"

Shoot. She hadn't meant to say that out loud. "Nothing."

"Dee," Sutton snapped. "*Who* are you avoiding?"

"Jagger. Apparently tequila leads to really bad decisions."

"Did you *do* the well-hung hippie?"

"*No!* And don't remind me of that." She'd done a pretty good job of not thinking about him naked, and now he was front and center in her mind again. "I might have sent him some incriminating selfies." She'd finally gotten up the courage to look at them. There were a couple of harmless kissy-faces, but then there was a full-on cleavage shot taken down her shirt and another of her wearing only her lace bra with a *take me, baby* look in her eyes.

"You did *not*." Sutton sounded as shocked as Deirdra had been.

"Blame the tequila! I've *never* sent those types of pictures to any man, and I'm absolutely mortified. And that's not the worst of it. He said I left him dirty voicemails, too."

"Oh my gosh. Dee!" She burst into laughter. "I'd give just about anything to hear those."

"Shut up. This is serious. What if he shows the pictures to other people? What if he shows our friends and laughs about them? What if he plays the voicemails for them? I don't even know what I said."

"What if he jerks off to them?"

"Sutton! You're not making this any easier. Now I'm thinking about his big hand around his . . ." She closed her eyes for a second, willing the thoughts away as her friend giggled. "I don't want to know what he did with them. I've been avoiding him since yesterday. Every time he comes near me, he gets under my skin in ways other people never do." *Bringing out parts of me I never knew existed.*

"You're totally into him, aren't you?"

"*No*. I don't know what I am. I think the whole work fiasco has messed with my head. Thankfully, Abby said Jagger is getting his RV back tomorrow, so he won't be hanging around at the house. But I don't want to talk about him." She pulled out of the driveway and headed for town.

"Fine. But if you ever decide to go full-on cougar and shag him, I want details."

"A five-year age difference hardly makes me a cougar. I'm hanging up now."

"Wait! I'll stop talking about him. What are you going to do about work? Find another job?"

"*Definitely.* There's no way I'm going to work my ass off for them after being overlooked for a job that I'm more than qualified to do, even though I hate the idea of interviewing. It's such an awful process, sitting for judgment, tooting my own horn."

"You're right, job searching sucks. I'm sorry your boss is an ass. You know any company would be lucky to have you. Did you start looking yet?"

"A little. I saw a few positions online this morning, but nothing jumped out at me."

"It'll take time. Maybe you can find something in Port Hudson, near me, or in Manhattan, near Leni."

"We'll see. On the upside, I just got to the library, and I get to spend three hours in my father's homeland. Jules was right about the virtual tours. They're really well done. I'm looking forward to this one."

"Take screenshots for me."

"Will do." Deirdra ended the call and headed into the library. "Hi, Shondra. How are you?"

"I'm well, thanks. I put you in room seven today. It's the fourth door on the left. Enjoy your tour."

"Thanks." At least she didn't have to worry about running into Jagger at the library. She could immerse herself in Paris, Versailles, vineyards, and according to the online brochure of the tour, endless fields of lavender as she toured Provence.

She pushed open the door and stopped cold at the elegance before her. The table was draped in white, and there was a vase in the center bursting with lilies and lavender, surrounded by plates of sandwiches with no crust, various cheeses, colorful macarons, and a bowl of raspberries and blueberries. Beside each dish was a fancy card with the names of the foods written in red in French—SANDWICHES DE PAIN DE MIE, PLATEAU DE FROMAGES, MACARONS, SALADE DE FRUITS, and more. There were cookies decorated to look like the Louvre and a basket of fresh bread that she could smell from the doorway. At one end of the table stood a metal Eiffel Tower, and in front of it was a framed picture of her parents. A lump formed in her throat.

She looked behind her, expecting to see Abby or Cait, but they weren't there. Her sisters and Sutton were the only people who knew she was watching the tour today. She hurried up to the entrance to see Shondra, who was grinning like a Cheshire cat. "Did Abby and Cait do all of that for me?"

"No, honey."

"Aiden?"

Shondra shook her head.

Deirdra was baffled. "Who, then?"

"I've been sworn to secrecy. Sorry." Her eyes lit up. "But it's amazing, isn't it?"

"Yes, and baffling. Thanks." She made her way back to the room and closed the door. She picked up the picture frame. It wasn't an actual photograph. It was a photocopy of a picture. Her parents were sitting on the steps of the Bistro. They looked so young; her mother couldn't have been more than nineteen or twenty, her father more than a decade older. He was twenty-nine when they met and her mother, eighteen. She had come to the island alone, and Deirdra had recently learned that she'd been drinking then, overwhelmed with guilt and sadness for being forced by her parents to give Cait up for adoption a year earlier. She'd gotten a job at the Bistro, and Olivier had helped her through her grief, and he'd helped her get sober. She'd also learned that they'd fallen in love quickly, but they'd waited a year before giving in to their feelings for each other.

She looked at her father's wild hair, which had started going white when he was in his thirties but was still dark in the picture. His unkempt beard was as scraggly as ever, and his joyous eyes were gazing lovingly at her tall, lanky but beautiful mother, with her shoulder-length sandy hair and the gap-toothed smile that Deirdra had almost forgotten she used to wear as proudly as a crown. Those happy memories were so distant, it was as if she were remembering someone else's life.

As she set the picture down, she noticed a red envelope by the cookies. She opened it, withdrawing a white greeting card with LET THE ADVENTURES BEGIN scrawled across the front in ink with stars, diamonds, and exclamation points hand drawn around it, and *Nous ne voulions pas que tu te sentes seule lorsque tu es au loin. Profite bien de ton voyage* scrawled across it, signed with the letter *J* and a tiny hand-drawn paw print.

Jagger.

Her heart skipped as she pulled out her phone and navigated to an online translator, typing in the French words and reading the English. *We didn't want you to feel lonely when you're away. Enjoy your trip.*

Something big and warm blossomed inside her. She couldn't believe Jagger had gone to so much trouble for *her*. Where had he gotten the picture of her parents? How had he even known she was going to be at the library? A little overwhelmed, she sat down to soak it all in.

This is what it feels like to be treated like I'm special.

She hadn't felt this way since she was a little girl. Feelings this good should be reserved for people who were more deserving, like Abby, who bent over backward to bring their family together, and Cait, who had been willing to risk her life to save Scrappy when she'd first found the stray pup drowning in a marsh, and Jagger, who took the time to try to get to know her and listened patiently as she unloaded. Hell, she could add just about everyone on the island to that list. The lump in her throat expanded. She *wanted* to be deserving, but the only place she felt worthy of being made to feel as though she stood out above everyone else was at work, where she went above and beyond to prove herself.

How did she get so messed up?

She picked up the phone to call and thank Jagger. Not just for *what* he'd done, but for how he made her feel. The trouble was, he was making her feel other things, too. Things she didn't know what to do with because their beliefs and lifestyles were worlds apart. She needed to think this through and calm her tripped-up heart before she ended up *doing the hippie* and becoming part of Silver Island's gossip trail.

As she set her phone down, she wondered if maybe she was making a bigger deal of what he'd done than he meant it to be.

She reread the note and looked at the picture of her parents and the food, flowers, and other decorations, and it was all too romantic, too thought-out and planned. She knew she was wrong.

This *was* a big deal.

A *very* big deal.

♥ ♥ ♥

Several hours later, her belly full of the goodies Jagger had made for her, Deirdra was still trying to untangle her feelings toward the unlikely romantic as she drove to Brant's parents' house. The one thing she knew for sure was that Jagger was right about taking advantage of the time she had off work to try to fix things with her sisters, and now that she knew how wonderful it was to feel thought of and special, she wouldn't settle for anything less for them. Starting with giving Cait an unforgettable engagement party.

She pulled into the Seaview cottage community and parked in front of Gail and Roddy's cute cedar-sided home. Their family had owned Seaview cottages and Rock Harbor Marina forever. Brant and his four siblings had grown up in Silver Harbor with Deirdra and their other friends. Gail and Roddy had moved to the cottage community after becoming empty nesters. Brant and his younger sisters, Tessa and Randi, also owned cottages there, while his younger brothers, Jamison and Rowan, lived off the island but visited often.

She grabbed her tote and headed up the porch steps to knock.

Roddy answered the door, and his sun-kissed face brightened. "*Deirdra*. How nice to see you." His longish gray-brown hair brushed the collar of one of his many brightly colored short-sleeved button-downs, which, as always, was open three buttons deep, revealing tufts of gray chest hair. "Get in here." He pulled her into a tight embrace.

"Hi, Roddy." His beard tickled her cheek.

"Come on in, darlin'. What brings you to our neck of the woods?"

She followed him inside. "I came to talk with Gail about Cait and Brant's engagement party. I know it's her bunco night, but I figured the rest of the ladies would want to weigh in on it, too. But don't worry, I'll be quick."

He chuckled. "Uh-huh. *Sure* you will." He slid a hand into the pocket of his faded and frayed jeans, rocking back on his bare feet, as if he had all night to chat. "Catch me up. How's life treatin' ya?"

He and Gail were two of the most laid-back people on the island, like Deirdra's father used to be . . . and, she realized, just like *Jagger*. She felt a tug in her chest and tried again to push thoughts of him away, but it was hard when he'd done something so special for her.

She didn't want to bog Roddy down with the unpleasantness of her job situation, so she went with an easy, and true for the moment, answer. "It's good. How about you?"

"*Good*, huh? Well, that's not telling me much, is it?"

How many times had he said those words to her over the years? He had a way of drawing out smiles *and confessions*, but Deirdra knew how to remain tight-lipped. "I'm fine, Roddy, really."

"Okay, we'll go with that. But you've spent a lot of years being *fine*." He leaned closer and lowered his voice. "Maybe one day you'll kick *fine* out to sea and jump on the *frigging fantastic* boat with the rest of us."

That drew a genuine smile. "If I'm lucky."

"You *are* lucky, sweetheart, and one day you'll slow down enough to see that." He pushed a hand through his hair. "I, on the other hand, have never felt luckier. One of my boys is madly in love, and soon we'll have a new daughter-in-law, which makes you family, and you know what that means."

She'd always loved his and Gail's warmth. "You've treated me like family for as long as I can remember."

"True, but this wedding will change things."

"I don't think you could treat me any better than you already do. Should I be worried about this *change* you're anticipating?"

"Probably. After this wedding, I won't let you off the hook so easily with that *I'm fine* malarky." He slung an arm over her shoulder. "Come on, let's get you to that hen party."

They made their way downstairs to the game room, and music blared as Roddy pushed open the door. *Magic Mike* was playing on a massive television. A loud collective cheer rang out, and Gail's arms shot into the air, her thick brown and silver curls trapped beneath a green visor. "Four of a kind, baby! That's what I'm talking about." She was sitting at one of three enormous poker tables with her mother, Millie, Shelley Steele and Shelley's mother, Lenore, and Margot Silver. Six other women sat around each of the other tables, and they were playing poker, *not* bunco.

Lenore, a tall, seventysomething blonde with a pixie cut, a flair for fashion, and a penchant for mischief, spotted them by the door and cleared her throat, nudging Gail, who was eagerly collecting money from the middle of the table. "Gate crashers."

The din quieted, and all eyes turned toward Deirdra and Roddy.

"Bunco, huh?" Deirdra shouldn't have been surprised, considering Lenore headed up the Bra Brigade, which was what the older of these women had called themselves since they were teenagers, when they'd first begun sneaking off to sunbathe in their bras. These seemingly sweet women also told their families they were going to play bingo on Cape Cod once a month, then returned with stamps on their hands from Pythons, a male strip club. The younger women in the room—the ones in their forties and fifties—had since joined the Brigade and had recruited many of their daughters, though as far as Deirdra knew, only the original Brigaders took part in the *bingo* outings.

Deirdra looked at Roddy. "How long have you known about these derelicts?"

"Who do you think taught my girl how to play? Have fun, sweetheart." He winked at Gail and headed out of the room.

Gail hurried over to Deirdra, her patchwork skirt swishing around her legs. "If you utter a word of this to my children, I'll have to kill you."

"I would never spill your secrets," Deirdra reassured them as Gail hugged her, and Shelley and Margot, the classiest—yet still down-to-earth—woman on the island, got up to greet her.

"Of course she wouldn't," Lenore called out. "Because she wouldn't want us to spill *hers*."

"*Mom*," Shelley chided her. Their mother's voluptuous friend had shiny auburn hair with cute bangs that made her look fortysomething instead of fiftysomething and a personality as big as her generous heart. She pulled Deirdra into her arms, squishing her against her ample bosom. "Hi, lovey. How are you?"

"Pretty good, thanks," Deirdra said as Margot, who was tall and elegant with perfectly coiffed light brown hair cut just below her ears, reached for her hand.

"I've missed you, honey." Margot gently embraced her.

Deirdra felt another tug in her chest, this time for the women who loved her despite her lack of love for the island.

"All right, ladies, let Miss Fancy Pants go." Lenore pushed to her feet and waved Deirdra over. "Let me look at you."

Deirdra went to her, standing tall for her appraisal. She was used to Lenore's scrutinizing, and appreciative, once-overs.

Lenore touched the sleeve of Deirdra's off-white blouse. "*Mm-hm.* Nice." Her gaze slid down Deirdra's black skinny jeans to her leopard-print heels. "I need to get myself a pair of those."

"Before our next bingo game," Millie said with a wink.

"Yes, *definitely.*" Lenore narrowed her eyes. "Now, Deirdra, my love, give us *all* the deets on why you're interrupting bunco night."

Deirdra arched a brow. "You mean your poker and *Magic Mike* night?"

"Let's not get caught up in minutia." Lenore lowered her voice. "Jules told me you were on the island. It sure took you a long time to come say hello."

"I just got here Saturday, and I helped Cait with her shop all day with everyone else."

"Yes, I know, and it is now *Tuesday*. We'd like to be higher on your priority list from now on. Am I right, girls?" Lenore looked around the room as the ladies nodded and called out their agreement.

Deirdra couldn't help but smile. "I'll try to remember that next time. I came to talk with Gail about Cait and Brant's engagement party, and I interrupted your game night because I figured you would all want to chime in."

"Wonderful! We've been tossing around ideas," Gail said. "We know mermaids and anchors are meaningful to them, and they love the beach and Scrappy, of course. We thought something nautical, maybe, but we haven't come up with anything perfect yet."

"I wish we knew some of their secrets," Shelley added. "That would make it easier to figure it out."

Margot settled into her chair. "Then they wouldn't be secrets, Shell."

"Sure they would. We know each other's secrets and they're still secrets to everyone else," Gail pointed out. "But we need to find something unique that's representative of their love for each other . . ."

As the ladies talked about Brant and Cait, Deirdra remembered a secret Cait had shared with her the night Brant proposed. She'd told her about dreams she'd had years before meeting Brant in which she'd seen a man who she now knew was Brant and a Paradise sign, which she'd realized was the surfboard that hung in Brant's house with the word Paradise written across it. "*Paradise*" slipped out before she could think to stop it, and everyone looked over.

"What, honey?" Lenore asked.

Deirdra could see the party playing out like a movie in her mind. "The theme should be paradise, and we should do it at Mermaid Cove, because that's Cait and Brant's special place."

"We could have a luau," Faye exclaimed from another table.

"That's a great idea, and it fits with the theme, but Cait is pretty low key. I don't think we should do anything too loud or overwhelming. She's never been the center of attention like she will be at the party. I think this should be a celebration that's different enough, it won't be easily replicated. What if we go for simple elegance, with a touch of paradise? We can use rustic wood chairs and neutral linens, centerpieces made from driftwood, using fronds, white flowers, and candles with sand in the bottom." The more she thought of, the more excited she became. "We can decorate with a hint of seashells and greenery, and what if we have friends and family write messages during the party and put them in bottles for Cait and Brant to open later? We can have a basket of bottles on each table, hang sparkling lights in the trees, and serve champagne and tropical drinks. Maybe we can find two of those enormous round-backed rattan chairs for them to sit in, too."

"Grant can help with the driftwood, and Wells has rattan chairs in the storage room at his restaurant," Margot said excitedly. Grant was an artist and Wells owned Rock Bottom Bar and Grill, by Rock Harbor Marina. "I don't know if you remember or not, but when Wells bought Rock Bottom, it was decked out with a Hawaiian theme. He kept most of the decor, and I'm sure he'd be happy to let us use whatever we need."

"I remember, and those chairs are perfect. I'll reach out to him." Deirdra made a mental note to do that. "Gail, does Roddy have an old anchor hanging around the marina that we can decorate? That would bring in the nautical side."

"My husband the hoarder?" Gail joked. "I'm sure he can pull together anything we need."

"I *love* this idea," Shelley exclaimed.

"Me too," Margot agreed. "It sounds very much like Cait and Brant."

"I'm sure Abby, Jagger, and I can come up with a tropical yet elegant menu," Faye offered.

"Be sure to have oysters." Lenore grinned mischievously. "We want them to have a *very* special night."

Everyone laughed, and as they discussed ideas and it all came together, they decided to keep the theme a secret from Cait and Brant so they would be surprised. Deirdra couldn't wait to tell Jagger.

Whoa.

Her thoughts skidded to a halt. *Tell Abby.* That didn't feel completely right, either. What was going on with her?

"Hello, Dee?" Lenore waved a hand in front of her.

"What? Sorry. I was thinking about the party." *Liar, liar pants on fire.*

"It's okay, honey," Gail said. "We were just wondering how long you were staying on the island."

"I'll be leaving after Cait's party." As she said it, she realized the need to flee that usually pushed her like the wind had been waylaid by the urge to make things better with her sisters, and that was a wonderful feeling. "Why don't I get out of your hair. I'll put all our thoughts in writing and email them to Gail tomorrow."

"Oh no, you don't, Fancy Pants." Lenore took Deirdra by the arm. "Someone get her a chair. She's probably got a wad of cash in that expensive tote just dying to be parted with."

"You want *me* to play poker with you?" Deirdra had been dragged into taking part in the Bra Brigade's sunbathing antics by her sisters and friends, but she'd never been invited into these ladies' private underworld like this. She felt oddly privileged.

"Afraid you can't hold your own?" Lenore challenged.

Deirdra scoffed. "Not even a little."

"How about you put your money where your mouth is." Margot set a chair beside her.

"You are *so* going to regret this. How do you think I paid for my books in college?" Deirdra put her bag on the floor beside her chair and rubbed her hands together as she sat down. "All right, ladies, what are the stakes?"

They dove in, and Deirdra quickly became more at ease as they cheered one another on and gave each other a hard time, all while reminiscing about life on the island and families who had lived there for generations. They talked adoringly about Deirdra's family, reminding her of how they used to get together with many of these ladies' families for boat rides, dinners, and birthday celebrations before her father died. They told stories of when Deirdra, Abby, and their children were young, laughing with each other for having made bets throughout the years about whose children would couple off as they grew up. They reveled in many of the good times Deirdra had tried so hard to keep at bay. They peppered her with questions about her nearly nonexistent personal life and shitty work situation, then rang out in her defense, ranting about her boss and building her up like she was the best damn attorney in the world. Around these supportive women, she sure felt like she was.

She got so swept up in their support, she told them what Jagger had done for her at the library, then immediately regretted it, because the conversation shifted to the ladies raving about Jagger, how kind and generous he was, *not to mention handsome . . .*

Not that Deirdra didn't agree with their assessments, but they made it impossible for her to stop thinking about him.

Hours later she was passed from one set of caring arms to the next as they said goodbye. They offered to help her find a job and tried to convince her to stay and work on the island. Several of them also *strongly* suggested she give Jagger a chance.

"I can't stay on the island, and Jagger is leaving when Abby closes the restaurant in a few weeks. Besides, the way he and I live is worlds apart."

"Things can change," Lenore said with a mischievous glimmer in her eyes.

"Not this, and can we please keep what Jagger did for me at the library just between us and not make me the talk of the island?"

Gail took her hand, squeezing it reassuringly. "You keep our secrets, and we'll always keep yours."

The other ladies agreed.

"Thank you, and thank you for tonight. I had a really good time."

"It was wonderful to spend time with you." Shelley hugged her. "It felt like we had a little of your mama back with us tonight."

That was a hard pill for Deirdra to swallow.

Gail walked her upstairs to the front door. "Do you remember the talent show you and your mom won?"

Deirdra's chest constricted as memories of dancing with her mother flooded in. "Of course."

"After you won, Ava told me you had fire in your belly and love in your heart, and that one day she hoped you'd meet a man with fire in his heart and love in his belly and be as happy as she and your father were."

"But that makes no sense. Why would she say that?"

"I didn't think it did, either, at first, so I asked her what she meant. She said your determination sometimes overshadowed your love for others, and that your soul mate's love for others would overshadow his determination." Gail hugged her tight. "You can close that door on Jagger, honey, but perhaps you shouldn't lock it just yet. It's okay to be the little girl in the tablecloth skirt."

Deirdra's chest tightened. She didn't think anyone else remembered when she used to make skirts out of tablecloths, trying to mimic her mother's bohemian flair. She looked into the caring eyes of the woman who had bandaged her skinned knees, fed her dinners under the guise of having made too much, and clapped for her at school events, and guilt nearly bowled her over. She felt more connected to Gail and the other women than ever before, and for the second time today she didn't feel worthy. Jagger must have opened something inside her that had been closed for too long, or maybe all the talk of family had dredged up too much emotion to contain, because her innermost thoughts tumbled out. "I've spent years trying to distance myself from this island and everyone on it. Why are you all still so nice to me?"

"Because you're not really trying to distance yourself from *us*, honey. We know you love us even if you can't let yourself feel it all the time. You're running from the pain Ava caused you, and we're just caught in the dust."

Tears sprang to Deirdra's eyes, and she willed them not to fall. "But you all loved my mother, and you know how I feel about her. Doesn't that bother you? Don't you resent me for it?"

"No, honey, we don't. We loved Ava very much, and we love you and your sisters. That'll never change. We don't stop loving people because they're hurting or they do things to try to push us away. That's when we hold them tighter, because that's when they need us the most."

CHAPTER SEVEN

JAGGER SAT ON the couch in the apartment above Abby's garage playing his guitar, trying to keep himself from dissecting the many possible reasons Deirdra hadn't reached out after her virtual tour of France. He'd been edgy all afternoon at work from trying *not* to think about it and had checked his phone incessantly like a freaking teenager. He'd tried reading and had answered a few emails, but he just couldn't concentrate. He wasn't looking for gratitude from her. She was fiercely independent, and he worried he might have irritated her by invading her private time. He just wished he knew if that were the case, so he could apologize.

Man, he was *never* like this, and he didn't know what to do with himself. He set down his guitar and paced the living room. Dolly lifted her head, looking at him like, *Are we going out?*

"Yeah, a walk. Good idea. Let's go." He got up and grabbed her leash as he opened the door, nearly plowing into Deirdra, her hand perched to knock. "Didi . . . ?"

Dolly pushed past him, putting her nose in Deirdra's crotch. Deirdra twisted away from her, laughing softly. "Dolly, *stop*. Are you sure she's not a boy?"

"Fairly certain. You're smiling. Does that mean you're not pissed at me?"

"Why would I be pissed?" She petted Dolly. "And why are you always shirtless? Are you busy right now? Do you have time to talk?"

"That's a lot of questions." He skipped over the first two, hoping to spend more time with her than a quick conversation in the doorway. "I always have time for you. Want to come in?"

Her gaze swept over his chest, a flicker of heat shining in her eyes. "How about if we talk out here instead?"

"Afraid you won't be able to keep your hands off me again?"

"*No*," she said too sharply, as if she really were worried about it. "It's just a nice night. But put on a shirt first."

He leaned in, turning that flicker into flames. "Or you could take yours off."

"That's *not* happening." She put her hand on his chest, keeping him from coming any closer.

"You really do have issues with nudity."

"I do not. You're *distracting*."

Good to know. "I think you could use a little distraction." He snagged his zip-up sweatshirt from the hook by the door and put it on as he stepped outside. "Better?"

"*Slightly.* You could zip it."

"Or you could enjoy the view."

Her eyes narrowed.

"Of the *water*." He pointed to the moonlight dancing off the inky water in the distance as they followed Dolly down the steps. "Let's sit in the grass and check it out." When they reached the landing, he looked at her high heels. "Want to kick those off?"

"Why?"

"Do you question everything?"

"I'm an attorney. It's my job to question everything."

"I'm not your client, and you're not at work. We're going to walk on grass. I just thought it would be more comfortable. Although I have to admit, you in leopard-print heels?" He whistled.

She looked out at the lawn for a moment, then met his gaze as she took off her heels and set them by the bottom step. She was quiet as they went to sit on the hill in the side yard, and he could practically see the gears in her head turning. Dolly lay down between them, and Deirdra stroked her back. "I'm sorry for questioning you. Some habits are hard to break."

"Especially the ones that have been ingrained since childhood."

"What makes you think I've questioned things for that long? Did my mother tell you that, too?"

"No. You had a lot of responsibility when you were younger. I just assumed you've always been inquisitive. What's on your mind, Didi? What brought you here?"

She gave him that look that said, *What have I told you about calling me that?*

"Sorry. I knew you as Didi through Ava well before I met you in person." He shrugged. "I guess some habits are hard to break."

"Touché." She tucked her hair behind her ear, her gaze moving to Dolly as she petted her. "I wanted to thank you for what you did at the library."

She sounded a little bashful, and he enjoyed how it softened her. "You're welcome. I was glad to see you hadn't really taken off."

"How did you know I was there?"

"I was doing some research at the library yesterday and saw you in a conference room, so I nosed around a little and found out you'd be there today."

Her expression turned curious. "That was really nice of you. It must have taken forever to make all of that delicious food. Where did you get the picture of my parents?"

"A gentleman never tells." He'd copied it from an old newspaper article he'd found while looking through archives of the *Silver Island Gazette*, but he kept that to himself. He didn't want her to figure out the real reason he'd been looking up her family in the newspaper.

"Nobody's ever done anything like that for me before."

"You're kidding."

She shook her head. "You don't have to feign surprise. I know I'm not for everyone. It's not like people are clamoring to do nice things for me."

"I'm not feigning anything, and I believe Abby clamored yesterday to get you to stay, and to make a family dinner in your honor. But you're right that you're not for everyone. Few people are."

"I think fewer people *aren't*. Look at you and all of our friends. Everyone around here thinks everyone else is the greatest thing since sliced bread."

"They think the same about you."

She rolled her eyes. "I have a hard time believing that."

"Why are you so hard on yourself?"

"I'm just realistic. They think I'm a pushy workaholic who only comes to the island under duress, and they're not wrong. That's why I can't figure out why you went to so much trouble for me when I haven't exactly been very nice to you."

"You really are hard on yourself. You've been more than nice to me."

She looked at him like he'd grown a second head.

"Everyone has their own brand of niceness." He bumped her with his shoulder. "You're still a nice person, Dee. You can be snarky and sarcastic, but that's part of your charm. Nothing is more attractive than confidence. I like that you're not easily swayed, and you can stand up for yourself. I had a great time the other night. Didn't you?"

"Yeah. I really did."

"Good." He wondered if that was hard for her to admit. "I feel like I finally got to see the girl Abby talks about."

"Abby talks about me getting tipsy on tequila?"

He laughed. "Not exactly. She misses you, and she misses the spontaneous sister she knew when she was little."

Deirdra gazed out at the water. "So do I sometimes."

"Maybe we can find her again."

She looked at him skeptically.

"Have some faith in friendship."

"I'm just not sure you realize how big of a job that would be."

"That's because you're not a *job* to me." He held her gaze as that sank in. "My eyes have been open since the day I met you. I know you're guarded and are carrying some heavy baggage. I get that, and I think your friends do, too. We've all been there, Dee."

She lowered her eyes. "Why did you do that stuff at the library for me? There are easier, more deserving women out there you can spend your time doing special things for."

"Because I don't believe the best things in life come easily or that people who are easy are very interesting. I dig seeing *you* smile, Dee. That's why I did it. I had fun putting it all together for you, knowing— or hoping—it would make your tour of France even better."

Her lips curved up, and she got that bashful expression again. "But you weren't there to see my smile."

"I'm seeing it now."

She was quiet for a moment, her eyes lighting up, but as silence stretched between them, her gaze turned troubled. "This is going to come out sounding colder than I mean it to, but I don't like to play games, Jagger. Are you just looking to *bang* me? That's okay if you are."

"Is it?" He chuckled, shaking his head. "You're a trip."

"You know what I mean. I like to put all the cards on the table."

"Oh, I see. *You* want to bang *me*. That's what this is really about."

She shoved him playfully. "I do not!"

"You do, but that's cool. I see you peeking at my chest right now."

"I am *not*." She laughed. "Seriously, though. Let's circle back to what you said about finding that spontaneous girl. What if this is who I am for the rest of my life? The person who rolls her eyes and doesn't have time for frivolities?"

"You just described half the population."

"That's not very hopeful."

"Here's all you need to know. That girl you miss came out to play the other night, which means she's not gone forever."

"You make me sound like a schizophrenic."

"I don't mean to. I was where you are once, and look at me now."

She plucked a piece of grass from the lawn and fidgeted with it. "I can't imagine you stressed out about anything."

"Trust me. I've been in that box before. There was a time when I worked like a fiend and had very little time for what mattered in life. I was miserable."

"I'd like to hear about that."

"About me being miserable?" he teased.

She shook her head. "*No.* About that time in your life. I only know what Abby has told me about you, which is that you were taught to cook by a world-renowned chef and you worked at some impressive restaurants, though never for very long. She said you don't want to get tied down with a full-time job, and you have a brother who has autism."

"That pretty much sums me up."

"Come *on.* I spilled my guts to you the other night. Tell me something about yourself. Abby said you go where the music takes you. What does that mean? Is music your real career and cooking is a side job?"

"You could say that. Music is my passion. It's in my blood. My mother was a pianist for the Boston Symphony Orchestra before staying home with us, and my dad plays the guitar and the saxophone, but just for fun. He was in a band in college."

"Wow. No wonder you like music."

"My mom swears I could play music before I could talk. I hear it in everything. Close your eyes for a second, and listen to the waves rolling onto the shore."

She closed her eyes and tipped her face up as she listened. She was so beautiful with the moonlight kissing her cheeks, when her lips curved up at the edges, he could almost feel her breathing deeper.

"Now listen for the brushing of the leaves on the trees," he said softly, and she tilted her head. "We've got a symphony serenading us all the time. We just have to listen for it."

Her eyes opened, and she shook her head. "I lived on this island for years and never heard it that way. Do you play other instruments besides the guitar?"

"Yes. I play the electric guitar, the bass, and the violin."

"Really? The violin? Do you play at hoedowns?" she teased.

Her snark hit him square in the center of the chest. "I can fiddle like nobody's business."

"I bet you can. Where do you play?"

"At festivals, restaurants, and pubs across the country. I've played at weddings and other events, too."

"And you make a living that way?"

"Sure. I don't need much money, and if I feel like going someplace and I don't have a gig, I pick up a cooking job for a while."

She pressed her feet into the grass and wiggled her toes as if the sensation were new, and something told him it just might be. "Do you play at the same events every year?"

"It depends what else I have going on." The way she rattled off questions made it easy to picture her at work, that brilliant mind looking for definitions, inconsistencies, and loopholes.

"So you don't have a set schedule?"

She looked at him like he was speaking a foreign language, and he had a feeling that in her world, he was. "God no. That'd stress me out."

She shook her head. "I don't know how you do it. Not having a schedule would stress me out. Have you traveled all over the world?"

"Not yet, but I'm going to. I've always dreamed of backpacking through Europe, but I've stayed in the States to be close to my brother, Gabe."

Her expression turned thoughtful, and she ran her palm lightly over the grass. "I'd love to hear about your family. Where did you grow up? It sounds like you and Gabe are close. What's he like?"

"Ah, the lawyer in you wants answers," he teased, earning a smile and a headshake.

"I'm trying to be more present for the people in my life, and right now you're in my life."

He cocked a grin, and she laughed. "If it'll get me more of those smiles, I'll spill my guts. I grew up in Boston, but we spent a lot of time at my grandfather's farm, which is about an hour away from my parents' house, and my brother is awesome. Gabe's two years younger than me, and we've always been close, but not in the same way as you and Abby or Cait. Gabe has nonverbal autism."

"Nonverbal autism? Does that mean he can't speak at all?"

"It's different for everyone. Gabe has learned to say a few rudimentary words, but it's not like he can string together sentences, and he knows some sign language, which is helpful, but he mainly communicates through devices, like an iPad with special software, and he doesn't experience the world as we do. The things we see and hear every day, like lights, cars, people, dogs barking, can be too much for him, and he can't always convey what he feels because there's a disconnect between what he feels or knows in here"—he tapped his head—"and getting that information across to others. He can get frustrated and have meltdowns, or even respond in physical ways that could harm him or others, when we don't understand what he's trying to tell us."

"That must be so hard on Gabe and your family. Do you mean he gets violent?" she asked carefully.

"I wouldn't say violent, because he's not trying to hurt himself or anyone else, and it doesn't happen very often anymore, now that we've all learned ways to communicate, and we understand more about Gabe and the things that cause trouble for him. But it can happen. We try to avoid situations that are overwhelming, but between communication difficulties and not having control of his movements, which makes him reliant on others, he has a lot going on, as you said, and like all of us, his needs will continue to change over time."

"I'm sorry. I honestly don't know much about autism."

"That's okay. The autism spectrum is kind of like the ocean. It's vast and fluid, and there are many aspects we're still trying to understand. If there's one thing I've learned about autism, it's that no two people experience it in the same way."

"What you just told me about how Gabe sees the world would be frustrating for anyone. I can't imagine how stressful that must be for him, much less for your family." She shifted slightly, facing him, as if she wanted to hear every word he said. "What was it like when you were growing up? How long did it take to figure out how to communicate with each other?"

"It took a long time to learn how to effectively communicate. Gabe wasn't correctly diagnosed until he was three and a half, and from what my parents have said, we were all floundering in those early years, trying to figure out how to communicate, learning what set him off, how to help him, that type of thing." She was listening so intently, he wanted to share more with her. "I remember as a kid I could sort of read him, probably the way any sibling could. But it was hit or miss, and it usually meant I'd done something that upset him and learned from it, like racing cars all over the living room until he lost it. Everything was a learning process in our house. Gabe would spend hours lining up our toys, usually cars, or he'd move one car along the same path over and over for hours. I wanted to play, so I'd snag a car from his line, and that would set him off. I got in a lot of trouble for being a kid, but I can't blame my parents for that. We were all learning."

"That makes me sad for you," she said softly, and touched his arm. "It had to be difficult. Did you feel slighted or resentful?"

A truth he'd never shared with anyone came easily with her. "Probably sometimes, but it didn't stick. I remember feeling bad for upsetting him, and it was a little scary sometimes when he'd get frustrated and violent because I didn't understand what was happening." Memories of those troubling emotions came rushing back. "I just loved him *so* much, all I wanted was to make things better, so I did what my parents did when I was sad or angry. I tried to hug him or share my toys. I didn't know he didn't like to be touched, or that he had no interest in my toys. But I learned that part quickly, because he'd throw them."

"Oh, *Jag*. That big heart of yours got you in trouble. That must have been stressful for both of you." Her brows knitted thoughtfully. "How did your parents figure out how to help him?"

"A lot of trial and error. My mom quit the symphony to stay home with us when Gabe was around three, before he was diagnosed. I remember her taking us to a park thinking it would make things better, cheer him up. But Gabe completely lost it when we got there. He made painful noises and banged his head with his hands repeatedly and flapped his hands as he wailed, which we later learned is called *stimming*. Gabe does it when he's overwhelmed. I remember kids pointing at him and adults giving my mom snide looks, like she couldn't control her child, which she *couldn't* because he didn't need controlling. *We* needed to learn about his perception of the world. We didn't know Gabe was trying to tell us that the sun was too bright, the swings were too grating, the kids were too loud, and that *all* of it caused him pain."

Sadness rose in Deirdra's eyes. "Poor Gabe. Your parents must have been beside themselves when they learned what he was really going through."

"They definitely were. My mom recently told me she carries a lot of guilt for not getting him to the right doctors sooner, but it's not like she or my father were thinking that he had autism. It wasn't even on their radar. His pediatrician wasn't even thinking it, or at least he never said it to them. But that was twenty years ago, and they were busy dealing with Gabe's digestive issues, which they later learned is common for kids with autism. They thought he had food allergies. He's been gluten- and dairy-free forever, which my parents think has helped."

"Weren't there other signs? You said he doesn't speak."

"You'd think that would tip someone off, but my parents said they didn't really notice anything out of the ordinary until he was about two, when he'd started withdrawing. He eventually stopped trying to mimic speech, and he lost interest in me and them. But his doctors were in a wait-and-see mode because he was so young. They said he was shy when he didn't respond like other kids did, or obstinate when he'd get frustrated and throw a fit. One doctor tried to get my parents to tough-love him." He scoffed. "My mom is the gentlest woman I know, and my father is the kind of guy who believes in reasoning, even with little kids. They wanted *no* part of tough love, but they never stopped searching for answers."

"Thank goodness they didn't. How did they finally figure out he had autism?"

"They took him to a child psychologist to see if there was anything they could do to help him learn to speak, and the psychologist recognized Gabe's behaviors and asked if he'd been evaluated for autism. That was when it all started coming together. Once they had a diagnosis that made sense, they got in touch with the right therapists, doctors, and teachers and met other parents with kids who had autism. With a lot of research, more trial and error, and all kinds of outside help, eventually they started to figure things out." He remembered how their lives started to change at that point, with more appointments for Gabe, more hope in the air.

Her eyes brimmed with empathy. "Your parents must have been relieved to finally have a diagnosis. But while Gabe was going to medical appointments and everyone was focused on figuring things out and helping him, what was it like for you? You were so young. Do you even remember?"

Outside his family, people didn't usually ask about how Gabe's autism affected Jagger. It was nice to share his side of things. "I don't think I'll ever forget. There was a lot going on, and I didn't know what any of it meant, but I felt changes. The constant tension that had settled into our house was easing, and I knew my parents were relieved. They said they were finally going to get help not just for Gabe, but for all of us. I remember being happy and hopeful." He gazed into Deirdra's caring eyes, and the genuine concern in them drew a harsh truth that he'd been hiding for so long it felt lodged into his bones. "I'm ashamed to admit this, but I think I believed they'd *fix* him, which made me as ignorant as those people at the park were. Nobody ever said that to me, and I was just a little kid, five and a half or six at the time. I didn't know how wrong that was, and I hate that I *ever* even had that thought." He wrung his hands together, unable to believe he'd actually admitted that, but the pull between them made uncharted territory seem not only navigable but safe. "I've never told anyone that before."

"Apparently the universe thinks we're each other's secret keepers or something. I think any kid in that situation might think the same thing. You couldn't have known any better at that point." She touched his hands, stopping him from wringing them, and he met her empathetic gaze. "I can see how guilty you feel, but you should forgive yourself. You were just a kid."

"Maybe one day I will." He paused, feeling the energy of their secrets twining together. "I realized pretty quickly that wasn't going to be the case, and we learned how to live as a family with autism, which might sound weird since we don't all have it. But we're all in this life together."

♥ ♥ ♥

The love Jagger had for his family was as beautiful as it was inspiring. Deirdra felt a little guilty for her feelings toward her mother. She'd always seen her mother's drinking as a choice, but alcoholism was a disease. Should she have been more compassionate? She didn't know the answer and tried to fend off those feelings.

"I don't think that's weird. It sounds like you have a great family. I didn't realize we had so much in common, but we both had challenging childhoods. I'm sorry I bitched about my life the other night."

"Don't be sorry. We all need to vent, and I'm a pretty good listener. You can bend my ear anytime."

She was tempted to tell him that the last couple of days had forced her to open her eyes and see herself more clearly. That she didn't love what she saw, and she wanted to be a better person. But she didn't want to make herself the focus of their conversation when he so clearly needed a friend, too. "Thanks, but I like getting to know you better, and I'd like to be here for you, too. Does Gabe still live with your parents?"

"Yeah."

"Is it any easier now?"

"*Easier* is a relative word. We all have needs and challenges. Gabe's are just more intensive than ours."

"You're right. I'm sorry. I don't know the right way to say things."

"You're not saying anything wrong. I was just explaining that we understand him better, and as a family, that makes things easier. But unfortunately, a lot of Gabe's frustrations are magnified by other people's ignorance. Since he doesn't really speak, and he has trouble with eye contact and controlling his movements, people assume he has severely limited cognitive functions. They often treat him as if he's not there, talking around him or speaking to him like he's a child. He *is* intellectually disabled, but he hears and learns from everything around him, just like we do. He may not think globally or socially, but he *can* think for himself. He has emotions and opinions, and he adds so much to our lives."

"I feel bad for him." The words didn't feel like enough. She wanted to fix those things for Gabriel, to make people understand him better.

"Don't feel sorry for Gabe," he said firmly. "Feel sorry for the people who miss out on knowing him, because he's fucking awesome. Being his brother has made me a better, more insightful and empathetic person. He's made me grateful for the little things in life, some of which he will never experience, and he's made me less judgmental on all levels. Even of myself."

The love and pride in his voice were as tangible as the earth beneath them. "Gabe sounds amazing, and you do, too, Jagger. Maybe I should hang out with you guys. I need some of those things you mentioned to wear off on me."

He held her gaze, his warm smile drawing her in deeper. "I think that can be arranged."

Dolly got up to walk around the yard, and Jagger moved closer, causing butterflies to swarm in Deirdra's belly. He was the first person to spark those feelings in so long, her nerves flared. She started to pick it apart, wondering, *Why now? Why him?* She'd never been attracted to a man like Jagger before, but she quickly realized that didn't matter, because she was pretty sure he was one of a kind. As his arm brushed against hers, those butterflies fluttered into her chest. She'd spent her youth proving she was strong and unpitiable and her adulthood trying to be the alpha female at work. It was strange and exhilarating to let that slip and allow herself to simply be a woman feeling things she hadn't ever felt before. Exhilarating *and* nerve-racking. She tried to distract herself with conversation. "What's life like now for Gabe and the rest of your family?"

"Life is good for all of us. Twenty years ago the doctors told my parents Gabe would never have a full life as they knew it, and today he has one. It's not the same life as you or I lead, but he's happy. He thrives on structure and routine, and he communicates primarily using an iPad with special software, as I mentioned. He has friends and a job he loves. We're still figuring out how to handle certain aspects of the future, but he's doing great, and we're all in good places."

"That's a real testament to your family's support. What are you trying to figure out?"

"Logistics, primarily. Sometimes the only thing that can calm him down is hearing me sing or play the guitar. That's how your mother met him. She and I were sitting right here on this hill talking when my father called on video chat because Gabe was having a hard time. I was playing my guitar, and Ava began singing along. Gabe didn't just calm down; he lit up. It was pretty incredible."

Deirdra tried to imagine her mother in the drunken state in which she'd lived, sitting on the hill with Jagger, the water kissing the shore below, stars shining down on them as she *lit up* someone else's life. But her visions were too clouded with heartache to conjure it.

Jagger leaned closer. "Is that difficult to hear because you feel ripped off when it comes to your mom?"

"A little," she admitted. "But I'm glad she was able to do something good for someone else. Was Gabe sad when she passed away?"

"He didn't know her that well, so there was no reason to tell him. When she was able to sing for him, she did, and he enjoyed it, but it wasn't like he ever asked for her. I'm that safety net for him."

"That's a good thing, right? That you're able to provide comfort?"

"Yes, but it comes with worries." He glanced out at the water contemplatively, then turned a warmer gaze on her. "If something happens to me, where would that leave Gabe? Am I too important? Is there such a thing?"

"I didn't think about that. That could be really hard on him."

"Exactly."

"But wouldn't that hold true for his living situation, too? What if something happens to your parents? Will you give up traveling and move to Boston to be with him?"

"I would, but we don't think that's the best answer, because again, he'd be relying on one person. But we're enacting a plan for that part."

"A *plan*? You mean your parents have a plan, right?" she teased. "Because you just go where the music takes you."

"Hey, Gabe's my number-one priority. I told you he's the reason I haven't left the country. I might not need a plan for myself, but I've pretty much always needed one for him."

"Do you even know what it means to have a plan?" she said in jest.

"Did you or did you not have delicious French food at the library?" He cocked a sexy grin, stirring those butterflies again.

"Okay, you got me."

He sat up a little taller, those confident, sexy eyes drilling into her. "Yeah, I do."

"Stop gloating and tell me about this supposed plan."

"The plan, right. Well, it's a two-part plan."

"Now you're stretching the truth, aren't you?"

"Not even a little. You might not believe this, but what has become a two-part plan started when I was a junior in high school. My parents were talking about college, which I had no interest in, and my future, and I started wondering what Gabe's life would be like as he grew up and what opportunities he'd have. I had choices, and I knew what I wanted, which was to see the world, play music, help save our planet, and experience everything life has to offer."

"That sounds like a dream life."

"It is," he said proudly. "Don't you have dreams?"

"Of course. I'm living them. I wanted to be a successful attorney, and here I am."

His brows knitted. "And . . . ?"

"And *nothing*. I don't have time for fluffy dreams."

"Fluffy . . ." He shook his head. "Don't worry, babe. We'll work on that, too."

She rolled her eyes. "Okay, *dreamer*. Tell me what happened with Gabe and the big two-part plan."

"I wanted him to have choices, too. But my parents had fought tooth and nail for every advancement he'd made, and they were stretched to the limit, not thinking that far ahead. I knew they would do whatever it took to make sure he had a great life, but I couldn't think about my future without worrying about his. I needed answers, so I asked him what he wanted. You know what he said?"

She could tell from Jagger's expression it was something remarkable. "What?"

"We pretty much grew up gardening with my mom and on my grandfather's farm. Gabe has always loved it, and ever since we were little, tomatoes have been his thing."

"Tomatoes?"

"Yes, ma'am. Years ago he entered a contest for growing the biggest tomatoes, and he won. Ever since then, he's been all about tomatoes. When I asked him what he wanted to do when he was grown up, he said, in not so many words, he wanted to grow the biggest tomatoes, and he wanted people to talk to him."

"Well, growing tomatoes should be easy, but the rest makes my heart hurt. It's such a simple request, but for Gabe, I bet it's everything."

"Exactly. Nobody wants a disability to define them, but any way we look at it, Gabe needs twenty-four-seven assistance, and that boxes him out of many situations. He could have just helped on my grandfather's farm. That would've been easy. It's familiar, and he's comfortable there. But it wouldn't give him a broader sense of acceptance, so I tried to figure out how we could help make that happen for him, which led me to thinking about other people with disabilities. At the time, I had been reading a lot about regenerative agriculture and was talking to my father and grandfather about moving the family farm in that direction—"

"Hold on. Regenerative agriculture? What is that?" She was having a hard time following, but she loved the passion radiating in his voice, lighting up his eyes, and practically lighting up the night.

"It's a holistic approach to regenerating, renewing, and improving soil functions based on geographical ecosystems. It wasn't used much in the US at that time, but it's made its way here. With our current agricultural practices, we only have about sixty years of topsoil remaining, which doesn't bode well for our food supply."

"Is that true? That's kind of terrifying."

"It is, which is why the changes have to happen now. I don't know about you, but I want to leave this earth better than I found it."

"Okay, don't judge me, but I'm so focused on the day-to-day, I haven't thought that far ahead."

"You and millions of other people." He leaned against her side, that sexy smile making her stomach flip. "Maybe I can wear off on you in that regard, too."

"One thing at a time, Mr. Save the World."

"Someone's got to try."

"In between music gigs, of course," she teased as Dolly sauntered over and lay at their feet.

"Is there any other way? Anyway, to make a long story short, that's when I came up with the concept for Homegrown Hearts."

"Which is . . . ?"

"On the surface, it's a regenerative farm, but at its heart, it helps people with and without disabilities who are interested in agriculture to find their way in the industry: helping high school graduates get into the right schools, offering mentorships, internships, full- or part-time jobs, helping people to understand opportunities in the field outside of farming. That kind of thing."

"That sounds incredible."

"It is, but it's so much more than simply an agricultural company. Gabe's opened our eyes to so many things that are wrong with our world. Everyone talks about increased awareness, but we should be taking it a step further and working on increased *acceptance* and less segregation for people with disabilities. That's why when my father and grandfather started the company, they made that part of their mission."

"Wait, this is a real company? You got them to actually start a company you dreamed up to help your brother when you were a teenager?"

"I just brought up the idea. My father is an agricultural engineer. He and my grandfather did all the due diligence and decided the world needed something like it. They expanded on the idea and made it all happen, using my grandfather's farm as a test site, and now they have three more farms in other cities with two more on the horizon."

"That's wild. And Gabe works there?"

"He does and he loves it. At Homegrown Hearts, people with disabilities work alongside people without disabilities. And they don't just employ people with autism. They have employees and volunteers with all sorts of disabilities. They also employ therapists, teachers, and aides, the same way they employ department managers, agriculturalists, and field workers. It's part of their business model. Gabe doesn't have a lot of social needs, but at Homegrown Hearts people look at and talk to *him*, not his aide, even if he can't look them in the eye or respond without a device or the help of his aide. He and dozens of other people are getting the respect they deserve. And the best part of all of it, other than the obvious environmental benefits, is the sense of community among the employees. They all have a common bond. They're following their passion for agriculture and making the world a better place in more ways than one."

Deirdra was floored. "I still can't get over your father and grandfather taking you seriously at that age."

"I think my father was secretly itching to get back to his farming roots, and my grandfather was in his sixties, so the timing was good. He'd been thinking about the future of the farm and what to do with it. It took a few years while they developed a business plan and got things going. My father retired from the company where he'd worked since before I was born, they formed the organization, raised seed money, and put it all into play. They've helped more than two thousand kids and young adults find or start their path to agricultural careers. They even have farm stands at each location."

"That's incredible. Do you work for them?"

"No. I don't want to be tied down like that."

"But doesn't the company's mission feed into your saving-the-world *non*-plan?"

"Yes, and they're doing good things, but I don't need to be part of it. I have other things I want to do."

"Like saving more of the world?" As she said it, it no longer felt like something she should be joking about. "If only you could save the world with your music. Unless you're also the secret brains behind the Arts for Autism Foundation. Abby told me that before you guys met, she saw you playing your guitar in Chaffee, and you were collecting donations for the foundation in your guitar case." Chaffee was an artsy town on the island not far from Silver Harbor.

"I'm not affiliated with the foundation, but I do try to raise money for several autism-focused charities. Maybe one day I'll drag you to one of the fundraising concerts my parents and I put on."

Her jaw dropped. "You put on *concerts*?"

"Only three or four times a year."

"Ohmygod. *Jagger.* Wait a second. Is that why they call you Jagger? Like Mick Jagger?"

He laughed. "You want to hear that story?"

"More than you can imagine."

"I was a bit rascally as a kid. Remember the girl's sister I made out with?"

"Third-Base Betty?"

He looked confused. "Her name was Mallory."

"Not in my head. She'll always be Third-Base Betty to me."

He grinned. "Well, *Betty* was a huge Rolling Stones fan, and I was too stupid to realize she wasn't looking for more than that one pity-driven make-out session. I snuck into her backyard the next week-end and set up my electric guitar with the amps and the whole deal and played 'Start Me Up' as loud as I could. I had no idea she was having a party."

"Oh no." Deirdra stifled a laugh.

"Oh *yes*. All the girls flocked to the window, and then the back door opened, and a sea of tough high school guys walked out. It started with 'Look at this kid. He thinks he's Mick Jagger' and ended with Betty's boyfriend, who we'll call Big-Biceps Bruce, hulking over me until I carried my things off with my tail between my legs. The nickname stuck."

"How embarrassing."

"Tell me about it. When I got back to school on Monday, word had spread, and everyone was teasing me. Even my family started calling me Jagger. So I decided to own it and asked if they wanted autographs."

She laughed. "That's genius!"

"I thought so."

"Oh, Jagger. I misjudged you so badly. You're not just a laid-back guy who doesn't give a thought to anyone else or to responsibilities. Why didn't you say anything?"

"Why would I? You're entitled to your opinion."

"Not when it's *wrong*. When Abby told me you never stayed at a job longer than a few months and that you wanted a *loose* schedule, I thought you were self-centered and flying through life by the seat of your pants."

"I am self-centered and flying by the seat of my pants. But aren't we all?"

"You're doing what you enjoy, but you're not selfish. I think I've cornered that market." *Just ask Abby.* "But I don't think I've *ever* flown by the seat of my pants. When Abby quit her job and moved back here with nothing more than a hope and a prayer, I thought she'd lost her mind. I definitely need to know I'm on stable ground and exactly where I'm heading at all times."

"But even the best-laid plans are partially built on a hope and a prayer, and aren't you kind of flying by the seat of your pants with everything that's going on in your life right now?"

She thought about that for a minute. She sure as heck didn't have a handbook for her job situation or her relationships with her sisters, and she *was* kind of flying by the seat of her pants with Jagger tonight, letting those butterflies in her belly swarm instead of swatting them into submission. "Maybe you're right. But there's one thing I don't understand. You said you've been where I am and felt boxed in, but you live your life freer than anyone I've ever known."

"It wasn't always that way. I knew what I wanted to do after high school, but I needed money to get there. My parents are great, but they weren't going to fund my travels, so during high school I bused tables at a fancy restaurant. After I graduated, the chef Abby told you about, Ross Denario, took me under his wing and spent a couple of years teaching me everything I know about cooking. He was a buddy of my father's, and I think he did it as a favor to him. My dad was always telling me I needed a backup plan in case music didn't pan out."

"I think I like your dad."

"You would like him. He's a real forward thinker. Anyway, Ross is a hard-ass and loses his temper over little things. Most people last about a minute under him, but growing up with Gabe taught me patience, so I lasted longer, and I ended up working as a chef for some high-end restaurants. I love cooking, but I was losing my mind. I worked my ass off to feed people who probably had enough money to buy small countries. I had no social life, and I couldn't just drop everything to play music for Gabe when he needed me."

"I understand what you're saying about Gabe. But as for the rest of it, that's what life is, isn't it? Working our butts off and fitting in fun when we can, even if it's few and far between?"

"I don't think so. Life is what we choose to make it. It would be a miserable world if work was everything. Is that how it is for your sisters?

For Aiden and Brant? Because I think they love their jobs, but they love their family and friends more. What about your parents? Was that how it was for them before your father died?"

Caught off guard by the question about her parents, she took a moment to think it over. Her father had been a remarkable chef and an even more enchanting host, chatting with customers and friends and always winking at her mother across the room or sliding an arm around her waist as he walked past. She smiled with a memory of catching them kissing in the office of the Bistro after school and hearing her mother's carefree giggles. "No, it wasn't like that for them. They loved working together."

"Whatever memories are bringing that shine to your eyes are the ones you should chase and hold on to. Hell, you should live in those memories." He reached over and tucked her hair behind her ear, his gaze soft and warm as he moved so he could see her whole face. "That right there is a *great* look on you."

She lowered her eyes, not used to getting such heartfelt compliments or being watched so closely. "Finish your story, charmer."

"In a second. I want to stay with *this* Didi for a minute."

She met his gaze, and *holy cow*. He was studying her with such reverence, it was hard to breathe, and all she'd learned about the kind, selfless man coalesced with the seductive glimmer in his eyes, wreaking havoc with her emotions. With the cool night air brushing her cheeks and her body heating up like a bonfire, she was drawn by something more powerful than anything she'd ever experienced and felt herself leaning in, wanting to press her lips to his, to taste all of that goodness. She wanted to be inside his bubble, to share his energy. Her heart raced as he leaned closer, his lustful gaze making her body hum with anticipation. She closed her eyes, unable to believe she was readying for his kiss and wanting it more desperately than she'd ever wanted anything. His warm breath whispered over her lips, and suddenly Dolly's cold, wet nose pushed between them, startling Deirdra. Jagger burst into hysterics, lavishing Dolly with affection and leaving Deirdra salivating for their near-kiss.

"I've never been *kiss blocked* by a dog before," Jagger said through his laughter.

"Maybe your wingdog is trying to tell us something." *Like don't add our names to the Silver Island gossip train. What was I thinking?*

"She just wants in on the action."

That makes two of us. Oh boy. She needed to get her head on straight. "No one said you were getting any action. Finish your story." *So I can stop thinking about kissing you.*

"Where was I?"

About to kiss me. "You were working as a chef."

"Right, and one day it hit me. My brother was boxed out of opportunities because of something he couldn't change, and there I was, miserably boxed in to a situation I had the power to walk out of. So I did. I'm thankful for everything Ross taught me, and my father was right. I needed to have a way to earn money, and I've fallen back on cooking a number of times on my travels, but there's a hell of a lot more to life than working . . ."

She tried to pay attention to what he was saying, but she couldn't stop looking at his lips, imagining how they'd feel, how he'd taste.

"*Dee?*"

His voice jarred her from her thoughts. Why was it ridiculously hard to stop thinking about kissing him? She shook her head to clear it and tried to remember what he was talking about. *Traveling*, that's it. "Is that why you live in an RV?"

A slow grin spread across his face. "There *are* advantages to owning a mobile living space."

She didn't want to think about how many women he'd banged in that thing. That thought brought to mind delicious images of Jagger in all his naked glory. *Lord have mercy.* Now she was thinking about banging *him*. Abby and Aiden were inside, probably in the living room, where they could see them if they looked out the window, and she'd almost kissed Jagger right there on the lawn. What else would she have done? If her body had any say in the matter, a hell of a lot more. She needed to get out of there fast and tried to distract herself from those thoughts while she figured out an escape plan that wouldn't seem rude. "Why have you been here all summer instead of traveling?"

"I came to the island to see Ava. I'd worked with her every summer for the last few years, and I didn't know she'd died. When I found out, I guess I didn't want to just take off. I needed to grieve, and helping Abby at the Bistro helped me come to grips with losing her."

Deirdra was astonished. She'd never truly grieved her mother's death, and he'd stayed on the island to do just that? She didn't want to think about what that said about her, but it didn't matter if she wanted to or not. The truth darted in and out like mosquitoes, leaving prickly reminders when she least expected it. Was it wrong that she wanted to lose herself in Jagger? Not just to stop thinking about her mother, or to see if his goodness could wear off on her, but because she was deeply attracted to the person he was. He was thoughtful and interesting, and he was funny and sexy. He made her think, feel, and *want* in ways she never had. She was tempted to throw caution to the wind and let herself get carried away with him. But she knew she shouldn't. Five-year age gap aside, having a fling with her sister's employee could have a disastrous outcome. Couldn't it? *Ugh*, she wasn't sure it could. Was she grasping at straws to find a way out of this?

Once again, she had no answers, which meant she should definitely get out of there until she figured it out. "So, tell me, traveling man, what's next? Where will you go when the restaurant closes for the season?"

"I'm finally going to fulfill my dream and spend a few months backpacking around Europe."

"Seriously?" She felt a pang of jealousy and had the strange inkling that she'd miss him. Neither emotion made sense. She had enough money to go anywhere in the world, and he was just a friend. *A friend I'm intrigued by and want to kiss and do a whole lot more with.*

Down, girl.

She swallowed hard, forcing herself to move past those thoughts. "That's exciting" came out a little too breathy. She hoped he didn't notice and cleared her throat, trying to regain control. "I guess you feel good about where Gabe is in his life now?"

"I do."

Is that amusement in your eyes?

He flashed a grin that was far too cocky for him not to have noticed, but thankfully, he continued talking. "Part two of the plan for Gabe is finally underway. My parents got together with a few other families they've known for years who are also looking for housing opportunities for their young-adult children who have autism. They're going to be purchasing a house where Gabe and two of his friends will be living, along with two teachers and two college students who will live there rent-free in exchange for helping with Gabe and his friends. It's going to take some time to find the right property, and my parents will transition Gabe slowly once it all comes together. He'll spend time at the house, have meals there, that kind of thing, so it's not culture shock for him when he eventually moves in, which should be about the time I get back to the States, so I'll be here if he needs me."

"That's quite a plan. When are you leaving?"

"A week from Sunday. I'll head to Boston to say goodbye to my family a few days before, then fly out Sunday morning."

That pang of missing him hit again. "That's the day after Cait and Brant's engagement party. Are you going to miss Abby's wedding?"

"Unfortunately, I am. It's too expensive to fly back for a weekend. I need to keep my reserve funds in case my family needs me to come back. But I've talked with Abby and Aiden, and they understand."

"Oh, I guess that makes sense." Why did it also make her sad? "What's your plan when you get to Europe? Or rather, your non-plan?"

"You're getting to know me, huh? There are a few regenerative farms I want to check out, and I'm definitely going to make it to De Kas, in Amsterdam, because it's one of the finest farm-to-table restaurants in the world. There are other sights I want to see, but I've got no schedule or firm plans beyond enjoying myself. I'll pick up work where I can and see how things flesh out while I'm there."

She was interested in what he was saying, but her lust-addled mind was stuck on *flesh out* and the images *that* brought to mind, weaving sexy possibilities into the time he had left on the island, which was crazy.

He leaned closer again, bringing a rush of heat. "You okay, Didi?"

"Yeah. *Mm-hm.* I'm good. *Great.*" She could command a boardroom in the blink of an eye, but somehow Jagger turned her rational thoughts to hot, sexy fantasies.

"What's on your mind?"

You, naked. "Nothing."

"Really? You seem a little distracted, or nervous. Am I making you nervous?"

"Gee, how can you tell?" came out laden with sarcasm before she could stop it, and she went for a quick save. "I mean, living without a plan makes me nervous. I could never live like you do." She stood up, readying to go inside. Dolly lifted her head, watching her. "I'm not good at that go-with-the-flow stuff."

Jagger pushed to his feet, stepping closer, making her heart thunder. "If you give yourself permission, I think you'd be excellent at going with the flow."

"I wouldn't." Her denial came out breathy and wavering.

"How about you let me be the judge of that?"

He placed his hands on her hips, slowly curling his fingers into her flesh, his piercing stare holding her captive as he tugged her against him. The air rushed from her lungs, and he brushed his lips lightly over hers, flooding her entire being with desire. His tongue slid along her lower lip, and a needy sound escaped. She felt him smiling and was surprised at how that hint of arrogance turned her on like a blowtorch. She didn't even try to hold back and rose onto her toes, taking the kiss she so desperately wanted. His mouth was hot and unforgiving, his tongue sweeping deep and demanding, battling for dominance. Her heart beat faster, and she clung to him, borrowing his strength to ward off the fear of letting him lead.

His kisses were firm and insistent, taking and giving in a blissful rhythm of deep and slow, then shallow and fast. She tried to keep up, their bodies grinding, moans escaping, desperate for more as he crushed her to him with one hand pressed firmly on her lower back. His other hand fisted in her hair, angling her mouth beneath his, taking their kisses impossibly deeper. Lust seared through her core, and her thoughts spun away. She'd never lost herself in a kiss, but this wasn't just any kiss. This was fire and ice, heaven and hell. This was sheer, torturous pleasure. The king of all kisses—unmatchable and addicting. Lust coiled low in her belly as his hand moved down her back, and he squeezed her ass *hard*. Another needy sound crawled from her lungs, and he slowed them down to a gloriously mind-numbing pace, mesmerizing her with every stroke of his tongue, lingering there in a blissful bubble of pleasure all their own.

When their lips finally parted, she clung to him, dazed and as turned on as if they'd been naked and she'd been touched all over. A cool breeze washed over her cheeks, and somewhere in the back of her mind the responsible woman she'd trained herself to be had her stumbling back, out of his arms. But when she opened her mouth to speak, lust took hold, and she had trouble stringing a sentence together. She motioned toward the house. "I'd better . . ." She sighed. "Get going." She swallowed hard, silently chiding herself for losing control, and that responsible woman shoved the nonsense-mumbling girl out of her way and held her chin up high. "I'm going inside before I get myself in trouble."

As she walked away on shaky legs, the excitement-seeking girl she'd long ago lost begged her to go back for more. She glanced over her shoulder at the man who was knocking her world off-kilter. He was bathed in moonlight, which made him even more enticing, but it was the wickedness dancing in his eyes that tugged at the spontaneous girl inside her who was trying to break free.

"I'm gonna like getting you in trouble, Didi."

Someone had better fashion her a chastity belt, because suddenly she wanted *Trouble* to be her middle name.

CHAPTER EIGHT

WEDNESDAY ARRIVED WITH clear skies and a heavy dose of reality. It didn't matter how much fun Deirdra had when she was with Jagger. She should *not* have kissed him. Jagger might be a dreamer and believe life was about seeing the world and experiencing everything it had to offer, but Deirdra was deeply rooted in the gardens of reality. She needed to figure out her career and finish planning Cait's party. She didn't have time for dirty fantasies like she'd had last night about a guy who wore more jewelry than she did and wore clothes made from hemp. She'd worked too hard to get where she was to lose herself in his world of fun banter and toe-curling kisses, which was why she was *not* going to think about Jagger in that way anymore.

Ever.

Feeling firmly back in control, she spent the morning scouring her contacts for colleagues she could reach out to and discreetly let them know she was entering the job market. Since she couldn't say she was seeking a more female-driven company and would never publicly disparage her boss, she settled on saying she wanted to branch out and gain new experiences.

With her job search officially underway, she went to work contacting rental companies for chairs and tables, linens, tiki lights, and other party supplies. She got sidetracked when she saw an ad for a restaurant and remembered Jagger saying something about De Kas in

Amsterdam. She started looking into it and ended up going down a rabbit hole, reading about the famous farm-to-table restaurant that used only local ingredients from either the adjoining hothouse, which she learned was a high-temperature greenhouse, or from nearby farms. It was easy to imagine Jagger running that sort of restaurant, making sure all the ingredients were fresh, and chatting with farmers and customers.

She was *not* supposed to be daydreaming about Jagger and forced herself to refocus on the party. She reached out to Roddy about finding an anchor, and he invited her to come see what he had on hand.

On her way to see Roddy, she stopped at the Sweet Barista, Keira Silver's coffee shop, and as she cut the engine, she spotted Jagger up ahead. He was walking down the hill toward the Bistro, wearing a striped boho hoodie with his guitar strapped over his back, with Dolly by his side. She was all too aware that her first thought wasn't her usual *There's the hippie*, but a breathy, excited *Jagger*. Butterflies swarmed inside her as their conversations and kisses came rushing back. She could still feel his firm grip on her hips as he'd hauled her against him and the tug on her scalp when he'd dragged her mouth where he'd wanted it. She'd never forget the hot swipe of his tongue over hers or the hardness of his arousal against her belly.

A knock on the car window nearly sent her jumping out of her skin. Cait peered through the glass with a perplexed expression. She looked down the hill where Deirdra had been staring and grinned.

Shitshitshit. Cait's tattoo shop was right across the street. Deirdra had been so lost in Jagger, she hadn't even given her a thought. He really was messing with her head.

She threw open the car door, and Scrappy barked up a storm as she stepped out. Dolly began barking, too. Deirdra looked that way just as Jagger turned around, and their eyes collided like thunder and lightning. He lifted his chin, waving casually, but there was nothing casual about the heat wave speeding up the road and engulfing her.

Cait waved to him, turning a curious gaze on Deirdra.

"Get that look off your face," Deirdra snapped as Scrappy tried to climb her legs.

"Sure. Right after you explain what I just witnessed."

"I have no idea what you're talking about. I'm just going to Keira's for coffee." She bent to pet Scrappy and stole another glance at Jagger, who was busy stealing another glance at her.

"You are the worst liar I've ever met. You're *blushing*, and you have that look in your eyes that Abby gets when she and Aiden come out of the office at the restaurant with their clothes all disheveled." Cait's eyes widened. "Ohmygod. You slept with him, didn't you?"

"Don't be ridiculous." She looked around to make sure the people coming out of Keira's hadn't heard her and lowered her voice. "But we might have kissed."

"You kissed *Jagger*?" Cait said far too loudly.

"*Shh!*" She glowered. "It was *one* kiss."

"It must have been a hell of a kiss to make you two nearly burst into flames like that."

"We did *not* almost burst into flames." She glanced down the hill again, catching only a second of Jagger's back as he walked out of sight, and her mind skipped back to last night and the things she'd learned about him and his family.

"You're totally into him, aren't you?"

Deirdra whipped her attention back to Cait. "No, I'm not. We were talking about his family and we just got carried away."

"If you say so, but if you ever look at *my* man the way you looked at Jagger, we're going to have issues."

They laughed as they stepped onto the sidewalk with Scrappy.

"Cait, you can't tell anyone about the kiss. You know how I feel about gossip. I don't even know why I mentioned it."

"Because you couldn't hold it in, which is another indicator that you're totally into him." Cait crossed her arms with a smug expression. "Maybe we can make a deal."

"Since when do we need deals to keep each other's secrets?"

"Since I have dirt on you, and you have something I want. Gail won't tell me any details about our party, so if you clue me in, I will keep your secret just between us. But if you don't . . ." Cait shrugged.

"You can't be serious. You're blackmailing me?"

"I prefer to call it coaxing you to share."

"Nice try, sis, but I have another deal for you. You'll keep my secret, or your party will suck."

Cait's jaw dropped. "You wouldn't dare."

Deirdra arched a brow.

"*Ugh!* I thought for sure you'd cave."

"I didn't get where I am by being a softy."

"How about just a hint?" Cait said sweetly.

"No freaking way. But I'll buy you something delicious from Keira's."

"*Fine.* I need to learn how to negotiate better."

"I can help with that." Deirdra reached for the door. "But as far as your party goes, you need to sit back and let us give you and Brant the magical night you deserve."

They chatted over coffee and muffins, and a little while later, Deirdra stood with Roddy in a storage area near the boathouse at Rock Harbor Marina, checking out an enormous antique anchor. "This is perfect, but it must weigh a ton. How can I get it to the cove?"

Roddy slid a hand into the front pocket of his khaki shorts. "I may know of a dapper gentleman with a bit of equipment who can manage that." He turned around, showing her the back of his green sweatshirt, on which HARBORMASTER was printed across the shoulders.

She laughed. "Of course. Thank you."

"When do you need it there?"

"The party is a week from Saturday at five. If you can get it there by three, that'll give us time to decorate it."

"Will do. I'll get it cleaned up. Would you like me to paint it?"

"I actually like the rugged look of it. It'll make a nice contrast against the flowers and other decorations that I'm going to use to spruce it up. Like Brant and Cait, rugged and feminine. I can't thank you enough, Roddy."

"It's my pleasure."

She looked around the storage area. Various engines, anchors, and other boat parts were scattered around the concrete floor. Metal shelves ran along two walls, littered with tools, more boat parts, and she had no idea what else. She spotted an iron mermaid on the top shelf, which would go perfectly with the party theme. "Where did you get that mermaid?"

"It was so long ago, I couldn't tell you. But you're welcome to take it."

"I'd love to use it for the party. I wonder if I can find a few more to use as decorations."

"Now, *that* I can help you with. There's a shop in Seaport called Everything Under the Sun, run by Saul Barker. He always has stuff like that on hand, and if he doesn't, he's the guy who can get it."

"You're a lifesaver. Thank you."

"No problem. I'll bring that little beauty when I drop off the anchor. Now, how about you tell me how you're doing? And don't give me that *fine* crap."

She loved his no-bullshit attitude. "I'm good. I'm having fun planning Cait and Brant's party, and later today I'm taking a virtual tour of Spain at the library." *If I could only stop having dirty thoughts about Jagger, I'd be great.*

"Those tours are all the rage."

"It sure beats jumping on a plane and finding out you don't like the place you've just spent a bunch of money to get to."

"Especially for a girl who hates to fly." He lowered his chin, looking at her in a way that said he knew all her childhood fears, which he did. "A little bird told me you took a hiatus from your job."

Cait. "Did this little bird have short black hair and tattoos?"

His beard lifted with his grin. "I cannot confirm or deny my sources. So, tell me, darlin', what's got the hardest-working girl I know taking several weeks off from the job she couldn't leave for more than a couple of days when her mother passed away?"

Deirdra winced. "You remember that, huh?" Thank goodness for Shelley, who had helped them with their mother's funeral arrangements. Deirdra had shown up the evening before to be with Abby, and she'd gone right back to Boston the next day.

"I have a good memory for things that are important, and you, m'dear, are very important."

He deserved the truth, and as they headed out of the storage building, she said, "I'm not taking time off for pleasure. Something happened at work, and I announced my hiatus, hoping to prove how much my company needed me. I thought I'd be back at work by now, but my plan backfired, and I realized I'm not as irreplaceable as I thought."

"I'm sorry to hear that. You know what your father believed about that, don't you?"

"About being irreplaceable?"

"Yes, indeed. He said there's only one place where a person is irreplaceable, and that's in the hearts of their loved ones."

She gazed out at the boats in the marina, warmed by the thought of her father's undying love. "I can see him saying that."

"You're young, Dee. You have many years ahead of you to climb your corporate ladders. You should enjoy this time off and make the most of it."

"I don't feel young, and it doesn't feel like I ever was."

His expression turned serious. "Oh *yes*, you were, and you were a firecracker, always looking for your next mountain to climb. Abby was content being by your father's side. But you were more like your mama, always busy and full of life. You've had something to prove since you were just a little thing. Hell, you learned to walk at ten months. I remember Ava chasing you all over creation. You'd think it'd drive her nuts, but she was tickled pink. She swore you were trying to prove you could outdo the older kids. And when you were seven or so, studying for spelling bees and practicing dance and roller-skating, she was right there by your side, helping you along and cheering you on. Yes, indeed, she was mighty proud of you, sure you were going to make a big mark on this world."

A gust of sadness pushed through her. "It's too bad that wasn't enough to keep her from drinking."

"Yes, it is. We all tried to help her find her way after your father died, but he was the very air she breathed. I've never seen anyone so lost without their partner."

"I guess he really was irreplaceable to her."

"Yes, but that doesn't mean you weren't. It means she was in over her head. The disease made her too weak to find her way to the surface in a sea of sorrow. I'm sorry for all you and your sister went through, Dee, and I wish I could have made it better for both of you."

"You did. All of you did in one way or another." She looked out at the boats, trying to quell the emotions rising inside her, and did what she did best—drew her shoulders back, refusing to give in to it, and held her chin up high as she faced him. "What's done is done, and she was right about making my mark on the world. I'm looking for my next job so I can do just that."

"That's admirable, and heaven knows we're all proud of you. But here's something to think about while you're standing at the crossroads of what was and what's to be." He paused as if he wanted her full attention, which she gave him. "Nobody gives a damn what you do for a living, as long as you're happy and you find your way back to see us more often. So, while you're talking with potential employers, just remember what your father said about family."

There's only one place where a person is irreplaceable, and that's in the hearts of their loved ones. "I'm not likely to forget that anytime soon."

"Good. For what it's worth, he never gave a hoot about you girls making your marks on the world."

"I don't know how I feel about that. Shouldn't parents believe in their children?"

"Yes, darlin', and he believed in you and adored you from the moment you were born. But to your daddy, you'd already made your mark where it mattered." He patted his chest over his heart. "He wouldn't have cared if you picked up trash for a living as long as you were happy."

Part of her wasn't even sure she knew what *happy* meant anymore, although that wasn't exactly true. Talking with Jagger made her happy. Kissing him made her even happier, and she was happy spending time with Cait and Abby, when she wasn't ignoring them for work.

"Okay, I take it back. Thanks, Roddy."

"Anytime. You take care now, darlin'." He hugged her. "Do me a favor. Remember to breathe before you jump back into that concrete jungle."

"I will, and I'll give Saul a call." As she headed for the parking lot, she pulled out her phone to google Saul's shop and saw a missed text from Jagger. Her pulse quickened as she opened and read it.

I've got a taste for trouble. How about an encore?

Yes, please hung on the tip of her tongue. She was giddy at the thought of kissing him again and turned on by his brazen and unexpected pursuit. Getting into *trouble* with Jagger sounded deliciously enticing.

Dirty, naked, throw-caution-to-the-wind trouble.

A car drove past, snapping her from her reverie. So much for being firmly in control. She thumbed out a response, *Sorry, but I'm on a trouble ban*, and sent it to him. As she climbed into her car, her phone vibrated with another text from Jagger. *That's too bad. It looked good on you.*

She sank back in the seat, thinking, *So would you.*

Hours later, as she headed into the library for her tour of Spain, she was *still* thinking about getting into trouble with Jagger. Shondra directed her to a small conference room near the back of the library. As she passed the room where he'd decorated and left her food, she wondered if *trouble* was waiting for her in Spain. She peered through the glass wall beside the door, and her hopes deflated. Trouble was nowhere to be found.

She didn't even want to think about why *that* bummed her out.

She settled in to start her tour, and as the host gave an overview, her thoughts traveled back to Jagger. She eyed her phone on the desk, thinking about texting him again, but what could she say? *I've lifted my trouble ban?* Did that sound desperate? She wasn't used to text flirting. Heck, she wasn't used to flirting at all. Men had never been a priority in her life. On the rare occasions when she had met a guy and was interested in him, they usually went to dinner, and they may or may not hook up, but she didn't have time for *flirting*.

Now she had nothing but time, and she wanted to flirt with Jagger. She liked their banter and the nervous, excited flutters he caused.

She looked at the phone to reread his texts, but noise coming from outside the room caught her attention, and she tilted her head, listening more intently. It was music. She pushed to her feet to check it out just as the door flew open, and Dolly ran in, followed by Jagger, playing his guitar and singing "Livin' la Vida Loca." He was dressed like a mariachi in a big black sombrero, a white shirt, and a red bow tie, a black waist-length jacket with silver embroidery around the hem, sleeves, pockets, and matching black pants with embroidery down the sides of his legs.

"*What* are you doing?" She couldn't stop grinning as she loved up Dolly.

Jagger kept singing and playing his guitar, the shine in his eyes saying he was loving her smile.

"*Shh!* We're in a library. We're gonna get in *trouble*." Thrilled and embarrassed, she went to close the door and saw Shondra and a few other people watching them with wide smiles. She shut the door and leaned her back against it as Jagger closed in on her, his voice lowering seductively as he sang, setting her entire body aflame.

He winked as he set down his guitar. "You ain't seen *trouble* yet."

"I said I was on a trouble ban." Her laughter betrayed her.

"And I'm here to break it." His eyes bored into her, and her laughter gave way to shallow breathing. His minty breath warmed her lips. The brim of his sombrero touched the door above her head like mistletoe trying to work its magic, and the edges of his very kissable lips quirked up. "What do you say, Didi? Ready to have some fun?"

"*Yes*" came out as a ridiculously happy, breathy whisper.

A slow grin curved his lips. "Cool. Let's get this party started." He lowered his voice conspiratorially. "But don't tell anyone this outfit is really from Mexico and not Spain."

You're worried about the origin of your clothes, and I'm thinking about ripping them off? "I can't believe you're *here*."

"Someone has to get you out of your own head." He dipped his face beside her, his manly scent sending shivers of heat down her spine. "And if I'm lucky, *into my bed*."

Even though she was cheering inside, she met his playful gaze and put on her best not-a-chance expression.

"*What?*" he asked with a chuckle. "It rhymes. Come on. You need to immerse yourself in the experience of Spain, not watch it on a computer." He extended his hand, looking handsome and fun, and too darn enticing. "Do you trust me?"

Yes. "Not even a little." She pocketed her phone and officially threw caution to the wind, slipping her hand into his.

"Smart, sweet thing. I wouldn't trust me, either." He picked up his guitar. "Let's go."

"Where?"

"To rustle up a little trouble, of course."

CHAPTER NINE

"I AM *NOT* walking around town in this." Deirdra stepped out of the dressing room in the local party supply and costume shop wearing a sexy mariachi outfit with a black sombrero with roses on the brim, a tight white shirt beneath a cropped black jacket with red fringe and roses on the breasts, tight black shorts with roses on the hips and red fringe that barely covered her beautiful ass, and the nude high heels she'd been wearing at the library.

She looked fucking amazing. Then again, when didn't she? Jagger had been so excited to surprise her today, he'd actually been nervous. But the way she'd lit up when he'd walked in on her at the library was worth every second of that anticipation.

"Then it's a good thing we already dropped your car at Abby's and went to the grocery store and the farm stand. You'll be happy to know there will be no more walking around town." They'd had fun at the grocery store picking out food for their fiesta, and at the farm stand he'd gotten a kick out of Deirdra's view of *good* produce—*the kind that someone else picks out*. He didn't like to leave Dolly by herself in the RV, but he'd known it would be a hard sell to get Deirdra out of the nice clothes she hid behind and into a costume, and he hadn't wanted any distractions.

Deirdra parked her hand on her hip. "Are you sure this is necessary? I mean, look at this thing." She turned in a circle.

"Oh, I'm lookin' all right. Damn, Didi." He took her by the hips, tugging her against him as he'd done last night, enjoying the flash of heat in her eyes. "You could set this place on fire."

She pushed at his hands. "And be the talk of the town? No, thank you."

"A'right, just let me get a picture." He whipped out his phone.

"Don't you dare!" She covered her face, turning her back to him.

"Oh yeah, that's a damn good view, too." He took a picture of her ass, and she glowered at him. He lifted his phone, catching that look, too. "That's a keeper."

"Jagger!"

"What? You have no idea how cute you are."

"I feel like a matador. All I need is one of those red cloths on a stick they use." She held her hands out to her right side, pretending to wave a cape. "Olé!"

"I'll *charge* you any day." He plowed forward, making her giggle as she twisted and turned out of his hands.

"Give me another one to try on, because I'm *not* wearing this out of here."

He grabbed another costume from the chair where he'd put the others he'd chosen for her. "Here, try this one on. But I'm buying the one you're wearing for later."

Her brow furrowed. "Later?"

"When it's just the two of us, and you're three sheets to the wind, drunk on *me*, not tequila."

She laughed. "You've got a big head on your shoulders."

"And, as you saw, an even bigger one down below."

Her jaw dropped. "You are not the laid-back hippie I thought you were. You're *bad*."

"That's another thing you bring out in me. If you're lucky, I'll show you just how fun *bad* can be." He turned her by the shoulders and

112

smacked her ass, earning a squeal and another glare. "Get in there and try that on. We have places to go and things to do."

She held up the hanger. "I am *not* trying on a belly dancer outfit."

"Why not?" He'd thought she might not notice until it was on.

She crossed her arms, cute as hell as she stared him down. "Are there even belly dancers in Spain?"

"Take life by the horns. Be a trendsetter." The scowl that earned made him chuckle. He took the hanger and handed her a different costume. "Fine. You win. That's a traditional dance costume."

She held up the two-piece outfit, wrinkling her nose. "It's *orange*, and it has *ruffles*."

"And it'll look hot as hell on you." He nudged her toward the dressing room.

"I can't believe I let you talk me into this." She went behind the curtain.

A few minutes later she came out looking sexy as sin in the vibrant orange cropped top and low-riding skirt. The top had three-quarter ruffled rainbow sleeves, and it tied in the middle just below her breasts, leaving her stomach bare and revealing deep cleavage he wanted to bury his face in. The skirt had rainbow ruffles running down a wide slit on the left from thigh to ankle, showing off one long, toned leg. His fingers and mouth itched to work their way up that leg to her sweetest spot.

"That's coming home with us, too."

"There is no *home with us*." She was trying hard to be firm, but her smile gave away her true desire. She covered her stomach with her arms. "I'm *not* wearing this. I feel naked."

"You look stunning."

She rolled her eyes, blushing a little.

He took her hand, pulling her into his arms, that flash of heat returning with a vengeance. Earning that look had just become his new favorite pastime. "It is now officially my mission to make you comfortable with your own nudity."

"*Pfft.* Good luck with that." Her eyes narrowed. "You have *one* more chance to find an outfit that doesn't make me feel naked."

He was about to make a joke, but the warning in her eyes held him back. He grabbed the costume he *knew* she'd wear, an off-the-shoulder black flamenco dress, and handed it to her. She disappeared behind the curtain.

"*Jagger,*" she whispered, hushed and urgent, from behind the curtain. "The hook is stuck."

He peeked in. She was wrestling with the hook at her hip. "Is this a ploy to get me in there with you? Because it's working."

She gave him a deadpan look. "I'm afraid I'll rip it. Can you help?"

He stepped into the dressing room, running his hand down her side as she struggled with the clasp, brows knitted, face pinched. Her skin was warm and soft, and he couldn't resist brushing his thumb over her ribs. Her breathing hitched and their eyes met, desire swelling between them. She was so damn sexy, it took everything he had not to push her up against the wall and kiss her.

"Stupid thing." She nervously tugged at the clasp.

He placed his hand over hers. "Let me."

As he tried to work the clasp free, she twisted in the tight space, trying to see what he was doing, her other hip rubbing against him. "I can," she said breathily, reaching down and yanking the material.

He snagged her wrist, and her eyes flicked up, dark and hungry. "If anyone's ripping this off you, it's *me.*"

Her eyes narrowed, and for a split second the world stood still, sounds of their lustful breathing competing with the thrum of desire. She grabbed his shirt, tugging his mouth to hers. *Oh yeah, baby, but now it's my turn.* He backed her up against the wall, bodies grinding, tongues tangling. She kissed him like she'd waited her whole life for this moment, and holy fuck, her eagerness made their kisses even hotter. He intensified his efforts, and she was right there with him, meeting him stroke for stroke. She clawed at his shoulders, arms, and head as they made out like they needed each other to breathe, driving him out of his mind. He grabbed her hands, pinning them out to her sides, and wedged his body between her legs, tearing the fabric at the clasp, her skirt held up by the pressure of their bodies pressed together.

"*Fuck*," he growled against her lips, and she giggled. "It's not stuck anymore."

She laughed harder, her head tipping back.

He took her face between his hands, soaking in her happiness. "I fucking love your laugh. I want to bottle it up so I can hear it all the time."

She trapped her lower lip between her teeth, but her joy was too bright to stifle.

He brushed his lips over hers. "Think anyone will notice if we stay in here all night?"

Her eyes flamed, and he slanted his mouth over hers, taking her in a slow, sensual kiss. Her needy moans made his cock throb. "Shh, baby. They'll hear you." He kissed her deep and devouringly, skimming his hands down her sides, and rocked his hips back, letting her skirt fall to the floor. He clutched her ass through her lace panties, lust scorching through him. "That's better. I fucking love your ass." He kissed her jaw and down her neck, giving it a long, hard suck.

She grabbed his arms. *"Jagger."*

He nipped at her earlobe, loving her sexy gasp. "Let me see that sexy flirt who sent me those dirty pictures." He reclaimed her mouth, taking her in a rough, demanding kiss. He felt her desire every time he took control, the sparks radiating off her, the hitch of her breathing, and the way her eyes pleaded for more. She clung to him, kissing him harder, vying for dominance. He fucking loved that, and he couldn't wait to one day give himself over to her. But first he wanted her to let him in, to relinquish control. He wanted her defenseless, vulnerable, open to every sensation, so she could see what she was missing by hiding behind that powerful facade. He slowed them down, sliding his tongue languidly over hers, grinding against her center, so she could enjoy the friction without rushing. She moaned into the kiss, rocking her hips.

"That's it, baby. Give yourself over to me." He took her lower lip between his teeth, giving it a not-so-gentle tug as he pushed one hand down the front of her panties. His fingers slid over her warm skin and through her wetness. "Shaved bare. So fucking hot."

She leaned forward, trying to kiss him, but he kept space between them, gazing deeply into her needy eyes as he pushed his fingers into her tight heat. Her eyes flared, and she gasped, panting as she rode his fingers. He loved the way she held his gaze. So damn confident it made him even harder.

"*Jag—*"

He silenced her with a penetrating kiss to keep other customers from hearing and used his thumb on her sweetest spot, still stroking the other tantalizing spot inside her, bringing her up on her toes.

"*More,*" she pleaded into their kisses.

She rocked faster, breathing harder, but he needed more, too. She gasped when he withdrew from between her legs to tear open her top, shredding the fabric. Her eyes bloomed wider, but she laughed, and he captured those sounds in another cock-hardening kiss as he unhooked the front clasp of her bra, freeing her gorgeous breasts.

"*Oh God, yes,*" she panted out as he dipped his head.

He pushed his hand into her panties, pleasuring her as he had before, while licking and sucking her nipple, earning one sinful sound after another. "Shh," he said against her breast, and she clapped a hand over her mouth. He couldn't wait to let that tigress free. He worked her faster with his hand, using teeth and tongue to take her higher, until her entire body trembled. Her hand fell away from her mouth, and her jaw hung open, eyes fluttering closed.

"Let go for me" came out as a demand, and the clench of her sex told him she loved it. "I want to feel you come." He pressed harder with his thumb on that sensitive bundle of nerves, speeding up his efforts. He grazed his teeth over her nipple, sucking it to the roof of his mouth, and her legs stiffened. Sucking harder, he fucked her faster with his fingers. She bucked wildly, and he recaptured her mouth as her heat clenched tight around his fingers. His cock ached to get in on the action. He stayed with her, teasing, taunting, thrusting his tongue into her mouth with the same passion as he wanted to drive his cock into her, until she went slack in his arms.

He kissed her softer, sweeter, soaking in the feel of her with no barriers, and brushed his lips over hers. "You're fucking beautiful, Didi."

Breathing hard, she blinked rapidly, as if she were still too lust-addled to focus. "What was *that*?"

"That was you being the sensual woman you were always meant to be." He lowered his mouth to hers in another tender kiss. "Next time it'll be my mouth, and we'll be someplace where I can hear all those sexy noises you had to stifle."

"Next time . . . ?"

"Oh yeah, sweet thing. We've only just begun."

♥ ♥ ♥

As Jagger drove the RV toward Lover's Cove, Deirdra tried to wrap her head around what had happened in the dressing room at the costume shop. She'd completely lost her mind, and Lord help her, she'd loved every second of it, even if she still couldn't believe she'd done it. They'd surely be the talk of the town tomorrow, because not only had he bought three of the costumes, a slew of enormous tissue-paper flowers, fringed red and yellow streamers, and other brightly colored decorations, but there was no way the shopkeeper had bought his story about the torn costume getting caught on his watch. Especially since he didn't wear a watch.

She petted Dolly, who sat between them, and tried to prepare herself for *that* gossip nightmare. It didn't help that Jagger had talked her into wearing the black off-the-shoulder flamenco dress out of the shop. She looked ridiculous with big red ruffles running at an angle from the top of her right thigh down to her left ankle, but he must have told her how hot she was a dozen times already, and that felt really good. She glanced at him as he drove off the paved road and along the dirt path that followed the beach all the way to the point on the far side of the cove. She'd like to tell herself that his dirty talk and that mind-blowing orgasm must have shaken her brains loose, but she knew it was more than Jagger's swagger that had her loosening her reins.

It was *him*, with his playful nature, alluring eyes, and ready-for-anything attitude. He was full of surprises, and not just with random acts of dirtiness, but with his good nature and honesty, his desire to make her smile, and, *yeah*, all that hotness didn't hurt. He'd shrugged off his jacket and taken off the bow tie and had tossed them on one of the orange benches by the small eating area in the back of the RV, and he looked incredibly handsome in the white dress shirt. But she kind of missed his hippie clothes, because that was who he was. *Go-with-the-flow Jagger.* His RV was exactly as she'd envisioned, only bigger and with more amenities. Including solar power, which she had to admit was genius, proving once again that Jagger wasn't as much of a non-planner as she'd thought, or as he made himself out to be.

She glanced behind her at the explosion of color that *was* Jagger's home. The floor was bright blue, and colorful tapestries lined the ceiling, boasting bright yellow stars, rainbow moons with faces, and a mishmash of other vibrant designs. There was a yellow closet behind the driver's seat, and sky-blue cabinets lined the space above the windows by the table. Just beyond was another small closet, painted red, and a full bathroom anchored the right rear corner. There was an entrance door behind the passenger seat beside a small kitchen with an oven, built-in microwave, sink, and more cabinets. The cabinets were yellow and green, and there were several photographs taped to them. Batiks hung open like curtains used to separate the bed from the rest of the space, and peace flags lined the rear windows.

Deirdra tried not to think about how many women Jagger had probably had in that bed. She'd never even allowed a man into her apartment, which was all tans and white, with sleek lines and pristine surfaces. At first glance, nothing about her and Jagger fit together, and yet here she was, in a ridiculous dress and happier than she'd ever been.

He parked at the point, turning an easygoing smile on her. "You're awfully quiet. Are you okay?"

"No," she said honestly. "I have no idea who I am when I'm with you."

"I can fix that. Deirdra de Messiéres, meet Didi de Messiéres, your inner self."

She giggled softly. "*Great*. You've unleashed the stripper. Please tell me you don't have a stripper pole hidden in here."

"Now, there's a great idea." He got up and went to the closet.

She narrowed her eyes. "There better not be one in there."

"I only wish there was." He withdrew four tiki torches and handed them to her before grabbing several more. Then he threw open the side door, and Dolly bounded out. "Come on, babe. Kick off your heels. We need to decorate for our fiesta."

"We're going to decorate *here*?"

"Hell yes. You can't have a Spanish fiesta without ambience." He stepped out of the RV and took her hand to help her down. "Nobody comes out this far. We'll have it all to ourselves." He cocked a grin. "I bet you've never been with a Latin lover before."

"Just because you think we're going to be lovers doesn't mean we are." Although her body ignited at the thought. "And you need a geography lesson, because people from Spain are not Latino. And neither are you. Wait. *Are you?*"

"Tonight I am." He waggled his brows, leaning in to steal a quick kiss. "Be right back." He set the torches down and disappeared into the RV.

While Dolly explored the decorations, Deirdra gazed back at the picturesque coastline and the twinkling lights of cottages in the distance. It was beautiful from that vantage point, far from the pain and disappointment she'd endured.

Jagger returned with a small folding table and two small speakers. "I'm digging that look in your eyes, babe."

His compliments were so genuine, she couldn't brush them off. "I haven't been out here in years. My parents shared their first kiss here. This is where my mom taught me to swim and where Abby learned to sail."

"Then I'm glad we're here. Now you'll have firsts about us from here that you can remember, too."

He said it like they were a couple who did things like remembering their firsts. She watched him as he set up his phone and speakers on the table and wondered if he said stuff like that to many women.

He turned on Spanish music and took her hand, twirling her into his arms. As he pressed his lips to hers, she was surprised that she didn't want to push the idea of remembering their firsts away. They danced together for a few minutes and then danced around each other as they erected and lit the torches, hung streamers and paper flowers along the side of the RV, and spread out a blanket on the sand. They put more paper flowers and other decorations around the blanket and made a small bonfire.

Jagger drew her into his arms again and began dancing, doing something between the tango and salsa. Dolly ran around them, barking and wagging her tail as he twirled Deirdra, the ruffles on her dress fanning out. Jagger had great moves. Thankfully, so did she, or at least she had a long time ago. She hadn't danced like that in years, but it was all coming back to her. She'd forgotten how much she enjoyed dancing like that. They laughed as they danced with no rhyme or reason. They shimmied and bumped and dirty danced as Jagger tugged her into his arms for toe-curling kisses between moves, losing themselves in the music and in each other.

Deirdra couldn't remember ever having so much fun. When he dipped her over his arm, she leaned up and kissed him. He brought her upright, kissing her more thoroughly, exploring her whole mouth with his tongue. His embrace was strong and possessive, and she felt protected. Like he thought she was *worth* protecting. How long had it been since she'd been held like this? Had she *ever*? His heart beat fast and hard against hers, their hips moved sensually, *eagerly*, to the beat of the music. She buried her hands in his hair, not wanting their kisses to end, but she needn't have worried. He seemed to be savoring their closeness as much as she was. How could someone so laid-back kiss so passionately? The longer they kissed, the farther away those thoughts flitted, until they disappeared altogether, replaced with a lustful fog. She felt herself melting against him, and *oh*, how she loved that unfamiliar feeling. When he broke their kiss, she mourned the loss. *No. Come back.*

His gaze was hot as fire and somehow also soft as an embrace. He touched his lips to hers again, twice, with such unexpected tenderness she felt even more special.

"As much as I want you, I can't let you take advantage of me right now."

She loved his humor. "Why is that?"

"Because I promised you a cultural experience that had more on the menu than *me*." He took her hand and kissed the back of it as he led her toward the RV. Dolly trotted beside them. "I have to warn you, some people say my paella is better than sex."

"That doesn't say much for your sexual skills."

"I never said it was better than sex with *me*." He nipped at her neck. "But I guess we'll have to test that theory."

She wondered how she'd gone from saying their being lovers wasn't a foregone conclusion to itching to get him naked. "Dancing, jokes, and making out. I like it. Is this what it's like to date a twenty-five-year-old?" She stopped in her tracks. *Date?* "I mean, to go out with. Hang out with?" Amusement shone in his eyes. "What do you call it?"

"Swiping right?"

"Oh *God*. Are you on those dating apps?"

"No. But you're so hung up on what you think those apps mean, I love seeing your reaction." He chuckled as they went into the RV and washed their hands.

"What I *think* they mean?" she asked as they set out the groceries they'd bought. "Everyone knows they're a direct line to sex."

"In many cases, but I'm not sure why that's a bad thing for some people." He grabbed cutting boards and pans from the cabinets. "Sometimes you've got to scratch an itch." He handed her a cutting board. "Why don't you start chopping the peppers and I'll do the onions?"

She began cutting a bell pepper, wondering if he'd lied to her. "So you *have* used them?"

"No, *Counselor*, I have not." He glanced over as he chopped onions. "Sex means something to me, and the people I get together with have to mean something, too."

"Come *on*, Jagger." *Chop, chop, chop.* "A guy who likes to keep things loose needs sex to mean something?"

"Do I seem like the kind of guy who makes shit up? That doesn't mean I wanted to marry them." He continued chopping, his tone casual. "It means I connected with each of them and wanted to be closer." He looked at her. "Doesn't intimacy mean something to you?"

She focused on chopping the pepper to avoid the depth of emotion in his eyes. Was it possible that he had higher emotional standards than she did? That made her feel funny, but she'd never hidden who she was, and she wasn't about to start. She met his gaze. "I don't have time for relationships, and to be honest, I don't trust them, so I guess I fall in the itch-scratching category. Not that I've been with that many men or relied on dating apps."

His expression didn't change, but the energy between them felt heavier. "That's a shame. Sex is so much better when it means something special." His lips quirked mischievously. "Maybe that will wear off on you, too."

"Don't hold your breath." *Chop, chop, chop.* "I don't have time for *special*." A sliver of guilt snaked through her, because she felt something more for him, even if she didn't want to name it.

"We'll see about that." He placed his hand over hers, stilling her knife. "You're going to chop that into smithereens." Setting her knife aside, he wound his arms around her, gazing deeply into her eyes again. "To answer your question, I call this hanging out with and getting to know the sexiest, most interesting woman on Silver Island, and in case you have any doubt, I *would* like to date you."

Her heart skipped, but her nerves prickled. "Dating sounds serious, like we're a couple. We're not serious. We're just . . ." She looked around awkwardly, scrambling for the right word. "I don't know. Having fun? Having a fling?"

"Sure, we'll go with that." He leaned in and kissed her. "Just don't fall in love with me, because I'd hate to break your heart."

His humor was addicting, too. "I don't think we're in jeopardy of that."

"You're right." He looked at the mess she'd made of the pepper. "I could never fall for a woman who takes her sexual frustrations out on peppers."

She swatted him. "I am *not* sexually frustrated."

He hauled her in for a deep, delicious kiss. "You are, but you won't be for long." He smacked her ass. "Now, move over, woman. Let a pro show you how it's done."

"What am I supposed to do?"

"Stand there and look pretty. Or I could get the stripper pole out."

And so began their fun, sexy-banter-filled evening. Jagger pointed out his family members in the pictures on the cabinets, giving her a little information about each of them. His parents looked a little straitlaced, like Deirdra probably looked to some people, and Jagger had definitely gotten his playful expressions from his grandfather. Gabe was a handsome guy, though he wasn't looking at the camera in any of the pictures. Jagger was funny when he caught her looking more closely at his family. *Stop checking out my brother. I know he got the looks in the family. Lie to me, baby. Lie to me.*

They ate dinner on the blanket beneath the stars, telling silly jokes and getting to know each other better. She swore him to secrecy with a pinkie swear and shared her plans for Cait and Brant's party.

"You should be a party planner, because it lights you up from the inside out."

She had no idea how to respond to that, or the way he was looking at her, like he was seeing her more clearly. She had a feeling he saw that look in her eyes, too, about him. "I am having a great time putting the party together, but that's because it's for Cait and Brant. I don't know if I'd be as excited if it were for a stranger. Do you enjoy cooking more when you do it for people you know?"

"I've never thought much about it." A wicked glimmer sparked in his eyes. "But now that you mention it, cooking for you definitely adds another dimension of pleasure."

He leaned in and kissed her for the dozenth time since they'd sat down on the blanket. He was so comfortable with his emotions, giving compliments, holding her hand, and stealing kisses, it pushed her to the very edge of her comfort zone, but she didn't want to escape. She wanted more of it, which made her a little nervous.

"This dinner is delicious. You could make a lot of money with a food truck, like Brant's brother Rowan, if the music and traveling thing doesn't work out."

"One truck is enough for me. If I were going to do my own thing with cooking, it'd be a small farm-to-table restaurant, with fresh, organic ingredients, and every meal would be a surprise for the customers, based on what was available from local farms."

"Like De Kas. I read up on that restaurant after you mentioned it to me."

"Didi de Messiéres, are you thinking about me when we're apart?"

She rolled her eyes. "Get over yourself. I like restaurants and got curious. Is opening a farm-to-table restaurant something you hope to do?"

"That's always been my pipe dream. I think all restaurants should be farm-to-table. It's better for our bodies, for the environment, and it's better for the cook's soul . . ." As he talked about what was involved in a true farm-to-table endeavor, he was about as passionate as he'd been when he'd told her about his family. "But running a farm-to-table restaurant takes a lot more time and energy than a regular restaurant, and I don't want to be tied to one place month in and month out, which is why it's a pipe dream." He raised his brows. "But now that I know I'm on your mind when we're apart, tell me, sweet thing, what other things about me have you been thinking about?"

"Smooth transition, charmer." They joked around as they finished eating, and when they carried everything inside to clean the dishes, she realized he'd totally disarmed her, just as he'd done the other times they were alone.

After cleaning up from dinner, they went back to the beach, and Jagger changed the playlist to pop music. "Hot in Herre" came on, and he broke into a dance, wiggling his fingers as he walked backward on the sand, beckoning her to join him. "Come on, sweet thing, let me see you shake those hips Shakira-style."

She fell into step with him, shimmying her shoulders and swaying her hips. He danced closer, singing and egging her on to do the same. As the lyrics left her lips, she couldn't believe she was singing without the mask of tequila. But if anything, he looked even more interested, which made her want to keep singing. Dolly barked, circling them, her tail wagging happily. Deirdra cracked up as they sang about taking off their clothes, and Jagger did a striptease, removing his shirt and giving her an eyeful of hotness. When that song ended, "Animals" by Maroon 5 came on, and he closed in on her, dancing seductively, spurring her on to get down and dirty, too. She snaked her arms over her head, swinging her hips in time with his. His hot hands slid down her waist and hips as he sang about her being his prey and wanting to eat her alive.

Yes, please. Devour me.

She shimmied down his body, heat pulsing through her veins. They danced through "Push It," "Moves like Jagger," and "Move Ya Body Girl." The longer they danced, the dirtier their moves became, and the more turned on she got.

"You stacked the playlist." She was only half kidding.

"Only for you, sweet thing."

When "Sexy and You Know It" came on, they were both out of breath, and they tumbled down to the blanket, laughing. Dolly bounded over and sat in the sand, tongue hanging out, as if she were waiting for the next round.

"I haven't danced that much in years." Deirdra flopped onto her back, grinning like a fool, her toes still moving to the music.

Jagger came down on his side next to her, resting on his elbow, his smile as genuine and engaging as the man himself. "Dancing is good for you. Why has it been so long?"

"Because I work for a living." She went up on her elbow, too.

"You're a hell of a dancer. You should do it more often."

She'd forgotten how good it felt to cut loose and to be appreciated as a woman. "I'll keep that in mind. I used to dance a lot when I was little."

He tucked her hair behind her ear as he'd done the other night, like he really wanted to see her face and they were a couple who did that sort of thing. She liked that. *A lot.*

"I know," he said softly. "You danced with your mom. Ava told me."

She lowered her eyes, her muscles tensing. "I don't want to talk about her."

"I know. I can't imagine how hard it was for you when you were growing up, and I don't blame you for being resentful. But carrying all that anger and hurt has to take a toll. You can unload on me, Dee. I'm on your side."

She met his gaze, and the honesty in them was inescapable. "Trust me, you don't want to hear about it."

"Actually, I do. I danced with your mom. Not like you and I did, but dancing with you was a memory she cherished, so I played along. I'm not defending her, but you should know that she regretted her weaknesses even if she wasn't strong enough to fix them. She knew she failed you and Abby, but she called you her savior."

A lump formed in Deirdra's throat, but anger nudged it free. "Because I made sure she didn't choke on her own puke?"

"No. She never told me about Cait or having given her up for adoption, but she used to talk about forgiveness a lot, and about leaving someone special behind because it was better for them. When I came to the island this past spring and learned about Cait, I realized that's who she meant, and it all fell into place. She said before falling in love with Olivier, she was empty inside, and that he filled that abyss for her. But she also said that when you were born, you brought another part of her back to life. I know she did wrong by you for a long time, but from what she told me, it wasn't always that way."

"I can't think about the better times. It makes me too angry that we lost them because we weren't enough for her."

He placed his hand over hers. "You're smart enough to know her drinking wasn't about you, even if it feels like it couldn't have been driven by anything else."

"I *know* that, but it doesn't change anything. You have no idea what it was like to be the *adult* at eleven years old. To make sure bills were paid and your mother didn't drink herself to death. To miss out on everything good in life and know your friends and their parents pitied you."

He put his arm over her, flattening his hand on her back as he drew her closer, so their bodies touched from thigh to chest, as if he knew her feelings came from a very lonely place, setting off more confusing emotions.

"You're right," he said softly. "I don't know what any of that is like, and it kills me that you do. But I *like* you, Didi, a lot. I like your feistiness and your confidence. I like that you're putting energy into trying to fix your relationships with your sisters and that you're not sitting back and taking the bullshit your boss did to you. And I really like the way you blush for no one else but me."

A smile tugged at her mouth.

"But all that resentment comes at a price. I worry that you're so intent on burying those bad memories, you're forgetting that she *did* mother you and show you love when you were younger and that you were wanted and adored by her. And I worry that you're not only blocking out the good times with Ava but the good memories of your father and Abby, too, because they're all part of the same fabric."

"My dad was nothing like her, and neither is Abby."

"But she's a part of them, just like she's a part of you. A family is woven with pieces of everyone—the good parts and the bad. You don't have to forgive her, but I hope someday you'll stop robbing yourself of those happier memories, because running on resentment can be a very lonely place."

Her thoughts stumbled. He truly understood the battle she faced every time she thought about her mother, and that made her feel vulnerable and validated at the same time.

"I got you a little something, and I hope you won't be mad." He reached behind one of the enormous tissue-paper flowers they'd set by the blanket and handed her a framed picture. It was a black-and-white photocopy of the photograph from the newspaper article featuring her and her mother when they'd won the talent show for their fifties-style dancing.

Her throat thickened. She could still feel the excitement of that night, jumping into her mother's arms when they'd won, the cheers from the audience, the way she'd felt on top of the world, and knew she couldn't have won without her mother. Her parents had made a big deal out of it, inviting all their friends back to the Bistro for a celebration. Tears threatened, and her heart swelled with the thoughtfulness of the gift, but it also struggled as the ghosts of her past trampled over those good memories. "Where did you get this?"

"At the library. That's what I was researching the other day when I first saw you there. That night was one of your mom's fondest memories. I thought it might help you to remember the good times."

"*Jagger.* I don't know what to say." She ran her finger over the picture, her heart aching for the mother she'd once adored. She swallowed hard, hating how vulnerable she felt, but with him, she didn't hate it quite as much. "Even if I wanted to remember times like this, what do you suggest I do with all the shitty feelings that come with the memories?"

"*Feel* them. *Experience* them, and then get that shit *out* of your system. Most people spend their whole lives running away from bad feelings, but that empowers the negativity, and it festers inside them, spreading like cancer, eating away at everything else. If you want to move past your pain, I think you have to first feel the hurt and rage and anything else it dumps on you, and then, instead of shoving it all down deep again, you kick its ass. Shout it out. Beat it out on a punching bag. Hell, kick something, break something, holler at your mother. You can't let all those bad feelings keep taking up space inside you, or you'll always live in fear of them."

She'd always thought that not thinking about the hurt her mother had caused meant she was stronger than the pain, but was she living in fear of it? Everyone else accepted her resentment as part of who she was or told her to just get over it. Nobody but Jagger had ever seen the truth, how that pain felt like a villain waiting to pounce. Even though it went against everything she'd ever believed, she wanted to get those bad feelings out of her system. But she wasn't a fighter, at least not in a physical sense, and she'd never been a yeller. Were there other ways to do it?

"I'll kick someone's ass if they mess with my sisters, but I'm really not that type of person."

"I know you're not," he said softly. "You can fool everyone else into thinking you're made of steel, but I see the truth. I know you're strong and determined, and if push comes to shove, you'd probably kick *my* ass. But in here . . ." He dipped his head, pressing his lips over her heart. "You just want to be loved, like everyone else."

"No, I don't. I don't trust love." She couldn't believe she'd said it, but there it was, her heart on a silver platter. How could she trust it when her own mother couldn't love her enough to care for her? How many times had she caught her mother looking at her and Abby with the dreamiest of expressions before their father died? Far too many to count, and nearly every time, she would tell Deirdra how blessed she was to be their mother. Her mother had filled her with so much love, she'd felt like the luckiest girl around, only to have that love obliterated by her father's death. She set the picture aside, resentment clawing at her again.

"I know that, too," Jagger said carefully. "Ava did a real job on you, babe. But just because you don't trust love doesn't mean you don't want it."

She lowered her eyes, feeling too exposed by yet another truth.

"Maybe you should think about writing her a letter," he suggested. "Get all those feelings out. Put them in a bottle and toss it out to sea, or set the letter on fire."

Who was this man who not only validated her feelings but also made her think about them? And the way he did it made her harsh thoughts seem a little less cutting. She thought about the unread letter her mother had left for her and realized that what Jagger described was probably exactly what her mother had done. "Did my mom tell you she left letters to me and my sisters?"

"No, but I may have suggested it to her a couple of years ago. I think it was the first summer we met. She was carrying so much guilt, it was hard to watch."

Hearing that her mother felt guilty caused more conflicting emotions. "I don't know when she wrote them. My sisters read theirs, but I haven't been able to read mine yet. I like the idea of writing her a letter, but I don't know if I can put all those bad things in writing. What if it makes them more real and then I can't bury them again?"

"They're already as real as they can be. You've already unknowingly given them too much power. You're an amazing person, Dee, and that resentment is holding you back from living your life." He kissed her softly. "Just think about it. No pressure. It's just a suggestion."

"Okay," she whispered, and he kissed her again, longer this time, bringing rise to warmer, better feelings, making her want to be even closer to him. "Why do I get so emotional with you? It's like you give me truth serum every time we're together."

"It's called connecting."

"But why? *How?* We're so different."

"I don't have those answers." He flashed a devilish grin. "But whatever you do, *don't* tell me I'm special, because God knows we don't want to go *there*."

He knew just how to make her laugh. "Shut up and kiss me." She tugged him down for a kiss, but he stopped short.

"Seriously, woman. We're *flinging*, remember? I can't make out with you if it has to mean something."

"Then we're good to go, *Jones*, because right now you're annoying the heck out of me."

His smiling lips came down over hers eagerly, mesmerizing her with the rough push of his tongue and his hands tangling in her hair, unearthing dark, needful urges. She loved that *edge* when he took control, so unexpected and thrilling. She kissed him harder, faster, but he refused her demands, slowing them down instead, kissing her more passionately in a languid, sensual seduction. He rolled her onto her back, his fingers tightening in her hair. *Yes, please.* He rocked his hips with each thrust of his tongue, and she felt every hard inch of his arousal. Desire burned through her, and she tried again to speed them up, grabbing at his back, pressing her hips against him.

"Give it up, sweet thing." Hungry eyes gazed down at her. "Just be with me. Don't try to control it. Let our bodies do what they want."

"Mine wants *you*."

"Yours wants to rush, to lead and control." He trailed kisses along her jaw. "Trust us. Close your eyes."

She had a fleeting thought about being an *us*, but he brushed his lips over hers, and her thoughts were lost in her effort to capture them. He was too quick and drew back. She opened her eyes, nearly coming apart at the emotions staring back at her.

"Close your eyes, beautiful, and just *be* with me. Don't go for the endgame. Try to enjoy every kiss, every touch." He took her in another sensually tantalizing kiss, whispering against her skin, "We'll get there when we get there, and I promise it'll be worth it."

Her pulse quickened at the idea of just *being*. She had no idea how to do that. It was a little scary, and she didn't know why. Did she always need to have a goal? Was it the idea of giving up control? She tried to figure it out, and another worry trickled in. They were lying on a public beach. "Someone might see us."

He kissed the corner of her mouth. "We're too far out to be seen."

"Are you sure?" She knew he was right, but she was still nervous.

"Positive." He touched his lips to hers. "I've spent enough time on this island to know nobody comes all the way out here."

"Does that mean you've done this before? Here with someone else?" Her stomach pitched.

"No. It means I've come out here when I wanted to be away from everyone." He kissed her again, slow and sweet. "I want to strip you of all your insecurities and show you how amazing life can be. But if you'd be more comfortable, we can go inside."

The responsible woman in her was ready to pack up the blanket and run into the RV, but Jagger had a way of nudging that woman away and bringing Dirty Didi out to play. "I'm okay out here. I'll try it your way."

His gaze heated. "*Our* way." He dipped his head, his tongue gliding along the shell of her ear, sending tingles all the way to her toes as he whispered, "You're safe with me. Close your eyes."

She closed them. Silent seconds without kisses or touches stretched to a minute or more, amping up her anticipation and her nerves. She fought the urge to open her eyes. "*Jag—*"

"*Shh.* Just be one with me."

She had no idea how to be *one* without being naked with their bodies fused together, but with him she wanted to learn. She focused on the weight and warmth of his body on hers and the cool breeze coasting over her heated skin. The scents of the sea mingled with Jagger's enticingly male scent, so unique and powerful, she wondered if she'd ever be able to smell the sea again without thinking of this moment. The sounds of the waves kissing the shore became white noise to their needful breathing. Just when she wasn't sure she could remain still any longer, his lips touched the hollow of her neck, warm, sweet, and surprisingly gentle. He lingered there, lavishing her with tender kisses, then trailing more along her shoulder, slowing to nip and *suck*. His every touch caused a rush of titillating sensations. She felt him shifting. Cool air hit the wetness his mouth had left, and goose bumps chased over her skin. He dusted kisses along her breastbone, and she arched her back, desperate for more, but his lips moved away. Her heartbeat thrummed in her ears, torturous seconds passing without a touch, heightening all her other senses. His fingers grazed her shoulder, soft as a feather, moving down to her breastbone, and heat flared in her chest. Lying on the beach, letting him explore her body, listening to his breathing, anticipating his every touch, was so intimate it felt dangerous and erotic. Knowing he was taking in her every reaction made her feel even more exposed, despite being fully dressed. She was way out of her comfort zone, but she trusted him, and she told herself to just *feel*.

Feel his openmouthed kisses on her flesh, every touch driving her desperation deeper. How could such simple touches cause so many emotions? She mewled and writhed, pleading for more, but with her efforts to speed them up, he drew back or slowed down, forcing her to endure the moments when his mouth and hands weren't on her and revel in the times when they were.

And revel in them she *did*, as he kissed his way down her arms, dragging his tongue along the crook of her elbow and the underside of her wrists. Lust pooled low in her belly. She never knew those spots could be so erogenous. She felt him shifting, straddling her hips, and her temperature spiked. Keeping her eyes closed was excruciating, but she felt electrified. She'd never been so turned on, and when he guided her hands above her head, holding them there with one of his, she nearly combusted. His mouth descended upon hers with dreamy intimacy, kissing her for so long, everything else fell away. She tried to free her hands, needing to touch him, but he tightened his grip on them.

"Don't rush us."

It wasn't a request, and she freaking loved that, too.

He brought her hands to his mouth, kissing her fingers, then licking each one, and *holy cow* . . .

He dragged her wet fingers over his chest. She felt his heart beating as hard as hers, his sexy dusting of chest hair tickling her fingers. He moved her hands lower, lingering on his nipples. They pebbled beneath her touch, and she soaked in his appreciative, guttural sounds. Her sex clenched, damp with desire. She felt him breathing harder as he guided her hands lower, his abs tensing as he dragged her fingers over them and brushed her palm over his erection.

"Soon," he said huskily.

Fireworks went off inside her as he kissed her palms, and she opened her eyes as he lowered them to the blanket. He took his glasses off and set them aside. She was salivating for a taste of him as he made his way down her body, touching, caressing, groping her breasts, ribs, and hips through her dress, as if he were memorizing the peaks and valleys of her body. She fisted her hands in the blanket to counter the rivers of pleasure rushing through her. She'd never been touched so intently and sensually. His hands were hot and heavy, traveling excruciatingly slowly down her legs, squeezing and stroking as he kissed her from thighs to ankles. She was barely breathing, lost in his touch and the appreciative sounds he made. His kisses were like pleasure-seeking missiles as his lips moved up her calf, sparking fires beneath her skin.

"I fucking love your legs." His voice was drenched with desire.

Too lost in them to think, she tucked that compliment away to revel in later. He found more places she didn't know could bring so much pleasure, his lips lingering on the side of her calf and just above her knee. When his teeth and tongue hit her inner thigh, her hips shot off the blanket. He gently pushed them back down and continued driving her out of her mind. She had no idea how she was keeping her eyes closed as he inched higher, kissing, licking, *nipping*, earning the neediest moans and gasps she'd ever made. His thumbs moved to the apex of her sex, rubbing her through her panties so exquisitely, she was embarrassingly close to orgasming. She writhed and rocked, pleasure burgeoning inside her. When he dragged his tongue along the edge of her panties, she reached for him. *"Jagger."*

He grasped her wrists, holding them against her hips as he teased and taunted around and through her panties, taking her right up to the edge of madness. She clenched her eyes shut, pleading for more, digging her heels into the blanket. But he was in no rush and continued exploring, pushing her dress up, nipping, kissing, and licking her belly and hips. Her body felt like a bundle of live wires, vibrating, humming, *igniting* with every touch. If this was what he meant by just *being*, she wanted to *just be* with him every minute of every day. His thumb returned to that magical spot, and she bowed off the blanket, chasing nirvana, which was just out of reach. He hooked his fingers in her panties at the hips, drawing them down and off. *Yes, yes, yes!*

"Do you have these in red?" His voice was husky and lustful.

She opened her eyes, and a wolfish grin appeared on his gorgeous face. He was dangling her panties from his finger. "I have colors you've never heard of. I *might* have a thing for sexy lingerie."

"Me too. I'm going to need to explore them *all*." His wanting eyes bored into her, his underlying playfulness setting the hook deeper, reeling her in as he twirled her panties on his index finger and flung them into the sand.

Dolly darted past, snagging her panties off the ground.

"No!" Deirdra sat up, but Jagger was quick to crawl over her, lowering her back down with his body as Dolly ran off with her lingerie.

"I'll buy you a new pair."

"They're *very* expensive."

"Then maybe you should go commando."

She laughed.

"*God*, Didi, your *laugh* . . ." He lowered his lips to hers in a smoldering kiss that went on and on, leaving her breathless as he slithered down her body and spread his hands over her thighs. "Your laugh, your *legs* . . ."

The greed in his voice made her insides sizzle. He visually drank her in, and those ravenous eyes found hers as his fingers teased over her wetness. "*Mm-mm. All* of you, sweet thing."

Her cheeks burned, and she closed her eyes as he lowered his mouth between her legs, nearly turning her inside out with the first slick of his tongue. It must have done the same to him, because he made a deep, growling sound that wound through her, heightening her arousal. She buried her hands in his hair as he used his tongue, teeth, and those masterfully capable hands in ways she'd never experienced, finding all of her secret spots, and *more*. She clung to him, breathing faster, trying to keep up with the scintillating sensations consuming her. He worshipped her there just as he had the rest of her body, sensual and intense, lingering in all the best places, drawing out her pleasure until she was moaning, pleading, *quivering*, barely hanging on to her sanity. He quickened his efforts, and her climax barreled into her like a speeding train. She cried out, writhing and bucking, enraptured with pleasure so intense, she was sure her heart would explode.

Just as she started to catch her breath, he moved up her body, savagely claiming her mouth while still working his magic down below with one hand. He tasted of sex and sin, summer and sunshine, the tantalizing mix sending her body into another frenzy.

He continued kissing her long after she came down from her high, holding her like she was *his*, whispering, "*So sweet . . . Beautiful . . .*" between kisses.

She told herself this was just a fling, just foreplay, but the lies tasted acidic. She'd never felt so cherished or heard so much emotion in a man's voice, and that brought an inescapable longing to *stay* in his arms. She didn't know what to do with those unfamiliar desires. They rattled her, scared her. She needed to turn off those feelings and put this night where it belonged—firmly in the just-a-fling category.

Jagger drew back, gazing deeply into her eyes, as if he'd felt a shift in her. He'd effortlessly torn down her walls, so when he opened his mouth to speak, she knew he'd say something touching and deep, and she kissed him, taking away his chance, urgently reaching for the button on his pants. But he grabbed her hand and tore his mouth away.

"Don't do that to us, Dee."

Justaflingjustaflingjustafling. "Do what? Take this further? You know you want to." She pulled her hand free, reaching for his button again.

He covered her hand with his, brow furrowed. "Tonight's not about sex. It's about you."

Her heart stumbled, but she tried to force her walls back up. "Trust me, you did *great* by me. I want to reciprocate."

"As much as I'd like that, I want this even more." He took her in another spine-tingling kiss, and when their lips parted, he ran his fingers down her cheek, looking at her like he wanted to say more. But no words came. He lay on his back and pulled her into his arms, resting her head on his shoulder, and kissed her forehead.

Her heart raced. "What are we doing?"

"Being close. We have plenty of time for more, but how many warm nights do we have left to stargaze together?"

"Stargaze?" He was doing it again, coaxing her into his seductive, unhurried bubble, and damn it to hell, she liked it. This was not good. She needed to regain control and shift them back into fling mode. She palmed his erection, tilting her face up to see his. "How about we get naked beneath the stars?"

Those kissable lips curved up. "I know you're not used to being put first or spending time in a quiet place, but just try it with me."

"All I ever do is put myself first."

"I know you think you do." He ran his hand lightly down her arm and laced their fingers together. "But really you put work first."

"That *is* putting myself first."

"No, babe. Letting me pleasure you and asking for nothing in return, allowing me to hold you without the need to chase the next thrill, and letting yourself be blissed out instead of stressed out is putting yourself first."

The way he saw things, and the things he said, made her wish she could feel that way, too. She wanted to be blissed out without feeling the need to flee, but she wasn't wired that way. "I'm not good at this."

"How can you know if you don't try?"

She closed her eyes, trying to find that sense of peace he seemed to live within, but her mind was racing. *Try to find my bliss? I don't even know what that word means. Why aren't you jumping at the chance to get me naked? Don't all guys want sex?* An awkward thought hit her. Maybe he wasn't that into her after all. She tried to push away that thought, along with all the insecurities it stirred, by letting her mind do what it did best and focus on her to-do list. *I'll look for more job openings tomorrow, then pick up the iron mermaids from Saul before going shopping with Abby and Cait. Shopping will be fun. I hope we find dresses quickly, so I can get back to planning Cait's party.*

Jagger lifted their joined hands and kissed hers.

Boy, it feels nice to lie here with you.

"Spend tomorrow with me. I don't work until five."

She wished she could, despite knowing that desire wasn't conducive to thinking in terms of a fling. "I can't. I'm running errands for Cait's party in the morning and going dress shopping with Abby and Cait in the afternoon."

He hugged her against his side. "Then go out with me Friday night."

She tipped her face up, and his hopeful smile stirred those butterflies again. "Do I have to wear a costume?"

He laughed. "Not this time."

"Okay. I'd like that. Thank you for tonight. I loved the fiesta, and the after-party was *hot*." She started to sit up, but he tugged her down for a kiss and kept her there.

"Yeah, *you* are hot, and I'm not ready for tonight to end."

Hm. Maybe you were just being a gentleman after all. "What did you have in mind? A little *sexy, sexy*?"

"I just want you to be with me. No agenda, no pressure, no worries."

"This might come as a shock, but I'm not great at turning off my brain. Do you have a trick for that?"

"Yeah." He pressed his lips to hers. "A little talking, a lot of kissing, some music, and if we're lucky, maybe we'll see a shooting star to wish upon."

"Wishing on stars? You are really"—*cute*—"something." Something she was enjoying, so she went with it. "Tell me about your tattoos. I know Cait did the one that says WHERE WORDS FAIL, MUSIC SPEAKS, and I assume it's for Gabe."

"It's for me as much as it's for Gabe. There were times that I felt guilty for being born without autism. I know that sounds weird, but I did."

Her heart ached for him again. "I think it sounds like you, not weird."

"Thanks. Anyway, my dad used to come into my room after Gabe was asleep, and we'd talk for what felt like hours but was probably only twenty or thirty minutes. He had a way of getting confessions out of me."

Like you do with me.

"I told him how I was feeling, and he said, 'Son, that's not guilt you're feeling. That's love.' I gave you the same advice he gave me, to feel whatever it was and get it out of my system. I was seven, and I said I wanted to write a song about it, but I had it in my head that I needed to know how to play the guitar, so he taught me. Gabe would sit for hours listening to me practice, and that's when we realized my music could help him. I finally wrote that song, and I played it for my family. Gabe asked me to play it over and over and over, and I did. That night when my dad came to talk to me, I told him how much better I felt, like I had finally connected with Gabe on a level we both understood. That's when he said those words to me. 'Where words fail, music speaks.'"

"I love that. And what about on your other side? The words down your ribs?" She ran her fingers over them. *Music. Nature. Family. Love.*

His gaze turned thoughtful. "Those are the things that we'll always have. If everything else in this world goes to shit, we'll still have what matters most." He kissed the top of her head and rested his cheek on it.

They sat in comfortable silence for a long time, and for once in her life, her mind was quiet, and she didn't feel the need to fill that silence.

Two hours later Jagger was sitting on the blanket playing his guitar, and she was lying with her head on his leg, gazing up at the stars and listening to him sing the song he'd written for his brother when he was only seven. The lyrics, and his love for his brother, were as honest and as real as Jagger, with an easy beat and tender words.

So much for using dirty deeds to push herself out of his enticing bubble.

He was blocking the exit, one dose of sweetness at a time.

CHAPTER TEN

DEIRDRA WOKE WITH a start, nervous about being the talk of the town and annoyed with herself for being in the position of having to worry about gossip. But that frustration was quickly buffered by an underlying happiness that she wasn't accustomed to. Jagger had tried to convince her to stay over last night, but she'd felt too much, and she'd been afraid if she stayed, those feelings would magnify and deepen.

She reached for her phone to check the time and saw a text from Jagger. Her nerves tingled as she opened it. *Wish you'd stayed. I could have had my new favorite thing for breakfast.*

She trapped her widening grin between her teeth, and another text popped up. *Found your panties. Want to come over and lose another pair?*

Did she *ever*.

But she wouldn't tell him that.

Jagger Jones was the very definition of a slippery slope, with his unique outlook on life, thoughtful surprises, and sexual talents. She couldn't stop thinking about the picture he'd given her and the things he'd said that made her swoon, *think*, and feel. Not to mention the way he'd kissed her senseless. She still couldn't believe what they'd done in that dressing room. That man was dangerous to her ability to think responsibly. She definitely needed to be more careful about losing her footing around him.

She tried to figure out how to respond to his text, and the first step in being firmly footed was to put a little space between them. This was only a fling. They didn't need to spend time together every day. They'd see each other tomorrow, and that was enough. They'd have a few drinks and maybe they'd have great sex. She *hoped* they'd have great sex.

Hm . . . Maybe they could see each other for a little while today.

Then that would be it. He'd be out of her system, and after Cait's party, she'd leave the island until Abby's wedding.

Her stomach knotted with thoughts of Abby.

She was sure her sister would say something over breakfast about the French cuisine Jagger had left for her at the library and all the other gossip she'd probably heard about by now. The thought of being gossiped about was enough to kick her back to reality and nix any lingering thoughts of seeing Jagger today. She sent him a quick response. *As fun as that sounds, I can't. I have a long list of things to do today.* As she climbed out of bed, her phone lit up with another message from him. *I'd like to be on that list.*

She'd like that, too. She tucked that thought away and went to shower.

To her surprise, Abby and Aiden didn't say anything unusual over breakfast. She wondered if she'd somehow flown under the radar of island gossipers and went about her morning. Her first order of business was moving into the apartment above the garage. Aiden and Abby hadn't had another loud tryst, but she wasn't taking any chances. After moving in and getting settled, she scoured the internet for jobs and submitted her résumé for two of them. Then she ran her errands, picking up supplies for Cait's engagement party. Nobody she'd run into had said a word about their dressing-room debauchery, the food Jagger had left at the library the other day, or his guitar playing yesterday.

It appeared the gossip gods were with her after all.

By afternoon, she was excited to spend time with Abby and Cait in Chaffee. The artsy town had always been a favorite of hers. Even though it wasn't far from Silver Harbor, it felt like it was a world away, with a large courtyard in the center of town complete with a beautiful fountain with a statue in the middle of it and surrounded by vibrantly painted three-story shops with wrought-iron balconies. There were no cars allowed on the cobblestone streets of the shopping district, which was another reason it felt like it was a world away. People rode bicycles or arrived on boats and set out on foot, like she and her sisters had. Aiden had brought them over on his boat and was picking them up later.

The short boat ride had reminded Deirdra of when she and Abby were young and would go out on the water with their parents. But as always, those memories were overshadowed by resentment. Deirdra had tried to allow herself to feel the pain, as Jagger had suggested, but it was too difficult. Maybe she'd try another time. That resentment had the power to ruin her entire day, and today was too important to let that happen.

She was in a fine mood now, as she and her sisters had a cocktail in the courtyard before shopping for dresses. Abby was telling them about a movie she'd watched last night, and she was so animated, waving her hands, beaming from ear to ear, her long brown hair bouncing over her shoulders, it sounded like it was the most glorious night she and Aiden had ever had. She looked cute in a red sweater and cut-offs, with strappy leather sandals, as did Cait in her holey jeans, blue T-shirt with WICKED INK emblazoned across her chest, and all her colorful tattoos on display. Then there was Deirdra, who knew she always dressed a little sharper than everyone else, wearing a pristine white T-shirt beneath her favorite short-sleeved fitted jacket, dark skinny jeans, and leopard-print heels. Her nice clothes, fancy car, and pricey loft had been ways of proving herself, but now she wondered if those things were setting her apart in the wrong way, expanding the divide she'd noticed at dinner.

"You must have gotten home really late last night, Dee." Abby sipped her drink. "I thought you'd be home after your virtual tour. Where did you go?"

"I want to hear about the tour. How was it?" Cait asked.

Deirdra wasn't ready to admit having been with Jagger, so she skipped over Abby's question. "It was fun."

"That's it? *Fun?*" Cait arched a brow. "What was it like?"

"It was festive and mostly focused on shopping, and a fiesta, at night, with lights, and dancing, and a *lot* of eating. *Devouring*, really." Her body warmed with the memory, and she took a quick drink. "It was spectacular."

"Wow. You must really like to watch people eat," Cait said.

Actually, I had my eyes closed, and it magnified everything. You should try it sometime. Deirdra stifled a grin.

"Was it better than Italy and France?" Abby asked.

"*Definitely.* Although France was really special, too."

"I might have to try one of those," Abby said. "So, where did you go after the library?"

She didn't want to tell a bald-faced lie, but a little white lie to keep from being interrogated wasn't bad, was it? "I ran into Jagger, and we grabbed a bite to eat."

"That sounds fun, and unusual. You went to eat with *Jagger?*" Abby asked.

"Well, he ate. I just went along for the ride." *And what a ride it was.*

"I'm glad you're making friends with him. Where else did you go? Aiden and I were up until about one o'clock, and you were still out."

Cait folded her arms on the table, looking at Deirdra with a mischievous grin. "Yes, Dee. Where were you and *Jagger?*"

Deirdra never should have told her they'd kissed. "We went for a walk on the beach." She downed the rest of her drink. "Ready to go look at dresses?"

"Not quite yet." Cait smirked. "You and Jagger walked on the beach until after one o'clock in the morning? Maybe *now* would be a good time to tell me the details of our engagement party."

Deirdra glowered at her. "I don't think so."

"Okay, you two, what's going on?" Abby asked.

"*Nothing*," Deirdra and Cait said in unison. Deirdra was grateful Cait didn't rat her out about kissing Jagger.

Abby's and Cait's phones chimed simultaneously. They picked up their phones and read their texts, exchanging an amused glance afterward before looking imploringly at Deirdra.

"Why are you looking at me like that? Who just texted you?"

"Jules," Abby said a little smugly. "She texted everyone. Why didn't your phone make a noise? Did you leave it on your *walk* last night?"

Deirdra's stomach pitched, and she fished her phone out of her purse. The ringer was off, and she'd missed texts from Jules and Jagger. "I must have forgotten to turn on my ringer this morning." She couldn't believe she'd forgotten. It was usually the very first thing she did when she woke up. Then again, she had been a little preoccupied with Jagger wanting to eat her for breakfast. She opened the message from Jules. *I heard a rumor about a hot hippie and a de Messiéres girl. Anyone care to fess up?*

So much for the gossip gods being on her side.

"Is there something you want to tell us?" Abby asked as their phones dinged in rapid succession.

Cait read the texts aloud. "Leni said if it's Abby, she'll kill her."

"As if I'd ever do that." Abby rolled her eyes.

Cait continued reading the incoming texts. "Daphne said *finally*, and Sutton said she didn't spill the beans." Daphne was married to Sutton's older brother Jock. Cait looked at Deirdra and said, "For the record, I didn't, either."

"Spill *what* beans?" Abby threw her hands up. "Did you and Jagger hook up?"

"This cannot be happening." Deirdra put her head in her hands, regretting yesterday because of the gossip and, at the same time, not regretting a second of being with Jagger. She flopped back in her seat and remembered the missed text from Jagger, but she'd have to tell him what was going on, and she wasn't ready to do that yet. Hell, she wasn't ready to live through it, either.

Their phones dinged with another text, and Cait read it aloud. "It's from Jules. *I'm dying over here. I've been holding this in since I saw Eden Lowe at Trista's café earlier. She was in the library yesterday when Jagger came in dressed in a mariachi costume to serenade Dee. How romantic is that?! Eden said they left holding hands. Dee! You've been holding out on us! Spill, woman.*"

"*This* is why I hate this island. I can't even have a little fun without everyone and their mother hearing about it." Deirdra picked up her phone and texted the group. *We're just having fun. It's not a big deal.*

"He serenaded you in the one place where silence is golden," Cait pointed out. "And you left holding hands. That's not exactly two people who don't want to be found out."

"I wasn't thinking, okay? It all happened so fast, and it was *fun*. There's something about him that trips me up and makes me stop thinking."

A text rolled in from Leni. *Oh, I get it. Poor Jagger isn't well hung.*

Abby and Cait laughed, but Deirdra felt oddly protective of him and furiously thumbed out a response, saying each word as she typed it. "He's *very* gifted in that department!" She added three eggplant emojis and sent it off.

Abby lowered her voice. "So, by *a little fun*, you meant having sex."

"*No.*" *Not yet, anyway.* "We're just hanging out." She felt a little bad for downplaying how much she liked Jagger, but she didn't want to make their fling into something it wasn't.

"Do you even know how to *just* hang out?" Cait teased.

"Clearly she's not just hanging out if she knows about his *eggplant*," Abby said as their phones dinged again.

Deirdra read Jules's text. *This just in! Dee, did you and Jagger get down and dirty in the dressing room of the party store? OMG!*

"Dee!" Abby's eyes widened. "In the dressing room?"

"Who are you, and what have you done with our sister?" Cait demanded.

Deirdra gritted her teeth, wondering when the next ferry to Boston was leaving the island.

A text popped up from Sutton—*Go, Dee!*—followed by one from Daphne. *I'm blushing for you, Dee.*

"I'm done. Can we please silence our phones and go look for dresses?" Deirdra turned her phone on silent and shoved it in her bag. She pulled out a wad of cash from her wallet, threw it on the table, and stalked off, leaving her sisters to chase after her while Jagger's voice traipsed through her mind—*I want to strip you of all your insecurities and show you how amazing life can be*—making thoughts of escaping the island far less appealing.

Thankfully, her sisters took the hint and dropped the subject. Two and a half hours and far too many dresses later, they walked out of Sophia's Closet, an upscale dress shop, with gorgeous cocktail-length dresses for Cait and Deirdra.

"I'm so excited," Abby exclaimed as she texted pictures of the dresses to Leni. "Dark champagne is such a classy color, and it looked great on both of you."

"Brant won't be able to keep his hands off Cait in that sexy little number." Deirdra wasn't kidding. Cait's dress was perfect for her slim figure, with a keyhole neckline, crisscross back, and pleated skirt, while Deirdra's was fitted, with a sweetheart neckline and lace overlay from shoulders to hem.

"Yours accentuates your figure," Cait said. "You really lucked out in the genes department."

"Oh please. You and Abby have great bodies. I'd give anything to have Abby's butt and your tiny waist."

"I'd give anything for your legs," Abby said.

Jagger's voice taunted Deirdra again. *Your laugh, your legs . . . Mm-mm. All of you, sweet thing.*

"Dee?" Cait tugged her in the opposite direction. "We're going into the lingerie shop." She pointed to the store Deirdra had just passed. "Thinking of Jagger's eggplant?"

More like his mouth. She followed her giggling sisters into the lingerie shop. "I'm glad we're here. I need new underwear."

"I bet you do," Cait teased. "But I doubt they carry hemp underwear here."

Deirdra rolled her eyes, making her sisters laugh, which made her laugh, too, and she couldn't hold the truth in any longer. "Actually, Jagger was very fond of my Fleur du Mal Charlotte Cheekinis. Unfortunately, so was Dolly. She ran off with my underwear while we were *busy.*"

Cait snort-laughed. "Welcome to life with dogs."

"I knew you slept with him!" Abby whispered.

"You knew *wrong*, smarty-pants." Deirdra lowered her voice, but there was no tamping down her smile. "We just messed around, but it was . . ." She sighed, unable to describe the magnificence of what she'd experienced with Jagger. "He's so real, and deep, which I didn't expect, and so laid-back, you know I'm totally out of my element with him. But I kind of really like him. That's weird, right? Me and the hippie? I don't know what I'm doing."

"It's not any weirder than me falling in love *at all* after everything I've been through," Cait reminded her. "And I'm so happy with Brant, I have to pinch myself most mornings to make sure I'm not dreaming."

"I know that's true. But I've spent my entire life staying out of the line of fire on this island, and now everyone's talking about me. I think this might be the dumbest thing I've ever done."

Abby took her hand, giving it a reassuring squeeze. "I know you're all about being smart, but sometimes it feels good to forget you're smart. Not that I think you getting together with Jagger is stupid. When you talk about him, you're happier, and you even look different. I think he softened your sharp edges."

Deirdra crossed her arms. "You mean my resting bitch face?"

Abby waved a finger at her. "You said it, not me."

"It's just so crazy. We haven't even spent that much time together, but I feel like . . . I would say he gets me, but that's not it. I think he gets *life*, and he sees and understands it differently than everyone else. Or at least than I do. And he's really thoughtful. I didn't tell you guys this, but when I went to the library for the virtual tour of France, he'd decorated the room and made me French food." As she told them all about what he'd done, the note he'd left, and the picture of her parents he'd given her, a sense of peace and relief came over her. It felt fantastic to share her excitement with them. "It was all so sweet, and I really like being with him and talking with him."

"Do you have a lot in common?" Cait asked.

"Sort of, in ways that aren't so apparent at first glance. We talked about Mom. He thinks I shouldn't block out all my childhood memories."

"I didn't know you were," Abby said.

Deirdra shrugged as they walked deeper into the store. "I can't help it. When I think of the good memories, I get angry at her for taking it all away."

"I understand that," Cait said.

"But that's not all Jagger did. He also made a copy of the picture from the article that was in the paper when Mom and I won that talent show together."

Cait and Abby exchanged an uneasy glance.

"I know what you're thinking," Deirdra said. "Don't worry. I wasn't mad at him for it. I was floored that he'd thought to do any of the things he's done for me, but especially giving me that picture since he knows how I feel about Mom. But I swear he puts me under some type of spell when we're together, because he somehow gets me to talk about her."

"That's good." Abby touched her arm. "That means you trust him."

"I do, but I have so much shit in my head about everything we went through with Mom, it's hard to make it through some conversations. Jagger thinks I should write a letter to her to get it out of my system."

"That's not a bad idea," Cait agreed. "A therapist once recommended I do the same thing to work through my past. I draw to get things out of my head. You might find writing cathartic."

"Have you read your letter from Mom yet?" Abby asked.

Deirdra shook her head. "I get in a bad mood every time I think about it."

"Don't stress. You'll read it when you're ready," Abby reassured her. "I think spending time with Jagger is good for you."

"I agree, plus orgasms are like magic pills," Cait joked.

"I'll second that." Abby high-fived Cait.

Deirdra had a feeling *Jagger* was her magic pill. Orgasms only took the edge off for a little while, but she was still thinking about him . . . and about writing that letter.

"So what's the real deal with you two?" Abby asked carefully. "Are you a couple?"

"No. This thing with Jagger is just a fling." A trickle of discomfort lodged in Deirdra's chest. "But we're going out tomorrow night, and I am looking forward to it."

"That's great," Abby exclaimed. "Aiden and I started as a fling. You never know what might happen."

Abby looked so hopeful, Deirdra had to try to bring her back to reality. "I'm not you and he's not Aiden, so don't give me that look."

"I'm just glad you're happy," Cait said.

"Me too." Abby hugged her. "I don't care if it's just a fling or the world's greatest love affair. Of course, I want you to have the world's greatest love story, but at least you're spending time with a guy you like, and that's *so* much better than staring at your computer all day. Come on, let's find some sexy things to tantalize our men with."

"Pick out something sickeningly sexy for your honeymoon as a gift from me, and, Cait, grab something to wear the night of the engagement party."

"You don't have to do that," Cait said.

"Shut up and let me spoil my sisters."

They converged on her in a group hug, babbling thank-yous and ridiculous comments about spoiling her back in the future. Deirdra pried herself free. "Enough mushy stuff. Go find something that'll melt the shorts off your men."

"Okay, are you going to look for hippie underwear?" Cait teased. "Hey, wasn't your father kind of a hippie, too?"

"And a chef," Abby pointed out. "Do you think our sister has daddy issues?"

Deirdra glowered, and Abby and Cait walked away still cackling.

As her sisters looked through displays of sexy undergarments, she pulled out her phone, ignoring the numerous texts from the girls, and finally read Jagger's message. *I guess people are talking about us because one of the waitresses asked if you and I were together. Sorry, Dee. I know you hate gossip. I'll tell them we're not seeing each other.*

His thoughtfulness definitely softened her. She felt changes happening right now, warmth spreading in her chest and the quickening of her pulse. This was her chance to put a stop to the gossip and end things between them.

A stab of longing moved through her. She wasn't ready to walk away from the one man she wanted to spend time with.

She typed a quick response. *I don't think you have to go that far.* Her thumb hovered over the *send* icon, her nerves pinging like a pinball machine. She glanced at her sisters, who were admiring a display of lace thongs as they chatted, no doubt about Aiden and Brant. For the first time in her adult life, Deirdra understood feeling giddy over a guy. She was only there for another week and a half—why the heck shouldn't she enjoy herself? The hell with the gossipers.

She sent the message, pocketed her phone, and went to join her sisters. "Those are sexy. Do they have them in red?"

♥ ♥ ♥

Later that evening, a cool breeze blew through the open window in the apartment above the garage, where Deirdra lay thinking about the great day she'd had with her sisters. They'd shopped for hours, hitting nearly every store in Chaffee, and after Aiden and Brant picked them up on the boat, they had dinner at Rock Bottom Bar and Grill. Cait had asked if she wanted to invite Jagger, but he'd had to work at the Bistro. Deirdra had secretly wished they'd gone there so she could have at least seen him, but even Abby, who loved that restaurant almost as much as she loved Aiden, needed a break from it sometimes.

Dinner was delicious, and Cait and Brant had done their best to pry information out of her about their party, but she was too excited about surprising them to give an inch. Deirdra had snuck away under the guise of using the ladies' room and had spoken to Wells about borrowing the rattan chairs. She'd been sure Wells would give her a hard time about Jagger, but either he hadn't heard the gossip or he knew better than to mess with her, because he was his usual flirtatious self and never mentioned the sexy musician/chef. They'd stayed long after they'd finished eating to listen to the live band. Deirdra had danced with her sisters, and of course her sisters had danced with their fiancés, leaving her wishing Jagger were there to joke around and dance with her, too.

Now here she was, in the bed where she'd found him naked and had turned tail and run away only six days ago, still wishing he were there with her. It wasn't even the making out she craved, although she definitely wanted more of that. She missed talking to him, listening to him play his guitar and sing, and Lord help her, because she even missed lying in his arms. In fact, she missed that the most.

She thought about texting him, but she didn't want to come across as clingy. She hated clingy people. But she was practically vibrating with nervous energy. Why couldn't she stop thinking about him? And why wasn't she freaking out about it? Or freaking out about her job? It was as if the wind had scattered *Jagger seeds* in her head, and they'd all taken root and tangled up her normally busy brain. Maybe a glass of wine would help quiet her thoughts. She slipped her feet into her fuzzy slipper booties and padded toward the kitchen. Her chest constricted at the sight of the pictures Jagger had given her lying on the counter. Oh, how she missed her father and the way her life had been when he was alive. She missed that little girl who was so full of hopes and dreams, she couldn't imagine life any other way. Claws of resentment prickled the back of her neck. She closed her eyes, breathing deeply, trying to let that longing rise to the surface, but the resentment was suffocating.

Forget wine. She needed air.

She headed for the door and saw Jagger's zip-up sweatshirt hanging on the hook. How had she missed that when she'd moved her things in? She put it on and pressed her nose to the sleeve, inhaling deeply. His uniquely rugged scent brought a different kind of longing. She went outside and sat on the steps, looking up at the stars, hoping the fresh air would clear her head. But her mind was stuck on Jagger. She wondered what he was up to tonight. Did he still park his RV at the Bistro as he had the last time she was on the island? She pressed the cuff of the sweatshirt to her nose again, missing him. That freaked her out a little, but not enough to quell the urge to use returning the sweatshirt as the perfect excuse to go see him.

Before she could talk herself out of it, she went inside and grabbed her keys. She hurried to the car and drove straight to the Bistro. Her stomach sank at the sight of the empty parking lot. She wasn't giving up and assumed he'd be parked by the beach somewhere. She drove along the road that ran parallel to the water. When she neared Lover's Cove, she drove to the sandy road they'd taken to the point, feeling excited when she saw his RV a little farther out. She threw the car into park, kicked off her slippers, and carried them as she hurried down the lane.

The ground was cool beneath her feet as she ran across the dirt, clutching her slippers to her chest. When she neared the RV, she heard music through the open windows, but the interior was dark. She made her way around to the side door, stepping over two of Dolly's toys. As she lifted her hand to knock, she glanced to her right and noticed a blanket and two tiki lights lying in the sand, bringing rise to an awful thought. What if he wasn't alone? *Ohmygod.* Why had she thought this was a good idea? Why would a man like Jagger ever be alone, when she'd seen women at the Bistro lusting after him as he played his guitar on the deck too many times to count?

Feeling foolish, and jealous, she turned to leave and stepped on Dolly's toy, which made a loud *squeak. Shit, shit, shit.* As she hurried away from the RV, she heard the door open behind her.

"Didi? Is that you?"

She froze, squeezing her eyes shut. *"No. I'm not Didi!"*

♥ ♥ ♥

There was no mistaking Deirdra's gorgeous hair or beautiful ass and legs in those skimpy shorts. If that wasn't confirmation enough, she was wearing the sweatshirt he'd misplaced with the Arts for Autism logo on the back. Jagger chuckled as he stepped out of the RV and headed toward her. "That's a shame, because she's pretty damn cool."

Dolly darted past him and tried to go paws-up on Deirdra, but she stepped out of reach and continued walking away, fending off his excited pooch with one hand and waving dismissively with the other. "Sorry. Go back to whatever you were doing."

He jogged past her, blocking her path, and drank in the embarrassment on her cheeks, feeling like a king because the woman who needed no one had sought him out. But why the hell was she running away? "Dolls, *sit*."

Dolly plopped onto her bottom, tail wagging, and Deirdra stared down at the ground, using one hand to shield her face, clutching slippers in the other. As if that did a bit of good. Beneath his sweatshirt, she wore a pink shirt with Too Glam to Give A Damn written down the middle. He wasn't buying it. She was there, after all.

He lowered her hand. "Miss me, Dee?"

She lifted her gaze, but it caught on his bare chest and slid down to his sweatpants.

His cock twitched at the heat in her eyes. "Like what you see?"

"*No.* I mean *yes*, but that's not why I'm here." She sighed heavily and met his gaze.

He stepped closer. "It's addicting, isn't it?"

"You are *not* addicting." She looked at him through her long lashes, her lips tipping up at the edges.

Always a fighter. He took her by the hips, pulling her against him, loving the sparks crackling around them. "Not *me*, sweet thing. The energy between us."

"It's *okay*, but I wouldn't say *addicting*." Her smile betrayed her.

"Then why are you here, if not for us?"

"To return your sweatshirt. I found it in the apartment."

She started to take it off, but he guided her hands over his shoulders instead. "You could have returned it tomorrow." He kissed her neck. "When we go on our date."

"I thought you might need it," she said breathily.

"The only thing I need is standing right in front of me." He spread his hands over her ass, holding her tight against him, and brushed a kiss to her lips. "Keep the sweatshirt. It looks good on you."

"I don't have to keep it."

He ignored that, knowing if she didn't like wearing it, she wouldn't have kept it on. "Tell me why you're running away. Did you come to kill me in my sleep because of the rumors going around and then think better of it? It's hard to be a highfalutin attorney from prison." That earned him a genuine smile.

"I shouldn't have come. I wasn't thinking. I got up to the door and realized you might not be alone, so . . ."

"Ah, you were jealous." Damn, he liked knowing that.

"No, I *wasn't*."

He arched a brow. "How about you try some good old-fashioned honesty and see what happens?"

"What happens is that I end up as front-page news."

"And that's bad because you're afraid it'll somehow diminish your badass-attorney status? You're allowed to be just a beautiful young woman having fun with a hot guy. But you'll have to make do with me."

She gave him a disbelieving look. "You know you're hot."

"I don't care if I am or not, unless it buys me more time with you." He decided to rile her up a little. "But I have to be honest. You *were* right about me being with someone else."

Her jaw dropped. "You *were*? Then why are you out here?" She tried to push out of his arms, but he held on tight.

"She's a real beauty, too, with big dark eyes, black spots, and a long tail."

She looked at Dolly, then scowled at him. "You jerk." She swatted at him, laughing, and he pulled her into a kiss.

"Come on, Didi, fess up. Why'd you really come here in the middle of the night?"

She stared at him for a long moment, her expression turning serious. "Because I couldn't stop thinking about you."

"Now we're getting somewhere, but you could have texted. I would have come to you."

"I didn't want to come across as needy, and . . . I just wanted to be near you, okay? I was in bed, and it felt weird, and I kind of wanted to be in your arms again."

"Kind of?"

"*Fine.* I wanted to be with you."

"In my arms, right? In these spindly things." He flexed his biceps, earning another sweet laugh. "Damn, Didi, your laugh gets me every time." He kissed her again, deeper and longer, feeling her go soft in his arms. "Come on, let's go inside and make your dreams come true."

"You are *so* full of yourself."

"You know you love it." They headed for the RV with Dolly. "Besides, I've got to be. There's no way a woman as spectacular as you would go for a guy who wasn't confident." When they got to the door, he knelt beside her. "Hold on to my shoulder. I'll help you get the sand off your feet."

"You're so laid-back, I didn't think you'd care about sand."

He began dusting off one of her feet. "I don't mind sand in the sheets, but I figured you aren't used to that sort of thing." He loved the way she got a little dreamy-eyed at that. She lowered her foot to the sand. "Give me your other foot."

"That's okay. You don't have to." She looked insanely sexy in the moonlight. "What's a little sand between the sheets, right?"

He pushed to his feet and swept her into his arms, kissing her smiling lips. "You're cringing inside, aren't you?"

"A little. But it's okay."

"Damn, I like you." He kissed her hard. "Better watch out, sweet thing. Next thing you know, you'll go full-on hippie girl."

"Not a chance."

They followed Dolly inside, and when he closed the door, shutting out all but a sprinkling of moonlight, Deirdra looked around nervously.

"Are you okay?"

"Yeah. It's just strange being in here like this."

"You mean with the intention of being in my arms?" He slid his arms around her waist, took her slippers, and set them on the table. "In my *bed*?"

She lifted one shoulder in a shrug so innocent compared to the confident, sensual woman he knew her to be, it endeared her to him even more.

"We can take a few blankets outside if you'd rather sleep out there."

"No. I want to be here, in your space."

"That's the honesty I was hoping for. Doesn't that feel better than saying you're here for any other reason?" He knew the answer and kissed her, feeling like the luckiest man on earth that she'd chosen to come to him. "Do you want a drink to take the edge off, or a glass of water?"

She shook her head. "No, thanks. Where is that music coming from?"

"Battery-operated radio by the bed." He slid the sweatshirt off her shoulders and tossed it on the table, then led her to his bed. Dolly beat them to it, her tail slapping the comforter. "*Floor*, Dolls." She jumped off the bed and went to lie down.

"Sorry to displace your girlfriend."

"I'll make it up to her." He set his glasses in the nook beside the bed and pulled back the covers. They climbed onto the bed, lying on their sides. He put his arm over her waist, pulling her closer, so they were nose to nose in the dark. "I'm really glad you're here."

"What were you doing when I got here?"

"Lying here wishing it was tomorrow night."

She smiled. "Really?"

"I told you I'm into you. Why is that so hard to believe?"

"Because most men are intimidated by me."

"Most men are insecure, threatened by your strength and your intelligence. I dig those things about you."

She blinked several times, as if she were processing that. "But you're so nice and thoughtful, and I'm not sweet like my sisters. I'm a workaholic who can't even pretend to understand the way you live."

"I'm not interested in your sisters, and I haven't seen you glued to your phone or your computer since we've been hanging out."

"Because when I'm with you, I'm not exactly thinking straight."

"How can you be sure? Maybe you're thinking straighter than you ever have." He ran his hand up the back of her shirt, pressing their bodies together.

Heat glowed in her eyes. "I can't be sure of anything when we're together. I don't know who I am when I'm with you."

"But look how much fun we're having figuring it out. And since I'm not buying that you're *too glam to give a damn* about anything, I want you to know that as long as we're hanging out, you're the only woman who will be in this bed. So don't hesitate to knock next time. Or even better, just walk in and crawl into bed with me, sandy feet and all." That dreaminess reappeared. She was wrong about being sweet. She exuded her own kind of sweetness, and that made her even more beautiful.

"I still can't believe I'm lying in your hippie van."

He rolled her onto her back. "You mean my shaggin' wagon?"

"*Ohmygod.* Do you really call it that?"

"Not always." He freaking loved riling her up. "Sometimes I call it my sin bin or my fuck truck."

"*Gross!* You probably have a different woman in here every week."

"*Hey*, come on, now. You know how I feel about connections."

"Yeah, but that could mean you have a few drinks and think a woman's hot so you sleep with her."

He could spend all night riling her up and calming her down, watching those green eyes go from soft to fierce and back again, and be perfectly happy, but he had to set the record straight. "That doesn't happen as often as you probably think." He touched his lips to hers, needing to slow her mind down enough for her to hear him. "Sometimes, when a connection is *really* special, it develops over time. Starting with watching an uptown girl whisper about me across a bonfire and wishing I could hear every word." He paused, letting his words sink in, and saw understanding rise in her eyes. *That's right, baby. It was you, the first night we met.* "It's knowing she's watching me play my guitar at the grand opening of her sister's restaurant even though she thinks I don't notice."

A sweet smile curved her lips. "Guilty."

He knew how hard the admission was for her, and it made it even more special. But what he'd failed to anticipate was how hearing her admit it would intensify his feelings for her. "It's playing my guitar surrounded by people on the deck of that restaurant and knowing every song is really meant for only one person." The emotions in her eyes deepened, and he brushed his lips over her cheek. "And sometimes it's being jealous of my dog, because she gets closer to you than I do."

She giggled. "I think *you* got closer last night, hippie boy."

If she only knew how it turned him on every time she called him that, she might not say it so often. "Don't worry, sweet thing, you're not just a notch in my belt." He dipped his head and whispered, "I don't even wear a belt."

She laughed.

He kissed her cheek. "Want to know what I think?"

"What?"

He skimmed his hand down her hip, giving it a squeeze. "You need a little hippie in you."

"That's too bad." Her eyes turned seductive. "I was hoping to have *a lot* of hippie in me."

Their mouths came together urgently, passion driving them into rough, demanding kisses, hands groping, bodies grinding. He wanted to slow down, to show her just how special she was, but he was too into her, too greedy for more. He broke their kiss long enough to peel off her shirt, instantly reclaiming her mouth. Her breasts pressed against his chest, sending heat searing to his cock. But he'd been thinking about her gorgeous breasts all day, and he moved lower, loving her breasts with his hands and mouth, licking and sucking, grazing his teeth over her nipple, earning one needy gasp after another. Those hungry sounds spiked through him as he kissed his way down her body and stripped off her shorts, her glistening sex drawing him in like metal to magnet. He feasted on her, rough and unrelenting, taking and giving, then taking *more*, making her tremble and writhe.

"*Ohgod. Jagger*—" sailed from her lips as she shattered against his mouth, her sinful sounds filling the air.

Her fingernails dug into his flesh, pain and pleasure slicing through him. Her every gasp, every moan and whimper, took him closer to the edge as she rode out her pleasure. When she came down from the peak, he stripped off his sweatpants and kissed his way up her body, taking her in a deep, sensual kiss. His cock wept for the warm haven of her mouth, but the all-consuming need to be as close as they could was too strong to deny. He forced himself to break away long enough to rise onto his knees and grab a condom from the cabinet above the window. He tore it open with his teeth, her eyes trained on his body. The hauntingly beautiful, unguarded look in her eyes got him all twisted up inside. He sheathed his length, and she reached for him as he came down over her. Their mouths fused in a sensual dance as their bodies came together inch by inch, until he was buried to the hilt. He'd fantasized about this moment all summer, but nothing compared to the rush of emotions engulfing him. "*Jesus*, Dee—"

She tugged his mouth to hers, cutting him off, but he knew by the intensity of her kisses that she was just as blown away as he was. She met his every thrust with a rock of her hips, their bodies moving in perfect harmony. Desire mounted with every swipe of their tongues, every thrust of his hips. She clung to him like she never wanted to let go, her desperation heightening every sensation. He pushed his hands beneath her ass, lifting and angling so he could take her deeper, and she arched her back, pulling her knees up and spreading them wider, knowing exactly what he needed. He'd never felt anything so incredible, and the urge to tell her as much was overwhelming. But she'd already let her walls down so far, he didn't want to scare her into putting them back up. Her head fell back, and he buried his face in her neck, kissing and sucking, earning one needful plea after another. Her urgency drew his release closer to the surface. He pounded harder, faster, their bodies slick from their efforts. Her knees clamped against his sides, and his name flew from her lips like a prayer. *"Jagger—"*

Her nails cut into his shoulders as her body clenched exquisitely tightly around his shaft, destroying the last of his control. Pleasure crashed over him like waves pummeling the shore, merciless and magnificent. Lustful praise spilled from her lips. *"Yes . . . so good . . . Jag . . ."* Her words carried him into a world so full of Deirdra, he didn't know where he ended and she began.

They lay tangled together for a long time afterward as their frantic hearts settled and their breathing calmed. Jagger kissed her softly, and her eyes fluttered open, blissfully hazy and beautifully sated. Neither said a word, but he felt her heart beating faster and knew she was trying to make sense of the emotions wrapping around them, just as he was. He needed to get up and take care of the condom, but he was afraid his sweet thing's mind would skip to what it meant that she'd come to him, wanting to be in his arms, in his space, and she'd hightail it out of there. But what choice did he have?

He brushed his lips over her cheek, dusting kisses there. "I'll be right back."

A small smile curved her lips as he climbed from the bed and went into the bathroom, hoping she wouldn't be gone when he came out. He washed up quickly, and when he opened the door, Deirdra was sitting up, holding the sheet against her chest as she reached for her shirt. He dove onto the bed and pinned her beneath him, earning the laughter that made his heart sing.

"Don't even think about putting clothes on your beautiful body."

"*Jagger.* I should go."

"You should stay."

"*Jag.*" She looked around, brows knitting. "I don't want things to be awkward."

"Then don't make them awkward."

That bashful smile he'd been graced with only a couple of times appeared, tugging at something deep inside him.

"I can't stay. That's not what this is."

"You came here wanting to be in my arms, and my arms got all excited. Now you want to let them down?" Her smile widened, and he tried to slide into that crack in her armor. "I know you *want* to stay, and I also know you're afraid of what it'll mean if you do." Her expression turned serious, so he went for humor. "I'm also pretty sure you're worried that if you stay, you might fall in love with me."

Laughter fell from her lips. "You're too much."

"I know it's hard to resist me, and the way we're vibing makes it even more difficult. But don't worry, sweet thing. I've got your back. I will *not* let that happen. We're *flinging*, not *falling*, so let's put that fear to rest and just enjoy being together. I promise your meticulously organized world will not collapse." He touched his lips to hers. "It might even look brighter in the morning."

Her eyes narrowed, but she put her arms around him, and he felt the air shift and lighten. "Have you ever considered a career in law? You're pretty convincing when you want to be."

"Does that mean you'll stay?"

"Will you let me put some clothes on?"

"Yes." As he lowered his lips to hers, he whispered, "But I'm just going to take them off again."

CHAPTER ELEVEN

THE SWEET AROMA of coffee drew Deirdra from a deep sleep and an erotic dream in which she was reliving last night's encore with Jagger. They'd gotten a little wild the second time around, trying different positions, and she could already feel a few well-deserved aches in places she'd never been sore before. She rolled onto her side, and a rough tongue slid up her cheek, chased by doggy breath. Deirdra squinted at the happy pooch beside her, perched to play. She groaned and rolled onto her other side.

"Dolly, are you stealing kisses again?" Jagger crawled onto the bed, eyes bright, like he'd been up for hours, but it wasn't even light outside. "*Damn*, Didi, you're even more beautiful when you wake up in the morning."

She melted a little inside. "You're dangerous. You could probably charm the panties off a nun."

He pressed his lips to hers, but she clamped her mouth shut. He looked at her like she'd lost her mind. "What kind of kiss was that?"

"The kind that saves you from my morning breath. What time is it?"

"Five thirty. I thought we could watch the sunrise. I made coffee."

Her heart skipped. "I haven't watched the sunrise since I was little."

"Then you'd better get your gorgeous butt out of bed so we don't miss it."

He leaned in to kiss her again, and she turned away. "Oh no, you don't, *missy*." He swept her beneath him, trapping her hands beside her head.

She futilely tried to stifle her laughter, turning her face to the side. "*Don't*. It's gross."

"I don't give a damn about your breath. I brushed my teeth. My minty freshness will conquer whatever you're worried about."

She shook her head.

"You stubborn thing." He chased her mouth with his.

"*Jagger!*" She wiggled and squirmed, dodging his lips and laughing.

"I want your lips on mine, so deal with it."

He said it like he'd never wanted anything more in his entire life, and that did crazy things to her insides. She'd forgotten how incredible it was to be truly wanted. He took her face between his hands and lowered his lips to hers. The hard press of his lips and the weight of his body lured her in, making her *want* and *crave* more of him. He brushed his thumbs over her cheeks as his tongue slid along the seam of her lips, too tempting to deny. She gave in to her desires, surrendering to their passion, kissing him feverishly.

His hands pushed into her hair, fisting tightly, and her whole body sizzled and burned. He drew back with a look so full of awe, she could barely breathe. "*Damn, Dee.* I don't want to stop."

She was wrong. She hadn't forgotten what it felt like to be wanted, because she'd never been wanted like this before. "Then don't."

♥ ♥ ♥

They missed the sunrise, and when Jagger led her into the shower with him, she didn't hesitate. They were insatiable for each other, and she'd never felt freer or happier in her life. He made them breakfast, and they ate it on the beach, she in her pajamas and Jagger in his hemp pants, shirtless and gorgeous. Dolly was lying a few feet away, chewing on a toy. With the sun warming Deirdra's cheeks, her toes in the sand, and Jagger's arm draped over her shoulder, she realized she hadn't thought about work or her phone, or anything other than Jagger, since last night, even *before* he'd screwed her senseless.

"Want to stretch with me?" he whispered against her neck.

"I think I'm well stretched, thanks."

He grinned. "Come on. A few yoga stretches will do you good."

"No, thanks. I just got more exercise than I've gotten in months. But you go ahead, hippie boy."

Jagger was always a sight to be reckoned with, but stretching all those lean muscles, with the morning sun kissing his skin and that glimmer of wanting her in his eyes? The man was nothing short of a force of nature.

When he finally drove her home, she went into the back of the RV to look for her slippers, and he followed, drawing her into his arms. "One last kiss."

They made out like horny college kids trying to eke out every second together. He was hard against her belly, his big hands groping her all over, making her wet and wanting again.

"I'll walk you up to the door," he said between kisses.

"No. I might not let you leave, and you have to be at work soon."

He groaned. "You're killing me."

He backed her up against the closet, kissing her feverishly. She pressed her hips forward, putting space between them, and slipped her hand into his pants, palming his arousal. He gritted out, "*Dee . . .*"

His warning was clear, but she was too turned on, wanting to give him as much pleasure as he brought her. She lifted his shirt and kissed his chest, whispering, "Shut the curtains."

He closed them and reclaimed her mouth in a savage kiss that set her entire body aflame. She untied his pants, pushing them to the floor, and backed him up toward the bed, kissing her way down his chest, licking and grazing her teeth over his nipples, earning sharp hisses and guttural moans. She pushed him down to the edge of the bed and fisted his cock as she dropped to her knees between his legs. She held his gaze, flames rising in his eyes as she licked the length of him, lingering on the broad crown.

"*Fuck*. Dee."

She lowered her mouth over his thick shaft, working him with fast, tight strokes of her hand as she sucked and teased. His hips rocked, and he grabbed her by the hair, growling, "*Look* at me." His demand made her wetter, but it was the wickedness in his eyes that had her working him faster, sucking harder, wanting to see him lose control.

"*Dee . . . fuck . . . I can't hold back.*"

She cupped his balls, giving them a tug as she took him deeper in her mouth, stroking tighter. Her name flew from his lungs like a curse, his hips thrusting hard as he rode out his release, and she took everything he had to give. His body jerked with aftershocks, and he tugged her up and into his arms, kissing her deeply and rolling them onto their sides on the bed. "Jesus, Dee." His eyes brimmed with emotion, and she knew he saw it in hers, too. He brushed her hair away from her eyes and kissed her softly, *intimately*, bringing rise to feelings so big, they rode on a cloud of fear. "This thing between us—"

She silenced him with a kiss. "I should go."

Disappointment rose in his eyes, causing a flare of discomfort in her chest. She couldn't afford to give voice to her emotions. Not when she knew how much heartache it would lead to. She pushed to her feet, but he took her hand and sat up, pulling her down on his lap. He was naked from the waist down, half-aroused, and totally focused on her, running his fingers through the ends of her hair with a warm expression, while her insides rattled nervously.

"Thanks for staying last night."

"I'm glad I did." She wanted to say so much more, but she held back. "See you tonight?"

"Absolutely. I'll pick you up at six. I have tomorrow off, so bring an overnight bag."

"Getting a little cocky, aren't you?"

He kissed her neck. "You know you're not going to want to leave me, and I want to spend the day with you. Bring sneakers."

"Are we going for a run?"

"Take off your lawyer hat and just go with it."

She wasn't about to pass up a chance to spend the day with him. "Okay." She got up and grabbed her slippers as he put on his pants. "What should I wear tonight? Where are we going?"

"Someplace fun." He drew her into his arms again, and boy did she like being there. "Wear whatever you want, because at the end of the night, I'm taking it off you anyway."

"You think so, huh?"

"I don't care if we get naked or not, but I have a feeling *you* do. You're always taking advantage of me."

She shook her head. "Okay, hippie boy. See you tonight."

He kissed her and smacked her butt as she walked out the side door. She feigned a scowl over her shoulder. On her way up the driveway, she noticed Abby and Aiden sitting on the front porch and froze. Aiden waved. Abby was grinning from ear to ear and pushed to her feet.

Deirdra pointed at her as she headed for the steps to the apartment. "Don't say it."

"Okay. I won't ask where your car is."

Deirdra froze. *Shit.* She'd been so preoccupied with Jagger she'd forgotten her car? She stalked back to the RV, her sister's giggles trailing behind her.

♥ ♥ ♥

"Knock, knock," Abby said as she walked into the apartment several hours later.

Deirdra looked up from her laptop as her sister sauntered into the living room, looking cute in jeans and a KISS THE COOK T-shirt. "Hi."

"Legally changing your name to Moonbeam?" Abby giggled and sat on the couch beside her.

Deirdra scowled. "*Ha ha.* I'm confirming an interview for next Thursday with Madeline King, who works for my company's biggest competitor."

"Oh wow. You're really quitting?"

"Yup. Working with Madeline would be a dream come true. She's a powerhouse who I could actually learn from, and the company is women-owned, and seventy-five percent of the staff are female. She said her colleague, a woman I had reached out to, told her I was looking. Their general counsel is going to be moving overseas for her husband's job. They hadn't even started looking for a replacement yet. But just in case that doesn't work out, I have a video interview on Monday with another company. The woman I'm meeting with is in the LA office until the end of the month, but she didn't want to take a chance that I'll find something else before then." She sent the email and sat back. "It feels good to be sought after instead of taken for granted. The new GC Malcolm hired called me this morning with questions about the merger."

Abby winced. "How did that go?"

"Fine. He seems sharp. Although not sharper than me."

"Then maybe you'll like working with him, and you won't have to look for a new job."

"Abby, I'm not looking because I think we won't get along. I realized it's time for me to make a change anyway. I shouldn't feel like I have to prove I'm better than a *man*. I should only have to prove that I'm the best person for the job, but I've always known a glass ceiling existed there. Now I just have to find a great job with a woman-run business that won't bore me to tears."

"You must have enough money saved to take a year off by now. Why don't you just quit and take your time finding a new job?"

"Because I can't fly by the seat of my pants the way you can."

"I know you can't—it was just an idea. I wish you'd move back here and start your own company or work for one of the attorneys or businesses on the island."

"Part of me sees how happy you and Cait are here and wishes I could be, too. But I'm not cut out for island life. Or at least not this island."

"But that thing we're not talking about tells me otherwise."

"Don't go there, Abby," Deirdra warned. She'd spent all day vacillating between being upset with herself for getting so lost in Jagger and his carefree world and being enamored with how wonderful she'd felt the whole time she'd been with him. She was so confused; she hadn't even told Sutton she'd slept with Jagger when she'd called. She needed to get her head on straight before talking openly about what she'd done.

Abby looked like she was going to burst. "How can I *not* go there? You never get caught up in anything outside of work, especially not guys, and you *forgot* your *car*."

"No kidding." She got up and paced, wondering if it was a mistake to spend tomorrow with Jagger but desperately wanting to. "That's *not* okay, Abby."

Abby popped to her feet. "Why not? You looked so happy when you came out of his RV. Even Aiden noticed it."

"That's because we screwed ourselves senseless."

Abby squealed.

"Would you *stop*?" It took everything she had to stifle the urge to gush about how wonderful, sexy, and fun Jagger was. But Abby was a dreamer, and she'd romanticize their time together. Deirdra was already having enough trouble trying to keep things in perspective.

"*No.* I won't stop. I'm excited. You're happy, and you're with a great guy who gets you out of your own head."

Deirdra stopped pacing and crossed her arms, needing a barrier between her and the truth. "He definitely knows how to do that. But

I can't be forgetting where I leave my *car*, for Pete's sake. That's what ditzy girls do, and that's *not* me. Hell, Abby, that's *never* been me. What I need is to find a new job and get back to my normal life."

"That's not what ditzy girls do. It's what a woman who's too caught up in being happy to think about anything else does, and that's *exactly* what you need."

"Don't tell me what I need."

"I'm going to tell you, because I'm the only one who can," Abby snapped. "I know you think you have to always be the sister who has everything in order and enough money in the bank *never* to feel like we did as kids. I was there, Dee. I know how you became who you are. I know you made sure I had food to eat every night and did my homework, and you got Mom to bed. You've been the grown-up since we were kids, and you have never stopped being that always-prepared person, which is admirable. I love who you are, and I'm proud to be your sister."

A lump formed in Deirdra's throat. "But I left you alone to take care of Mom."

"I *told* you to. You deserved to start your life. But I wasn't being a martyr. I knew I'd get my turn. I wasn't in a rush like you were. Shelley had to practically kick me off the island to get me to go. So *stop* feeling guilty for leaving. If I had wanted you to stay, I would have told you. But you've always been too bullheaded to see what's right in front of you. You're so focused on your next goal, you plow forward and find reasons to regret it later, even when there's no need to regret anything. But I think that's part of how Mom screwed us up. She made us not trust people, or even ourselves."

"I trust myself." The knee-jerk reaction wasn't wholly true.

Abby made a disbelieving face. "If that were the case, you'd know you never in our entire lives have done wrong by me. And you're too stubborn to see what you need, so listen carefully." She closed the gap between them, holding Deirdra's gaze. "You deserve to be happy. You don't need to be perfect all the time. Not for me, or anyone else."

Tears welled in Deirdra's eyes, and she struggled, willing them not to fall.

"You said you're just having a fling with Jagger." Abby's tone softened. "What's wrong with having a great time with him for the next week and a half and *then* getting a job, taking more of your hiatus before carrying on with your normal life? You can go back to working twenty-four-seven and wait another nineteen years to smile like this again, but at least you will have had this amazing time with a great guy to look back on."

Deirdra's thoughts stumbled. Nineteen years? Had it really been that long since she'd been happy? *No.* Of course it hadn't. Her work was stimulating, and she felt like she was part of something important, with daily accomplishments and a nice paycheck. She was happy. Maybe not the same type of carefree happy as she'd been this last week with Jagger, but that wasn't reality, and it certainly wasn't sustainable, considering she hadn't been working.

But Abby was partially right.

Cait's party was next weekend, and then Deirdra could take off and go anywhere she wanted. *Wait.* No, she couldn't. Forget her hiatus. She had to go back to Boston and find a job. Then she'd give her notice, finish out her stint at her old job, and start the new one. She'd be bored on a long vacation anyway. With a solid plan in place, why not enjoy the time she had left on the island with Jagger?

"Are you okay?" Abby asked. "I didn't mean to upset you."

"You didn't. I was thinking about what you said."

"Is that good or bad? I know you've never been carefree, and you probably never will be, but being a little less worried about what you have to do next and paying a little more attention to just having fun would be good for you. It's only a week and a half, and you deserve the break."

"You're right. There's no reason not to enjoy myself for the next ten days. I'll just have to work harder to keep my head on straight. But if I forget my car again, I'm outta here."

"Yay!" Abby hugged her. "Maybe we can have a triple date this week, all six of us. We can have dinner on the boat or head out to Bellamy Island and have a cookout. Or maybe we can go dancing at Rock Bottom, since Jagger wasn't with us last time. Or we could plan an evening on the Cape, since you like upscale places. I need to look at schedules. Jagger works Sunday and Wednesday morning, but I work until six both days, and I know Cait is booked with full days of tattoos next week, so it'll probably have to be an evening."

"Slow down, sis. That all sounds great, and I definitely want to find time to get together with everyone, but I still have things to do for Cait's party." She told Abby her plans and what she had left to do. "I hired Tara Osten to take videos and pictures at the party." Tara was the mayor's daughter. She was a few years younger than Abby and worked as a freelance photographer. "She told me that Gail arranged for an engagement announcement in the newspaper. I never would have thought of doing that, and I'm sorry I never did it for you. I should have."

"Don't worry about that silliness. Shelley had one put in the newspaper for us. You were in Boston at the time, and I guess I forgot to mention it."

"I want to know those things, Abby. I feel so out of the loop, and I know it's my own fault. But I want to be in the loop."

"*Aw.* I love that, and I promise from now on you'll be kept in the loop on everything."

"Thank you. I'm glad Shelley did it for you, but I'm going to up my sister game from now on. When you and Aiden decide to have babies, I'll make damn sure I'm the one who sends in the announcements." They both laughed. "Hopefully, I haven't forgotten anything for Cait's party. I spoke to Jules this morning about the centerpieces, since she holds those centerpiece-making classes at her shop, and she said she'd help us make them. She said she could get a great deal on everything we need—vases, candles, fake fronds, and all the other decorations. She also asked Grant to get a bunch of driftwood and make it pretty for us. She is amazing, isn't she?"

"She's the party queen. I'm so excited to do this with you, and for Cait. What you have planned is perfect for her and Brant. You put a lot of thought into it."

"Thanks. It feels good to put as much effort into this as I usually do for work. I was thinking, we should ask Gail and Brant's sisters to help with the centerpieces. Randi called me yesterday, asking about the plans. I apologized for sort of taking over, but she said between Tessa's flights and her diving schedule, they have no time to do much of anything." Tessa was a local pilot, and Randi was a marine archaeologist, currently working a diving expedition with famed treasure hunter Zev Braden off the coast of Silver Island, where he'd discovered the wreckage from a pirate ship that sank in the 1700s.

"We should also ask Shelley, because she's done so much for us, and you know she'll want to do something special for Cait."

"Right. Good idea. Maybe I should just ask Jules to put out a call to anyone who can make it. We're thinking about doing it around four on Tuesday. Do you think you can make that work?"

"I'm the boss. Of course I can." Abby wiggled her shoulders proudly. "Where are you doing it?"

"I thought we'd do it at the house."

"I don't think that's a good idea. Cait might show up, and we can't do it at Gail's in case Brant stops over."

"I'll ask Shelley if we can do it at her house." Deirdra took out her phone and texted Shelley. "It's getting late. I have to get ready for my date with Jagger." Excitement bloomed inside her. "Want to help me pick out something to wear?"

"Yes, definitely. Where is he taking you?"

"I don't know. He wouldn't tell me, but I've liked every surprise he's planned for me, so I'm sure I'll like this one, too."

"I love Jagger," Abby said dreamily.

He's easy to fall for. "He asked me to spend tomorrow with him, so I won't be home tonight." She pointed to the overnight bag by the door as they headed into the bedroom. She'd packed a cute, casual outfit and sneakers, as he'd requested.

"So he *is* a planner?"

"Only when it comes to other people's lives. But he doesn't seem to plan things for himself. Except he does have solar on his van, so there's that."

"*RV*," Abby corrected her. "And that's important planning."

"True, which is why it's weird that he lives by the seat of his pants in other ways. Did you know he's going to Europe for a few months after you close the restaurant and he has absolutely no plans for where he's staying or how he'll earn money or anything? He doesn't even know exactly how long he's staying."

"I knew he was traveling, but he never said where he was going. He really has no plan for any of that?"

"Nope, and he's not bothered by it, either. He said he'll pick up jobs when he can. It obviously works for him. He's been doing it for years. I just don't get it, since he made sure his brother had his future planned out before he was even out of high school." She told Abby about Homegrown Hearts.

"Maybe that's why Jagger doesn't plan his own life. From what he's told me about Gabe needing structure, it sounds like he's doing the things his brother can't. The same way you live your life in a way Mom couldn't. Does that make any sense?" Abby picked out a dress and looked thoughtfully at Deirdra. "Try this on."

Deirdra thought about what Jagger had said about Gabe being boxed out of opportunities as she put on the dress. "He said something similar, so yeah, I guess it does make sense." She looked in the mirror at the fitted sheath. "This is too dressy." She took it off and tossed it on the bed.

"Want to wear something hippieish? I might have a peasant blouse."

"You cannot be serious. I don't do peasant blouses."

Abby laughed. "Just offering. I thought you might want to fit in with his hippie world."

"We're having a fling, not getting married." She looked over her blouses. "And he is a hippie, but he's not the guy I thought he was. I thought he had no ambition or direction, but he does, sort of. He's really into saving the environment, and he's passionate about it, but he's not looking to make a career out of it." She pulled a sweater off the shelf and put it on, but it felt too bulky.

"Not everyone has to climb corporate ladders."

"I know. Actually, he did make some plans for his trip to Europe. He wants to see a few farms and go to a famous farm-to-table restaurant. Why would he plan *that* and not figure out a way to make money?"

"Because that's Jagger. You just told me that he cares about the environment. It's obviously more important to him than money. There's nothing wrong with that."

"I didn't say there was." Deirdra tried on a pair of slacks, but they were too dressy, and she tossed them onto the bed. "I like that he has such altruistic aspirations, probably because it's so different from how I live. I'm intrigued and baffled by the way he lives, which reminds me. I wanted to ask you about something. Remember how Dad used vegetables from our garden at the restaurant?"

"Of course." She tossed her a blouse and jeans.

As Deirdra put them on, she said, "Jagger said he's always wanted to have a farm-to-table restaurant, but he doesn't want to be tied down. I haven't mentioned this to him yet, so don't say anything, but is that something you'd be interested in for the Bistro? I was reading about it, and this morning I did some research on organic farms around the island and on the Cape. I think you could pull it off."

"That would be a dream come true, but sourcing quality ingredients isn't easy, and to do it right would take a lot of relationship building and coordinating, which I don't have time for."

Who was better with people than Jagger? "What if a consultant did that for you?"

"You mean Jagger?"

"*Maybe.* I don't know if he'd even be interested. I'm just thinking out loud."

"It's an interesting idea. I would love to offer organic meals. But it adds to the cost of goods and time for food prep, which would mean higher prices, and if I offered exclusively farm-to-table meals, the menu would have to be changed. It's a big undertaking, but that's not a deal breaker. That's what Dad always wanted, and there's nothing like it on the island. You've kind of got me excited about the idea."

"Would you have to offer exclusively farm-to-table? Couldn't you plan some meals that were farm-to-table on certain days and make them special offerings?"

"I can do anything. As I said, I'm the boss." She eyed Deirdra's outfit. "You can't wear that. It looks too *city.*"

They chatted about the idea as they picked out outfits and Deirdra tried them on. Half an hour later, she tossed a blouse on the mountain of clothes on the bed and sighed. "Why am I so nervous about what to wear? I never have this much trouble picking out clothes."

"Because you really like Jagger, and you're already wearing the things that matter." She motioned to the red lace lingerie Deirdra had bought when they were in Chaffee.

"There is a lot of truth to that statement." She looked at the sister who knew only how to be open and honest and decided it was time to do the same, even with herself. "I like him a lot, Abby, like so much, it's scary."

"Oh, we're allowed to talk about this now?" she teased. "I figured you did since you came home in some kind of orgasm coma this morning. How did you end up in his RV, anyway? You were home when I went to bed."

"I couldn't stop thinking about him." Deirdra picked through her clothes again. "I've never thought about a guy as much as I think about him, much less missed someone. I can't explain it, but I *really* wanted to be with him."

"You don't have to explain it. That's the great thing about falling for someone."

"I didn't say I was falling for him."

"Right," Abby said sarcastically, and handed her a V-neck cropped white sweater with bell sleeves. "Try this with the suede miniskirt and suede ankle boots. What was it like? Sleeping in the RV, not the sex."

Deirdra pulled on the sweater. "Weird at first, being surrounded by his hippie stuff." She stepped into the miniskirt. "I had a moment of feeling too old. But it was just a quick blip on my radar."

"You're only thirty."

"I know, but I've always felt older than people my age to start with, and he's only twenty-five."

Abby looked up at the ceiling. "Thanks for making her grow up too soon, Mom. Now Jagger will have to screw her senseless all week to undo that damage."

Deirdra laughed. "I would *not* complain about that. But honestly, he's so playful and easy to be with, by the time we got in bed, the RV and our age difference didn't matter." She put on ankle socks and slipped her feet into the boots. "And in the morning, I woke up to Dolly licking my face and sand in the sheets."

"Oh no. You hate to be sandy."

"Right?" She shrugged. "But then there was Jagger, wanting to watch the sunrise with me, and suddenly the sand and the dog slobber didn't matter, either." She turned toward Abby, who was beaming. "What do you think? Do I look okay?"

"I don't think I've ever seen you look more beautiful."

"Really?" Deirdra looked down at her outfit.

"It's not the clothes, Dee. It's you. You're glowing, and you're going to knock Jagger's socks off."

That made her all kinds of happy. "I feel sorry for Aiden if you focus on knocking his *socks* off. I'm aiming for something a little higher."

Abby giggled, and they began putting away the clothes that were on the bed. A knock on the door sent Deirdra's heart into a frenzy. "He's here. Are you sure I look okay? What if I'm overdressed?"

"When have you ever cared if you were overdressed? You really are nervous. It's cute."

"Stop it. You're making me more nervous. Come on." She headed out of the bedroom, took a deep breath to calm her nerves, and opened the door.

Her stomach flipped. Jagger looked delicious in a white linen button-down with the sleeves rolled up to his elbows, revealing tanned forearms, and dark linen pants. His clothes were a little wrinkled, and in addition to his bracelets, he wore a slim leather necklace with a tree of life charm and another, shorter beaded necklace. On any other man, the jewelry might look out of place or feminine, but with Jagger's pitch-black scruff, gorgeous eyes, and sexy smile, it looked artsy and nomadic, making him even more enticing. Why had it taken her so long to see him for who he really was?

"Hi, Jag." Her voice was so breathy she didn't recognize it.

"Hey, sweet thing." His eyes took an appreciative stroll down her body. "*Mm-mm.* You look gorgeous." He leaned in and kissed her cheek, whispering, "Taunting me with your sexy legs?" He nipped her earlobe, sending sparks racing along her flesh. "Hi, Abby. How are you?"

"I couldn't be better." Abby looked like she wanted to cheer for them. "Where are you going on your date?"

"Someplace special," Jagger said.

"Let me get my purse." Deirdra went to the kitchen to get her purse.

"Is this your overnight bag, sweet thing?"

She grabbed her purse, and when she turned back, Jagger was holding her bag behind Abby, who was facing her and mouthing, *Sweet thing? I love that!*

It was all Deirdra could do not to laugh. "Yeah, that's my bag."

They followed Abby down the stairs, and as she headed inside the house, Jagger took Deirdra in his arms and kissed the hell out of her. He kept her close, speaking huskily. "How is it possible that I missed you so much when we're just *flinging*?"

She cleared her throat to try to quiet the excited girl inside her. "I don't know, but you'd better get that under control, hippie boy. I don't do clingy."

"Not clingy, just honest." He patted her butt. "Let's go, *Miss Independent*. Our next adventure awaits."

"Where's Dolly?"

He draped an arm over her shoulder as they headed for the RV. "In the shaggin' wagon."

"Watch it, hippie boy."

He opened the door, and Dolly greeted them with a big pink bow around her neck.

"Look at this pretty girl." Deirdra loved her up. "*Jagger*, she's beautiful."

"She got dolled up for our first date."

And just like that, she got all melty inside again. She climbed into the passenger seat. "What smells so good?"

Jagger leaned in and kissed her. "I made a meal for a few friends earlier."

She found that interesting and wondered who the friends were, but she wasn't about to ask, because that crossed a clingy line. She did ask where they were going, and he refused to tell her. They chatted as he drove along the coast, and she couldn't hold in her excitement about her talk with Abby. "I can't stop thinking about your pipe dream. You're so passionate about it, I'd hate to see you turn your back on it altogether, so I was thinking . . ."

"Uh-oh."

"Just hear me out. I know you don't want to be tied down to any one place, and I'm not suggesting that you do. I did some research, and I think farm-to-table is something you and Abby could do at the Bistro, even if only on special days or for special meals. I was thinking you could do it when you visit here in the summers, if you continue to visit the area."

He looked astonished. "Hold on. You *researched* my pipe dream?"

"Yes, and I mentioned the idea to Abby. She seemed interested, but she said it takes a lot of coordinating and scheduling, which gave me another idea. A few actually."

"You talked to your sister about it?"

"Please don't be mad. I was just excited about the idea and wanted to feel her out."

"I'm not mad, Dee. I like that you thought of me."

"Good, then let me tell you my ideas. You obviously need to make money wherever you go for your music gigs, or travels in general, and you're passionate about farming the right way and farm-to-table eating. What if you combine the two and consult with restaurants to help them get set up for farm-to-table? You'd have to commit to putting that infrastructure together, but you wouldn't have to necessarily be in one place while you did it."

"I'd have to meet the farmers and check out the farms."

"Okay, that's doable, but the rest—setting up schedules and such—you could handle remotely, right? And that got me thinking that even though you don't like to plan, you did make plans to see farms and a restaurant while you're away, which tells me that you can plan if you're interested in the end result. So, what if you research the areas you're traveling to and see if there are farm-to-table restaurants where you can work if you need money? That way, if you do have to work, at least you'd be working with something you believe in. Another idea was that you could see if there are any restaurant or café owners that you can talk to about moving toward farm-to-table."

"You really *have* thought about this."

"I know. You know how you said I should be a party planner because it lit me up from the inside? That was only because I'm doing it for Cait, but you lit up about this, Jagger. I know it all sounds crazy, but there are so many ways you can be part of what you love without giving up traveling, your music, or the ability to drop everything and be there for Gabe. I'm sure there are obstacles that would need to be addressed, but as a consultant, *you* decide if you want to work with one client or twelve. You decide the location, the time and effort you'd put in." The more she talked, the more excited she became. "It's all in your hands, and you'd only be tied down in the sense that you're putting together a process and then maybe doing quarterly check-ins, or semiannual visits, to ensure it's running smoothly. You don't even have to do that. It can be a turnkey operation, where you set them up and walk away."

"But I'm the idea guy, not the make-it-happen guy."

"Don't sell yourself short. I don't believe for a second that all you did was drop an idea for Homegrown Hearts and walk away. You're too passionate about Gabe and the environment not to have had your hands in many of those pots. But even if you did, look at the other things you do: playing concerts and opening your guitar case at town squares to raise money for autism. That's a guy who makes things happen. And don't forget, I've seen firsthand what you can do. You brought France to life for me at the library, and you made a Spanish fiesta with all the trimmings, and both were spectacular."

"I'm intrigued, Dee, but I wouldn't know the first thing about how to start something like that."

"You spent half an hour telling me about how farm-to-table restaurants work. You *know* plenty, Jagger. You've just never envisioned yourself in the roles I mentioned, the same way I've never imagined allowing myself to think about the good memories from years ago. If there's one thing I'm learning from you, it's that life is what we make it, and sometimes that means reimagining parts of ourselves."

He looked at her with a serious expression.

"I'm sorry. I'm not trying to change who you are or how you live your life. They're just ideas. And if it all sounds like too much, you can just write it all down so you have it years from now when you look back on our time together and think, *Deirdra might have been onto something.*"

He laughed. "You're definitely onto something. You've given me a lot to think about."

"I know it's a lot, and I don't expect you to jump on it. I just thought there might be ways you could see the world and save it at the same time."

He reached across the space between them for her hand, looking at her like she was a gift, setting off those butterflies again. "You're amazing, and thoughtful, and too damn smart and beautiful for your own good. Thank you. I will think about it."

CHAPTER TWELVE

DEIRDRA WAS EXCITED to see what Jagger had planned for their date. She was even more curious when he drove into Seaport, a small fishing town known for its old-fashioned New England charm. There were no elaborate homes or historical monuments and no fancy court-yards or luxurious shops, but what the town lacked in materialism, it made up for in character. They drove through the center of town, passing quaint cottages that had once been home to fishermen and were now shops and restaurants, their residential driveways and fences still intact.

Deirdra pointed to Everything Under the Sun. "I was at that shop yesterday picking up iron mermaids for Cait and Brant's party. The guy who owns it is a sweetheart."

"Saul? Yeah, he's a cool guy."

"You know him?"

"Sure, and his wife, Nina. Or as most people around here call her, *the cookie lady*. Kids flock to her at the community breakfasts. Little do they know she puts vegetables in those cookies. I almost got the recipe from her once, but she refused to give it up."

Deirdra imagined him trying to charm a recipe out of her. She'd never be able to resist. "I forgot about those cookies and the breakfasts. Does Goldie Gallow still host them at her family's bed-and-breakfast by the old lighthouse at Gallow Pointe?"

"Yes. She's a riot. Eighty years old and still rockin' on." He pulled off the main road, passing more cute cottages with bountiful gardens.

"How much time do you spend here? You seem to know everyone."

"I wouldn't say everyone, but I've made some good friends over the years. And you're about to meet some of them." He turned down a narrow gravel road.

A parking lot and an old clapboard building came into view at the end of the street. The massive structure was built on a hill, with piers holding up the right side. Concrete steps led to a double-door entrance, flanked by three enormous glassless windows with hinged-at-the-top shutters propped open with long pieces of wood, like heavy eyelids hanging over them. SEAPORT DANCE HALL was painted above the doors, and black cables and wires ran from the outside of the building to nearby electrical poles.

Jagger drove toward the far side of the packed parking lot, passing a swarm of elderly people on the side of the building, milling about and sitting at picnic tables. A handful of women wore bright red hats. Dolly craned her neck to see out the window and barked.

"It's okay, Dolly." Deirdra petted her. "What are we doing here?"

"Going on our date." He parked beneath the shade of a large tree and cut the engine, turning in his seat with that easy smile.

"Here?" She looked at the people on the lawn, none of whom looked younger than sixty.

"Yeah. Once a month the Red Hat Society hosts a seniors' dinner and dance. I'm playing with the band tonight. I figured we'd eat a great dinner, you can meet some of my friends, and I can watch you dance your sexy little ass off." He cocked a grin. "And you can walk around like a proud peacock, knowing you have a backstage pass to the hottest guy in the band."

This was so *very* Jagger, and he made it sound fun. "Okay, let's do this."

"A'right! Didi is in the house." He pulled her up to her feet and kissed her. "We'll have a blast. Let's grab the lasagna and get out there."

"These are the friends you cooked for?" Why did that make her like him even more?

"Sure are. Everyone brings something to share for dinner." He slung his guitar strap across his chest and leashed Dolly, and they carried two large pans of lasagna toward the gathering.

This man was full of surprises, and he looked so happy, she knew these friends were important to him. "Tell me about this band you're in."

"It's a boy band, and the ladies dig us, so prepare yourself for competition. We call ourselves the Crotch Rockets."

She laughed, but he looked serious. "You're not kidding, are you?"

Someone shouted, "Jagger's here!" and a loud cheer rang out.

A tall, skinny woman hurried toward them. She wore a long-sleeved black shirt with a zipper down the front that was open dangerously low for a woman who looked to be in her seventies, colorful stretch pants, and black knee-high boots. Her white hair was cut in a shag, like Joan Jett, her eyes were heavily made up, and her lipstick was bright red. A tiny woman with thick, curly gray-blue hair, wearing a sparkly black-and-gold blazer, caught up with her, also heading their way.

Jagger leaned closer to Deirdra. "The tall woman is Goldie, and the shorter one is Estelle."

"*That's* Goldie? Gosh, she's changed. I remember her as being a plumper grandma type."

"I told you she was a trip."

A heavyset man with a white goatee hollered, "Gerry, you'd better get over there before you lose Estelle to Jagger," causing an uproar of jeers.

"Who is that big guy?"

"Big Dick. He plays the drums in the band." Jagger pointed to a skinny man with tufts of white hair sticking out from under a black baseball cap with CROTCH ROCKET written across the front. "That's

Gerry, Estelle's boyfriend. He's an old stoner, and he can play the hell out of a guitar. He doesn't play with the band anymore, but sometimes we can coax him into playing a song or two."

"Hi, honey." Goldie loved up Dolly with one hand as she leaned in to kiss Jagger's cheek, leaving a little lipstick behind.

Estelle pushed her aside. She couldn't be more than five feet tall. "Let me in there." Her voice was as rough as sandpaper. She went up on her toes, and Jagger met her halfway so she could kiss his cheek. "Hello, handsome. I know you missed me these last few weeks."

Jagger chuckled. "Yes, I did."

"I see you brought the goods." Estelle took the pan from him. "And a *hotsy-totsy*. Good for you." She looked Deirdra up and down. "With a body like that, I know you can give him a run for his money between the sheets."

"*Estelle*," Goldie chided her, turning a sweet smile on Deirdra. "You'll have to excuse our friend. When she turned eighty-three, she decided she'd earned the right to say whatever comes to mind."

"And I have," Estelle said proudly.

"That's okay. You're right, Estelle. I *can* give him a run for his money. Thank you for noticing," she said cheekily. "I'm Deirdra. It's nice to meet you both."

"I'm Goldie, and you look very familiar."

"You might remember me from when I was younger. My parents owned the Bistro in Silver Harbor, Olivier and Ava de Messiéres. They brought my sister Abby and me to a few of your community breakfasts when we were little."

"You're little Didi? No wonder you're such a looker." Estelle lowered her voice. "I knew your parents—that gorgeous Frenchman and his *very* young wife. He was the envy of all the men and she, of all the women. I was sorry to hear your mother passed away. Poor thing had a rough go of it."

"*Yes*, I remember your parents and you and your sister," Goldie said. "You were a feisty young thing, chasing boys around and giving orders."

Jagger cocked a brow.

"They probably stole my cookies," Deirdra said.

"Everyone loves Nina's cookies," Goldie said. "I don't get over to that side of the island much, but I have fond memories of your family. I'll never forget the way your mother looked at all of you."

"Oh *yes*." Estelle nodded. "I remember that look."

Deirdra braced herself, knowing exactly what was coming, because if she tried hard enough, she could still conjure her mother's younger face, her mossy-green eyes filled with so much love it was palpable.

"Like she was seeing each of you for the first time," Estelle said. "Goldie, you said something to her about it once, remember?"

"I remember." Goldie smiled, as if she were remembering the moment. "She said she couldn't get over how lucky she was to have been blessed with such a beautiful family."

Jagger laced his fingers with Deirdra's. It was nice to be with someone who understood how even kind comments could sting, but she tried to push away that sting and feel the warmth she used to when she'd see that look in her mother's eyes. Her pulse quickened, and she squeezed Jagger's hand again, borrowing his strength as she rode out the moment. He made it a little easier.

"We should get over to the buffet so you two can eat before the dance," Goldie suggested.

As they followed the ladies toward the buffet, Jagger said, "Sorry about that. I should've anticipated that people here might say something about your parents."

"It's okay. I took your advice. It wasn't easy letting myself remember that look without the bad feelings creeping in. But it worked for a minute, and it was kind of nice to remember something good about my mom."

"That's awesome, babe. I guess having a little hippie in you was good in more ways than one." A wolfish grin appeared. "I can't wait to see what else we can unlock in you."

"Calm your jets, hippie boy. It won't be a striptease."

Goldie and Estelle ushered them to the buffet table, and as they were loading up their plates, Saul came over to say hello and introduced Deirdra to his wife, Nina. Several other people also stopped by to greet them and shower Dolly with attention. A few of the men asked Deirdra to save them dances. She and Jagger's friends got a kick out of him giving them a hard time, saying things like, *Back off, dude, she's taken*, and *Watch yourself. I'm not afraid to take a senior citizen down.*

They tied Dolly's leash to a tree by a picnic table, where they ate with Estelle, Goldie, Big Dick, who was a real jokester, Gerry, who was even more laid-back than Jagger, and Arthur, a short, salt-and-pepper-haired gentleman who played the piano with the band. Arthur spoke to Jagger like a father might, asking about his travels, how his money was holding up, and if he needed anything. Gerry doled out advice on getting musical gigs and places to visit when he was overseas, and the ladies treated him like a grandson, doting on him, telling him to eat more, and asking how his family was doing. They brought Deirdra into their conversations and began doting on her, too, and asking about Abby. She told them about Abby and Aiden, and the Bistro, and then she told them about Cait. Their sadness for what Ava must have gone through after giving her up gave Deirdra pause about her harsh feelings toward her mother.

Jagger was so comfortable with his friends, and with Deirdra, holding her hand, touching her leg, and offering her tastes of food he had on his plate that she didn't have, it made her feel comfortable, too. This was by far the best first real date she'd ever had, and it had only just started.

Jagger got a call and pulled out his phone. "It's my mother on FaceTime. Excuse me for a second." He grabbed his guitar, which he'd set down by the table, and walked away to take the call. Dolly tried to follow him.

"It's okay, Dolls. He'll be back." Deirdra petted her as Jagger lowered himself to the grass, looking at his phone. She loved that he put his family first and vowed once again to continue trying to do the same.

"Don't worry, sweetheart," Gerry said. "When he says it's his family, it always is."

"I'm not worried. It's not like that between us."

"Why the heck not?" Estelle asked. "When you've got a good one on the line, you've got to set your hook and stake your claim, or someone else will."

"Not everyone thinks every other woman is after their man, Estelle." Goldie shook her head.

"You're wrong, Goldie," Estelle insisted. "Women always want what they can't have. Men, too. You've got to protect what's yours, right, Ger?"

As they debated relationships, Deirdra stole another glance at Jagger, playing his guitar with his phone propped up on the case. He looked different when he played for his family, happier. He was such an upbeat guy, it was hard to imagine there was another level of happiness, but there it was, radiating from him like the sun.

"Gabriel must have needed him," Goldie said. "Didi, have you met his brother?"

Her knee-jerk reaction was to correct Goldie about her name, but she was getting used to Jagger calling her Didi, and she realized they'd known her as Didi first, too. "No. I don't know his family. Do you?"

"I haven't had the pleasure of meeting them, but through Jagger I feel like I have," Goldie said.

Deirdra had lived on the island for eighteen years before moving away, and she knew only a handful of people outside of Silver Harbor. Jagger had been there only a few weeks on and off during the last few years, and he'd managed to know her mother, possibly better than she had, and become entrenched in this community. "How did all of you meet Jagger?"

"Gerry and Estelle met him one night when he was playing at Whit's Pub down on the wharf a few years ago," Big Dick explained.

"Yup. That's right." Gerry nodded. "He had to take a break to play for Gabe, and when he came back, instead of starting up again, he explained why he'd had to stop playing and told us all about his brother."

"We were so taken with him," Estelle said. "He got everyone in the place talking about their families, their jobs, grandkids. He and Little Dick got to talking about some newfangled way of farming, too."

"Little Dick would have talked about his farm all night if he could've." Gerry shook his head. "That boy was born to farm."

"Little Dick?" Deirdra tried not to sound amused. "That's an unfortunate nickname."

"If you knew my son, you'd understand why it doesn't bother him." Big Dick patted his chest with both hands. "He's a whole lotta man. Just like his dad."

There was a murmur of agreement and chuckles.

Gerry said, "Little Dick was the one who told Jagger about our dances. We'd lost a band member the previous month, and Jagger offered to play at the next dance. We couldn't pay him or anything, and he was still all in."

"He's been playing for us a few times each summer ever since," Goldie said. "He can't always make it to the island for our dances, but we sure enjoy having him around when he can."

"I think he enjoys it, too," Deirdra said.

"Yes, he seems to," Goldie agreed. "He's an interesting young man. There are many sides to him, and we have yet to find a bad one."

Deirdra watched Jagger set down his guitar and pick up his phone, talking with his family, his vibrant smile still brightening the evening. *Yes, there are, and I have a feeling I've only scratched the surface.*

♥ ♥ ♥

Jagger played a second song for Gabriel, and by the time he said good-bye to his family, the crowd was heading inside. He made his way over to Deirdra, who was standing by the entrance with his friends, holding Dolly's leash, and slipped an arm around her waist. "Sorry to leave you alone for so long. Gabe wanted to hear a couple of songs."

"I didn't mind. Is Gabe okay?"

Jagger petted Dolly. "Yeah, he's fine. He wasn't upset. He seemed to just want to touch base. Do Cait and Abby call you often when you're in Boston?"

"We text more than calling. I'm usually working and distracted, so calls are hard. But you're wearing off on me, and that's one of the things I'm going to pay more attention to when I go back to work."

"I'm sure they'll appreciate that." He had a feeling she needed to close that gap even more than they did. "Let me run Dolly to the RV. I'll be right back."

When he returned, they followed the crowd into the rustic dance hall, and Deirdra said, "They told me about Little Dick. Does he farm the way he would need to for farm-to-table? If so, maybe you could talk to him about working with Abby if she decides to do it."

"That magnificent brain of yours never stops, does it?" He'd been blown away by her ideas and even more so that she'd come up with them as a way for him to do the things he loved without losing his freedom to travel and play music.

She whispered, "You're pretty good at making it stop when we're alone."

"Damn right." He tugged her into a kiss.

"We've got a good crowd tonight," Goldie said as people began settling in around tables surrounding the dance floor.

Deirdra looked up at the lights in the rafters and around the stage at the far end of the room. "This is so much bigger than I expected."

"That's what all the ladies say." Big Dick roared with laughter.

Arthur grabbed his arm. "Let's go, Romeo. We've got a show to put on."

"I'll be right there." Jagger drew Deirdra into his arms as Arthur and Big Dick headed up to the stage. "Are you cool with this?"

"Yes. I'm fine. I like your friends, and it'll be fun fangirling over you when you're onstage."

He grinned. "I freaking love that."

Goldie and Estelle sidled up to them. "Don't worry, honey. We'll take good care of her. Estelle has been stacking Didi's dance card."

"That's right, with everyone but my man." Estelle winked at Deirdra. "Remember what I said about claiming your hunky hippie. Come on, Goldie. Let's get a table and let them smooch."

Jagger had never wanted to be tied down in the way Estelle implied, but when it came to Deirdra, he sure liked the idea of it. "Don't go finding a new fling partner while I'm up there."

"Don't tell me what to do, hippie boy."

Her confidence and that sexy smirk were like an aphrodisiac. He gave her a quick kiss and headed up to the stage. When they began to play, he couldn't take his eyes off Deirdra swaying in her seat, her head bobbing to the beat as she chatted with Goldie, Estelle, and a few other ladies. This time, he *had* stacked the playlist with a few of the songs he knew Deirdra had danced to with her mother, hoping they might coax out more of those good memories.

When they played "Wake Up Little Susie," Gerry and Estelle headed to the dance floor, and two gentlemen asked Goldie and Deirdra to dance. Deirdra stole a glance at Jagger on her way over, and he winked. She swung her hips, and the elderly man twirled her around. He said something to her, and she threw her head back with a laugh. Jagger wished he could hear that magical sound, but the music was too loud.

When the song ended, Deirdra glanced at him again, their eyes colliding with the heat of a thousand suns. She flipped her hair over her shoulder, giving him that slightly bashful, insanely seductive smile she shared only with him.

As the night wore on, she danced with Goldie and Estelle, and half the men in the place took their turn spinning her around the dance floor. It was hard to believe this was the same buttoned-up woman Jagger had first met in the spring. She was like an entire meadow blooming all at once, outdazzling everything around her, and he felt damn lucky to be with her. He could watch her dance all night long, but it was torture not having her in his arms, especially now that he knew she was as consumed with thoughts of him when they were apart as he was of her. As much as he enjoyed the event, he was glad when it was time to play the last song.

Jagger set down his guitar and took center stage, speaking into the microphone. "It's about that time, ladies and gentlemen, and tonight a special guest is going to play the last song of the evening. Let's hear it for everyone's favorite rocker, *Gerry Fast-Fingers Dixon!*"

Cheers and applause rang out as Gerry sauntered up to the stage and Big Dick and Arthur set up the amps for his electric guitar.

Jagger stepped away from the microphone. "Thanks, man. I really appreciate this. You remember what to say?"

Gerry clapped him on the shoulder. "Whaddaya think, I'm senile? Get your ass off the stage and go get your girl before one of these Viagra munchers steals her away."

Jagger headed over to Deirdra, who was watching his every move, as Gerry announced, "This song goes out to our good friend Jagger Jones and his gorgeous *flingmate*, Didi de Messiéres."

Deirdra's cheeks reddened, eyes wide, as Jagger took her hand and pulled her up to her feet. "This song is for you, sweet thing."

He gave her a quick kiss and led her out to the dance floor, taking her in his arms as the guys started playing "Beast of Burden." He held her close, their hips swaying. Her eyes smoldered as he sang about wanting to make love to her. Other couples joined them on the dance floor.

He sang about Deirdra putting him out of his misery, and she laughed. The glorious sound brought his lips to hers. When he sang about her claiming he wasn't her kind of guy, Estelle shouted, "She's wrong!" and laughter rolled through the room.

Jagger twirled Deirdra and gathered her against him, gazing into her eyes, the pulse of their connection beating louder than the drums as he sang the last verse. Applause rang out, but they were lost in a moment he wanted to hunker down in for the winter. Deirdra's eyes were soft and dreamy, and she was holding him like she never wanted to let him go, and to his surprise, he hoped she wouldn't.

"If I were any other girl," she said softly, "it might be hard not to fall for you."

"If you were any other girl, I wouldn't want you to." He lowered his lips to hers, kissing her tenderly, and before she could think too much or get too nervous about what he'd said, he led her off the dance floor, where they were immediately engulfed in conversation with his friends.

A while later, after many hugs and a lot of good-natured ribbing, they made their way back to the RV. Dolly was sacked out on the bed, but when she heard them come in, she leapt off to greet them. Deirdra lavished his pup with attention as he put away his guitar. He put his arms around her from behind and kissed her neck. She smelled like sunshine and happiness. "How do you feel about an ocean view tonight?"

"That sounds great."

They took Dolly for a walk, then drove out to the beach. Dolly bounded out of the RV. Deirdra took off her ankle boots and socks and followed her outside. Jagger sat on the step to take off his shoes, watching Deirdra draw in the sand with her toes. She twirled around with her arms stretched out to the sides and tipped her face up to the moon. She was so damn cute. It was easy to imagine her as a little girl doing the same. His sweet thing was rediscovering herself, and that warmed him to his core.

"I never used to like sand between my toes." She set those smiling eyes on him as she walked over. "But I'm kind of loving it now."

She sat on his lap, and he ran his hand down her leg. "I'm glad, because the beach looks good on you."

"You like my sandy feet?"

He squeezed her foot. "I like everything about you, but I noticed that when we're at the beach, you seem happy, and that looks good on you."

"I think that has more to do with you than the beach."

"I like hearing that almost as much as I dig the new easygoing vibe you're giving off."

"I'd better get that in check so I don't lose my edge."

He chuckled. "You couldn't lose your edge if you tried. It's what makes you stand out above everyone else. Your confidence is one of the sexiest things about you." He ran his hand along her thigh. "Almost as sexy as your gorgeous legs." He pressed his lips to hers. "Did you have fun tonight?"

"I had a great time. I liked watching you play, but I'm onto your sneaky ways. I know you stacked the playlist."

He started to respond, but she silenced him with another kiss.

"It's okay. I like you even more for it, but don't expect me to wear a Crotch Rocket hat anytime soon."

"Aw, *come on*. What kind of fangirl are you? How about a T-shirt?"

She lowered her face so they were eye-to-eye. "*No*, hippie boy."

"A tattoo that says *Crotch Rocket Groupie*? I know a great tattooist."

"How about you shut up and kiss me?"

She didn't have to ask twice.

CHAPTER THIRTEEN

DEIRDRA SAT ON the beach between Jagger's legs early Saturday morning, happier than she could ever remember being, and she was in no hurry to move. Her hair was pinned up in a messy bun, and she was wearing one of his big, comfy sweatshirts. They were bundled up in blankets, a cool breeze sweeping off the water as they drank coffee and watched the waves roll in. She couldn't imagine a better way to start the day or a better way to end one than the way they had last night, making love for hours.

She petted Dolly as she lay beside them. The sneaky pooch had gotten into the bed with them in the middle of the night. Deirdra couldn't blame her. Next to Jagger had become her favorite place to sleep, too.

Jagger kissed her cheek. "What's on your mind?"

"That I'm pretty sure you put drugs in my coffee."

"Because I wore you out last night and you've got a hippie hangover?"

She giggled. "I do have a hippie hangover, but that's not what I meant. The stress that usually consumes me when I'm on the island feels like it's a world away when I'm with you."

He slipped an arm around her belly, hugging her. "The universe knew you needed me in your life."

"My dad used to say stuff like that." She'd forgotten how much she'd loved hearing her father talk about the universe and all its power and beauty, but she had, as much as she loved hearing Jagger talk about it. She had a feeling Jagger was right. There had to be something bigger than both of them bringing them together because Jagger was everything she'd never thought she wanted, yet every day she wanted him more, which proved how little she knew herself.

"You haven't said much about him. What was he like?"

"A lot like you, laid-back and happy. You've seen pictures of him, with his wild hair and ponytail and those eyes that were always smiling. He loved being near the water. He said it calmed him, although I don't remember him ever raising his voice. He was always hugging us, laughing about something we did. Sometimes he'd talk to me in French. I had no idea what he was saying, but I loved listening to him speak his native language. His voice was deep and a little rough, and he had a thick accent. Everything he said sounded beautiful." Sadness pressed in on her.

Jagger must have felt the change, because he held her tighter. "It's okay, babe. Ride it out. I've got you."

"I miss him so much." She hadn't said those words in years, and they brought the sting of tears. "He was *so* in love with our family, and with my mom. Even as a kid I could feel it." Another confession vied for release, and she didn't want to hold it back. "I know I said I don't trust love, but there was a time when I couldn't wait to fall in love because they made it look so good. They made it look easy, like it was the best, most natural thing in the world." She tried to swallow past the lump in her throat.

"I think they made it feel that way because when it's real, it is easy and natural." He held her tighter. "Let yourself feel the sadness. It keeps his spirit alive and fills those empty places inside you."

She closed her eyes, wondering how he always seemed to know what she needed. She breathed deeply as the sadness took hold and resentment toward her mother bullied its way in.

"Feel that, too," Jagger whispered in her ear, as if he'd felt that shift in her, too.

Her chest burned, but she allowed herself to feel the hurt and was glad that pushing past the resentment wasn't as difficult as usual. She felt safe with him, but she also felt more vulnerable than ever, and a little embarrassed. "Sorry I'm so weird."

"You're not weird. You're human." He kissed her softly. "We don't have to talk about your dad if it's too hard."

"I'd like to tell you about him. Thanks to you, I think I'm getting a little better at not wanting to kill someone when I think about that time of my life. Besides, he was a great father, and he deserves to be remembered that way. I'm sure my mom told you that he was an artist, a painter. Abby has some of his paintings hanging up at the house."

"Ava showed me some of his paintings. Do you have any at your place in Boston?"

A knot formed in her stomach. "No." She could say they didn't go with her decor, but that wasn't the real reason she didn't have them, and she was pretty sure Jagger knew that, so she offered no further explanation. "He loved talking with customers, and he used to paint on the deck of the Bistro, talking with them while they ate. He was genuinely interested in everything anyone said." She looked at Jagger. "Like you. You listen like you're memorizing every word."

"Only with you."

"No, I've seen you do it with others. It's a good trait. You make people feel special the way my dad did."

"Thanks. I like knowing that." He held her gaze, and there were so many emotions looking back at her, her heart stumbled. "Your parents must have been at the restaurant a lot."

"They were, which left Abby and me free to ride our bikes and see our friends. I was always getting into trouble."

"I knew I saw a troublemaker lingering in you."

"You did *not*."

"Yes, I did, and I still do. It's a vibe you give off, but I think you only show it to me. Even before we got together, you'd narrow your eyes and look at me like you wanted to cut loose and play in my world, but not because it was fun. I think you wanted to show me up."

"You mean like you weren't doing it right, and I could do it better?" How did he know her so well already?

"Yup. But then I realized it was only a plan to get me naked."

She laughed. "I did *not* have that planned."

"Don't deny it. You know you wanted to get me naked."

"Half the girls on the island want you naked. That's not a far leap for you to take."

He kissed her neck. "So you admit it."

"I plead the Fifth." She giggled. "What are we doing today?"

"Are you bored already?"

"No, not at all. I could sit here for hours."

"Look at my city girl going with the flow."

She leaned back against his chest, smiling up at the sky. "It feels good to do nothing with you."

"You're doing some very important things. You're enjoying the fresh air and the sounds of the sea, and you're realizing how much you like being with me."

That was the truest statement ever made. "You say the funniest things."

He nipped at her earlobe.

"I *do* like being with you." She turned and kissed him. "But don't tell anyone. I have a reputation to uphold."

"Look at Deirdra trying to wrangle Didi into submission."

They sat in the cool morning breeze, smooching and chatting for a long time. When Jagger got up to do his yoga stretches, he pulled her to her feet. "Come on, sweet thing. Time to breathe new life into your lungs."

"My lungs are just fine, thank you."

He touched his forehead to hers. "Just try a few stretches with me. I think you'll like the way it makes you feel."

"Fine," she relented. "I'll try, but don't laugh at me if I can't do them right."

He showed her how to do several stretches and yoga poses, making sexy innuendos when she bent over and kissing her between movements. As he showed her poses, he reminded her to breathe, and when she did a pose wrong, he carefully guided her into the correct position. She was fairly certain yoga wasn't supposed to rev her up, but doing anything with Jagger had that effect on her. Sexiness aside, she liked doing yoga with Jagger. With the sun warming her cheeks and his capable hands guiding her, it felt intimate and special experiencing something new and different with him.

When they finished, he took her hand, pulling her in close. "What did you think?"

"I loved it. It's amazing how a simple adjustment can really make you feel the stretch. I feel like I'm breathing deeper and am more aware of my body."

"I thought you'd like it, and for what it's worth, I've never been more aware of your body." He kissed her, sending thrills skittering through her chest.

They went inside to shower, and Dolly climbed onto the bed while Jagger led Deirdra into the bathroom. She caught a glimpse of herself in the mirror, grinning like a giddy girl of eighteen as they stripped off their clothes. They stepped into the insanely small shower, and what started as a slow, sensual kiss turned into a tangle of hungry kisses and greedy gropes. His big hands slid down her back, holding her tight against him as he ground his hips, his hardness pressing into her belly, sending her body into a frenzy of desire. A deep growl slipped from his lips into hers, and she fisted his arousal, giving it a few tight strokes, earning more of those seductive sounds. She slithered down his body, taking him in her mouth and working him with her hand, loving his fingers tangled in her hair and the lustful sounds he made.

"*Damn*, baby." He made a tight, torturous sound. "You're too fucking good at that. I don't want to come yet."

He hauled her up, crushing his mouth to hers, and his hand moved between her legs. His fingers pushed in deep as his thumb went to work on the magical spot that sent her soaring, gasping, *pleading*. She cried out his name in the throes of passion, and he lowered his mouth to her breast, sucking and teasing, taking her right up to the peak again and keeping her there so long she was sure she'd explode.

When she finally came down from the peak, she was shaking with a bone-deep ache to be as close as they could be. "I need *you*." She palmed his cock again.

"I don't have a condom." He began kissing her neck, her chest, her breasts . . .

She was on the pill, and she'd always used condoms to be extra safe, but she didn't want to with Jagger. She didn't want anything between them. Just as she started to say she was on the pill, his mouth covered her sex, shattering her ability to speak. She clung to his shoulders, illicit moans spilling from her lungs as he licked and flicked, sucked and fucked, sending her spiraling over the edge again. She dug her fingernails into his flesh, her body racked with pleasure so intense, she could barely breathe.

Her eyes fluttered open as he caressed, groped, and kissed a path up her overly sensitive flesh, every touch sparking fires, and reclaimed her mouth. He tasted of sex and lust and something deep and true that was as scary as it was thrilling. Oh, how she loved kissing him. He put his all into kissing, the same way he did everything else, drawing her in like a starving woman to a hearty meal.

"We gotta get out of here," he gritted out between kisses. "I need to be inside you."

She couldn't wait another second. "I'm on the pill."

His eyes widened, then narrowed, his lips quirking up. "Thank *Christ*."

He reclaimed her mouth, fierce and aggressive, and lifted her into his arms, lowering her onto his arousal. She was aware of every sensation, every breath they took, every inch sliding deep inside her. The pressure and closeness were overwhelming. He tightened his grip, his heart slamming against hers. She'd never felt anything so intense, so *right*, and it scared the hell out of her.

"*Fuck*, baby, feel—"

She silenced him with an urgent press of her lips, and they began to move. Electricity scorched through her with every thrust of his hips as they fell into sync, devouring each other like they needed the other to survive. She used his shoulders for leverage, riding him harder, *faster*, trying to outrun the emotions—his and hers—braiding together, winding around them, binding them as one. But there was no escape. They seeped under her skin, driven deeper as her back hit the wall and he pounded into her. He grabbed her bottom so tight, shocks of pain and pleasure ricocheted through her. She knew she would bruise, but she was too lost in them to care as the world spun away and they surrendered to the soul-drenching drafts of their connection, riding it all the way to the heavens and back.

She went boneless in his arms, the sounds of their hastened breathing and frantic hearts mixing with the soothing splash of warm water raining down on them.

"*Jesus*, babe. What's happening to us?" He turned with her in his arms, leaning his back against the wall, his arms wrapped tightly around her, and pressed his cheek to her chest. "It's like you're a part of me. Do you feel it?"

She tried not to respond, to hold back the feelings stacking up inside her, thundering through her body, clawing for release. This was only a fling. She wasn't supposed to feel so much, but it was torture holding it in. He lifted his face, his eyes brimming with emotions vaster and deeper than the sea. She wanted to dive into them, to drown in them, and the truth broke free. *"Yes. I feel it, too."*

They were only five little words, but in his eyes, and in her heart, she knew they changed everything.

♥ ♥ ♥

Later that morning, as they drove out of Seaport, Deirdra felt more alive than ever, and a bit terrified by how much she felt for Jagger and how quickly it had happened. She gazed out the window, trying to push the worries away, and noticed that everything looked more vibrant than ever. The leaves were greener, the sea bluer. Was it possible that being this happy could transform the way she saw things? Or had she always been too resentful and busy to notice the island's beauty before? She looked at Jagger, and even he looked happier than usual, which was crazy, since he was always cheerful. Maybe that should add to her worries, but she wanted to stay in this brighter place, because soon enough he'd leave for Europe and she'd go back to her life in Boston, and their time together would be a distant memory. That brought a sting of sadness, but also a trickle of relief. She hadn't relied on anyone since she was eleven, and that relief told her she hadn't completely left her safety zone.

Jagger drove along the coast to Silver Haven, but instead of driving toward town, he went to the marina, and she asked, "What are we doing here?"

"I figured you might want to get off the island for a while. We're taking the ferry to our next adventure."

Excitement bubbled up inside her. "And where would that be?"

"Provincetown." Provincetown was an artsy town at the tip of Cape Cod. It was a haven for artists and the LGBTQ community, known for its eclectic shops, galleries, nightclubs, and street performers.

"Really? I *love* P-town. I haven't been there since I went with my parents when I was little. Do you go there often?"

He looked at her as he put Dolly's leash on. "I haven't been in a few years, but I thought it would be fun to go together."

Her heart sang. Although she had a feeling they could pick through trash and it would still be fun if they did it together.

Half an hour later, they stood at the railing on the ferry, with Jagger's arm around her waist and the brisk sea air prickling her skin as Silver Harbor faded in the distance, taking with it the weight of her past. They talked and kissed as they cruised toward Provincetown. Jagger took selfies of them and texted them to her, *So you won't forget me when I'm gone.* She didn't want to think about when they would go their separate ways, and she intended to revel in the time they had.

"Look." Deirdra pointed to Pilgrim Monument in the distance.

When they docked at the pier, Deirdra's pulse kicked up as she took in the artist cottages along the pier and the people milling about. They followed the crowd off the ferry, and she felt like she was stepping into a dream. With the exception of the fun she'd been having with Jagger, it had been forever since she'd done anything other than work.

"This is so exciting. How much time do we have?"

"My day is yours, babe. As long as I'm back for work tomorrow, I'm cool."

They looked through all the artists' cottages along the pier and made their way to Commercial Street, where every shop looked like a two- or three-story house, each one a different shape, painted in bold purples, blues, reds, yellows, and every other color under the sun. Vibrant banners hung over the street announcing evening shows, and throngs of people meandered on the sidewalks and in the streets. Dolly panted happily as they passed other people with their dogs.

They looked through shops and galleries, stopping to listen to street performers play music in front of Town Hall and watch pantomimes and magicians on the lawn of the library. They had pizza for lunch and shared delicious pastries from the Portuguese bakery later in the afternoon. They held hands, and Jagger pulled her into alleyways and store nooks for quick make-out sessions, leaving her weak-kneed and wishing they were alone. She'd never felt so high.

As they made their way back through town, Deirdra found a bracelet with a whale's tail for Cait and earrings with dangling gold utensils for Abby. "I wish they were here with us," she said as they left the jewelry store. "Maybe when you come back from your trip, we can get together and bring them." She caught herself sounding like they were a real couple and backtracked. "I don't mean like a couple, or like we'll pick up where we left off when you come back or anything. I just thought it would be fun to go with everyone."

He pulled her closer, nipping at her neck. "You miss me already, don't you?"

"Get over yourself, Jones." *Sarcasm, the great pretender.* "I just figured *you'd* miss *me*, and I didn't want you to feel funny about asking if you could see me again, because even though this is just a fling, we'll still be friends."

"That was awfully thoughtful of you," he teased as they went into the next store. "You could come with me to Europe, and we could see each other every day."

She knew he was joking, but she couldn't deny the pang of wishing she could be that frivolous. "I have a real job, remember? And I hope to have a new one by then. I'm heading to Boston Thursday for an interview." She turned to look at him, and over his shoulder she saw an old-fashioned metal sign with TOMATOES written in script above two enormous tomatoes. "Oh my gosh, *look*." She tugged him over to it. "You have to get it for Gabe. You said tomatoes were his thing."

Jagger had been grappling with how much he felt for her and how important she'd already become to him, and those feelings were deepening every minute they were together. He'd only been half kidding about her traveling with him, and now he took another hit to the heart with her thinking of his brother. "They are. He'd love it."

She plucked the sign off the shelf and hugged it to her chest.

He couldn't resist drawing her into his arms and kissing her. "I have an idea. I need to go home sometime this week to say goodbye to my family. Let's go to Boston together Thursday morning. I'll visit with my family while you're interviewing, and then you can come meet them, have dinner with us, and we can give that to Gabe together."

Her brows knitted. "You want me to meet your family?"

"Why not? I know your family."

"I don't know, Jagger." She sounded as torn as she looked.

"You want to, Didi. I can *feel* it. You're just afraid of what it means." *Just like you were afraid to say you were falling for me at the dance.* "It doesn't have to mean anything more than I love being with you, and I know you like being with me. We've only got a week left together. Let's not waste it." He touched his forehead to hers. "Say you'll come with me."

"But—"

He silenced her with a tender press of his lips. "No buts unless it's yours in my hands."

She smiled, but it was a troubled smile. "I don't want to give your parents the wrong impression."

"My parents or us?" He didn't wait for an answer. "Stop thinking like a lawyer. This isn't a contract or a deal. It's two people having a great time together and wanting to soak up every second of it."

She took a deep breath, brows still knitted. "Okay. I'll meet them. But you can't tell Abby. She'll get too excited and turn it into something it's not, and then it'll get awkward."

"I won't." Although he wanted to shout it from the rooftops. There was no tamping down his joy. Not even when Deirdra dragged him into a dress shop because she saw a tropical-print dress and forest-green wrap in the window that she *had* to buy for Cait for her engagement party. She was so excited, she sent a picture of it to Abby to make sure she also thought it was the right style for Cait. Abby loved it and asked her to find a dress for her, too.

An hour later they left the store with three dresses, because he'd found a hell of a sexy dress for Deirdra that brought out her eyes, accentuated her gorgeous figure, and was higher in the front than the back, leaving her long legs uncovered for him to adore. She insisted he get a white linen shirt with a tropical print that she said would look great on him, and she promised all sorts of dirty things if he'd wear it to the party.

He'd wear it every day if it earned him more of her.

They ate dinner at a quaint outdoor restaurant, where Deirdra shocked the hell out of him by asking to speak to the chef, then proceeded to tell the chef she was doing research on intimate restaurants on the Cape and asked if he'd ever considered a farm-to-table menu. She was so damn sharp, he was in awe of her.

They walked hand in hand on the beach by the pier and caught the last ferry back to the island. They cuddled on a bench on the covered deck of the ferry with Dolly at their feet, kissing and watching the moonlight dance off the water. "I hope my sisters like their gifts."

"They will because they're from you."

"I hope so. I feel bad for ruining Abby's dinner the other night. Those dinners are so important to her and Cait, and I'm realizing how important they are for me, too. I want to make it up to them, and I have a crazy idea. Are you free Wednesday night?"

He waggled his brows. "What'd you have in mind?"

"*That*, later in the night, but I was thinking that we could surprise them with a family dinner. Abby's working until six, and I know she said Cait has a busy day, but I think she usually stops tattooing by five or six. We could clue in Aiden and Brant to the surprise, and you and I can cook the whole thing together."

"You mean I can cook and you can watch?"

"*No.* I want to cook, too. You can do the chopping if you're worried, but I want to do this together and cook like Abby does, putting my heart into it. I always buy things for them, but I never do anything special that takes more effort than money."

"You're planning Cait's engagement party. That's pretty damn special."

"I know, but I want to do more. I want to show them they're important and make up for hurting Abby's feelings and ruining the dinner she worked so hard to make. I want to do it all from scratch, and if you're willing, I want to do it with you. I was thinking that I could even pick apples at the orchard in the morning and bake an apple pie with extra cinnamon for dessert. It's Cait's favorite."

"Have you been holding back on me, Betty Crocker? I haven't gotten any sweets from you."

"You've gotten plenty of *sweets* from me." She patted his cheek playfully. "Besides, I might suck at baking. This will be my first apple pie. I'm going to look up how to make it on YouTube. What do you think? Can you help me with dinner?"

"First of all, forget YouTube. You've got me. I think it's a great idea. I have to work from eleven to three, but I'll go with you to the orchard if you want, and I'd love to help make dinner."

"Really? That would be great. We need to plan a menu." They spent the rest of the ferry ride coming up with a menu and grocery list.

Jagger made her promise to get the freshest vegetables at the farm stand.

When they got back to the RV, he put Dolly inside and drew Deirdra into his arms for the millionth kiss of the night. "I don't want to take you back to your apartment." He kissed her again, long and slow, savoring their closeness. "Stay with me tonight, or I'll stay with you. I don't care where we are. I just don't want the night to end."

"I was hoping you'd say that so I didn't sound clingy if I said it."

"Don't hold back, baby. I have a feeling I'll like clingy when it's you doing the clinging." He brushed his lips over hers, whispering, "Say you'll stay."

"I have to go by the apartment for clothes."

"Done."

She flashed a coy smile. "Think we can get a room with an ocean view?"

"This is the only view I need." He squeezed her butt. "But if my girl wants an ocean view, then an ocean view she'll get." He lowered his lips to hers. He deepened the kiss, needing more, but he knew in his heart he could kiss her every minute of the day and it would never be enough.

CHAPTER FOURTEEN

"GET ON MY shoulders so you can get the apples up top." Jagger crouched on the ground in front of Deirdra.

It was Wednesday morning and they were at Silver Island Orchard, picking apples for tonight's dessert. Deirdra had clued in Aiden and Brant, and they were helping them to pull off their surprise tonight at Abby and Aiden's house.

"I am *not* getting on your shoulders. I'm too heavy."

He pushed to his feet, his eyes dark and seductive, causing flames that riled the butterflies that had been permanently nesting in her belly for almost two weeks. "I hold you up in the shower while I make you come so hard you can barely breathe." He grabbed her butt, and her body threw a little party, anticipating the sinful things that usually followed. "I think I can handle having you on my shoulders." He leaned closer, speaking huskily into her ear. "If you take off those jeans and the sexy lace panties I saw you put on this morning, I'll show you what *else* I can do with you on my shoulders."

Holy fudge. Yes, please . . .

A devilish grin curved his lips. "By the look in your eyes, I know what I'll be having for dessert tonight, and it ain't gonna be apple pie."

She giggled. "Darn right it's not. You can't open that naughty door and expect Dirty Didi not to run through it."

"Damn, sweet thing. We're never going to get any sleep now that I know that." He lowered his lips to hers in a toe-curling kiss. "Now, climb on before I drag you behind that old barn."

She held his gaze. "That sounds better than getting on your shoulders fully dressed."

He grabbed her hand and took off running down the row of apple trees toward the barn. They were both laughing as they ran past a group of people talking in front of the barn on their way around to the back. His mouth claimed hers so passionately, her back slammed into the rough wood wall. He broke the kiss, eyes full of worry. She pulled his mouth back to hers, loving that he was concerned about her but desperate for more kisses. This was bliss. This man, his kisses, the cloud of joy she'd been floating on for days.

The sound of someone clearing their throat startled them apart. The burly orchard owner stood a few feet away, arms crossed over his flannel shirt, chin low, eyes serious.

"Sorry, sir." Jagger laced his fingers with Deirdra's. "I'm just crazy about my girl, and I get carried away sometimes. But can you blame me? Look at my sweet thing. She's not just beautiful—she's the smartest woman I know."

Ohmygod. Deirdra shot him an incredulous look, cheeks burning, and turned a sweeter expression on the farmer as she dragged Jagger toward the orchard. "We're sorry. It won't happen again." She felt a giggle coming on at the absurdity of *her*, of all people, being caught making out in such a place, but the man fell into step beside them, sobering her up real fast.

"I understand getting caught up in the heat of the moment," he said kindly. "But the missus is worried about the kids around here getting an eyeful of something they shouldn't."

"We understand, and again, we're very sorry." Thinking fast, Deirdra tried to turn the conversation around. She threw her shoulders back and focused on the idea she'd had Monday night when Jagger was working, when she'd researched Little Dick's farm and read up on the orchard. "I read online that your orchard has been pesticide-free for five years. Have you ever thought of working with restaurants that offer farm-to-table menus?"

The orchard owner looked at her like she was speaking a foreign language.

Jagger looked at her like she was brilliant. When they'd seen each other Monday evening, she'd told him she was researching organic farms, and he'd shown her what he'd been working on when the restaurant had been slow the last few days, flooring her with a notebook full of farm-to-table ideas for the Bistro.

That look he was giving her was all it took for her to continue her sales speech. After a long discussion, they exchanged contact information, then Deirdra and Jagger went back to picking apples. Jagger draped an arm around her shoulder. "You just proved me right."

"About what?"

"That you're the smartest woman I've ever known." He pressed his lips to hers. "Sorry I got you in trouble, but I'd do it all over again."

"I'll have you know that in thirty years I've *never* been caught making out on this island like that." She went up on her toes, whispering, "But I'd do it again, too."

He grinned and raised his brows.

"*No.* We have apples to pick before you go to work, and after last night, this island has enough to gossip about." After making the centerpieces with Abby and their friends, they'd gone to the Bistro for dinner. Jagger had been playing his guitar on the deck with a gaggle of single women around him, when he'd looked her dead in the eyes and dedicated a song to his sweet thing. She'd never thought she'd want to be claimed so publicly, but she'd never been prouder—or more unsure of who she was. She felt trapped in a dream she never wanted to wake up from.

They went back to picking apples. Every time she bent over to put an apple in the basket, Jagger smacked her butt, rubbed against her, or made a sexy joke. They joked and kissed, and when they were interrupted by a call from Sutton, Deirdra stepped away to answer it. "Hey, Sutton. I was going to call you this afternoon."

"I bet you were. I have a bone to pick with you," Sutton said firmly, although Deirdra could hear her smile. "I heard all about the centerpiece making and the dinner that followed at the Bistro. When were you going to tell me that you and Jagger are together?"

Deirdra cringed. "I'm sorry. I've been so caught up in Cait's party planning and—"

"Doing the hippie," Sutton teased. "It takes seven seconds to send a text saying you got down and dirty with him. This is major news, and I found out from *Jules*."

"It's not major news. It's just a fling. We're going our separate ways after Cait and Brant's party." She glanced at Jagger carrying the basket of apples, looking casual and handsome in hemp pants, wiping one hand on his Henley, and she was hit with the longing she felt every time she thought about their time together coming to an end.

"*Fling* my butt. Jules said he was playing his guitar last night and he dedicated the song 'Missing Piece' to his *sweet thing* in front of everyone, and he was staring at *you*."

Happiness bloomed inside her anew. "He did, but it's still just a fling, and I swear I was going to call you after we got back from the orchard, when Jagger goes to work."

"Did you say *orchard*?"

"Yes. We're picking apples. I'm planning a special dinner for Abby and Cait tonight and baking a pie."

"Baking? Now I know you've lost your mind. Do you have a fever? Did you ingest something that turns your brain to mush?"

Jagger glanced over and blew her a kiss. She warmed all over. "Yeah, I have. It's called *Jagger*."

"Oh my gosh, *Dee*. You're totally falling for him, aren't you?"

She didn't even try to lie. "I don't know what I'm doing. All I know for sure is that I really like being with him, and I wish we had more time. I know he's not like the guys I usually go out with, but he's better, Sut."

"Better than the guys with fancy apartments and nice cars who can afford to take you to nice places?"

"Yes, and I know how that sounds after making fun of how he lives for so long. But he's passionate, and smart, and insightful, and he's playful in this sexy way. We have so much fun together, and we talk about *everything*." *Things I haven't even shared with you.* "I never expected to feel this way, but being with him is changing me. Every morning we wake up with a view of a different beach. By the time he goes to work, or I get started on whatever I need to do, I swear it's like we've spent hours easing into the day, when all we've done is lie there in each other's arms, or had coffee on the beach watching the sunrise, or taken Dolly for a walk, or done yoga, or all of those things."

"Wait. There are way too many parts of what you just said that I don't understand. You're staying in his RV every night?"

"*Mm-hm.* I like it better than the apartment."

"Of course you do. The apartment doesn't have a sensational *schlong* like Jagger does."

"It's more than that. Some nights we lie beneath the stars on the beach and don't even fool around. We just . . . I don't know. I must sound crazy to you."

"Yes, you do, especially since you despise sand touching any part of your body. But you also sound happy and a lot less stressed."

"I *am*, and I'm spending more time with Abby and Cait, too, which I love. I always feel guilty about not seeing them enough. The three of us had lunch on Monday." She told Sutton all about the jewelry and gorgeous dresses she'd bought for Cait's engagement party and how she planned to surprise them with the gifts the day of the party. "And

I saw Abby last night when we made the centerpieces. Wait until you see them. They're gorgeous. The party is going to be phenomenal, right down to the last detail. I can't wait to see Cait and Brant's reactions to it all."

"Jules sent me a picture of the centerpieces. They're amazing. I haven't heard you this excited since your last promotion."

"I know. It turns out I really like doing things for my sisters, and I have no idea who I am when I'm with Jagger, but I really like that, too. I can't wait to see you at the party."

"I'm looking forward to seeing this new you, but you haven't mentioned your job. What's going on with it?"

"Ohmygosh, I forgot to tell you. I decided to cancel my hiatus because I need to find a job, and if I do, I need to give notice, but things are looking good on that front." She told her about the video interview she'd had Monday, which had gone incredibly well, and the interview she'd lined up with Madeline King for Thursday. "I've spent hours the last few days combing social media and news briefs to learn everything I can about Madeline. I want to blow her away."

"You'll nail the interview for sure, but, Dee, you just said you really like Jagger. How are you going to just walk away after the party?"

"What do you mean? My life is in Boston, and his is wherever the wind takes him. We both know there's no endgame with us." *No matter how much it will hurt to say goodbye.*

"Babe!" Jagger pointed to another row of trees and headed that way.

"Hey, Sut. I've got to go. I'm missing out on all the apple picking. But do me a favor?"

"Buy you overalls?"

"I wish it were that simple of a request."

"Don't worry, Dee. I'm already planning on checking on you after you two go your separate ways. We'll get through this, the same way we got through your mom's drinking all those years. You can lean on me, and nobody will ever know about the tears you cry or the curses you utter."

"I hope this won't be as torturous as that was." She had no experience walking away from a man she cared so deeply about.

"It's a different type of heartbreak. It's going to suck, but I'll be there to make it suck a little less. Want me to bring tequila?"

"No, thanks." She headed for Jagger, her heart already aching. "It's probably better to feel the pain than to numb it." She had a feeling there wasn't enough alcohol on earth to numb the pain of missing Jagger.

CHAPTER FIFTEEN

DEIRDRA HAD BEEN a nervous wreck all afternoon, wanting everything to be perfect for their family dinner. After Jagger got off work, he showed up at Abby and Aiden's house freshly showered, with a bouquet of flowers for the table and a world of calming words and kisses to bring Deirdra down from the ledge. They made the pie using his mother's recipe, which she was surprised to learn included vodka, and they were having so much fun joking around as they made it, she accidentally knocked the bowl off the counter. Much to Dolly's delight, apples covered in brown sugar, butter, and all the other ingredients had gone flying. Deirdra and Jagger had laughed so hard, both had tears in their eyes.

They did their best cleaning up as quickly as they could and started over.

Now the pie was done baking, the kitchen smelled scrumptious, and they were making dinner. Jagger was adding mint and shrimp to the spinach salads, while Deirdra mashed potatoes. She glanced at the clock, and her nerves spiked again. "They'll be here in twenty minutes. Don't forget, we're not mentioning that I'm meeting your family. Abby will make too big a deal out of it. Are you sure we shouldn't start the steak and asparagus? What if it's not ready in time? Don't forget to add sliced almonds and cranberries to the salads."

"Take a breath, babe. It only takes ten minutes to cook them. We're right on schedule. I won't mention you meeting my family, and I've got the salad covered."

"Are these mashed enough?"

Jagger wiped his hands on a dish towel and wrapped his arms around her from behind, kissing her cheek. "They're perfect, and so are you."

"I'm a mess. I should change before they get here." She had flour and who knew what else on her jeans.

The front door opened, and Deirdra stilled.

"What smells so good?" Abby's voice carried into the kitchen seconds before she and Aiden, who looked panicked, appeared in the doorway.

Aiden said, "I'm sorry. I tried to stall," at the same time Abby said, "Dee? What is all of this?"

"It's okay, Aiden," Deirdra reassured him. "It was supposed to be a surprise family dinner because I ruined the last one, and I know how much they mean to you. But it's not ready, and I really wanted to clean up before you got here. I'm sorry it's such a mess."

"You guys did all this for us?" Abby asked.

"I just helped pick apples for the pie." Jagger put his arm around Deirdra. "Didi made the pie, and she's making every bit of dinner, too."

Abby looked at the pie. "Is that apple pie with cinnamon and sugar on top?"

"Cait's favorite," Deirdra said.

"Dee . . ." Abby looked like she was going to cry.

Deirdra steeled herself against the emotions bubbling up inside her. "No tears, *please*. It's just dinner."

"It's so much more than dinner." Abby threw her arms around her. "Thank you." She peeked into the pot and looked at the salad. "You're mashing potatoes? Is that shrimp on the salad?"

"Yes, and we're having grilled steak and asparagus. Now please get out of here so I can finish cooking and clean up."

"Not a chance. I haven't seen you cook since you used to make me mac and cheese. I'm parking my butt right here and watching." Abby sat at the table.

"I think this calls for wine." Aiden reached for wineglasses and looked in the paper bag on the counter that was full of apples. "Are you feeding an army with apple pie?"

"We were having so much fun this morning, I didn't want to stop picking apples, and since the farm is organic, I thought Abby could use them in pies for her first farm-to-table menu item."

"That's a *great* idea," Abby said. "But you know I haven't committed to anything yet. I forgot how pushy you can be when you get an idea in your head."

Deirdra rolled her eyes as she got the milk and butter out of the fridge.

"I think the term Abby was looking for is *determined.*" Jagger kissed Deirdra's cheek.

"Thank you." Deirdra warmed with his support. "Abby, I still think you should strongly consider it. There's a farm right in Seaport that can work with you, too."

"You know how busy I am," Abby said. "I don't have time to set up everything necessary to really make a go of farm-to-table."

Aiden set a glass of wine beside Deirdra. "I think it's a phenomenal idea. I'll work on her."

"Awesome, but farm-to-table was Jagger's idea, so the kudos go to him." Deirdra sipped her wine.

Aiden handed Jagger a glass. "Great idea."

"Thanks. Dee, we should finish up the potatoes." Jagger told her how much of each ingredient to put in the mashed potatoes and slid the cutting board with the garlic she'd chopped closer to her. "Abby, there's no pressure from me, but if you ever decide to go farm-to-table, I'd be happy to help you set it up."

"From Europe?" Abby teased.

"Actually, yes. I talked with my father about it, and he's willing to visit and check out farms while I'm away. I'd still manage the process and be in close contact with the farmers, but he'd do the physical inspections."

"Really?" Abby and Deirdra said in unison.

Deirdra was floored. Jagger had shared his ideas for consulting, but she hadn't known he'd been this serious.

"I was going to tell you later tonight," Jagger said to Deirdra. "I spoke to my father this afternoon. He thought a small test site was the perfect way to start."

"To *start*? You're seriously thinking of consulting with restaurants?" Deirdra was excited for him.

"Possibly, on a very limited basis. There are legalities that need to be handled first and logistics to be worked out, but I think your idea is genius, and I can probably help a couple of businesses a year without it hindering my travels or my music."

Deirdra squealed and hugged him. "I'm so happy for you! This is amazing."

"How can I *not* offer up the Bistro as your test site?" Abby jumped up to hug him. "I'll help any way I can."

"I know a good finance guy if you need to hammer out numbers," Aiden offered.

"Thanks, man." Jagger took a drink. "I'll probably take you up on that."

"Let's see if I'm as good at making garlic mashed potatoes as I am at coming up with business ideas." Deirdra held a spoonful of potatoes up for Jagger. "Taste this. Is it too garlicky?"

He tasted it. "It's *almost* perfect. I'd add a little more salt and garlic."

"Are you sure?" Deirdra tasted the potatoes. "Oh yeah, you're right."

"That'll teach you to doubt me." He smacked her butt and stole a kiss.

"You guys are too cute," Abby said as Aiden pulled her into his arms.

We really are.

Being with Jagger and sharing their coupledom with her sister wasn't something Deirdra had ever imagined for herself. But standing in Abby's kitchen with Jagger by her side and laughter in the air made it easy to imagine more nights like this, hanging out as couples with her sisters, seeing that look of pride in Jagger's eyes when he said supportive things, stealing kisses and holding hands.

She cut herself off from riding an unattainable fantasy down a slippery slope and mentally added *family dinners* to the list of things she'd miss when she left the island.

The front door opened, and Brant's voice boomed through the house. "Houston, we have a problem."

"Oh no. I was just about to cook the steak," Deirdra said as Brant walked into the kitchen, his blue baseball cap shading his worried eyes.

Brant's brow furrowed. "*You're* cooking? Is that safe?"

Abby giggled, Aiden and Jagger tried to stifle their amusement, and Deirdra rolled her eyes.

"I told Cait I had to pick something up from Aiden, but she's talking with Randi on the phone and waved me off when I tried to get her to come in. Do you think she knows Dee's cooking?" He chuckled.

Deirdra placed the steaks in the pan and pointed the fork at Brant. "I wouldn't make fun of my cooking if I were you. You had *one* job. To get my sister here at six. And you left her in the car, while I made your fiancée's favorite pie under the direction of a *very* talented chef. Cait will be so full of goodness when you leave here tonight, she'll be an easy mark for your charms. You should thank me and *then* get your cheeky dimples outside and bring her in here."

♥ ♥ ♥

The evening passed with easy conversation and good-natured ribbing. Everyone raved about dinner, and the pie was a big hit. Cait was on her second piece, but while Jagger was thrilled for Deirdra that dinner had gone off without a hitch, the compliments on her cooking weren't the headliner for him. It was Deirdra herself. Gone was the woman who had distanced herself from group fun and had carefully peered out from behind her walls, like it was her against the world. She held his hand, whispered inside jokes, and blushed when he stole kisses. She was finally showing her relaxed, easygoing side, which he believed to be a big part of her *true* self, to her sisters and friends.

She was telling them all about their dates in Seaport and on the Cape. "But while all of that was beyond fun"—Deirdra leaned closer to Jagger—"none of it compares to waking up with this man and an ocean view. You guys should really consider investing in RVs."

Damn, he loved hearing that.

"You have been giving Jagger a hard time about sleeping in a hippie van since the night you met him, and now you want us to buy one?" Cait finished her wine. "I think I need more wine. I must be in the twilight zone."

"It's an *RV*, thank you very much," Deirdra said, causing everyone to laugh.

"Does this mean you're going to start braiding flowers into her hair?" Aiden teased. "You could start a new fashion trend among attorneys."

"Want to borrow some of my mom's clothes?" Brant asked.

"You can make fun of me, but you don't know what you're missing. It's been a nice change." Deirdra looked at Jagger, her smile fading.

She didn't have to say a word to explain the sadness rising in her eyes, because he felt it in his bones. *I'll miss you, too, sweet thing.*

"That reminds me," Abby said. "I have to show you what we found when we finally went through the rest of the boxes from Mom's old junk room. I'll be right back."

As Abby went inside, Aiden said, "We found some real treasures, and Abby's been excited to show you guys."

She returned with a shoebox. "Wait until you see these old pictures." She handed everyone a handful of pictures, and they started going through them, all of them talking at once.

"Look how little you guys were," Cait said. "I wish I could have known you then."

"Can you imagine how different we'd be if we'd all grown up together?" Abby looked thoughtfully at them. "Dee, you wouldn't have been the oldest. I wonder how that would have changed you."

"I wouldn't have had to be your personal pillow." Deirdra held up a picture of her and Abby in the back of their father's car. Abby was fast asleep with her head on Deirdra's shoulder, and Deirdra was pouting.

Everyone laughed.

"I wish my girl could have grown up here." Brant reached for Cait's hand. "I'd have made you my girlfriend in first grade and never let you go." He leaned in and kissed her.

"Aw, that's so sweet," Abby said.

They showed each other pictures, and Abby and Deirdra told stories about some of them.

"*What* is happening here?" Cait held up a picture.

Deirdra couldn't have been older than six or seven. Her hair was a tangle of waves, and she had a big white flower tucked behind her ear. Colorful fabric was wrapped around her lower half like a skirt, hanging unevenly to the tops of her feet, on which were bright red high heels several sizes too big. A white blouse billowed around her tiny frame, sleeves rolled up to reach her wrists, the bottom knotted at her waist. Several long necklaces hung around her neck, and she was holding a handful of flowers in one hand, their roots dangling like threads. Her other hand was on her hip, and a wide smile showed off a missing front tooth. Abby stood beside her wearing yards of blue fabric with colorful polka dots and a floppy blue hat that almost covered her eyes. She was holding up the brim of her hat, gazing at Deirdra like she was a queen.

Abby snagged the picture. "Those are our tablecloth dresses. Remember how you used to *love* dressing me up?"

She handed the picture to Deirdra, who looked it over with a thoughtful expression. "I had to do something with you. You followed me around like a puppy."

She showed the picture to Jagger. He'd seen that same joy in Deirdra's eyes more times than he could count since they'd come together. "I've got to hear more about these tablecloth dresses."

"Dee wasn't always into designer clothes and high heels. She loved our mom's bohemian style, and she used to dress up and prance around pretending to be her. She could whip up outfits out of *anything*—our dad's shirts, scarves, blankets." Abby pointed to the picture in Jagger's hand. "She made her skirt and my dress out of tablecloths."

Jagger covered Deirdra's hand with his own, knowing the memories might be difficult for her. "Sounds like my girl's always had a little hippie in her."

Deirdra smirked and leaned closer, whispering, "There's only one hippie who's ever been inside me, and we both know there's nothing little about you."

Jagger chuckled and kissed her.

"Care to share with the class?" Cait teased.

Deirdra picked up her wineglass. "Absolutely not." She looked at the picture again and squeezed his hand. "This picture reminds me of how much I loved who our mom was back then."

It was crazy how proud of her he was for having the strength to admit that hard truth in front of everyone.

"Mom was always smiling," Abby said.

"And up for anything, remember?" Deirdra looked at the picture again, joy *and* sadness brimming in her eyes. "We could have told her we wanted to dance naked under the stars, and she'd have set an alarm just so we didn't miss out. She loved to dream, like Abby."

"You used to dream, too," Abby said carefully. "Of things other than being a corporate success."

Jagger squeezed Deirdra's hand. "I'd like to know those dreams."

"They were silly little-girl dreams," Deirdra said, but something in her eyes told him they weren't silly at all.

"I like silly dreams. Come on, Didi. What did the little girl in the tablecloth dress dream about?"

She picked up the picture, studying it for a minute, a small smile curving her lips. "She wanted to go to her daddy's homeland and see all the places he talked about. She wanted to crush grapes with her feet and make wine, and get a puppy, because we were never allowed to have one. Our dad was allergic."

"And she dreamed of *love*," Abby said in a singsong voice.

Deirdra's eyes narrowed in a warning.

"Don't look at me like that." Abby touched the picture. "That was your wedding dress and my bridesmaid dress, remember?"

"Whoa." Cait looked curiously at Deirdra. "There was a time you wanted to get married?"

"If you knew our parents, you would understand." Deirdra shook her head. "They made love look easy and like it would last forever. The same way you guys do."

Her sisters exchanged a glance Jagger couldn't read, but the way Deirdra's eyes were narrowing told him she could.

"Don't look at each other like that." Deirdra sipped her wine.

"I have *no* idea what you're talking about," Abby said with feigned innocence, and she and Cait giggled.

"You and Jag make things look pretty easy, too," Aiden pointed out.

Deirdra turned a warm, caring gaze on Jagger. "Jagger has a way of making everything look easy."

"You're easy to be with, sweet thing, and you make everything better."

She leaned in and kissed him.

Abby groaned. "You guys are *so* happy. I wish Dee wasn't going back to work, and I wish Jagger wasn't going away. You could have so much more together."

Deirdra looked at Jagger, her feelings radiating off her as inescapable and real as the moon in a pitch-black sky. He couldn't imagine *more* when what they had was already bigger and more powerful than anything he'd ever thought possible. But he knew where they stood.

This was all they could have, and he needed to start coming to grips with that.

As if Deirdra had read his thoughts, she lifted her chin, the emotions he'd seen reluctantly giving way to something a little more distant.

There it was. The cutting edge that was always at the ready. She might fool everyone else with that protective coat of armor, but he knew the sweet, sensitive parts of her that lay beneath, and the combination of tough and tender in his beautiful, feisty woman had already stolen his heart.

CHAPTER SIXTEEN

JAGGER LACED HIS fingers with Deirdra's on the ferry ride to Boston on Thursday morning. Things had changed between them, and it was not because she was dressed to the nines in a crisp white blouse and fitted navy blazer with a matching skirt, her hair and makeup done to perfection. She'd tried her damnedest to put distance between them last night at Abby's, but when they'd gotten back to the RV, that steel will of hers had fallen away, and they'd been closer than ever. Their kisses had been deeper, more meaningful, their lovemaking more intimate. They'd clung together, whispering in the dark for a long time afterward, bound by an underlying hum of desperation as they pretended their time together wasn't dwindling faster than a burning wick and Sunday wasn't looming behind them like a villain with an axe just waiting to sever their connection.

This morning, she tried again to distance herself by showering alone, but she'd called him in to join her a minute later. The great pretender had met her match, and he didn't want to let go. He looked down at Dolly, lying by Deirdra's feet. From the way she'd been sticking to Deirdra like glue, he didn't think she wanted to let her go, either.

"I still can't believe I forgot my car *again*. I always bring my car on the ferry back to Boston, but we were so caught up in each other, and I was so nervous about the interview, I didn't even think about it when we took the RV." Deirdra leaned against his side on the bench seat. "You really have made a mess of my brain, hippie boy."

"Nothing could mess up that beautiful brain of yours." He kissed her softly. "Want some money for an Uber?"

She smirked. "I think I can handle it. Are you excited to see your family?"

"Yes, and excited for you to meet them."

"You don't think it's going to be weird?"

"Introducing my fall fling to my parents?" He nipped at her earlobe. "I think it'll be fun."

She narrowed her eyes. "Your *fall* fling? Is that how you classify me? Who was your summer fling?"

"You might know her. She was a sexy thing with a body that could make a dead man come."

"Seriously?" Deirdra scowled. "You can stop now."

He whispered, "She only existed in my fantasies. Her name was Didi."

"You are such a butthead." She pushed him away.

"Is that a legal term?" He tugged her back for a kiss. "You were smart not to put on lipstick until after the ferry ride."

"I know how dangerous those lips of yours are."

He ran his hand up her thigh. "Too bad I couldn't convince you not to wear panties. I could have sent you into that interview *very* relaxed."

She took his hand in hers and rested them on *his* leg. "I think you mean hot and bothered and craving more. Knowing you, you'd tear my suit in the process."

"You had no complaints last night." He lifted her hand to kiss the back of it. "Are you nervous about the interview?"

She shrugged one shoulder. "Kind of. I have a lot riding on it, but Madeline pursued me, which means I have a leg up."

"I love it when you have a leg up." He waggled his brows, and she laughed. That gorgeous sound did him in, and it took everything he had not to tell her how he really felt about going their separate ways. "I'm going to miss your laugh. I want to rewind time so we have another two weeks."

She rested her head on his shoulder. "Me too. I'd like to stay in our cozy fling bubble and put off real life for a while."

He chewed on that as the ferry cruised into Boston Harbor, but the closer they got to port, the louder his emotions spoke. If she got that job offer today, there wouldn't be a hope in hell that she'd consider following her heart instead of her head.

"We can." He tightened his hold on her hand, praying she wouldn't pull away. "Come with me to Europe."

"That would be nice, huh?"

"I'm not kidding. We're great together, and you're at a crossroads in your career anyway. The timing is perfect."

She lifted her head from his shoulder, sorrow brimming in her eyes. "You know I can't."

"Why not? You deserve to take some time for yourself instead of rushing back to fourteen-hour workdays. Come with me and explore the world, see the places you dreamed of as a little girl."

She bristled, and Dolly lifted her head, watching them. "I have a career, remember? A career I worked my ass off for. I can't just give it all up to go backpacking through Europe. This is . . ." She paused, pain staring back at him. "This was supposed to be a fling, nothing more. We agreed to that."

"And then we fell for each other," he said, harsher than he meant to. "Things change, Dee. I've changed. You've changed, and don't tell me you haven't, because I see and feel the truth."

She pushed to her feet and strode to the window. He grabbed Dolly's leash and followed, aware of other passengers watching them. He put his arm around Deirdra, feeling her tense up, but he didn't let that deter him. "Please hear me out."

"We've been seeing each other for less than *two* weeks," she whispered sharply.

"So what? Your parents fell in love the first time they saw each other. Look me in the eye and tell me you don't feel a hell of a lot for me."

She swallowed hard but remained silent.

"I'm not asking you to marry me, and I know I'm not a billionaire like Aiden, or even well off like Brant. But I love you, Dee. I love your snarkiness and your sweetness. I love your stubborn streak and the way you give me crap but look at me like you want to devour me. And I love that you're reconnecting with your sisters. God, baby, I love how you feel in my arms and how I feel in yours, and I *know* you love it, too."

"Jagger." Her eyes teared up. "I don't want Aiden, or Brant, or anyone other than you."

His heart soared. "Then come to Europe with me. I don't want to go without you. It'll feel like something's missing. Everything will be half as bright and half as interesting without you by my side. Take a chance on us, sweet thing. Take a leap of faith. For once in your life, follow your heart instead of your head."

"I want to." Her lower lip trembled, and a tear slipped down her cheek. "But I'm not like you. I can't just leave my safety net behind and free-fall into a life of unknowns. It goes against everything I've ever done."

"No, it doesn't. It goes against everything you've done since your mother forced you into adulthood at eleven years old." He pulled out his wallet, withdrew the picture of her and Abby in their tablecloth dresses, and held it up. "But it feeds *this* girl's spirit, and damn it, Deirdra, she is a bigger part of you than you think, and you deserve to be happy."

"I *am* happy," she said shakily, swiping at her tears.

"Are you? Or are you working yourself to death, barely seeing your family, and loaded down with guilt because of it?"

"But that's *life*, Jagger." Her voice escalated, tears streaking her cheeks as the ferry docked. "I've been on the other side of it, scrounging to make ends meet, and it might seem romantic, but it sucks."

The sting of her words sank in, momentarily taking him aback. "Has it sucked being with me? Have you felt like you've been scrounging?"

"*No*, that's not what I meant. I *love* being with you. I just . . . I can't go backward."

He was gutted, and it took a minute to find his voice. "I guess we really are different. I don't see it as going backward. I see it as a huge step forward, finally getting out from under the cloud Ava cast over you. The one that caused your fear of not being seen as important enough if you aren't working harder than everyone else."

She lowered her gaze, sniffling.

"I thought you were done running from your feelings, but if you want to turn your back on us, on what you feel for me, then it's probably best if we end this now."

She lifted teary eyes, shaking her head as the ferry began deboarding. "I wasn't supposed to fall for you."

"But you did, and I fell for you, and if we feel like this after almost two weeks, imagine how we'll feel in two months, two years. Change your mind, baby. Say you'll come with me."

Tears rained down her cheeks, her lips trembling. "I can't," she said just above a whisper.

Jagger embraced her for what he knew would be the last time, his heart breaking. He took her beautiful face between his hands, gazing into the green eyes that were etched into his heart. "Know this, sweet thing. You might not *think* you know who you are without your attorney hat on, but you do. Since we've been together, you've shown me and your sisters exactly who you are, and there's no woman more spectacular on this earth. You *are* important to so many people outside of work. You're important to *me*." Her tears puddled against his hands. "You are truly unforgettable, and I will always love you." He pressed his lips to hers, fighting the lump in his throat and the crushing pain in his chest. "Goodbye, my sweet thing."

CHAPTER SEVENTEEN

HOLD IT TOGETHER. Just hold it together.

Deirdra kept her *head down as she pushed through the restroom doors on the ground floor of the building where her interview with Madeline King was taking place in fifteen minutes. How the hell was she supposed to handle sitting in an interview when she felt like someone had carved her heart out with a saw? The thought brought another rush of tears. Why hadn't anyone warned her that ending things with Jagger would hurt so much? She tore paper towels from the dispenser, silently cursing everyone she knew, trying futilely to dry her eyes.*

She looked in the mirror at her red nose and puffy, bloodshot raccoon-eyes, but it was Jagger's face she saw, his hopeful eyes turning sadder as she'd made the worst decision of her life, sucking her into their depths of despair as he'd said, Goodbye, sweet thing.

Tears sprang from her eyes, and she swiped at them again, the rough paper towel scratching her skin. She'd always been an expert at shutting down her emotions, but this was like trying to stop a speeding train. Her phone chimed. She dug it out of her purse, hoping it was Jagger and, at the same time, hoping it wasn't, because if it was, she'd never pull herself together. She had missed messages from Cait, Abby, and Sutton. Two must have come in when she was in the Uber flooding the back seat with her tears.

She opened Abby's message first. *Good luck with the interview! I snuck pics last night. Don't kill me, but I love you guys together.* Another message bubble popped up with two pictures of Deirdra and Jagger. In the first, they were standing in the side yard holding hands and gazing into each other's eyes. Her heart beat faster at the emotions leaping off the image. The second picture was of them kissing. She could still hear what he'd whispered to her after that kiss. *I wish I could kiss you for the rest of my life.*

More tears spilled from her eyes. How could she have been stupid enough to think she could bundle up all those emotions that had been taking root inside her and simply walk away with a kiss and a wave?

She looked up at the ceiling, breathing deeply, steeling herself against the unbearable pain consuming her. She knew she'd done the right thing by turning him down. It didn't matter how much money she had in the bank. She couldn't just take off and go traipsing around Europe. What would happen when she came back? How would that look on her résumé? She'd been tempted to ask Jagger to stay, but she knew what it felt like to have her dreams stolen out from under her, and she'd never do that to him.

But she couldn't do that to herself, either, by pining for a man she couldn't have without giving up everything she'd worked so hard for. If she could pull herself together when she was eleven, after the death of her father and what was essentially the death of her mother as she'd known her, she could do *this*.

Telling herself she was going for her brass ring, she steeled herself against the pain, wiped her eyes, lifted her chin, and straightened her spine. *I can do this.* She was *not* going to be like her mother and fall apart because of losing the man she loved.

Oh God, I love Jagger.

She closed her eyes against another rush of tears, telling herself there was no reason to cry over something that could never be. Her hands curled into fists, and the mantra *I am not my mother. I don't need a man to survive* ran through her head, louder and louder until it pushed all the emotions that weakened her down deep. When she opened her eyes, images of Jagger flashed before her—his loving face when they made love, his smile, which always drew one from her, the funny way his scruff twitched while he was sleeping, like he was even happy in his dreams—weakening her resolve.

I am not my mother. I don't need a man to survive.

She tried bullying those images away, but she was warring with her heart, playing an unwinnable game of tug-of-war. But reality was a mystifying contender, and she grasped at it, despite wanting to run from it. She would always have the memories she and Jagger had made, but if she didn't get her ass in gear, she'd lose out on her dream job.

She gritted her teeth. *Okay, Deirdra, pull your shit together. It's now or never.* She quickly checked the messages from Cait—*I know you don't need luck, but I'm sending you some anyway. Love you*—and Sutton—*Make this interview your bitch! You've got this!* She'd added a muscle-flexing emoji.

"Damn right, I've got this." Deirdra shoved her phone in her purse, pulled out her makeup bag, and did her best to hide the proof of her shattered heart.

♥ ♥ ♥

Madeline King's windowed corner office was outfitted for a queen, which was fitting, since she had the poise and grace of one, sitting tall behind her desk, her dark hair pulled back in a severe bun, wire-framed glasses perched on the bridge of her nose, hands folded neatly in the lap of her black Armani dress. Deirdra knew the designer because she'd spent far too many hours thinking about the twelve-hundred-dollar designer threads each time she'd passed them in the window of Neiman Marcus last month. After experiencing a simpler life with a man who gave his extra money to charities and didn't need to prove himself to others with a fancy job or an expensive home, the idea that she'd blindly spend that kind of money on a piece of clothing to prove herself made her uneasy.

But today Deirdra needed all the help she could get to pull herself together, and whether she liked it or not, she was most comfortable in her own skin in expensive clothes and posh offices such as this. They were her safety zones, where decisions were made based on facts and legalities, and gray areas and emotions didn't come into play. She'd snapped into business mode and turned her professionalism, and her confidence, up to perfection the minute she'd walked in and she'd shaken Madeline's hand, rattling off an excuse of having forgotten to take her allergy medicine to make up for her puffy, red eyes.

The interview had been going beautifully ever since.

Madeline was careful not to ask questions that infringed on the confidentiality of Deirdra's current employer, although she'd touched on how they would navigate around those issues if she were to work for them. Deirdra said all the right things, impressing Madeline with her knowledge and expertise, and she was straight with her about wanting a clear vision of potential future growth.

"How far you progress will be completely dependent upon your ability to increase your scope of influence over our executive teams." Madeline lifted her chin. "The more effective the increase, the more prominent your role will become."

Deirdra reassured her that working weekends and evenings wasn't an issue, but the acidic aftertaste of that assurance brought back her conversation with Jagger, when she'd declared her happiness. She'd told herself she wasn't really lying. She loved the legal work she did, but spending time with Jagger had shown her a different type of happiness that was fulfilling in ways she hadn't even realized she'd been missing. He'd shown her how incredible life could be with someone she cared about and how much closer she could be to him and her sisters if she wasn't always volleying work during her limited time off.

As Madeline told her about the corporate infrastructure and benefits, Deirdra's mind lingered on Jagger. He'd seen right through her, calling her on that fib the same way he'd called her on everything else she'd tried to hide behind.

"How does that sound to you?" Madeline asked, jarring Deirdra from her thoughts.

"It sounds like exactly what I'm looking for." *A massive distraction from walking away from the man I love.*

"I was hoping you'd say that. I've followed your career for several years, and I cannot think of a better, more qualified person to step into the position of general counsel." She opened her desk drawer and withdrew a manila envelope, sliding it across the desk. "I think you'll find our offer to be very generous."

Deirdra knew the interview had gone well, but she hadn't expected to get an offer right away. She tried to hide her shock as they finished talking, and half an hour later, when she headed out of the building, validated in her importance and elated with her success, she was flying high.

She took out her phone to text Jagger with her good news, then stopped cold, sadness enveloping her. Jagger had made her special even before they'd come together, and he hadn't done it based on her education or experience or what she could do for him. Longing burned in the center of her chest, and tears threatened. She gritted her teeth, willing them not to fall. Since when was she a crier?

Since Jagger showed her it was okay to feel something other than *strong*.

She'd done way too much crying this last week and a half. Yes, it was cathartic, but this nonsense had to stop. Their fling was *over*. They'd both known it would come down to this. She just needed to focus on the here and now, and there was no room for weakness in the world in which she lived.

She started to text her sisters, focusing on sharing her good news to perk herself up, but as she typed the message, she just couldn't do it. She wasn't in a celebratory mood, and if they called to congratulate her, they'd hear that, and all hell would break loose because she'd be forced to tell them what had happened with Jagger, and she'd end up in tears again. She clicked the Uber app, and as she put in the address for the ferry, she realized she wasn't ready to go back to the island, either. Everything would remind her of Jagger.

She entered her home address.

Couldn't someone have warned her that she was getting in over her head? Why hadn't *she* seen the signs? She paced the sidewalk, knowing damn well why she hadn't seen them. For the first time in her life, she'd been too happy and had felt too free to worry about anything at all. And now she felt flayed open and left to bleed out.

Oh God. Was this what Mom felt? Magnified a million times over since she and Dad had been together for so many years?

Did love *really* have the power to obliterate a mother's love for her daughters and everything else around her? Deirdra would never forsake her sisters for Jagger, the way her mother had turned her back on her and Abby. Did that mean she didn't really love him?

Her heart thudded harder, driving the ache deeper.

But she knew better.

Her mother was weak, but Deirdra was a survivor.

♥ ♥ ♥

After half an hour in the back of an Uber, spent ping-ponging between beating herself up for turning down Jagger and giving herself hell for questioning her decision, Deirdra was ready to scream. She walked into her apartment—her fortress, her other safe space—and stepped out of her heels. She shrugged off her blazer and dropped it and her purse on the table by the door.

She protected her apartment with the same vehemence as she'd always protected her heart, and it had always brought a sense of comfort and accomplishment with its pristine winter-white walls and counters, tan sofas, and perfectly placed glass-topped coffee and end tables, so different from her mother's nightmarish junk rooms and cluttered living spaces. But as she went into the living room, with a dream job at her fingertips and a future she could count on, the apartment felt as lonely and barren as her heart.

Was *this* really everything she'd ever wanted? Jagger had a hundred stories about people he knew and places he'd gone, each one more interesting than the next. But what did she have? Lists of work-related accomplishments? Each one as boring to anyone other than herself as the next? Twenty years from now Jagger would have even more stories and probably adorable little hippie children with shaggy hair and hemp clothing, who said things like *dude* and *chill*. Her sisters were getting married and would be taking honeymoons with the men they loved, eventually having children and taking them on trips and planning their weddings.

Twenty years from now Deirdra would have a stack of accomplishments higher than the building she lived in. And she'd *still* be lonely.

What had Jagger done to her to make her question everything she'd ever known about herself? What did he know about life? He was twenty-five and lived hand to mouth. *While feeding others from the same pockets.*

What had she ever done for others?

I practically raised Abby and made sure Mom didn't kill herself.

She'd been thrust into those roles. Did they even count? It felt like she'd spent a lifetime doing things for others. But it wasn't a lifetime. She was only thirty.

Yesterday she'd felt young and free.

Today she felt old and trapped in those whitewashed walls.

I'm losing my freaking mind. She needed a drink and stalked into the kitchen, opening and slamming cabinets, looking for something, anything with alcohol. Why couldn't she be like every other thirty-year-old and have a wine collection? She opened the cabinet above the refrigerator, spotting a champagne bottle with a gold bow on it. *Perfect!* She snagged the champagne Malcolm had given her when she'd gotten her promotion last year, and as she twisted off the metal twine that held the cork in, she silently ranted.

It wasn't Jagger making her question herself. It was her damn mother. *She* was the reason Deirdra had buried her dreams of finding the love of her life, someone who would look at her like her father looked at her mother and would play songs just for her. Jagger had touched the soul of the girl she'd been, but she'd grown into a woman and no longer fit.

The cork *popped*, flying across the room and startling Deirdra, bubbly spilling all over her clothes. *"Shit!"* She held the bottle away from her body, looking down at the mess, and a flashback of finding her mother in the kitchen with a bottle tipped to her lips, alcohol spilling down her front, sent chills down her spine.

Tears sprang from her eyes. She went to the sink and began pouring the champagne out, a sob falling from her lips. Jagger's voice didn't just whisper. It shouted through her mind. *You can't let all those bad feelings keep taking up space inside you, or you'll always live in fear of them.*

She let go of the bottle, clinging to the sink, and looked up at the ceiling, seething at her mother. "Look what you've done to me. You stole everything good that I ever was and made me into somebody I don't like. I can't even give you shit or ask you why, because you drank yourself to death, leaving me in this fucked-up place without any answers."

Tears streamed down her cheeks as a familiar tune came through the walls of her apartment. She wiped her eyes, listening to her neighbor blaring one of her mother's favorite songs, "Please Read the Letter." An incredulous laugh tumbled out, and she glanced up at the ceiling again. *Are you shitting me? If you've been watching me this whole time . . .*

Her heart raced as she made her way to her bedroom and went into the closet. She pushed a trembling hand beneath a pile of sweaters on the shelves and withdrew the letter her mother had left her. The sight of her name in her mother's loopy handwriting brought a lump to her throat. She opened the envelope as she went to sit on the bed and finally read the letter.

> *My sweet dancing girl,*
> *I don't expect that you'll ever read this letter, but if you*
> *do, I know I'll feel it up in heaven.*

Deirdra closed her eyes against another rush of tears. Somewhere deep inside her, she'd always known her mother had felt her resentment, but the confirmation slayed her. She took several deep breaths, knowing she deserved the stab of pain in her chest, and forced herself to continue reading.

Breathe, sweetheart. If I know you, you're feeling bad about putting distance between us, but please don't. That was my fault, not yours. You did what you had to in order to survive, and I would never hold that against you. How can I be anything but tremendously proud of my dancing girl, when I've caused you so much pain?

Deirdra swiped at the tears running down her cheeks.

You always knew what you needed, and you held your chin up and pushed through like a champ, caring for me and your sister as if you were the parent. I am so sorry, Didi, and I will forever regret putting you and Abby in such a horrible position. I know nothing I say can take away the pain I've caused, but if you're reading this, it means I'm gone, and you need answers. Why did I let myself drink so much? Why didn't I ever tell you about Cait? Why didn't I tell you I was sick?

Deirdra steeled herself for the answers.

The answer to the first two questions is that I was too weak. Too weak to find my footing after your father died and too weak to admit what my parents had made me do. I was ashamed of not being strong enough to keep from drinking, but your father had been my anchor, and I was lost without

him. I guess I was trying to drown myself for all these years.
And as far as Cait goes, I carried a lot of shame for giving
her up, and I had already disappointed you so much. I
couldn't handle letting you girls down more than I already
had. You're stronger and smarter than me, Didi. I have no
doubt that if you'd been in my situation, you'd have moved
heaven and earth to find a way to raise your baby.

More tears flooded Deirdra's eyes. Her mother was right, but not
because Deirdra was stronger than her. Deirdra had simply been born
to better parents who had put love above all else.

The last answer is a little more complicated. You and
Abby had given up so much for me. I know if I told you
I was sick, you might not come home to care for me, but
you'd hire the best doctors and you'd keep tabs on me from
afar, the way you always have. I know you love me, Didi.
I feel it in the way you look at me, and I hear it in your
voice when we talk. But I also hear, see, and feel the dam-
age I've done. I couldn't put any more of a burden on you
and your sister. What you may not realize, sweetheart, is
that by not knowing about my illness, you allowed me to
fade away gracefully and be with your father.

Her mother might not have been strong enough to stay sober, but
dying alone? Without anyone to hold her hand, to tell her it was going
to be okay? That had to be terrifying, and it must have taken herculean
strength. Deirdra swiped at her tears and continued reading.

You unknowingly saved me for a second time. The first
time was the day you were born. I wasn't sure I could

ever love another child as much as I loved Cait, but then I held you in my arms and nearly burst with it.

I'm sure you have more questions, and I wish I knew what they were so I could answer them. Hopefully I've given you enough to finally climb out from under the mountainous hell I put you through and live the life you were always meant to.

Read that last line again, Didi.

Deirdra didn't reread the line.

I know you didn't read it again.

Deirdra rolled her eyes.

Don't roll your eyes at me, Deirdra Lynn.

Deirdra smiled, picturing her mother standing with her hand on her hip, shaking her finger at her.

Hopefully I've given you enough to finally climb out from under the mountainous hell I put you through and live the life you were always meant to. Ha! I made you read it again.

A laugh tumbled out with a sob.

You've always been more of a leader than a follower, marching to your own beat, sneaking out your window to sit on the hill in the side yard, probably plotting out your life, wishing it were different. Yes, I know about you climbing out your window, hanging by your hands on the sill, and then dropping and rolling. I'm surprised you never noticed the piles of leaves that used to appear out of nowhere beneath to soften your fall. But I guess you were too sidetracked back then to see them. I also know that's how you hurt your ankle when you were thirteen and told me you tripped going into the shower. I might be a drunk, but I'm still your mother, and mothers have a sixth sense when it comes to their children. That's how I know you're probably still running from everything I put you through, afraid if you slow down enough to smell the flowers or dance in the streets, you'll end up with nothing, or someone will come out of the shadows and say you're a slacker like your mother.

Have no fear, sweetheart. You are too smart and too resourceful to end up with nothing. Even as a little girl, you could make clothing out of scraps, and what other little girl could successfully negotiate with the mayor to change the annual children's talent show to the annual Silver Island talent show, so we could dance together?

Deirdra's tears dripped onto the letter, and she turned her face away, wiping her eyes.

You're too strong and sensitive to others to ever become me, as you proved every day of your life by caring for me and Abby. I'm sure you're wondering why I'm giving you a check for so much money, separate from your inheritance. It's yours, Didi. When I asked you to stop sending it and you continued, I told myself I would use it for rehab one day, but as you know, that day never came. I want you to know that I never spent a penny of it on alcohol.

Deirdra read that part again through the blur of tears, having no idea what her mother was talking about. She looked in the envelope, and her heart nearly stopped as she withdrew a cashier's check for thirty-eight thousand dollars. She quickly did the math and realized her mother had never spent *any* of the money she'd sent. She remembered what Abby had told her about the island families having taken care of their mother, by ordering food for parties and tacking on thousands of extra dollars and other sneaky ways they'd found to ensure she could make ends meet. She remembered what Gail had said about holding the people they loved tighter when they were hurting, because that was when they needed them most. Swamped with emotions, she turned back to the letter.

> *I would give anything to relive all of our good moments and erase all of the bad. But since I don't have superpowers, I can only tell you how I feel and hope it helps.*
>
> *Please listen carefully, Didi. I am proud of you, and your father would have been so very proud of the woman you've become. But you are so much more than a brilliant attorney. You're a kind, generous, loving daughter, sister, and woman, and one day you're going to find that love of your life you used to dream about. He'll see through that stormy facade you wear so well to the music of your soul and the love in your heart. Grab that happiness by the horns, sweetheart. It's time to leave the ugliness of our past behind and embrace the beautiful, long life you are destined to have. Take the trips you've always dreamed of, dance until you're so full of joy, you glow with it, and know that Daddy and I are always with you.*
>
> *Shine on, baby girl.*
> *All my love,*
> *Mom*

Deirdra sat there for a long time, feeling something deep and hidden inside her opening up as she thought about her mother and what kind of strength it must have taken to write that letter. She waited for resentment to take hold, but while she felt a host of other emotions—relief, gratitude, sadness, love—resentment was nowhere in sight.

She folded the letter and put it in the nightstand drawer, feeling a little lost. She didn't know who she was without the weight of resentment holding her down, much less how to move forward. Jagger's voice came to her rescue. *If you want to move past your pain, I think you have to first feel the hurt and rage and anything else it dumps on you . . . Maybe you should think about writing her a letter. Get all those feelings out. Put them in a bottle and toss it out to sea, or set the letter on fire.*

Write a letter. That's exactly what she needed to do.

She hurried into her office and sat at her desk. She had no idea what to write, but when she put her pen to paper, the letter wrote itself, her emotions spilling over one page onto a second and a third. By the time she was done, the sun was going down, and she knew what she had to do. Her mother might be right about her being more than just a brilliant attorney, but Deirdra knew what she was and wasn't capable of, and she could no sooner go traipsing through Europe on a hope and a prayer than she could wear open-toed shoes after Labor Day.

Some things simply weren't meant to be.

Clearheaded and confident in her decision, she rolled up the letter on her way to the kitchen and shoved it into the champagne bottle. She fished around in her miscellaneous drawer—because she refused to call it a *junk* drawer—and found masking tape, using it to cover the top of the bottle so the letter wouldn't fall out. Then she ran to get her phone from her bag by the door.

She paced the foyer with a bounce in her step and a hammering heart and made the call that would solidify her future.

"Hi, Madeline, it's Deirdra de Messiéres . . ."

CHAPTER EIGHTEEN

AS THE SUN went down, Jagger sat on his parents' back porch with Gabe and his grandfather, messing around with his guitar, while Dolly was inside getting spoiled by his parents. Usually nothing could pull Jagger's attention away from Gabe, but Deirdra had knocked the wind from his sails. Every time he strummed a few chords, he saw her watching him as he played just for her on the beach or in bed late at night, those sharp green eyes smiling back at him, and in the next second reality crashed over him, her beautiful eyes wet with tears as they went their separate ways.

How the hell was he supposed to say goodbye to the woman he loved and his family on the same day?

His parents and grandfather had known something was wrong the minute they'd hugged him. He'd told them what had happened, but he hadn't told Gabe. He'd hoped the gut-wrenching ache would have lessened by now, but it had only grown stronger. He knew Gabe felt the tormented energy he was giving off, but selfishly, Jagger didn't want to walk away. As much as he usually helped Gabe settle down, his brother did the same for him. He needed to feel the closeness of family right now, and he tried like hell to put his heartache into perspective. Gabe might never fall in love, or experience the magnificence of a love so powerful it was almost too much to take. Jagger knew he should feel blessed that he had experienced it at all, even if only for a couple of short weeks. But the pain was too sharp, the longing too deep.

Gabe signed, *Why sad?*

Their grandfather glanced at Jagger, gray brows raised in question, his message clear. *Maybe you should tell him.*

Dolly bounded out the back door, followed by his parents, their gazes moving between the three of them. Jagger petted Dolly as she passed on her way to his grandfather.

"What's going on?" his mother asked, giving Jagger's shoulder a squeeze. She'd been hovering around him all day, in the skirt and sweater she'd probably picked out with meeting Deirdra in mind. His father had been studying him all day, too, the way he had when Jagger was young and had tried to keep his troubles to himself.

"Gabe wants to know why I'm sad." He'd never lied to Gabe, and he sure as hell didn't want to be one of those people who treated him like a child who wouldn't understand his grief. But how could he tell him the truth without risking upsetting him? He looked at the parents who had taught him how to love and had rallied behind him and Gabe their whole lives, and at his grandfather, who had doled out advice about everything from the importance of following his heart to farming for as long as Jagger could remember, and he knew that whatever Gabe's reaction was, they both had a world of support. Jagger looked at his brother and hoped for the best. "Gabe, the reason I'm sad is that someone I know became even more special to me recently, and I had to say goodbye to her today. It was hard to do."

Gabe rocked, his eyes downcast, his head jerking to the side. He signed, *Mouth cute.*

"Did he just ask if she had a cute mouth?" Their grandfather chuckled.

His father shook his head. "I don't think so."

Gabe rocked more forcefully, shaking his head vehemently, and signed it again.

Jagger racked his brain, trying to figure out what he meant. *Mouth cute. Mouth cute. What the . . . ?* And then he remembered what his mother had said about Deirdra. Gabe's memory never failed to blow Jagger away. "That's right, Gabe. The mouthy but cute one."

His father and grandfather laughed.

"Oh my goodness," his mother said. "I think Jagger prefers the word *feisty*, which means lively and determined, like your brother." She winked at Jagger.

Feisty was a perfect word for Deirdra, as were *smart, sexy, kind,* and *vulnerable*. So damn vulnerable she ran away. Jagger remembered the antique sign she'd found for Gabe and added *thoughtful* to that list of words. Damn, he missed her. He wondered how she was holding up. Was she as devastated as he was? How had her interview gone? She should be back on the island by now. Had she told her sisters what had happened? He'd always believed in allowing himself to feel whatever came at him, but making sure Gabe was okay took priority over experiencing his heartache.

"But don't worry about me, bro. I'll be fine." Jagger excused the lie, because telling his brother he was sure he'd come out of this a different person would only confuse him. "I have a present for you, Gabe." He opened his backpack and withdrew the antique sign. His family *ooh*ed and *aah*ed, making a big deal over it as he gave it to Gabe, wishing Deirdra were there to see the light in his brother's eyes.

Gabe rocked faster, touching his chest repeatedly.

"That's right, buddy. It's yours." Jagger wanted to hug him but knew better. Sometimes, like before leaving for an extended time or when he returned from weeks away, he'd warn Gabe a hug was coming and pull him into his arms, enduring the agonizing sounds his brother made and the guilt that came with it. Because *Jagger* needed those hugs, and even though he knew it was uncomfortable for Gabe, he hoped in some soul-reaching way they did some good for his brother, too.

"That was very thoughtful, Jagger," his mother said.

"Actually, Deirdra spotted it for him."

"Sounds like my kinda gal." His grandfather pushed to his feet, patting his stomach. "How's dinner lookin'?"

"Like a feast waiting to be eaten," his mother said. "Ready to eat, Gabe?"

As she and Gabe went inside, admiring his sign, Dolly bounded after them. Jagger slung his backpack over his shoulder. He reached for his guitar, but his father beat him to it.

"How are you holding up, son?"

Before he could respond, his grandfather clapped a hand on his back. "Jag's gonna be just fine. He'll go after her and show her what's what."

"He's leaving the country for months, Pop," his father said.

"*Eh.*" He waved his hand dismissively. "Absence makes the heart grow fonder. I had to court your grandmother for a year before she'd give me the time of day."

"You don't know Didi, Gramps. She doesn't waffle on decisions. Once she makes up her mind, that's it."

"Then you'd better get your ass in gear and rethink that trip." His grandfather went inside, and Jagger headed for the back door.

His father touched his arm, keeping him outside. "Talk to me, Josiah. What are you thinking?"

"That I wish I were wired differently, but I wouldn't last a week in the city while she worked a hundred hours." He bit back the fire in his gut and paced across the patio. "And damn it, Dad. I don't think she belongs there, either. I mean, she does in one sense because she's a lawyer, and from what I've been told, a damn good one. But if you knew her and if you'd *seen* the person she's been with me, you'd understand why I say that. This can't be *it* for us. It can't be over. I wouldn't feel like this if it wasn't real and meant to be more."

"I haven't seen you riled up like this over anything other than your brother."

"I *know*. That's just it." His hands fisted as he paced, his heart racing. "I feel like a piece of me was ripped from my chest, and the worst part is that I know she's going to be miserable stuck in those offices day and night. I have to do *something*. Maybe Gramps is right and I should postpone my trip. It would suck without her anyway. I have to go see her. I have to tell her she's making the wrong choice. She always wanted to go to France. It's where her father is from, and I could *feel* how much she wanted to say she'd go with me today on the ferry. But she was forced to grow up so damn fast. Being saddled with responsibility is all she knows—"

"No, it's not."

Jagger spun around at the sound of Deirdra's shaky voice. She stood in the doorway with his family gathered behind her, holding a champagne bottle with tape covering the top and a big gold ribbon around it. Her hair was wild and tangled, her blouse and skirt stained. Her eyes were bloodshot and puffy, her makeup was smeared beneath them, and she was still the most beautiful sight he'd ever seen. His heart thundered in his chest. "*Sweet thing.* What're you doing here?"

She came to him, tears spilling from her eyes. "Being saddled with responsibility was all I knew, but that was before we got together. Now I know what it feels like to watch sunrises, sleep on sandy sheets, and be woken up by Dolly's kisses. Now I know what it's like to fall asleep in your arms and to kiss your lips, to love you and be loved by you. I don't know how it happened so fast, but now I know how it feels to do yoga with my best friend and know that if I need to cry, he'll hold me and tell me it's going to be okay. You were right about needing to feel all the bad stuff about my mom. I read her letter, and I wrote my own." Tears streaked her cheeks as she held up the bottle. Inside was a wet, loosely rolled letter, the ink smeared. "But it wasn't to my mom. It was to you. I'm sorry it took me so long to figure out that I wouldn't suddenly go back to being that little girl who had to fight for everything in life if I chose to be with you and be happy. I love you, Jagger, and if you still want me, I want to take that leap of faith and go with you to Europe. But I can't do it the way you want to."

His mother gasped, and relief nearly bowled Jagger over. "I love you, Didi. I'll do whatever you need, babe. Just tell me what you need."

"You better hear it before you agree." She laughed softly, swiping at her tears. "I need a plan. Not a solid itinerary, but at least a general idea of things so I know we're not sleeping in the streets. And we need to come back for Abby's wedding. Just for the weekend. I'll pay for our tickets, but I can't miss her big day, and I don't want to go without you."

"*Done.* We'll plan, and we'll come back. What else?"

"I want to crush grapes with my feet, and I want to bring Dolly."

"Grapes, feet. Got it. We're at the end of the grape harvest, but I swear we'll do it right after we arrive, and Dolls already has a ticket. What else?"

She shrugged, tears spilling from her eyes. "I really need you to hold me right now, because I'm scared shitless."

Jagger gathered her in his arms. "I am *never* letting you go." He sealed his promise with a kiss. His mother's sighs and the others' upbeat murmurs were drowned out by the sound of his heart gathering all of its broken pieces, swelling with love as it came back together.

"I like this gal," his grandfather said. "She *is* feisty."

Deirdra smiled a little bashfully at his family. "I'm sorry for interrupting your night." Her eyes found Jagger again. "But I couldn't stand the idea of losing you."

"You couldn't lose me, but you did save me from having to kidnap you." That earned a sweet smile from her and laughter from his family.

"As I said inside, honey, it's okay. We're happy you're here." His mother smiled warmly. "Jag, Deirdra hasn't met Gabe yet."

Jagger gazed into the eyes of the woman he loved, feeling like he'd been given a new lease on his already wonderful life, and introduced her to the other half of his heart. "Didi, this is my brother, Gabe. Gabe, this is the special friend I told you about, Didi."

Deirdra walked over to him. "Hi, Gabe. I'm so happy to meet you. I hear you're the best tomato grower around. Maybe one day you can show me your gardens."

Gabe kept his eyes trained on the ground as he shocked them all and gave Deirdra his version of a hug, touching the side of his body to hers and resting his head on her shoulder.

Jagger didn't think it was possible to feel more for Deirdra than he already did, but just like that, he fell a little harder for his girl.

CHAPTER NINETEEN

"OH, JAG—" DEIRDRA curled her fingers around the edge of the counter, a rush of pleasure burning through her core as Jagger devoured her. His beard abraded her thighs, but she didn't care. They hadn't been able to keep their hands off each other since she'd taken that giant leap of faith to turn her life upside down. Or rather, turn it *right-side up*, as Sutton had said when she'd called to give her the news.

Jagger reached up with one hand and squeezed her nipple, sending bolts of fire between her legs as he feasted on her. He grazed his teeth over that sensitive bundle of nerves, and her hips shot off the counter. She cried out, loud and lustful, glad they were parked at the point of Lover's Cove, where nobody could hear them. He grabbed her ass with both hands, tugging her to the edge of the counter, and spread her legs wide, lapping and licking, until her entire body shook with desire. She grabbed his head, holding him there. *"Don't stop."* She arched and moaned, writhing against his mouth as the world spun away in an explosion of raw, violent pleasure. *"Jag—"*

He stayed with her, loving her with his mouth, making sinful, gratuitous sounds as she rode the endless waves of pleasure. Just as she started floating down from her high, he kissed and nipped her inner thighs, sending shocks prickling up her center. He pushed to his feet, shoved his pants down, and drove into her in one fast thrust. They both cried out, hips rocking and gyrating as he loved her mouth as exquisitely as he loved her body, carrying them into a love-drenched world of ecstasy.

They clung to each other, their bodies ravaged, jerking with aftershocks as they came back down to earth. Jagger kissed along her shoulder.

"Best welcome home, *ever*," Deirdra panted out. It was Saturday, and she'd only just walked into the RV after spending the afternoon with Gail, Randi, Tessa, Shelley, and Jules, setting up for Cait and Brant's engagement party at Mermaid Cove, when Jagger had given her one of his predatory looks, and what had started as a hello kiss had quickly turned to carnal desire.

He grinned. "Dirty Didi has turned me into Jacked-Up Jagger. I can't get enough of you."

"You don't hear me complaining, but we'd better hurry or we'll be late, and I've got Cait's and Abby's dresses." She and her sisters had planned to get ready for the party together. They'd been shocked and thrilled for her and Jagger when she'd texted them Thursday night, and they'd all gotten together for a celebratory breakfast yesterday morning.

"Then let's get a move on, sweet thing."

He kissed her again, stepping out of his pants, and helped her off the counter. Dolly lifted her head from where she was lounging on the bed as Jagger led Deirdra into the bathroom. Dolly was used to their sexy antics by now.

Thirty minutes and one sexy shower later, Deirdra's hair and makeup were done, save for her lipstick, which she no longer wore around Jagger's very kissable lips, and they were parked outside Cait and Brant's cottage. While Jagger took Dolly out, Deirdra carefully put Cait's and Abby's dresses into gift boxes and slid them into the large gift bags with their other gifts. She put her makeup case in her tote bag, gently rolled up her dress, and as she put it in her bag, she glanced out the window at Jagger. His hair was still damp from the shower. He was wearing the linen shirt they'd bought in Provincetown—white with a pale green, blue, yellow, and pink tropical print—his brown hemp drawstring pants, and leather sandals, and he took her breath away. He'd spent all day making food for the party with Abby and Faye and texting Deirdra sweet and sexy messages. She sighed inwardly, unable to believe that beautiful, thoughtful man was hers, and *this* was her new life, filled with love, family, music, and going with the flow.

As she stepped out of the RV, Jagger turned with the easy smile that stirred butterflies in her belly. "Let me help you."

He stalked toward her, dragging his eyes slowly down her body, reawakening her desires. They'd just had an orgasm marathon. How could she possibly want him again so soon?

"Keep looking at me like that, and you *will* be late with their dresses, because I'll carry your sexy ass right back into the RV."

She giggled and held up a gift bag between them. "*No*, you will not."

He lowered her arm, pulling her into a kiss. "Don't worry, sweet thing. I can wait for our private after-party. But don't think for a minute I've forgotten the sexy favors you promised me if I wore this shirt."

"I'm counting on it, but we have so much to do before leaving for our trip, I'm nervous about getting it all done. Our sheets have more sand in them than the beach. Maybe I should wash them while I'm here. Kill two birds with one stone? I was thinking—"

He silenced her with a toe-curling kiss. "I love that sharp brain of yours, but this is Cait's big day, and *you* worked hard to put it all together. I don't want you to think about anything other than enjoying your time with your sisters. You're not alone anymore, babe. You don't have to do it all. I'll get up early and wash our sheets tomorrow morning before we take off."

As anxious as it made her to leave too much until the last minute, she *was* trying to stop feeling the need to control every little thing in her life. "You're right. What's a little more sand between the sheets?" At least they wouldn't have to worry about where to wash their clothes when they were in Europe. She'd already scoped that out, along with places to stay in each area they wanted to see, and she and Jagger had made a list of all the places her father had talked about. But they didn't make specific plans. As nervous as that made her, she was learning to go with the flow, and like their morning yoga stretches, she was starting to love it.

"That's my girl."

"I'm nervous about the party, too. You'll make sure the food is set up pretty?"

"Of course."

"Thank you. Why do I feel like I'm missing something?"

"Because you are. A farewell kiss from your hippie boy." He kissed her again, longer and deeper, leaving her a little fuzzy headed.

"I *love* my hippie boy," she said dreamily.

"And I love you, sweet thing." He squeezed her butt. "I'll meet you at the party, and we can scope out bushes to sneak behind and make out."

"Okay, see you there." She glanced over her shoulder as she headed up the walk. Jagger leaned against the doorframe, looking at her like she was his princess. She tripped on the walk and stumbled, finding her footing just as Jagger's arms circled her.

"I didn't think anything could trip up the great Deirdra de Messiéres."

"Haven't you heard? Didi left her in Boston. You're stuck with Dirty, *Trippy* Didi."

"I love Dirty, Trippy Didi, but she doesn't exist without Deirdra, and Deirdra is the woman who first caught my eye. I love all of you, babe." As his lips came down over hers, the front door opened and her sisters ran out.

"Okay, lover boy, that's enough smooching," Abby said as they descended the porch steps. Her hair was French braided over one shoulder, and she'd already done her makeup. "If we don't get ready soon, I'm going to have to start feeding Cait shots."

"Sorry, but I don't want to miss my own party." Cait's hair was wet, her face makeup-free. She took Deirdra by the arm, dragging her toward the house.

"Have fun," Jagger called as Dolly trotted over to him. He blew Deirdra a kiss and winked. "See you in the bushes, babe."

"In the bushes?" Abby asked as they walked inside.

Deirdra giggled.

"Look at you, giggling like a schoolgirl," Abby said.

"And beaming like a lighthouse," Cait added. "Love sure looks good on you."

"It does, doesn't it? Now I understand Abby and Aiden's loud sex-capades. Sorry I'm a little late, by the way. We got *busy* and lost track of time."

"That's okay. I'm just a nervous wreck. I'm not used to being the center of attention, and Abby's talking about how we should do my hair, and I don't *do* my hair." Cait was talking a mile a minute. "Let's get ready in my bedroom. I hate being nervous. I'm seriously thinking about eloping at this point, because if I'm this nervous for our engagement party, I can't imagine how I'll be at our wedding."

"You are *not* eloping," Abby said.

"We'll make sure your hair looks like *you*—don't worry. I got you each a little something. I hope you like them." Deirdra put her tote bag on the bed and handed them the gift bags.

"You didn't have to do that," Cait said.

Abby peered into the enormous gift bag. "But we're really glad you did."

"I am, too. I hope you like them, but if you don't, that's okay. Open the small boxes first."

Abby's eyes bloomed wide. "There are small boxes?" She and Cait dug through the tissue paper in their bags and carefully opened their small gift boxes.

"Oh, *Dee*. This is beautiful." Cait looked awestruck as she admired her whale-tail bracelet.

Abby squealed. "Where did you find these? I *love* them. Look, Cait, they're little utensil earrings."

"I found them in a cute jewelry shop in P-town."

"Thank you!" Abby hugged her and put them on.

"Will you put mine on?" Cait handed Deirdra the bracelet, and Deirdra put it on her. "It's so pretty. I can't wait to show Brant."

"I'm glad you like it. Open your other present. You too, Abby." Abby knew she'd bought her a dress, but Deirdra hadn't shown it to her yet. They tore open their boxes, giggling, the air buzzing with their excitement.

Cait held up her strapless tropical-print maxi dress with a for-est-green background and forest-green wrap. "Dee, this is too much. I can't believe you got me a dress. It's gorgeous, but I have one from last year I was going to wear."

"It's not too much. It's your special night—you should have some-thing new—and it was too perfect to pass up."

"You're going to look amazing in it, Cait. The green will bring out your eyes." Abby held up her cream-colored halter-top dress with a tropical print along the hem and at the waist and squealed. "I *love* it!"

Cait and Abby hugged her and thanked her over and over again, raving about their dresses. It was astonishing how much Deirdra enjoyed those hugs, instead of feeling like she needed to break free and get back to work.

"Want to see my dress?" Deirdra took out her dress and showed them the tropical-print off-the-shoulder hi-lo dress with billowing sleeves that Jagger had picked out.

"It's beautiful," Cait said.

Abby touched the gauzy skirt. "It'll look amazing when you dance with Jagger. Did I mention how much I love you guys together?"

"Only about a million times since I told you I was going to Europe with him."

"We're just happy for you." Excitement rose in Cait's eyes. "I just figured out the theme of the party! It's a Hawaiian theme, right? A luau?"

"Close, but not quite. The theme is *paradise*, and I went for elegant simplicity instead of a loud luau. I hope that's okay."

"Oh, Dee." Cait teared up.

"No waterworks, please," Deirdra said even though her own emotions were thickening her throat.

Cait wiped her eyes. "I can't help it. It's absolutely perfect. Thank you."

"You're welcome. But we'd better get a move on."

Just as Deirdra said it, the front door opened and Gail's voice rang out. "Where are our lovely girls?"

"In the bedroom," Cait answered, looking at Deirdra and Abby in confusion.

Deirdra had met Gail and Shelley yesterday afternoon for coffee at Shelley's house to thank them for always being there for her and to give them her good news. They'd been elated for her and Jagger. They'd talked for a long time about life and love, and although it had been a difficult conversation at some points, it had also been wonderful to hear the stories they shared with her about her parents, when they'd first met and throughout the years. When she'd gone home—*home!*—to meet Jagger at the RV, she'd told him everything, and she'd cried again. He'd held her and soothed her, helping her heal the way he'd been doing all along. She didn't know how well she'd do living in an RV when they came back to the States, but with Jagger by her side, she had a feeling anything was possible.

Gail and Shelley appeared in the doorway. Deirdra feared something had gone wrong with the food setup. "Is everything okay?"

"Perfectly *perfect*, as usual," Gail said as they sashayed into the room. She looked pretty in a colorful knee-length, bell-sleeved frock with a flower barrette in one side of her thick curls.

"You didn't think we'd let our girls get ready without their surrogate mamas, did you?" Shelley's auburn hair cascaded over her shoulders in waves as bold and gorgeous as the blue crisscross-bodice dress printed with tangles of gold ropes and green fronds she wore. Her bangs gave her a sassy look, as did the sexy midthigh-length underskirt and transparent overskirt that hung to her ankles.

"We were just about to put on our new dresses." Abby held hers up.

Shelley sighed. "Now, *that* is a party dress. Come on, girls, we need to get you ready before Brant loses his mind."

"He wasn't nervous this morning," Cait said.

"Oh, baby doll, he's not nervous about the party." Gail looked lovingly into Cait's eyes. "He can't wait to celebrate with his bride-to-be. Now *chop-chop*."

There was a flurry of activity and chatter as they put on their dresses. As Abby began doing Cait's hair and Deirdra applied her makeup, Gail and Shelley raved about how much fun the party would be and how hard Deirdra had worked to pull it all together. Their mother would be so thankful that her best friends were taking care of them. As Deirdra made up Cait's eyes, she saw her mother's eyes gazing back at her and felt a pang of longing, wishing Ava could be there to see Cait and Abby on their big days. She allowed herself to feel that heartache, and the vault inside her that had begun opening when she'd read her mother's letter opened further, bringing an unexpected surge of love for her mother and for these women. Blinking away tears she hoped no one would notice, Deirdra looked up at the ceiling. *I wish you were here for me, too.*

"I still can't believe you're going to *Europe*," Abby exclaimed, pulling Deirdra back to their conversation.

"I can't believe you're the same woman who couldn't take a day off work for years on end," Shelley said.

"What can I say? Maybe I have some hippie in me, too. It does run in our family."

"I don't know about *that*," Abby said. "But you have had a lot of a certain hippie in you lately."

They all laughed.

Gail put a hand on Deirdra's shoulder. "I'm glad our table-cloth-wearing girl is finally getting to live the life she always wanted."

"After what Malcolm told her, I'm glad she's changing directions and going away with Jagger," Cait said. "I don't want to know what a burnt-out Deirdra would be like."

When Deirdra had called Malcolm to give her notice, they'd talked for a long time, and he'd said he hadn't passed her up for the job because of her qualifications. He'd feared she was going to burn out if she kept up the pace at which she'd worked, and he'd said there would always be a place for her there. She'd felt bad for jumping to the wrong conclusion, and although she knew he was right about his worries, her gut told her that maybe Malcolm was also covering his butt, because there was not a single female top-tier executive in the company.

"Do you know how lucky you are that he allowed your two-month hiatus to serve as your notice?" Shelley asked.

"I know. I swear the career gods were with me Thursday."

"So were the love gods," Abby pointed out.

"Yes," Deirdra agreed. "They definitely were."

Gail and Shelley exchanged a knowing smile, and Gail said, "I have a feeling *they've* been working their magic since you and Jagger first met."

"I think you might be right," Deirdra agreed. "Hey, maybe the love gods had a talk with the career gods. I still can't believe Madeline wants me to consult. I mean, talk about having it all." When Deirdra had called to turn down the job, Madeline had said she'd be a fool to let Deirdra walk away when she had so much expertise in the field and asked if she'd be willing to consult on an as-needed basis. "It's the perfect solution to keep my foot in the door."

Abby looked at her curiously as she finished doing Cait's hair and set down the brush. "What do you think, Cait?"

"Oh, Cait, you are stunning," Gail said.

Cait admired herself in the mirror. "You guys are miracle workers. I *love* it. Thank you for not making me look plastic. I look like me, only prettier."

"You're always beautiful, Cait," Deirdra said. "Just ask Brant."

"You're all gorgeous," Shelley said. "I can feel Ava and Olivier smiling down on you right now. They would be so proud of each of you."

The three of them looked at each other, with their beautiful new dresses and in-love smiles, happiness billowing off them, and Abby said, "Gorgeous or not, we'll be the happiest women there."

"You'll definitely be three *of* the happiest, but you'll be joining Shelley and me, who have been married forever and are right up at the top of that list with you," Gail agreed.

"And I think Jules and Daphne might have something to say about being included in our happy list," Shelley chimed in.

"Absolutely. Gosh, it feels good to be so in love and surrounded by all of you." Abby looked thoughtfully at Deirdra. "I love seeing you so happy, but I have to ask: Should I be worried about you? Are you thinking of going back to work seventy hours a week next summer when you're back from Europe?"

"Right now *no*, definitely not. I love Jagger, and he loves me. We know we're great together, and we both want this. But we aren't going in blind or lovestruck. Well, we *are* lovestruck," she admitted. "But we're realistic. We know there'll be bumps in the road. How can there not? Neither of us has lived with anyone in a very long time, and we're hoping for the best."

"I understand, but trust me, you are two peas in a pod," Abby said. "You'll be great together forever."

"We think so, too," Deirdra said vehemently. "We just can't predict the future, so we're taking it day by day, and having that consulting job kind of takes the pressure off, which is nice."

"Because you were terrified of letting go of everything you've worked so hard for and leaving it all behind?" Cait asked.

Abby gazed thoughtfully at Deirdra. "Because it's a big change for her, and even though she's all in with Jagger and learning how to go with the flow"—she took her sister's hands—"we all know how hard it is to come out from under our stormy pasts and accept that the skies aren't going to suddenly open up and drown us again."

Deirdra teared up. "I won't let that happen. I love you guys so much. I'll be your umbrellas."

As she pulled them into her arms, Cait and Abby said, "And we'll be yours."

♥ ♥ ♥

Cait and Brant's party had been hopping all night. The sounds of tropical music, happy conversations, and true love hung in the air. Jagger finished checking the buffet table and gazed across the beach at the love of his life chatting with her sisters and petting Dolly, who thanks to Brant's niece, Joni, had a mermaid tail strapped to her butt and a plastic flower tied to her collar. Deirdra glanced his way, her sweet smile lighting up his heart. He swore she got more beautiful every day, and tonight, in that sexy dress, surrounded by friends and family, she was absolutely stunning.

They were in paradise all right, and not just because Deirdra had done a phenomenal job of decorating with lanterns in the trees, elegant table settings, the gorgeous centerpieces the girls had made, and rustic hand-painted wooden signs reminding guests to leave their sandals at the entrance, sign the guestbook, and take a moment to write Cait and Brant a note and put it in one of the tiny bottles with gold ribbons on the tables. Everyone had raved about the entire setup, and Cait and Brant had been in awe of their magical night. They especially adored the anchor decorated with red and white roses, with a mermaid's tail wrapped around the bottom.

Jagger thought it was all lovely, but it wouldn't matter if he and Deirdra were in the middle of the desert. As long as they were together, paradise would never fail to exist.

He chuckled inwardly, knowing his sweet thing would need running water, a roof over her head, and the ability to call her sisters. That was okay, because a woman like Deirdra should be able to count on those things at a bare minimum. The truth was, if she hadn't chosen to be with him, he'd have postponed the trip and gone back to the city with her until she realized what he'd already known. Not only were they meant to be together, but she had a lot of living left to do and dreams to be realized instead of shutting herself off from the beautiful world around her.

Roddy, Brant, and Aiden stepped into his line of vision, bringing him back to the moment. They headed his way in their tropical shirts. Roddy wore tie pants, like Jagger's, while Brant and Aiden wore slacks. Brant was also sporting quite a smirk. He'd been ribbing Jagger all night about Deirdra.

"Your gal did a hell of a job putting this party together," Roddy said as they sidled up to him. "I've never seen a real grass-hut bar. Where did she get that?"

"She had it made for the party. I didn't even know about it until this morning when it was delivered." Jagger had been as floored as everyone else was. But he had a feeling that years from now, when their lives were fully intertwined and they shared everything, she'd still find ways to surprise him and everyone else around her.

"She thought of everything," Brant agreed. "I'm glad Tara caught Cait's reaction on video when we first got here, because I've never seen her so shocked. Dee really outdid herself, and we appreciate it."

Jagger was stoked that they were having such a good time. "Thanks, man. I'll be sure to mention that to her."

"I heard the girls staking claim to the iron mermaids," Aiden added. "And the messages in bottles are a *great* touch."

Jagger thought about the champagne-soaked letter Deirdra had written him. Thursday night, after they'd gotten back to the island, he'd asked her what it had said. She'd told him she'd written all of the things she'd said to him when she'd gotten to his parents' house. Then last night she'd confessed that there was one more thing she'd written in the letter; she'd thanked him for loving her. She'd said she knew how precious love was, and she never wanted to take a second of it for granted, to which he'd said, he knew how precious *she* was, and he'd never take her or her love for granted, either.

"Now that we're past the pleasantries." Brant lifted his chin in Deirdra's direction. "What are your intentions with our girl while you're overseas?"

Jagger decided to rib him right back. "A gentleman never tells. Why? You looking for pointers in the bedroom?"

Roddy laughed, and Aiden stifled a chuckle.

"Shit," Brant said with a grin. "I was kissing girls behind the boathouse before you were out of diapers."

"Hey, man, if you're all about quantity, that's cool." Jagger smirked. "Nothing but the best for my girl. I'm *all* about quality. Satisfaction guaranteed, *all* night long."

Roddy cracked up, and Aiden tried not to.

Brant tried unsuccessfully to keep from laughing. "What I'm hearing is that you got a problem with quantity."

Jagger ran his hand down his shirt, holding it against his stomach, which made the bulge in his pants appear even more prominent, and arched a brow at Brant. "Want to put money on that?"

They cracked up, and Aiden muttered, "Guess I'll be the only adult on the beach tonight," making them laugh harder.

"Looks to me like you boys have competition." Roddy motioned to several of Cait's burly, tatted-up biker friends, the Wickeds, flirting with Deirdra, Abby, and Cait.

"Aw, hell no. That's *not* happening." Brant grabbed Aiden and Jagger by the arm, dragging them toward the girls. "Let's go."

Jagger went along with them, but he'd met the Wickeds at the grand opening of the Bistro, and he'd since played his guitar at their restaurant/bar, the Salty Hog, on Cape Cod a few times. Those men were *not* all talk, but they weren't assholes, either. Jagger might be jealous, but he wasn't worried about losing his sweet thing to one of them—or any other man, for that matter.

As they approached, Zander Wicked, the biggest flirt of all, stepped between Deirdra and Abby, flashing an arrogant grin that put Brant's to shame. "How's it going, boys? I figured since my Caity Cat's off the market, I'd slide into first place with these lovely ladies." He put his arms around them.

"In your dreams, hot stuff." Deirdra moved out from under his arm and reached for Jagger's hand.

"I'm taken, too!" Abby practically ran to Aiden.

"Aw, come on." Zander laughed.

"Not sorry, dude," Jagger said, pulling Deirdra closer.

"You should be sniffing around those trees." Cait pointed to Randi and Tessa, standing with Sutton and Leni a few feet away. "They've been checking you guys out all night, and they're single."

"Yeah, baby. Let's go, guys." Zander and his brothers and cousins walked away.

"Those are my sisters." Brant started toward them.

Cait grabbed his hand, tugging him back. "They're also grown women who don't need your approval to flirt with my friends."

"You gotta learn to let them grow up, or they'll rebel," Aiden said. "Just ask my sister."

As the others chatted about what it meant to be an older brother to sisters, Jagger gathered Deirdra in his arms. "Everyone loves what you've done for Cait and Brant."

"It's pretty great, right?"

"Almost as great as you are." He kissed her. "I've got a bush all picked out for us when you're ready."

She laughed, gifting him one of his favorite sounds. He nuzzled against her neck as Joni darted past in her mermaid costume with Scrappy on her heels. Scrappy was wearing a brown bodysuit with green fronds hanging over his head. Dolly took off after them.

"Joni is so darn cute," Aiden said as they watched her and the dogs weaving through the crowd. "I can't wait to have kids." He pulled Abby closer. "Want to start thinking about it, or trying, on our honeymoon?"

Abby gazed up at him. "Maybe we will."

Brant and Cait exchanged a loving glance, and Brant said, "Maybe we should start thinking about that, too."

"Yeah," Cait agreed. "Maybe we should."

All eyes turned to Deirdra and Jagger. He looked at the woman he wanted to spend the rest of his life with, and as much as he hoped to one day have children with her, he was in no rush to share her just yet. He opened his mouth to say as much, and they both said, "Maybe we won't," making everyone laugh.

Jagger pressed his lips to hers, turning her laughs into a sweet, sensual kiss.

"No kids?" Aiden asked.

"Maybe someday," Jagger said.

"For now we just want to be free to go where the wind takes us." Deirdra laced her fingers with Jagger's and whispered in his ear, "Let's go, hippie boy. There's a bush with our name on it, and I feel a breeze coming on."

Jagger's heart was full to near bursting as they ran across the cool sand, laughing and kissing, serenaded by the music in the air and the whispers of their hearts.

CHAPTER TWENTY

DEIRDRA AWOKE TO the sound of children giggling, sunshine streaming in through the curtains, and Jagger's warm, naked body wrapped around hers. Dolly lay on blankets beside the bed and lifted her head as the giggling children ran by the charming guest house where they'd been staying for the past week just outside the village of Moustiers-Sainte-Marie, in the heart of Verdon Natural Regional Park in southeastern France, where her father had grown up.

They'd been traveling for three and a half months, wandering through the cobblestone streets and picturesque countryside of Europe. They'd danced in the streets of Spain, kissed in the Eiffel Tower, walked from Charing Cross Station to Buckingham Palace to watch the Changing of the Guard, and enjoyed the sunset by the river Thames and the Rhine. They'd visited remote farms, fascinating markets, medieval churches, elaborate castles, and interesting museums, falling truly, deeply, and even more desperately in love by the day. Jagger had played at a number of cafés and pubs, and they'd met so many amazing people and learned about such a variety of cultures, Deirdra never wanted to go back to her boxed-in, boring life in Boston.

The children ran by again, and Deirdra moved to peek out the window, but Jagger tightened his hold around her belly, pulling his knees up behind hers, so not even air could fit between them. "Where do you think you're going, sweet thing?"

"Absolutely nowhere. I was just going to look out the curtains." She turned in his arms, meeting the playful expression that made her heart skip. Jagger's hair had gotten shaggier, his scruff bordered on a beard, and when he kissed her, the sparks he caused were as hot as ever. "I love it here."

This was their second visit to Moustiers-Sainte-Marie. They'd met the owner of the property, Sylviane, when they'd first landed in Europe and had come to France to catch the end of the grape harvest. Sylviane was in her sixties and had known Olivier. She'd shared wonderful stories of his younger days and of the grandparents Deirdra had never had a chance to meet, and she'd invited them to stay in the guest house. Not only had Deirdra's dream of stomping on grapes come true in the very best way—in her father's hometown, with Jagger by her side and Dolly watching on—but they'd made a good friend and had come back last week to celebrate both Sylviane's and Jagger's birthdays.

He brushed his lips over hers. "Here in this *bed*?"

"In this bed, in your arms, and in this amazing place with the olive-tree garden where my father used to play and Sylviane's giggling granddaughters right outside our window."

Sylviane's daughter, Céline, and her three little girls had been living with Sylviane since Céline had lost her husband last year. Her daughters adored Deirdra, Jagger, and Dolly, often showing up at their door to play with Dolly or with a basket of pastries in an effort to entice Jagger to play his guitar and Deirdra to dance with them.

Jagger ran a hand down her body, giving her hip a squeeze. "You have that look in your eyes, like when you didn't want to leave Cadaqués."

She sighed and rolled onto her back, remembering the gorgeous nature preserve in Spain where they'd hiked for hours and made love beneath the stars. They had planned on staying there for only four days but had ended up staying for two weeks. "That was magical."

He ran his finger along her cheek, a sexy smile playing on his lips. "*Mm-hm.* That's where my buttoned-up girl became my starry-eyed lover." He kissed her slow and sweet and oh so perfectly. "I'm getting the feeling you want to cancel next week's trip home."

"I don't want to cancel the trip." They hadn't been back to the States since Abby's wedding. Aiden had gone all out, giving Abby the wedding of her dreams. It was so beautiful, even Jagger had teared up.

It was a good feeling to hear the word *home* and finally know what it meant. Her *home*, the place where she saw herself living for years to come, was by Jagger's side, wherever that might be. But her home was also on Silver Island, with her sisters and the friends who had always been there for them, even when Deirdra couldn't accept their help. She'd discovered a new home, too, with Jagger's family. She'd gotten to know them well these past few months. Gabe and his grandfather had even given her a virtual tour of the farm. She'd tried singing for Gabe, but Gabe would have no part of it. She didn't blame him. Deirdra's voice was grating even to herself. But Jagger loved it, and that was more than enough for her.

"I miss everyone, and we need to be there for Gabe when he moves out of your parents' house and for you to help Abby get ready for the grand reveal of the Bistro's special farm-to-table days." Deirdra had made good use of the money her mother had left her. She'd given it to Abby to help fund the Bistro's move toward farm-to-table. With Jagger's and his father's help, Abby was well on her way. Deirdra wound her arms around Jagger. "But I was talking with Sylviane and Céline about what it's like in the summers, and I was thinking that we could come back in June or July so we can see the summer farmers' markets and festivals."

"My girl's got the travel bug. What about your consulting work?"

She'd taken on one consulting project a month after they'd gotten to Europe, but her heart hadn't been in it. After completing the assignment, she'd told Madeline she wanted to hold off on doing any more consulting until she was back in the States. "I've been thinking a lot about that, too. I *love* our life, and I know it'll be different when we're in the States, but I want to take my time and figure things out. I thought I'd take a page out of my hippie boy's songbook and keep things loose."

He nuzzled against her neck, shifting over her as he laced their fingers together, pinning her hands beside her head. "You want to keep things loose, huh?"

She giggled. "I don't want to get tied down."

"I got news for you, sweet thing." He nudged her legs open and brushed his lips over hers, rocking against her center in a mind-numbing rhythm. "You're tied to me forever."

She loved teasing him. "You think so, do you?"

"I *know* so." He took her in a deep, passionate kiss, sending heat waves through her core. She lifted her hips, needing more, but he continued teasing and taunting, kissing her into a moaning, writhing mess of desire. "Tell me you're mine." His breath was hot against her mouth. "Or I might have to tie you down to this bed and never let you go."

"Now, *there's* an idea." She giggled, and his eyes flamed as his lips came down over hers in a fierce and hungry kiss that turned slow and sensual and beautiful.

"Damn, baby," he whispered against her lips. "I love you so much I ache with it. Kissing you on Abby's lawn was the best decision of my life."

"Why?"

"Because I knew once we kissed, there would be no turning back."

She gazed up at the man who had changed her world, and her heart, and there was no holding back her love. "Being with you was the best decision of my life. I'm yours, hippie boy, today, tomorrow, *forever*."

He lowered his lips to hers as their bodies came together, and she knew with every fiber of her being that she was finally living the life she was always meant to live, with the man of her dreams, who not only heard the music in her soul and saw the love in her heart, but had become a part of them.

A NOTE FROM MELISSA

I hope you enjoyed Deirdra and Jagger's story as much as I enjoyed writing it and getting to know Jagger's family. While creating Gabe's character, I spent many hours researching nonverbal autism and feel it is important to point out that autism is a vast spectrum, and no two people's experiences are identical. What works for one person, another might find controversial. This book was written with that in mind, and I hope as you read the story, you recognize that Gabe's family has done what they felt was best for him.

If this is your first Silver Harbor book, you might enjoy starting at the beginning of the series with Abby and Aiden's love story, *Maybe We Will*. You can find a downloadable map of Silver Island, family trees, and series checklists for all of my books on the Reader Goodies page on my website (www.MelissaFoster.com/RG).

If you'd like to read more about the Silver Island Steeles, Silvers, and Remingtons, you can find some of their stories in the Steeles at Silver Island series, which is part of my Love in Bloom big-family romance collection. If you're curious about the Wickeds, you can read about them in The Wickeds: Dark Knights at Bayside. And if you're curious about Randi's diving expedition, pick up *Searching for Love*, a Braden & Montgomery novel featuring treasure hunter Zev Braden and chocolatier Carly Dylan. In *Searching for Love* you can get to know the beloved Bradens and spend time on Silver Island.

If you're a binge reader and prefer to start at the very beginning of the Love in Bloom big-family romance collection, the collection offers characters from all walks of life, from billionaires and cowboys to blue-collar workers, and begins with *Sisters in Love*, the first book in the Snow Sisters series. Each of my books may be enjoyed as a stand-alone novel. Characters from each series make appearances in future books, so you never miss an engagement, wedding, or birth.

Be sure to sign up for my newsletter to keep up to date with my new releases and to receive an exclusive short story (www.MelissaFoster.com/News).

Happy reading!

~Melissa

ACKNOWLEDGMENTS

Writing a book is never a solo adventure. I'd like to thank the many people who shared their experiences with me about having autism or caring for or working with people with autism, and more specifically, nonverbal autism: Dr. Sheila Iseman, SCI Educational Consultants; Maria Ott, Partnership for Extraordinary Minds; Danielle Wright and her extraordinary son, Brady, who writes the *Hostage to Silence* blog; Terren Hoeksema; Rosalie Perez; Carol Dillingham; Rochelle West; and Stephanie MacLellen. There were several others who have chosen to remain anonymous, and I am grateful for their input.

I'm forever grateful for my assistants, friends, and family for your generous support and endless patience. Heaps of gratitude go to my wonderful editor Maria Gomez and the rest of the professional and talented Montlake team. My books would not shine without the editorial expertise of Kristen Weber and Penina Lopez and my capable proofreaders.

If you'd like to get a glimpse into my writing process and talk with me about my Love in Bloom romance collection, please join my fan club on Facebook, where I chat with fans daily (www.Facebook.com/groups/MelissaFosterFans).

To keep up with sales and events, please follow me on Amazon and sign up for my newsletter (www.MelissaFoster.com/News).

ABOUT THE AUTHOR

Photo © 2013 Melanie Anderson

Melissa Foster is a *New York Times*, *Wall Street Journal*, and *USA Today* bestselling and award-winning author of more than one hundred books, including *The Real Thing* and *Only for You* in the Sugar Lake series. Her novels have been recommended by *USA Today*'s book blog, *Hagerstown* magazine, the *Patriot*, and others.

She enjoys discussing her books with book clubs and reader groups, and she welcomes an invitation to your event. Visit Melissa on her website, www.MelissaFoster.com, or chat with her on Instagram @MelissaFoster_Author, Twitter @melissa_foster, and Facebook at www.facebook.com/MelissaFosterAuthor.